MW00699315

SLOW SIMMER

THE WAY TO A WOMAN'S HEART ROMANTIC COMEDY
(COMING HOME TRILOGY BOOK 1)

SHERIDAN JEANE

Slow Simmer
Copyright © 2023 by Sheridan Edmondson
All rights reserved.
First published in Medina, Ohio, United States by Flowers & Fullerton.

ISBN-13: 978-1-63303-020-6 (Trade Paperback)

Library of Congress Control Number: 2023903610

Cover Design by Earthly Charms
This book is a work of fiction. Names, characters, places and incidents are the
product of the author's imagination or are used fictitiously, and any resemblance to
actual persons, living or dead, business establishments, events, or locales other than
existing city and street names is entirely coincidental.

The scanning, uploading and distribution of this book without permission is a theft
of the author's intellectual property. If you would like permission to use material
from this book (other than for review purposes) you may contact Sheridan@
SheridanJeane.com. Thank you for the support of the author's rights.
All rights reserved, including the right to reproduce, distribute, translate or
transmit in any form through any medium by any means.
Copyright © 2023 by Sheridan Jeane
All rights reserved.

To my amazing children, Xan and Ashley.
Being a mom has been one of the most rewarding and challenging roles of my life. I tried to impart some nuggets of wisdom to you, but you ended up teaching me even more.
Love you to the moon and back!

BIBLIOGRAPHY

Contemporary Romances

The Way to a Woman's Heart series - the **Coming Home** trilogy

Slow Simmer
Here's the Scoop
From Bitter to Sweet

———

Coming in 2024
The Way to a Woman's Heart series - the **Destination Wedding** trilogy

Too Much On My Plate
Say Cheese!
Turkish Delight

———

Historical romances

Gambling On a Scoundrel

Secrets and Seduction series:

* Lady Cecilia Is Cordially Disinvited for Christmas
*(only available via Sheridan's VIP club)
It Takes a Spy…
Lady Catherine's Secret
Once Upon a Spy
My Lady, My Spy
Along Came a Spy

NO PARADE

FORD

I yawned and stretched, making my back crack. I'd been up since 4 A.M. to make it to the airport for my flight from Los Angeles to Pittsburgh. My body told me it was almost midnight, even though the clock in my rental car said quarter to nine.

Other than some obligatory holiday visits, I hadn't spent much time back home since high school. What can I say? I tend to be a workaholic. It comes naturally. I'm a lot like my dad that way.

Wasn't that my real reason for coming home though? Guilt about that emotional distance from my family? Dad in particular? A couple of weeks ago, my sister and brothers started hammering me with texts.

> Hailey: Something is off with Dad. None of us can get him to talk. It's your turn.

> Max: I'm panicking here. Dad's losing interest in Ross Film Productions. This isn't good.

> Sean: You need to check in with Dad. Something's wrong, and you were always his favorite. Talk to him. Even better? Go see him.

Me: I'm on it.

Of course, I'd ignored the part about coming home. A conversation should handle it. Dad and I had never had trouble talking. Easy enough, right?

Not exactly. Maybe it had been too long since we'd had a real heart-to-heart, but when I'd called, Dad had avoided any personal questions and kept changing the subject. He'd only wanted to discuss the film his production company was shooting in Italy. I finally realized my sister and brothers were right. If I wanted answers, I'd have to talk with Dad face-to-face.

I decided to suck it up and spend a few weeks back in my hometown. I needed to choose my next film, and Dad usually had good advice. In fact, spending some time away from Hollywood would probably do me some good.

That was before I'd been ditched by Dad on my first night back.

Well, maybe ditched was too strong a word, but I couldn't think of a better one. After I landed, I saw the text from him saying his flight back from Italy had been delayed. He'd be back tomorrow.

Right now, I just wanted some dinner and a bed.

I stepped out of my car in the restaurant's parking lot, and the peaceful silence took me by surprise. Here, a stone's throw from the Ohio River, the only sounds filling the night came from the light breeze blowing through the trees, and water lapping against the riverbank.

I was so hungry, my stomach gnawed at my insides. A formal-looking restaurant glowed through the second-floor windows, but the bar on the ground floor looked more appealing.

As I pulled open the restaurant door, I glanced down at my phone to check for messages. I glimpsed a pair of red Converse high-tops directly in my path an instant before I plowed into the woman wearing them.

I grabbed hold of her elbow to steady her as I glanced up and met her startled brown eyes. She was cute with her brown hair pulled back into a ponytail. The vibrant blue tips of her hair caught my attention. I also took note of her jeans, nicely proportioned body, and snug-fitting red, white, and blue Wonder Woman t-shirt. It was a good look on her. Her easygoing comic book style didn't seem typical for the preppy little town of Sewickley, but maybe things had changed more than I'd realized since I'd been gone.

She staggered back. Her takeout bag slipped from her arm, and I barely managed to keep it from falling

"Sorry." I tucked my phone away as I passed the bag back to her. "My fault." I flashed my well-honed Hollywood smile.

This woman immediately pegged my smile for what it was—nothing more than an attempt to placate her. She clutched the delicious-smelling bag of food to her chest and scowled, a sour expression tightening her pretty mouth. "Walking while texting? What, are you twelve?" Her warm body slid past me as she headed toward the parking lot.

Harsh, but deserved. "Can I make it up to you? Maybe buy you a drink?"

Whirling around to face me, she narrowed her eyes. "Do you actually expect that line to work?"

Before I could reply, she held up her hand to stop me.

"Don't answer. I'm not interested." With that, she tossed her blue-tipped hair, turned, and strode away, her ponytail swishing like I didn't stand a chance.

I'm clearly losing my touch.

I let the door swing shut as I turned to face the restaurant's vacant hostess station. According to the chalkboard sign, the kitchen would be open for another twenty minutes, so I scanned tonight's house specials.

Ribeye. That would hit the spot. I bypassed the stairs leading to the second-floor restaurant and entered the bar.

My gaze immediately focused on the striking view of the Ohio River through the large, garage-door-sized windows at the far end of the room. The full moon reflected off the rippling water. Lamp-lights glowed on the bridge in the distance, completing the picturesque scene.

I claimed a vacant barstool with a view of the riverscape and inhaled the irresistible aroma of grilled steak. A dark-haired, broad-shouldered man pushed through a door behind the bar, but he halted the moment he laid eyes on me. "Ford Ross? Is that you?"

I jerked my head back in surprise. "Conner? Conner Gillette? What the hell? You work here? It's great to see you." I stood and held out my hand.

He reached across the bar and pumped it up and down. "I don't just work here. I'm half-owner." He flashed the same easy-going smile I remembered, his short brown hair still stuck straight up in the front. "Congratulations, man. I saw you won best director at Sundance. That's amazing. I watched your acceptance speech on YouTube."

I sat back down, a pleased grin splitting my face. What can I say? I'm damned proud of that award. "Thanks, man. It was an amazing night."

"You in town for long?"

I relaxed in my seat and rested an arm on the bar. "Not sure yet. A few weeks at the least." It really all depended on how things went with my dad.

I ran my hand through my too-long, light brown hair, my fingers catching in the slight wave I'd inherited from my mom. It was a sure indicator that I needed a cut. The wave annoyed me when I let it get this long, but I was bad about getting a haircut when I wasn't filming. The makeup and hair crew always kept it neat and trim—one of the perks that came with being a director.

"I'm surprised you're in town," Conner said, leaning onto the bar to face me. "With that win, I'd have thought you'd be busy landing a film with a major studio."

"There's this thing called a cell phone," I lifted mine from the bar and waggled it from side to side. "You should get one. It lets

4

you talk to people even when you're on the other side of the country."

"Smart ass, eh? So you're a hot commodity?"

"What can I say? Everybody loves a winner." And they avoided losers like they had leprosy. "All I need to do now is figure out which film I want to tackle next. It's getting down to decision time. I need to pick something soon."

Conner seemed to remember himself. "Did you just stop by for a drink, or did you want something to eat? The kitchen closes soon."

"I want your ribeye special, medium-rare, and that amber ale you have on draft."

"You should get the truffle fries too. They're beyond belief."

"Load me up."

Conner knocked his knuckles on the bar, served my beer, and then disappeared through the swinging kitchen door, presumably to put in my order.

I took in the rest of the room with a director's eye for a set. The huge open windows, the stage in the corner with a door behind it so the band could load in without disturbing the patrons, the many tables... this place was clearly set up as a music venue. Conner had spent years traveling with his band, and it showed in the room's layout.

A minute later, Conner reappeared, but this time he came around to my side of the bar to sit next to me. "What brings you to town?"

A guilty conscience? I glanced down, not wanting to tell him I was worried about my dad. That was family business, and I didn't want to invade Dad's privacy. "It's been a long time since I've taken any real time off. The Sundance win messed with my head. It changed a lot of things for me and put me in the public eye. I need some time to think."

I was surprised to hear myself say that. Was it true? Was I feeling overwhelmed? Strange how avoiding one truth made me blurt out another one. "Dad's flight back from Italy was delayed.

He won't be back until tomorrow, so I'm staying with my sister."

Conner relaxed against the back of his barstool and took me in. "Italy? Nice. Vacation?"

I let out a laugh. "Never. He's working. I don't know the last time he took a vacation. His production company is filming there. My sister offered to put me up in her guest room since Dad isn't here, but she's out with her family right now. She suggested I stop by here to grab dinner before coming to her place, but she didn't mention you owned it."

I'd always assumed Conner and his band would hit it big. The guy had a stellar voice and could play guitar like he'd sold his soul to the devil. Seeing him running a restaurant seemed wrong somehow, but maybe I didn't know him as well as I thought I did. Besides, people change. Priorities change. Life does that to all of us. I'd married Chelsea, and then she'd driven that point home when she'd walked out the day after our second Christmas together. Nothing lasts forever. Especially not relationships.

"We opened Not a Yacht Club a year ago. Things are going great, knock-on-wood." Conner rapped his knuckles against the glossy bar top. "As you can see, Tuesdays tend to be pretty quiet, but if you come back later in the week, we'll be packed."

"Love the name…Not a Yacht Club. Back when we were in high school, I remember you saying you weren't the yacht club or country club type."

"You remember that?" Conner asked, looking pleased. "Yeah. I thought a bar and music venue would be a nice alternative the posh country clubs around here."

I raised an eyebrow. "That doesn't track. I saw your upstairs restaurant through the windows from the parking lot. White tablecloths. Great view of the river. Looks pretty posh to me."

Conner flashed a grin. "Thanks. We have all our bases covered here. I thought it would be funny if we added a kayak rental place. A kayak is as far from a yacht as you can get and still be a boat."

A let out a chuckle. "Wouldn't that clash with that high-end restaurant of yours?"

He shrugged. "Maybe. Or maybe I can figure out how to make it a classy kayak rental place."

I liked the idea. "This town's the place for something as offbeat as that. Who's your partner?"

The kitchen door swung open and a tall, brawny, dark-haired man in chef's whites appeared. Conner gestured toward him. "You remember Dante, right?"

"Dante Bastiano?" I jerked my head back in surprise. "*Mi amico*! What the hell are you doing here? I thought you still lived on the West Coast." We'd been friends since the day we'd started first grade at Middlebridge Academy and swapped cookies during lunch, but we'd lost touch over the past few years. A pang of guilt pierced me. When was the last time I'd called him? I couldn't even remember. "If I'd realized you were the chef, I would have ordered one of your Italian dishes. Your mom's lasagna is still the best I've ever tasted."

"Thanks, man. I'll let her know you said so." Dante's pale gray eyes flashed with good humor as he rounded the bar to greet me. "Moved back here a couple of years ago. Good to see you, Ford. Congrats on Sundance." Dante's scarred hand—a chef's hand—engulfed mine in a firm shake.

"Thanks. You two are business partners? How'd that happen?"

Conner shifted on his barstool to face me. "It all came down to timing and luck. We got to talking one day, and when we realized we had similar ideas about opening a new restaurant here, we decided to partner. The rest is history. As the chef, Dante handles everything food-related, and I take care of everything else. It works since I can't cook worth a damn."

"You should know how to cook if you're gonna run a restaurant." Dante sounded annoyed.

Conner shrugged. "So you keep telling me—and I keep ignoring you."

A man in jeans and a collared shirt with a "Gillette Construction" logo on the chest strode in from the parking lot and dropped onto the stool next to Conner. He looked like Conner, even down to the close-cropped hair. He had to be Kincaid, Conner's younger brother. It had been years since I'd seen the kid. Well, not a kid anymore.

Kincaid clasped his hands together in supplication and shot Dante a pleading look. "I know it's past nine," Kincaid said. "Tell me it isn't too late to grab dinner."

Dante scowled. "My assistant is already closing things down in there. I'll have him throw another ribeye on the grill next to the one I'm cooking for Ford, but you need to grovel."

"Thanks, man," Kincaid said. He glanced at me and gave me a nod, but I don't think he recognized me.

"Either get here before nine or learn to feed yourself," Dante said as he headed back into the kitchen.

Conner shifted on his barstool to face his brother. "Didn't your girlfriend sign you two up for a weekly couples' cooking class? Why aren't you there tonight?"

Kincaid shrugged. "She cancelled after last week's lesson. They wanted her to cut up raw chicken."

"Is she vegetarian?" I asked.

"No. Touching raw meat grosses her out. She has a weak stomach. You should've seen the way she reacted when I came home with stitches on my hand after I tore it open at a construction site. She can't stomach the sight of blood."

"Bro." Conner raised one eyebrow. "Can you say, *high maintenance*? Why'd you let her move in with you when her roommate kicked her out? You should have told her to stay with her parents." He made an irritated sound. "Didn't you also tell me she never cleans up after herself in the kitchen or bathroom? I know you're a neat freak. You gotta be beat by the time you get home from work each day. Being her maid must suck. She's making you her bitch."

"Fuck you," Kincaid tossed back. "At least I *have* a girlfriend."

2

A HERO'S WELCOME

FORD

The Next Day

As I walked through Sewickley's trendy business district towards my house, my phone rang. "Ford! Why don't you ever answer the phone?" Sheila's voice squawked into my ear.

I held my cell phone away until she calmed down. "I could say the same thing to you." I walked around a rack of trendy clothing on the sidewalk outside the shop entrance. "I left you three messages. The time difference between the Netherlands and Pennsylvania is a pain in the ass. You're impossible to reach."

"I guess we both suck at using phones," she said. Thankfully, Sheila understood the challenges of keeping in touch while maintaining a grueling shooting schedule and didn't resent my occasional extended silences.

I wanted to take a look around before Kincaid arrived, so I quickened my pace. "How's your girlfriend?" I asked.

"Who, Deirdre?" Sheila asked. "She's ancient history. She dumped me when I wouldn't cast her in my flick. What the hell are you doing in Pennsylvania? If you needed a break, why didn't you come to Amsterdam? Going home never works. You should know that by now."

"I thought it was a good time to catch up with my family." I kept it short, not wanting to give Sheila too much information.

Dad had returned to town earlier today, but strangely, he didn't want to see me today. First, he didn't want me to stay with him, and now he was telling me to wait until tomorrow to visit. Was work really so important to him? Despite his request, I decided I was going to stop by later this afternoon. My siblings thought there was something off, and I was beginning to think so too.

Staying with my sister long-term was not a desirable option, as she was already bossing me around as usual. On top of that, her home was currently in chaos due to the ongoing renovations. I needed a quiet place to work, and after meeting Kincaid at my house later, I'd decide whether or not to move my furniture out of storage and stay there for a while.

"Don't tell me you're in Sickly right now!" Sheila exclaimed. "Please, tell me it's not true."

I grimaced. "You're butchering my town's name to irritate me. It's pronounced Seh-wick-lee. And yes, I'm here."

"What the hell are you doing there anyway?"

"I want to spend some time with my dad. We've been out of touch," I explained, feeling guilty for not speiding time with him sooner. Dad had a heart attack five years ago, and instead of coming home to help out, I had put my work first. Hailey, Sean, and Max had to manage everything on their own. At the time, I was in Norway on a tight shooting schedule, and I'd justified my decision to delay coming back by convincing myself that Max had the business end of things under control, and my presence would only confuse the chain of command at Ross Film Productions. Looking back, I realized that had been selfish. It was long overdue for me to step up. "I feel guilty. I haven't seen him much these past few years. We've both been busy."

"Going home is the worst," she said, using her mock voice of doom.

"You sound jaded."

Sheila sighed so heavily that I could feel her breath move my hair through the phone. "That's because I am jaded. My last visit home turned into a traumatic nightmare. Dad turned my girlfriend into my ex-girlfriend in the span of five minutes. Why couldn't I have been born into your family? Your dad is awesome. Not a homophobic bone in his body. Lesbophobic, I should say."

I let out a huff of laughter. "Dad's pretty laid back. He rolls with things rather than letting them eat at him." As a parent, that had not always been the case. He had never been satisfied with the nannies and other caregivers he had hired after Mom died, and I had grown used to coming home to find that he had fired the one I had just started getting attached to.

"I thought your issues with Don tended to focus more on professional boundaries."

"True," I said with a laugh. "He had strong opinions about my films." I dodged a couple of pedestrians as they scurried past me, moving fast. Had my laid-back hometown changed so much? This was strange behavior for a Wednesday afternoon. Everyone should be ambling, not scrambling.

"Had?" Sheila said. "As in past tense?"

"He's changed since his heart attack." When I finally glanced up and spotted the enormous bank of dark clouds, I felt like a fool. How could I have forgotten western Pennsylvania's spring rainstorms? Too many years in Southern California, that's how.

"What's wrong? Is he feeling okay?"

As a store clerk bustled out to the sidewalk and shoved a wheeled clothing rack back inside the shop, a large raindrop hit the back of my hand. I glanced up and was rewarded with another one directly in my eye. I rubbed away the droplet. "I'm not sure." I veered towards the nearest shop entrance to wait out the storm, but the lingerie in the display window changed my mind, so I hurried on down the street. I could just imagine the shopkeeper's curiosity as I perused a display of lace thongs. No thanks. With my luck, she'd post a video of me on Instagram or TikTok and label me a creeper.

"Is that why you're really there?" she asked. "To help your dad?"

"I need to reconnect with him and see how he's doing, but—"

"But?"

"I need to take a break and avoid the spotlight for a while. Sewickley seems like the perfect place to hide while I read through scripts. I've already eliminated seven options, and I'm in the process of narrowing down the rest," I explained, hoping to avoid the rain as I looked through the large glass window of the next storefront. Unfortunately, it was a hot yoga studio filled with women in athletic wear doing the cat-camel stretch, offering me no refuge. I started jogging down the street, hoping to find a dry spot.

"Aha!" Sheila exclaimed, sounding like an overacting Sherlock Holmes uncovering an important clue. "That explains why you keep calling me. You're in desperate need of my expert advice and insight when it comes to choosing a script."

Just then, the sky opened up and dropped everything it had on my head, immediately drenching me. It was time to stop being picky and find a dry spot. I yanked open the very next door, not caring where I was. The door chime jangled in irritation at my rough treatment, and I wiped my face in the crook of my arm. When I looked up, the colorful covers of comic books assailed me from every side, and I let out a groan.

Superman.

Figured.

"Don't groan at me," Sheila said peevishly. "It isn't my fault I'm smart and you're predictable."

I rubbed my wet hair and smoothed it back into place. "It isn't you. I just walked into a store to escape the rainstorm. I'm in a comic book shop, surrounded by pictures of Superman." I glowered at a Superman poster. "It's like the guy's stalking me. Maybe it's karma bitch-slapping me and telling me I need to make a decision."

An ash-blonde mom hovered near her equally pale-haired

sons. She shot me an annoyed glare and then turned her back. What was *her* problem?

"Do tell!" Sheila's voice took on a cultured British inflection.

I grinned at her posh accent. "Are you filming a period piece?"

"Is it obvious? So what if I like to immerse myself in a project? A director should dive in so deep that the mood oozes from her pores."

"Ooze away."

She resumed her British accent. "Tell me about your crossroads, my good man. Set the stage. Explain your conundrum to me."

"With that Sundance win..." I broke off mid-sentence. The mom was still staring at me, but now she looked as though she was trying to place me. Had we been classmates?

It was possible.

It was also possible she recognized me from *Entertainment Weekly* or *Here's the Scoop*. I'd really rather not chitchat with a fan right now.

I turned my back to her and lowered my voice so it wouldn't carry. "I need to decide how to leverage my situation. Should I keep trying to find a script and produce my own film, or take a shot directing the big-budget action film I'm about to be offered?"

Sheila let out an excited squeal. "*Superman*! I heard McCormick Studios was considering you for the remake. Is it true?"

I glanced down and saw the Man of Steel comic staring back at me from the rack in front of me. I grimaced. "You heard right."

"And you're hesitating, because..." She dragged out the word.

I scowled at the caped superhero. "Because Superman has already been done. Too many times."

"Have you read the script?"

"Not yet, but I've heard rumors that McCormick is pushing for an origin story remake," I said, scanning the nearby display rack with its rows of Superman comics. "It's frustrating how Hollywood keeps playing it safe and sticking to the same tired superhero stories just for the sake of box office hits. And don't even get me started on the cookie-cutter writing, complete with the same snarky comments. It seems like studios won't even consider investing in something original or innovative. There's a reason superhero origin stories are always so popular. They're the only ones with any character development."

"That's not true," Sheila chided. "The Marvel franchise has plenty of character development."

I turned to face the room with its rows upon rows of comics.

"And all the characters sound the same in those movies. What about Batman and Superman? They have excellent origin stories with strong character arcs, but the sequels have never lived up to the originals."

"The Spider-Man and Marvel crossovers have been great."

I shook my head. "A fluke. But yeah, that's Marvel for you." I let out a frustrated sigh. "I want something unique. Fresh. And the budget to do it right."

"Fluke? You can't keep using that word. I don't think it means what you think it means."

I chuckled at her Princess Bride reference. "I hear you. But you have to admit that for most superhero movies, the main characters remain fixed. Static. On the rare occasion when a writer is permitted to develop the character, the powers that be end up wiping the slate clean in a sequel with some retcon bullshit. Too much of this comic book junk is garbage." I made a derisive noise. "Characters need to develop, to change, to overcome some internal issue. Otherwise, they're flat and boring."

The pretty cashier behind the counter shot me a fierce scowl. I'd recognize that irritated expression anywhere. Her brunette ponytail with blue tips confirmed it - she was the woman I nearly slammed into at the restaurant last night.

She was even better-looking than I remembered, wearing a different Wonder Woman t-shirt today. Her deep brown eyes and blue-framed eyeglasses looked hella sexy. I had to give the store owner credit for putting someone as beautiful as her at the register. It must lure in comic book nerds in droves...unless she frightened them off with that terrifying frown.

A little brown-and-white dog sat on a cushion next to the counter, watching me intently, its tail unmoving.

I tried my Hollywood grin on her again, but her scowl deepened. Tough room. I needed to work on my charm.

I turned my back on her so I could focus on my conversation, but I must have startled the mom standing nearby because she took a quick step back.

"True, but that's not necessarily what audiences want," Sheila pointed out. "They want to see their favorite heroes doing what they do best: saving the world and kicking butt."

"I know, I know." I rubbed my temples, feeling a headache coming on. "But I'm not interested in making movies just for the box office. I want to create something that will last, something that will be remembered."

Sheila gave a dramatic sigh. "Ah, the age-old artist's dilemma. Fame or art?"

I rolled my eyes.

"What movies are you considering if you're not doing the Superman thing?" Sheila asked.

I shrugged. "Maybe one of those twisted psychological things. I love killing people. The bloodier, the better." Something clattered to the floor on the other side of the comic book rack, but I couldn't see what was happening. A moment later, I heard a whispered conversation.

"But you just did one of those," Sheila protested.

"That's why I'm considering McCormick's offer, but only if I can figure out how to breathe some life back into a dead thing that's on life-support."

The bells on the door jingled, and I glanced over to see the mom I'd noticed earlier pushing her two blond-haired sons out into the rain. She paused next to the big plate glass window, and her panicked gaze locked on me. Her eyes widened when they met mine, and she immediately redoubled her speed and disappeared from view.

Had she recognized me? I hoped she wasn't off to announce it on Facebook or something. Normally, this sort of thing doesn't bother me, but I was here to get some downtime and be with my family. I'd prefer to avoid any attention.

The cashier came out from behind the counter, her hands clamped to her hips. She stalked toward me, giving me a glimpse of those amazing denim-clad legs I fondly recalled noticing last night. When my eyes traveled up, and I finally met her gaze, I realized the bundle of fury in tight black jeans and red Chucks had murder on her mind.

My murder.

"Sheila, I'm gonna have to go. Something's come up." I slid my phone into my pocket.

The shopgirl glared at me, hands on hips and feet spread wide, mirroring the Wonder Woman poster on the wall with the caption "Be the hero of your own life." Damn, she was hot.

"Really?" she snapped. "*Now* you end your call? *After* driving my customers away in the middle of a rainstorm? Why couldn't you have done that before walking into my store? Who do you think you are to come in here using foul language and talking about murdering people in front of those kids? Not to mention badmouthing Superman and comic books en masse!"

I recalled my conversation with Sheila and winced inwardly. She was right. I had mentioned murdering someone. No wonder that mom had freaked out. "Sorry about the murder comment. I'm a movie director. I'm not actually plotting any crimes."

She remained unimpressed. "You drove away my customers."

My eyebrows shot up as I shoved the Superman comic back onto the display rack. "Did you ever consider they couldn't find anything worth reading?"

She glared at me, her face reddening. That sound. What was it? It was coming from *her*. Was she *grinding her teeth*?

"Considering those kids spend their entire allowance here

every week, I sincerely doubt that's true," she said in clipped tones. "It was you. I don't know if it was your murder comment or the fact that you reinforced their mom's doubts about letting her sons read comics. It took me weeks to convince her to encourage her kids to read things they found engaging. You might have singlehandedly cost me two regular customers, not to mention depriving those kids of their favorite things to read."

Chastened, I opened my mouth to apologize—

"But what the hell. Drive away all my customers. Shut down my store. Why should *you* care if I go bankrupt?"

I raised my eyebrows as I glanced around the tidy shop, seeing it in a different light. "You own this place?"

Her little dog approached and sniffed my foot. I'm pretty sure my shoe outweighed the little guy. Those enormous upright ears were so big, I was surprised they didn't make him topple over.

The shop owner visibly bristled. "Why do you find the fact that I own a comic book store so inconceivable?" She crowded forward as she levelled an ice-cold glare. "Is it because I'm a woman?"

I backpedaled, holding up my hands in surrender. "It's just that you're so—well—you're attractive. I tend to associate comic books with—"

"With what?" she demanded.

I hesitated. "With nerds," I blurted out. "You don't strike me as a nerd."

She attempted a glower of pure annoyance, but a small smile tucked into one cheek as she nudged her glasses back up her nose.

I reconsidered her superhero t-shirt and blue hair. "Well... I suppose you're slightly nerdy around the edges."

The little dog sat and stared up at the woman worshipfully, then turned an irritated gaze toward me. Apparently, I was even pissing off small animals.

She held up one hand as if to stop me. "I'm not interested in some pretentious stranger's assessment of me, my looks, or my nerdiness, so keep your opinions to yourself. And where do you get off judging the entire comic book industry?" She folded her arms. "I bet you haven't read them since you were a kid. Don't tromp around my store dissing them if the only way you experience them is through movies."

She waved her hand around at the books in her store, then realized I wasn't arguing. She peered at me, seeming to reconsider her abrasive attitude. "Don't get me wrong, there are some excellent films out there, but too many directors aren't willing to take a chance on anything new. They keep doing remakes and poorly conceived sequels. Look at yourself, dude." She emphasized her point with a finger-jab at my chest.

The little dog's entire body wilted, and he padded back to his pillow. He shot me a reproachful glance before plopping down on his stomach. I considered joining him.

"Theater attendance is at a twenty-year low," the sexy, blue-haired dynamo continued, not done with me yet. I folded my arms and leaned against a rack, getting comfortable. She was kind of hot when she got all intense like this. All that intelligent, nerdy sexiness was really growing on me.

"On-demand movies are king. Profits for the top studios have dropped by something like forty percent in the past decade. I know my facts. I did market research when I was designing a video game." She shook her head in mock dismay, but her eyes, her intense brown eyes, drew me in and wouldn't let me go.

"Face it," she continued. "The movie industry is in trouble. Your monolithic production companies aren't keeping up with changes in customer preferences. You people keep giving us warmed-up leftovers instead of creating films that are fresh and new. If I want something original these days, I watch one of the subscription services or play a video game. I rarely find anything original in a movie theater."

I could only stare at her, astonished. This woman had just eviscerated me and my entire industry. She had made excellent points too, ones I had been worrying about lately. Wasn't that what I had just griped about to Sheila?

"What's wrong?" she asked, lifting her chin in a bring-it-on gesture. Damn, she was sexy with her flushed cheeks and slightly askew ponytail. "You can dish it out, but you can't take it? If you're going to walk in here and announce that comic books are drivel, I think I should be allowed to come to your next movie premiere and tell everyone the film industry is dying."

I closed my mouth with a sharp click. "You're remarkably opinionated."

"It isn't opinion. It's fact. Go look it up. If you want to be relevant, why don't you try making something original? What about the Stan Lee comics in the Marvel universe? They're huge hits because they don't keep rehashing the same origin story. There are plenty of examples of other comics that were turned into successful films. What about *Scott Pilgrim Saves the World*? *Men in Black*? *Snowpiercer*? *Three Hundred*? For the love of god, what about *The Walking Dead*? They were all based on comics."

Had this woman handed me the answer I needed? For some perverse reason, I found myself arguing with her. Maybe it was because I liked what that spark of irritation did to her eyes.

"Not necessarily all of those were successful. Certainly not as successful as Superman."

"Which *Superman*?" Her brown eyes snapped. I'd lay money she was enjoying our argument too. It had been ages since I'd had an intellectual debate about these subjects. I wanted to lean in, but I was afraid she'd back away. I wanted her closer. Much closer.

"There have been at least a dozen Superman movies," she pointed out. "Check the box office numbers for every single one. Sure, any Superman film will capture die-hard fans, but you won't convince most people to spend their hard-earned money and precious time watching something old and tired. The movies I mentioned might not have been huge box-office hits when they were first released, but every single one of them had staying power."

I made a mental note to track down not only the box office numbers but also the gross revenues for the movies she had mentioned. Maybe I should ask my dad. He could reel off the numbers from memory without needing to check.

"Try reading something original and creative." She strode past me, and I caught her intriguing spicy scent. She started plucking comics off her racks. She frowned at her selection, hesitated, then grabbed one more before holding them out to me. "Here. All new. All fresh. All original."

I stared at the stack of comics, then at her. This intelligent, vibrant dynamo not only wasn't intimidated by me, but she also spoke her mind. No holds barred.

Damn, that was sexy.

I flashed a genuine smile as I took the stack she offered. "We got off on the wrong foot. Let's start over from the beginning. Hi. I'm Ford Ross."

She continued to frown at me. When she finally relented, she relaxed her shoulders and held out her hand. "Mara Stellar. Welcome to Ghost of a Chance Comics."

3

TRAITOROUS LIBIDO

MARA

The devilishly handsome man wrapped his hand around mine.

Well, damn. He even had sexy hands. Strong. Firm. Smooth.

I forced myself to release it. The rain had abruptly stopped, and now a bright beam of sunlight splashed across Ford's medium-length, light-brown hair, highlighting the slight wave at the nape of his neck. With that strong jawline and those full lips, the man was too delicious to be real.

I didn't trust him. Someone who looked as good as he did had to know it.

The door chimed again, and my heart skipped a beat as I spotted Randall, a twelve-year-old with a notorious reputation for stealing. Today, he had two younger boys in tow, both looking nervous and fidgety. I recognized Gabe and Marcus from previous visits, but I had never seen them with Randall before. As they walked between the shelves, their wet sneakers squeaked on the floor, echoing in the quiet store.

"If you'll excuse me," I said with a sense of urgency, "I need to keep a close eye on this situation." I quickly moved to my favorite surveillance spot near the register, hoping to spot any suspicious activity using the convex mirrors above the bookcases. But as I looked around, I realized that the mirrors didn't cover all areas of the store, and I cursed myself for not repositioning them sooner.

I tried to steady my breathing as I watched the boys out of the corner of my eye. They seemed to be browsing innocently, but I knew better than to let my guard down. Randall was a skilled thief, and he always had a plan. I couldn't afford to let him out of my sight, especially with two younger boys with him.

Out of the corner of my eye, I noticed Ford examining the stack of graphic novels I'd handed him, giving each an approving nod. He set them on the counter before turning and heading back into the rows of merchandise to browse.

The man confused me. After the way he'd dismissed everything I cared about, I should want to keep my distance from him, but my libido didn't seem to agree.

"Irritating libido," I muttered.

The last thing I needed right now was to get involved with a man. I had the bad habit of letting their needs take over in a relationship, and I didn't have time for that right now.

Even so, the guy was ridiculously good-looking. It would be nice to take this opportunity to watch him unobserved, but I really needed to stay focused on those boys. I surreptitiously watched the security mirror again.

Marcus held a comic book in his hands and stared down at it with a frown. When he set it back on the shelf, Randall shot him a glare. The boy immediately wilted, intimidated. Then he took in a sharp breath, snatched up the comic, and shoved it clumsily under his jacket.

My heart sank. I needed to act fast.

The fledgling thief made for the door, but I darted forward, placing myself between him and his escape. To my surprise, Ford stepped into the aisle where the other two boys were standing, subtly blocking their path to the door. Zephyr followed at my heels, tongue lolling.

"Can I help you?" I asked in my best "mom" voice, letting him know I didn't approve of his actions.

The boy paled. The comic book slipped out from beneath his jacket and landed on the floor with a smack.

"Uhh—" Marcus backed away from the evidence with a look of pure terror on his face.

I picked up the copy of Ironman and brushed it off. "Since you obviously want this one, let's head over to the register so you can pay for it."

The other two boys widened their eyes in a feigned display of shock and dismay. Zephyr looked on with good-natured interest.

When Marcus stood frozen in place, I rested my hand on his back and gently guided him toward the counter. With a well-timed glance at one of my convex mirrors, I spotted Randall, the ringleader, put a comic back on the shelf.

"Smart decision, Randall," I called out to him, my voice low and serious. "I wouldn't have been lenient with you a second time. Your mom will be hearing about the wise choice you just made. Or should I say, narrow escape?"

Zephyr growled softly, sensing my tension.

Randall's face reddened with surprise as he tried to stutter out a response. Without another word, he edged around Ford and bolted out the door with Gabe in tow. My gaze lingered on their retreating forms, making sure they didn't stop to grab anything else on the way out.

As I turned back to the counter, a self-satisfied smile tugged at the corners of my mouth as I rang up Marcus's purchase.

But the boy wouldn't meet my eyes.

"That was your one and only do-over, Marcus. Don't let me catch you trying to steal from me again. I won't call the police this time, but I will call your mom. You should reconsider who you hang out with."

The boy blanched. "You know my name? You know my mom?"

I gave him a stern look. "I make it a habit to learn the names of all my customers. It's my superpower. Tell your other friend Gabe to stay out of trouble."

"Superpowers," he murmured, his eyes round with wonder.

"You're welcome to come back—as long as you promise you won't step over the line again. I won't hold a grudge," I said, hoping to end the interaction on a positive note.

He tapped his chest. "I promise. And—and I'm really sorry about what I did."

I let out a small sigh of relief as he scurried out the door. "At least one thing turned out right today," I said, glancing at Ford.

The man stared at me in open admiration, then grinned and cocked an eyebrow. "Did you know you're posing like Wonder Woman right now?" he said, breaking the tension and injecting a bit of levity into the moment.

I rolled my eyes, feeling my cheeks flush with embarrassment. "Seriously?"

FLUSTERED, I dropped my hands to my sides, hiding my embarrassment by leaning down and giving Zephyr a pat of approval, my ponytail concealing my face. My glasses started sliding off my nose, so I had to stand back up or risk looking even more ridiculous. Here it came again, that lack of self-confidence whenever I found myself attracted to someone. I could go from self-assured business owner to fumbling idiot in a flash.

Smooth. Very smooth. Geez, I was such a nerd. He'd called it. Why hadn't I worn my contact lenses today? Oh, *right*—because I'd stayed up all night working on that coding gig to pick up some extra money and now my eyelids felt like sandpaper.

"Did you enjoy the comics I chose for you?" I asked, switching back to business mode.

"You chose well. I'm impressed."

"You chose well," he replied, flashing me a smile that made my insides melt. Not good. "I'm a huge fan of Neil Gaiman, but I've only read his books. Never his graphic novels."

Made sense. A few of Gaiman's stories have been turned into movies. He'd even written some Doctor Who episodes. My heart gave another thump as I realized that Mr. Sexy Hotshot Director and I had something in common. Neil Gaiman.

Shields up.

"Our mutual love of Gaiman doesn't make us besties after the way you drove off some of my customers," I said, attempting to scowl but failing as a grin spread across my face.

Traitorous libido.

He handed over his stack of comics. "You're turning me into a convert. You obviously have excellent taste. I'll take them all, plus these, please."

As he added copies of *Snowpiercer* and *Ghost* to his purchase, I stilled when I saw the grayscale cover of the latter. My self-confidence faded away, and I began ringing up his purchases almost robotically.

Ford's gaze roamed around my store, and I wondered if he'd notice how low I was on stock. "I see Superman is still a staple," he commented, his expression thoughtful.

"He always will be," I replied.

His gaze locked on a collectible figurine in my display window. "Is that one of those bride-and-groom cake topper things?"

I cast a fond glance at the little statue. "From the Lois and Clark wedding. It's a custom order. The bride plans to pick it up this weekend. It's a surprise for the groom."

"She must be head over heels for the guy if she's willing to make Superman her wedding theme," he observed.

I shot him a sidelong glance. "There you go again, judging things without having all the facts. I'll have you know those two lovebirds met nearly a year ago at my grand opening, when they both reached for the same comic. It was love at first sight. I don't think you could convince her not to have a Superman-themed wedding. They're even writing their own superhero-themed vows." Pausing, I quoted,

"'Every lover is, in his heart, a madman, and, in his head, a minstrel.'"

Ford's eyes flashed. "Did you just quote Neil Gaiman to me? *Stardust*?"

I responded with an approving grin. "There's hope for you yet. I think you might have a true nerd's soul buried under that polished exterior."

"Maybe." He hesitated. Did something deeper flash in his expression, or did I imagine it? It was almost as if I'd surprised him today and given him things to think about. Even as I watched, that instant of vulnerability disappeared. "Thanks for the help." He glanced over his shoulder and speared me with that megawatt Hollywood smile. "I mean it."

Acting on a sudden impulse to escort him to the door, I came out from behind the counter.

Ford pulled a pen and a business card from his pocket, scribbling something on the back before handing it to me. His clear blue eyes met mine. "This has my private email and cell number. I'll be around town for a while, visiting family. I grew up here." He hesitated, then said, "Add me to your email list. You have one, right?"

My fingers brushed his smooth, warm hand as I took the card. Touching his skin sent an electric charge through my body. *Holy swoon, Batman.* I all but snatched the card from him.

His mouth twitched as though he'd picked up on my reaction to him.

"'Add me to your email list?'" I raised one eyebrow. "I bet you say that to all the girls." I gave my ponytail a toss.

With a grin, he closed the door, causing my door chime to jingle—as well as all my girly bits.

Stupid libido.

I wasn't fool enough to fall for good looks, easy charm, and a killer smile.

I stopped in my tracks. *Was I?*

4

BOOK CLUB

MARA

I drove up the long driveway to Lianna's house for book club and parked behind three other cars at the edge of the grass. Her sprawling house sat at the top of a huge hill, overlooking one of the country clubs. I turned off my Mazda, and the abrupt halt of the air-conditioning made me feel the thick, post-rainstorm heat all the more. I got out of my car, feeling the humid air clinging to my skin. I was running late, so I still had on the t-shirt and black jeans I'd worn to work.

Looking around, I didn't see Scarlet Smith's car. I had been hoping to corner the mayor and ask about Ford Ross. Scarlet probably knew him since they had both grown up in this town and were around the same age. Besides, she was notoriously well-informed. If Mr. Hollywood Director was trouble, she'd let me know.

But Ford Ross was intriguing. Sexy, too, and intelligent, which was like catnip to me. I couldn't help thinking about him, even though I knew that men as intense and driven as he seemed to be could complicate a woman's life. Complications were the last thing I needed right now. My world was a big enough mess already, and I could only blame myself for that. My self-confidence seemed to exist only when I was managing the store. In all other areas, I was a hot mess, constantly second-guessing myself.

Since I knew Lianna never expected her guests to stand on ceremony, I walked in without knocking and followed the sound of voices toward her kitchen. When I stepped through the doorway, I spotted all my friends heading out the patio door.

Lianna's open and welcoming demeanor put me at ease. When I'd moved here a year ago to take over opening the store, we'd immediately hit it off. When I'd revealed my computer background, she'd wrapped me in a hug and declared we'd be lifelong friends. She'd been right. She'd become my go-to person for after-work drinks or girls' nights watching Netflix when her husband was out of town.

Now, Lianna waved for the others to go on outside before hurrying over to greet me. "I'm so glad you're here." As she enfolded me in one of her amazing hugs, her long, wavy brown hair tickled my shoulder, bringing with it the light scent of lilacs. "The only person who's missing is Scarlet."

I let go of her and nervously rubbed my hands down my jeans, grazing the outline of Ford's business card in my pocket. I hoped Scarlet wouldn't be a no-show. "Is she coming?"

"She'll be here. She said she'd probably be late. Mayoral duties." Lianna crossed to the small counter just off the kitchen that served as a bar. She raised an empty wine glass. "Can I pour you something? We were just heading outside to enjoy this gorgeous weather. Spring is off to a great start."

"Gorgeous weather? Only if you're a tree frog—or maybe a salamander." I eyed Lianna's lightweight summer dress with envy. "It's way too hot and humid."

"To-may-to, to-mah-to. I've been cooped up in the office all day and I'm dying to get some sun."

I examined the wine bottles arranged on the bar, one of which dripped with enticing droplets of condensation. "I'll take some of that chilled pinot grigio."

Lianna attached a round red, white, and blue wine charm that reminded me of Captain America's shield onto the stem of my glass, poured a generous amount into it, and handed it over.

"Enjoy," Liana said. "It's just us girls tonight. Paul's out of town again." The lines between her eyebrows deepened as she frowned. "At this rate," she muttered almost to herself, "I'm beginning to think I'll never get pregnant."

That came as a surprise. "I didn't realize you were trying." Lianna was one of my closest friends. Why hadn't I known she was trying to have a baby?

Some friend you are, Mara.

Lianna glanced away. "Sorry. I shouldn't have brought it up. You didn't know because I've kept it to myself. I'm getting frustrated, though. Not being able to conceive makes me feel like a failure, which is stupid, I know. I guess that's why I never mentioned it." She hesitated, then blurted out, "We've been trying for nearly three years."

And she'd never once mentioned it to me before? Why now? "I'm sorry. That has to be hard."

She shrugged. "It is what it is. At least not having kids means I can pour myself into my work. It's a good thing I like my job. I do wish Paul didn't have to travel so much for work, but other than that, I love my life."

Lianna worked as a program manager for a large software company. I knew from my experience in the video game industry how demanding managing an IT project could be. I still missed it sometimes. But it wasn't a life most people would covet.

I envied Lianna's passion for her job. Too bad I didn't feel the same way when it came to running Ghost of a Chance. Too often, I resented the amount of work I had to devote to it.

"Do you ever wonder if you work too hard?" I asked, voicing the question I'd been asking myself lately.

Lianna raised one eyebrow. "And you don't? You don't have any employees to share the burden, and you haven't taken a single day off since you opened that place."

"I know, I know. But in my defense, I'm closed every Sunday and Monday."

"Right. And you spend those days doing bookkeeping or marketing or website maintenance. You've been picking up some freelance work too, right? Don't try to fool me, Mara. You wouldn't recognize free time if it bit you in the butt."

I offered a faint smile, trying to muster up some energy. Lianna was right. The past year had been grueling, with relentless work to get my store off the ground, but it felt like I'd barely made any headway.

Lianna let out a dramatic sigh and gestured toward the French doors. "Speaking of free time, we should go outside and join the others. Rose recruited a new member."

As I stepped onto the patio, the sweet scent of freshly mown grass hit me, carried on a cooling breeze. Except it wasn't a natural breeze, it was from an electric fan. Lianna had set up a couple of them to cool the seating area, and I stepped in front of one, feeling the breeze ruffle my ponytail.

The patio was a charming little oasis. Colorful cushions were scattered around a low table in the center, surrounded by potted plants bursting with pink and purple blooms. I couldn't help but smile at the sight. Three book club members and an older woman I didn't recognize watched me from their cushioned seats.

We were a diverse group, which made our monthly gatherings entertaining. Apart from me, Lianna, and our missing mayor Scarlet, today's group consisted of a bubbly librarian, a brainy cancer researcher —plus this new member who appeared to be quite a bit older than the rest of us. I pegged her as being in her late seventies. The rest of us ranged from our late twenties to early thirties.

I succumbed to the gravitational pull of the food tray on the low table. The loaf of crusty Italian bread looked like it had been baked fresh this morning. The dipping bowl of oil was dotted with bits of roasted garlic and spices, and the blocks of various cheeses and dish of kalamata olives beckoned to me.

I greeted the group with a playful, "Greetings, earthlings," as I grabbed a plate and loaded it up with snacks.

Courtney lifted her wine glass, adorned with a white cancer-awareness charm. "Hi, Mara."

I teased her with a smile, "Cured cancer yet?" But Courtney didn't bat an eye as she tucked her long red hair behind her ear. "Not yet, but I'm inching closer."

I loved spending time with these women. They challenged me intellectually, which was something I missed from my former job. Just a year ago, I'd been a hotshot code-slinger and game developer. My business partner Destiny and I had been rising stars in the video game industry.

I took a deep breath, reminding myself that I'd made the right decision. When I left the video game industry to open Ghost of a Chance, I'd sold my half of our startup to Destiny and used the funds to open the store. It hadn't been a smooth transition, but it was a dream come true.

I stepped closer to the low stone wall that separated Lianna's elegant stone patio from the sloping lawn, captivated by the sight of two horseback riders crossing the open field below. Dressed in black equestrian helmets and tall riding boots, they were a picture of grace and power.

With a contented sigh, I claimed the spot next to Courtney on the sofa, setting my Captain America wine glass beside her cancer awareness one. Lianna took the chair at the head of the table, glancing around to introduce the newest member of our eclectic book club.

"Mara, this is Gertrude," Lianna said, gesturing to the elegant woman to her right.

To my surprise, Gertrude immediately rose to her feet and extended her hand. Despite being my grandmother's age, she moved with the grace and energy of someone in her thirties. Suppressing my groan at my tired feet, I pushed myself up from the couch to shake her hand, impressed by her agility. "Great to meet you. How did you learn about our book club?"

"I saw a flyer at the library," Gertrude replied as we sat back down. She glanced at Rose, who sat at the foot of the table.

The oscillating fan caught Rose's humidity-frizzed reddish-brown hair, and she brushed it away from her face. "We talked about finding more members, so I made a flyer and put it on the library's bulletin board. Gertrude volunteers there, so we talk a lot." As Rose spoke, the breeze from the fan carried the scent of freshly mown grass, making me long for the cool, open fields below the patio.

"We see each other at yoga too," Gertrude pointed out.

"Which is why I got you a yoga charm for your wineglass," Rose said, tipping her head toward the glass. "Each of us has a unique wine charm so we don't mix up our glasses."

Gertrude lifted her glass in a toast. "Thank you. It's perfect."

"Gertrude, I'm impressed you've already read the book. Not all our members manage it," Courtney said, giving Lianna a pointed glance with her catlike green eyes.

"I do my best," Lianna defended herself. "I usually read *most* of the book."

"Or you watch the movie adaptation," Courtney added, arching one elegant eyebrow.

"Busted," Rose said, grinning and waggling a finger at Lianna. "Hey, we've all pulled that trick. We won't judge."

The French doors opened, and Scarlet strolled through them, dressed in a red suit as vibrant as her name. Her sophisticated bob haircut completed her poised look. Memories flooded back as I recalled our first encounter when I'd gone to the zoning office to open my store. She'd warmly welcomed me to the community, and it hadn't seemed as though she'd been going through the motions and mouthing polite words. She'd really meant it. She was happy to have me here. Over the past year, she regularly stopped by the shop to see how I was doing.

"You sure know how to make an entrance," I greeted her, my sore feet forgotten for the moment.

Lianna stood up and joined me. "It's always a pleasure to see our illustrious mayor."

Scarlet beamed at us and gave us quick hugs. "Sorry I'm late. I was judging the Gettysburg Address competition."

Rose's interest was piqued. "I know a few eighth graders who planned to compete. How did they do this year? Was there a clear winner?"

Scarlet's face lit up. "There was this one boy who stood out. Although all of them had memorized the Gettysburg Address, he delivered it with such emotion that it was hard to believe he was so young. He was simply exceptional."

I wondered if Ford had taken part in that contest when he'd been a boy. Lianna returned to her chair, so I took the opportunity to pull out Ford's business card and hand it to Scarlet. "Do you happen to know this guy? He stopped by my shop," I said.

Scarlet took the card and studied it closely. Her eyes went wide. "Ford Ross is in town? Wow. He's a local superstar. Heck, that's an understatement. He's a *national* star. I'll have to give him a call and welcome him back."

Rose let out an excited shriek. "Ford Ross is in Sewickley? I just saw his photo in *Here's the Scoop*. That guy is so *hot*. So was his date. He's always out with some new actress."

Hot certainly described Ford, with his wavy light-brown hair and his too-charming smile. The tall, slim, toned slice of gorgeousness filled out a pair of jeans in an enticing sort of way. Let's just say, the man had excellent ass-ets. When he'd aimed that damned smile at me, it had made my knees go weak.

Suddenly, my brain locked onto a key part of what Rose had said. "What do you mean when you say, 'some new actress?'"

"According to *Here's the Scoop*, since his divorce, there have been a string of them. He's never dated anyone for long," Rose said with a shrug.

I furrowed my brows as I reached back and pulled my ponytail tighter.

Lianna arched an eyebrow. "You read *Here's the Scoop*?"

Rose shrugged. "Sure. *People*, too. And *E! Online*." She toyed with the little book charm on her wineglass. "We have all sorts of magazines in the library. I might love books, but I also adore looking at photos of beautiful people on the red carpet."

Gertrude set her napkin on the table and sat up straighter. "As in, the red carpet at a movie premiere?"

"Yes!" Rose squealed. "Ford Ross won an award at Sundance for best director. He's a hot commodity. Can you believe it? A Sewickley native!"

"His movie was great," Scarlet said, her pride and pleasure apparent in the warmth of her voice. "The theater here in Sewickley brought it back for a repeat showing after he won."

My head was spinning. Red carpets, movie stars, awards - it was all so overwhelming. I plopped down clumsily onto the patio cushion. Ford's life sounded vastly different from mine, and he sounded a bit too famous for my tastes. Not to mention, Rose's comments suggested he was a womanizer. I didn't want to get mixed up with someone who ran through women like they were nothing more than discarded tissues. Not after the way Doug had cheated on me.

I stopped myself, not wanting to dwell on Doug. I crossed my legs, leaned against the arm of the sofa, and forced myself to relax.

Scarlet sat between me and Courtney, and Courtney turned to her. "I don't watch movies or follow the entertainment industry, so why does Ford's name sound so familiar?"

"Hmm." She thought for a moment. "Maybe because he was friends with your brother Conner?" Scarlet suggested, setting her wineglass with its silver gavel charm on the coffee table before leaning back against the sofa cushions. "Ford was in the same grade as me and Conner, but he went to the private school, Middlebridge Academy. Since I attended the public school, I probably wouldn't have spent much time with him if our families hadn't belonged to the same country club. My mom and dad hosted regular fundraisers for my uncle's senate campaign. Ford's dad was a contributor."

"Now I remember him," Courtney said, nodding. "We met at Conner's graduation party."

Scarlet glanced around the table. "Am I the last to arrive? Sorry if I kept you waiting."

Courtney clinked her wineglass with Scarlet's. "We'd never start without you, Madam Mayor."

"Let's discuss the book before we get distracted again," Scarlet said. "We're bad about that. Lianna, you chose the novel we read this month. Do you have some discussion questions for us?"

As the conversation turned to the book club selection, I let out a sigh of relief. It was nice to focus on something other than Ford's celebrity status and womanizing reputation. I took a sip of my wine, savoring the dry, crisp taste, and leaned back into the patio cushion.

Thirty minutes later, Gertrude let out a satisfied sigh. "I have to admit, I haven't picked up a romance novel in years. This book has been a great reintroduction to them. Back when I used to read them in the eighties, all the heroines were virgins, and all the heroes were nothing but manipulative man-whores."

I couldn't help but laugh at her choice of words. "I think you're going to fit into our book group perfectly."

Gertrude beamed at me. "This book was a refreshing change from the ones I read back then. She was such a strong heroine. I need to start reading them again."

Lianna pierced a kalamata olive with her fork. "I'll let you look through my collection before you leave." She munched on the olive. "I have scads of them."

"We're meeting at your place next month, right, Mara?" Scarlet asked. "What book should we read? You get to choose."

I perked up. "I've been looking forward to this. I want us to read a graphic novel called *Watchmen*."

Rose bounced in her seat. "Oh! That's a popular one. We have two copies in the teen library." She looked at Lianna. "HBO did a reboot, but it's nothing like the original comic. Their miniseries is great, don't get me wrong, but you can't watch it instead of reading the graphic novel. They're completely different. Someone made a movie version of the comic sometime around 2009 that sticks closer to the original story, though."

"Is the 2009 movie any good?" Lianna asked as she tapped on her phone, taking notes.

Rose shrugged. "Good enough."

Scarlet simply raised her eyebrows at me.

I knew her well enough to interpret that look, and I sent her a sharp glance. "Don't be such a snob. Comic books have had a huge influence on our culture. If you want examples, look at all the superhero movies being made these days." Was I actually holding up a movie franchise as an example after the way I'd ripped apart the entire industry only a few hours ago? Go me. Hypocrites unite.

Lianna waved a dismissive hand. "Scarlet, you're just being Scarlet again. You're always too worried about what people think about you."

Scarlet shrugged as she selected a piece of cheese from the tray on the table. "I'm a politician. What do you expect?" She popped the cube into her mouth.

"I bet it's killing you that we read a romance this month, huh?" I teased. "What if someone caught you? Having to read a comic book must be driving the knife even deeper." I arched an eyebrow in challenge.

"Ha. Ha." Scarlet enunciated in a forced voice. "Very funny. I'm not that bad."

"Of course you aren't, love." I patted her hand. Was it possible to pat someone's hand sarcastically? If so, I might have pulled it off, because Scarlet yanked hers away. "It isn't your fault that your uncle's a senator and you've always had to be perfectly proper in every way."

Scarlet shot me an irritated scowl. "You make it sound like a bad thing. Shouldn't we all be on our best behavior at all times? It's called *being mindful*." I'd heard that well-worn adage from her many times. Someone had clearly drilled it into her over the years.

Scarlet's phone rang, and she checked the screen before standing up abruptly. "Can you excuse me for a minute? It's my uncle. He almost never calls except on the weekends," she said, scooting past Mara and heading back into the house to take the call from Senator Smith.

Rose glanced at her phone. "It's getting late. I should leave if I want to get to sleep at a decent hour."

That broke things up. Everyone started heading home. Ten minutes later, I pulled into the lot behind my building. I walked down the alley to my front door, conveniently located right next to the entrance of Ghost of a Chance.

Through my store's big plate glass window, I spotted a light still shining from behind the counter. Damn, I must have forgotten to turn it off. I quickly punched in the security code and let myself in.

I paused next to the cash register and pulled Ford's business card from my pocket, staring down at it. Rose's revelations about him earlier made me hesitate. Did I really want to get involved with someone like him? Sure, he was good-looking and seemed interested in me, but could I trust him? After what happened with Doug, I couldn't take any more chances.

But then again, maybe Lianna was right and I needed to get a life. Maybe I should put myself out there and try dating again. I tossed the business card on the counter, determined to find someone else to go out with.

Just not Ford Ross. That man was a bad bet, and I wasn't willing to take that risk.

5

A QUICK DINNER

FORD

The next evening, I hauled the final two black garbage bags out the French doors of Dad's enormous pastel and chintz 1980s-style lower level of the main house. I'd spent a long day of sweaty, physical labor clearing things out down there. It was a relief to finally have it done.

Considering how many people Dad had on payroll to maintain this place, I had never understood why he let the lower level get into such a state of disrepair. He had a maid who cleaned twice a week, plus a groundskeeper. Why couldn't he hire someone to clean out the basement?

Years ago, when my siblings and I were teenagers, he'd told the maid to stop cleaning the lower level. We kids were supposed to take care of it ourselves. That never really happened though. The place had just become a dumping ground for all our crap.

I work out regularly these days and am in decent shape, but man, clearing out all that junk wore me out. It had taken all day, but I'd managed to clear away most of the years of accumulated crap. With four kids in the house, we'd had our share of interests growing up. Skating, skiing, fencing, karate, football, lacrosse, and all the associated equipment and clothing. Mom had always handled donating the no-longer-needed items, but after she'd died, all that discarded or outgrown stuff had been shunted here and ended up filling every available space—sort of like that insulation foam spray that filled all the cracks and crevices.

I even found the hockey stick I'd broken back in third grade in a corner of the unused home gym. It brought back memories of my childhood and made me feel a little sentimental.

Dad had worked with me down there for a while and had helped me sort through all the stuff we'd tossed down there. He'd even agreed to donate a couple of now-empty bookcases.

I dropped the garbage bags next to the row of neatly arranged trash cans. The groundskeeper would load them onto the tractor and haul them to the end of the long driveway on trash day. I'd deal with the items to be donated myself.

With a groan, I arched my back in a stretch. Today had been a good day's work.

I stood there for a moment, taking in the deep reds and golds of the setting sun over the golf course that adjoined my dad's place. The stunning vista still took my breath away. I was fortunate to have grown up in such a magnificent home. Built in the 1800s by one of the old-time Pittsburgh steel barons as a summer residence, the interior was opulent beyond belief. The walk-out basement, however, was an ugly blemish on the otherwise impressive estate. It didn't match the elegance of the rest of the house at all with its soaring ceilings, mullioned windows and intricate woodwork.

A line of trees hid the nearby stream where I'd often gone exploring as a kid with my younger brothers. Salamanders and frogs abounded there among the lost golf balls. I collected them and passed them along to my dad. I'd managed to keep him supplied with free balls for years.

With some reluctance, I abandoned the view and turned back to my dad's place. Now that I'd cleared out the basement, I needed to convince him to hire someone to clean and paint it.

As I walked up the steps to the French doors, I couldn't help but feel that the neglected, out-of-place lower level was a reflection of my father's disinterest in life. It was as if he'd locked away a part of himself down there, disconnected from the rest of the house and his family. Maybe he was depressed. Maybe he just needed someone to help him see the light and bring him back to the vibrant person he used to be. I couldn't help but feel that renovating the lower level was a symbolic gesture, a way of showing my dad that I cared about him and wanted to bring some brightness back into his life. Those worn tropical print sofas from the 80s had to go, and the biggest guest bedroom down there was a red, white, and blue Laura Ashley nightmare. It was time for a fresh start, a new beginning for both of us.

My stomach rumbled and I checked my watch. Damn. It was nearly 8:30 already. When I'd made plans for the day, I'd originally assumed that Dad and I would spend it together and I'd eat dinner here.

At first, everything went according to plan. Dad had been enthusiastic about it, and had even helped me carry those bookcases out to the garage so we could donate them, but a few hours ago he'd turned a little pale, and started perspiring heavily. He'd said I was wearing him out.

That had sent me into a panic. "Is this too much for your heart?" I'd asked. After his heart attack five year ago, he'd seemed to spring back to full health pretty quickly, but maybe letting him help carry bookcases to the garage had been a bad idea.

He'd scowled at me and waved away my concern. "Of course not. My heart's fine. I just need to exercise a bit more. I guess I'm more out of shape than I'd realized."

Dad rubbed his chest in a distracted way. Was that gesture a habit he'd developed since his heart attack, or did it indicate something more? A moment later, he'd run a hand through his hair, wiped his forehead with his palm, and then mumbled something about an appointment he'd just remembered. He'd darted for the staircase leading back to the main level of the house before I could pry any details out of him.

An hour later, I'd gotten a text from him saying he'd gone out and wouldn't be home until late. I was on my own.

If his heart was fine, then perhaps the issue was emotional. Had I pushed him too hard to purge the basement? Did he get upset because he didn't want to get rid of all that accumulated junk? Or maybe I had simply asked too many personal questions, like when I inquired about his health and happiness.

Despite my attempts to get to the bottom of things, Dad had stonewalled me all afternoon, insisting everything was fine. I sighed, feeling like I was going in circles trying to figure out what was bothering him. My stomach growled, reminding me that I needed to eat. I decided to call my brother to see if he wanted to grab dinner.

"Hey, bro," Max said on the other end of the line, barely audible over the blaring siren.

"You sound like you're out somewhere," I said.

"I am. I just ate and I'm driving home. Hold on. A firetruck is passing me."

The wail slowly faded. "Sorry, bad timing on my part," I said once it was quieter. "I was calling to see if you wanted to grab dinner."

"Maybe tomorrow?"

"Sounds good. While I have you on the phone, do you remember Conner and Dante? I knew them back in high school. They started a restaurant in Sewickley."

"Sure, Not a Yacht Club. I've been there, that place is fantastic."

"Dante is starting a men's cooking class on Monday nights. Would you be willing to be my cooking partner while I'm in town? It'd be a great way to spend time together."

He let out a laugh, "You only got to town yesterday and you already signed up for a cooking class? Damn, you move fast. I thought you didn't know anything about cooking."

"I don't. That's why I'm taking a cooking class."

Max chuckled, "Well, at least we get to eat what we make,

right? Sure. Count me in. Could be fun. Monday, you said? I'll pick you up at Hailey's house and drive you there."

As we ended the call, my stomach growled, reminding me of my hunger. I knew that this time of day, my sister would be winding things down and getting my niece ready for bed, so I decided not to bother them for dinner. The memory of last night's easy camaraderie and those French fries covered in truffle oil and freshly grated parmesan cheese drew me in like the alluring scent of an expensive perfume.

Besides, there was always a chance that I'd bump into a certain sexy comic book purveyor at the restaurant.

Twenty minutes later, I found myself sliding onto a barstool at Not a Yacht Club as I set my copy of *Sandman* on the bar—just in case I couldn't find anyone to talk to.

The bartender placed a cocktail napkin in front of me. "What can I get you?"

"What's good for dinner tonight?" I asked.

"Are you a fan of spaghetti and meatballs? Our chef uses his grandmother's recipe. It's truly excellent."

I'd often ended up at Dante's house during mealtimes growing up. Good timing was my forte, as was my preference for excellent food. His grandmother's sauce was one of the best things I'd ever tasted. "I'll take it, with an order of those truffle fries." I spotted a bottle of wine I recognized sitting behind the bar. "And pour me a glass of that cabernet sauvignon as well."

He served my wine and then headed into the kitchen. There were more people in the bar than last night, but I didn't see anyone I knew. It felt strange to be out in public and have no one recognize me. That never happened in Los Angeles.

The only other person sitting alone at the bar was an older man with a sour expression. A guitar case rested on the floor next to him, and he hunched over his plate like a feral dog as he shoveled down his dinner.

It looked like I'd be eating alone. With an air of resignation, I turned to *Sandman*, and in a few moments I found myself immersed in a world where the personification of sleep was being held captive in a glass prison.

I was vaguely aware of someone claiming the stool next to mine. Suddenly, Mara appeared. "I see one of my comics has sucked you into its world," she said with a smile. "Be careful. Those things can become addictive. Pretty soon you'll be hiding a stash of them under your bed."

I glanced up into those gorgeous brown eyes that had been haunting my thoughts all day. They flashed with humor, and a pleasant warmth settled in my chest. She was exactly the person I'd hoped to see here tonight. "I'm trying to banish a personal prejudice that was skewing my perception of an entire genre." I tilted the comic to reveal the cover. "This is setting me straight."

Mara grinned. "I'm glad to hear it. You never know what you might discover if you open yourself up to something new. You aren't entrenched in your prejudices. That's good to know."

"Not when a clever woman takes the time to set me straight." Our eyes locked, and I leaned in as something seemed to flash between us. A moment of connection.

"How was your day?" she asked.

My reflexive smile felt tight. False. "Good question. A bit of an eye-opener, I suppose. I haven't spent much time at home in a few years, and things have changed a lot—with my dad, I mean."

She raised her eyebrows. "Is he okay?"

"I'm not sure," I admitted. "He seems healthy enough, but my sister says he sometimes cancels his appointments and holes up in his house for a day or two. She's worried about him."

I hesitated, unsure if I should continue, but something about Mara made me want to confide in her. Maybe it was the way she listened, or the warmth in her eyes. Whatever it was, I found myself speaking before I could second-guess myself.

"I don't know if it's physical or emotional," I said. "Maybe something subtle and pernicious—like depression."

Mara's expression turned sympathetic. "That's tough," she said. "Have you talked to him about it?"

I shook my head. "I've tried, but no luck so far, but I've only been here a day."

"Well, keep trying," Mara suggested. "Sometimes just knowing that someone cares can make a difference."

I nodded, feeling a weight lift off my shoulders. Mara's words had a soothing effect on me, and I found myself relaxing in her presence. For the first time in a long while, I felt like I could breathe easy. "Don't we all see our parents in a different light as we get older? More as peers?"

"I suppose that all depends on whether or not your parents still treat you like a kid," Mara muttered. "I wish I'd opened my store farther away from mine—like on the other side of the country."

Her comment made me wonder about her relationship with her parents.

Conner's arrival interrupted our conversation, and his demeanor towards me was guarded. "Mara—good to see you. Dante's working on your order. It's nearly ready." He turned to me with a sly grin. "I see you've met Hollywood. He isn't bothering you, is he?" His words were teasing, but his tone held a hint of warning.

Mara didn't seem fazed by his comment. "I have," she said, meeting my gaze. "He stopped by my store yesterday and stocked up on some excellent reading material."

Conner rubbed the back of his neck, just below his close-cropped hair. "I hear your dad did CPR on some guy who keeled over in the grocery store last week. Did he make it?"

Mara nodded. "Last I heard, the guy was doing great. Mom told me all about it."

"Your dad's really something," Conner said. "He's a real asset to the community. I bet you're proud."

Mara's smile was tight, as if there was more to the story than what she was willing to reveal. "Absolutely."

Conner turned to me. "Her parents moved here a few years

ago, but it's like they've lived here forever. Mara is a more recent transplant."

"That's right," she confirmed. "I've only been here a year." Her discomfort was palpable, and I wondered what had led her to this small town.

Dante came through the kitchen door carrying a white paper bag and set it on the bar in front of Mara. "Your order's ready," he said, and headed for the kitchen.

She grabbed it and stood. "Thanks."

"Enjoy," Conner said.

"See you around," she said. Her eyes lingered on mine for a moment before she turned and headed for the exit.

I watched her saunter out the door, her denim-clad hips swaying, her ponytail gently swinging, and her carry-out bag swinging from her fingertips. I couldn't seem to look away.

Conner came around the bar and sat on the stool Mara had vacated, blocking my view. "You two were looking cozy just now," he said.

Well, at least he was direct. "I like her."

"Yeah, I could tell. Just be careful with her. She and my sister Courtney are tight." Conner rubbed the side of his nose. "Mara hasn't been in town long, but her parents moved here a few years ago while she was still in college. They've put down roots in the community, with her younger sisters attending Sewickley High and her mother volunteering frequently. I wouldn't mess with her if I were you."

"I don't mess with people," I said, slightly annoyed by the implication.

Conner's gaze shifted past me, and his expression darkened. "Hold that thought. I need to talk to that musician before he leaves. I've received too many complaints about him."

I glanced down the bar at the morose-looking man I'd spotted earlier and saw him toss back his drink. "Mr. Sunshine over there? What's wrong? Isn't he any good?" I asked Conner, gesturing towards the musician.

"He's great. Talented as hell, but he's an asshole to pretty much anyone who talks to him." Conner shook his head. "I hate this part of the job," he muttered as he walked away.

My phone vibrated, and I pulled it from my pocket. When I read the name, I stilled. I took a moment to compose myself before answering. "Hey, McCormick. How are things on the West Coast?"

McCormick let out a huff of laughter. "The weather's perfect and the traffic sucks. You know. The usual. What the hell are you doing in Pittsburgh?" His voice held a faint sneer as he said the city name.

"Don't knock it 'til you've tried it."

"They have snow there, right?"

"Only in the winter," I said.

"I assume you'll be back in L.A. long before then."

"I know you like the snow," I countered. "You ski. Remember Lake Tahoe—two years ago? The outdoor hot tub at the house we rented? You managed to drag your half-naked ass out there in sub-zero temperatures for a soak every single night after you got off the slopes."

"True, but it's more fun to bust your balls about being in Pittsburgh."

Why did Californians always act as though no place outside their state was worth living in? I should be used to it by now, but McCormick's comments still rankled.

"That's bullshit!" The outburst from the morose musician startled me.

I turned away from the unfolding drama and focused on my call. "Pittsburgh's a great city. If you try it, you might actually like it. It's lush and green with miles of untouched forests. Nothing like the endless acres of brown out there where you live."

"You live here too."

That brought me up short. "Good point. I guess coming back here has me connecting to my roots again."

"Whatever. I wouldn't know. I'm a third-generation Californian, and proud of it." McCormick cleared his throat. "I guess you already know why I'm calling."

My chest tightened. Was that anticipation I was feeling? It felt tinged with... dread. But that couldn't be right. I had been waiting for McCormick to make me an offer for days now. "Probably, but I wouldn't want to make assumptions."

"Spoken like a cautious man."

"I don't like misunderstandings."

A series of harmonious thumps and bumps caught my attention—especially since they seemed to be moving toward me. The now angry musician stormed toward the exit, banging his guitar case against every chair he passed.

Conner watched him leave, feet wide and arms crossed, looking frustrated. He caught my eye and shrugged. "Some people can't take constructive criticism," he said. With a resigned expression, he headed into the kitchen, probably to inform Dante they'd need a new musician for Wednesday nights.

"I want you to consider this Superman movie I'm producing," McCormick said, pulling my attention back to the conversation. "You're on my shortlist to direct it. In fact, with your Sundance win, you're at the very top. You interested?"

I relaxed into my chair. "I could be."

McCormick hesitated for a beat. "What has you on the fence?"

"I haven't read the script yet." I scratched my chin, thinking carefully about my words. "I know you want an origin story remake, but making a Superman movie that's fresh and new could be tricky. You know me. I want great writing, strong dialogue, an original plot, and well-structured character arcs."

McCormick let out a low, rumbling laugh. "You artist types. I just want a successful movie. I'll FedEx you a hard copy of the script. What's your address?"

I stifled my gut-level reaction to his dismissive attitude. We "artist types" cared about those things because they were what made a movie great. I let my breath out slowly and then gave him my mailing address.

"Got it," McCormick said.

As the bartender set my truffle fries and the plate of spaghetti and meatballs in front of me, I inhaled deeply, enjoying the delicious smells. I pulled the phone away from my face and said, "You can bring the check now." I was suddenly feeling restless and needed to take a walk to think things through.

I returned the phone to my ear just as McCormick said, "It'll arrive tomorrow. Call me back within the week to let me know if you're interested."

A knot twisted in my gut. I only had a week to make a decision, and I'd hoped for more time. But showing interest wasn't the same as committing to the film. "Sounds good," I said.

As I ended the call, I checked the clock on my phone. It was already nine here, meaning it was around three in the morning in Amsterdam. I wouldn't be able to call Sheila now, but if I waited a couple more hours, I could catch her before she left for the day's film location.

I tore into my meal, and by the time Conner joined me, I was nearly finished. He snagged one of my last remaining truffle fries, but I let it slide since he looked downtrodden. "I need to hire a new musician," he said. "That guy won't be coming back."

"I guessed as much." I took in the cozy atmosphere of the bar and set some cash on top of the bill. "It feels good to be back in Sewickley."

"I get you, man," Conner said. "I felt that way when I came back to town a couple of years ago too. It's why I decided to stay and open this place."

I tucked *Sandman* under my arm as I rose to my feet. I was one of the last remaining customers in Not a Yacht Club, and the large garage door sized windows facing the river were closed, making the room feel a bit stuffy. I needed to clear my head and sort out the jumbled thoughts that swirled around in my mind. Between McCormick's offer and my concerns about Dad's health, there was a lot on my plate. It was looking more and more like my siblings were right. Something was off with my dad, and I needed to get to the bottom of it.

"See you on Monday at Dante's class," I said to Conner.

He groaned. "Why did you have to remind me?"

"Dante's right. You should know something about cooking if you're going to run this place."

"Yeah, yeah." He let out a heavy sigh. "Maybe it won't be so bad. Do you plan to stay in town long?"

I hesitated. "That's the big question, isn't it? You have a talent for getting to the meat of things. You missed your calling—you should have been an investigative journalist." I tapped my knuckles on the glossy bar top with a sharp rap. My frustration was mounting because I still didn't know how to help my dad.

"Does that mean you're thinking about staying?"

"I'll let you know once I figure it out." I headed toward the door, needing to take a walk to clear my mind.

6

A BIG DEAL

MARA

Rain pounded the pavement outside, a familiar sound that had become a constant presence in the past few weeks. The dismal weather had taken a toll on my store's revenue, leaving me with a sinking feeling in my stomach as I settled onto the stool behind the counter. I scowled at the rain through the large picture window, wishing it would let up for once.

I knew I should be using my downtime more productively than sulking, like tackling the depressing balance sheet. With the store's sales slipping, I needed to find a way to turn things around, or risk becoming another failed-business statistic. Perhaps another *Magic the Gathering* event at Dante and Conner's restaurant would do the trick.

The chime of the front door interrupted my thoughts, and a glimmer of hope flickered within me. Maybe a customer had finally decided to buy out my entire inventory. It wasn't entirely impossible.

But the person who stepped through the door wasn't a customer. It was Courtney, who never failed to lift my spirits. Despite the dreary weather, she looked immaculate in a tailored suit and black polka-dot rain boots.

"Welcome, *chica*," I said, springing up from my stool to give her a hug. I relieved her of her wet umbrella and placed it in the stand. "You don't come to my store as often as you used to."

"I know, sorry about that. Now that I'm the lead researcher for my team, I don't have much free time."

"Wow, that's impressive. I bet you'll cure cancer in no time," I said, half-jokingly.

Courtney smiled. "Wouldn't that be amazing? In the meantime, I'll read that graphic novel for this month's book club."

"*Watchmen*!" I exclaimed, excitedly leading her through the rows of shelves. "It's still pretty popular, even though it came out back in the eighties." I handed her a copy. "It's a classic."

"It looks interesting," Courtney said, examining the cover. "It's one I've been meaning to read."

I guided her back to the front of the store and positioned myself behind the counter. "You won't be disappointed." I glanced at the clock. "You're usually at work this time of day. What brings you around?"

"I had my monthly lunch with Kincaid at In Vino Veritas, so I thought I'd stop by before heading back to work."

"How's he doing?" I inquired.

"You know my brother. Busy, busy. He says he met with that movie director you mentioned, Ford Ross—" Courtney paused, watching me closely as if to gauge my reaction. "—and the guy hired him to do some painting and minor repairs to a house he owns here in town."

"For realz? Good for your bro. His construction biz is really kickin' it." Butterflies battled it out in my stomach at the thought of Ford staying in Sewickley, but I couldn't help but feel skeptical. "How long do you think Ford Ross plans to stick around?"

Courtney's lips curled into a satisfied smile. "Hard to say. According to Kincaid, Ford usually rents out his house, but it's empty right now. Apparently, he plans to live there for the next few weeks instead of with his family. I feel sorry for the guy. Can you imagine having to live in your sister's guest room?"

I cringed at the thought. "There's no way I could ever live with anyone in my family again. I'd rather sleep in my car. Dad would drive me right over the edge with his constant sniping."

"I need my own space where I can unwind at the end of a long day." Courtney placed her copy of *Watchmen* on the countertop.

I scanned the barcode. "By the way, book club members get a ten percent discount."

"Thanks, Mara, but you don't have to do that." Courtney waved away my offer, using a Jedi mind trick like Obi-Wan-Kenobi.

"What's the point of owning a store if you can't help out your peeps?" I put her purchase in a bag since it was still pouring outside.

"Thanks," Courtney said, grabbing her umbrella from the stand. "I gotta bounce. I have a meeting in half an hour."

Back at my computer, I once again stared at my balance sheet, but I wasn't in the mood to deal with it right now.

Giving in to a moment of weakness, I clicked away from my spreadsheet and opened my browser. A quick search brought up the *Here's the Scoop* website—the trashy celebrity gossip magazine Rose had mentioned at book club. Pages of photos of Ford Ross filled my screen.

Rose was right. In every single photo, Ford stood arm-in-arm with a different stunning woman. The two things all his dates had in common were their extreme beauty and their gorgeous dresses.

Oh... and Ford. Make that three things.

I felt like the website had just taken a wiki-leak all over me.

My phone rang, and I glanced at the screen. Of course, it was Dad. This should be the dollop of poo icing on a craptastic day.

"Hi, Dad. What's up?" I said cheerfully. Might as well start out that way, because we'd only go downhill from here.

The door chime jingled as the mail carrier pushed inside. She handed me a rubber-banded bundle and then picked up the outgoing mail before leaving with a distracted wave.

"Hey, pumpkin," Dad's voice boomed. "How are things?"

Maybe Dad would be nice for a change—I could hope.

While I was at it, I might as well buy a lottery ticket and dream big.

"Things are good. The store is quiet right now since it's raining, but I'll have to ring off if someone shows up."

The stack of bills and junk mail included a larger envelope hand-addressed to me—Marilyn Stellar.

Curious, I ripped it open and upended it, spilling the contents on the counter, and a glossy magazine with a yellow post-it note on the cover slid out.

"I'm sure your customers could manage without having you breathing down their necks."

I bit off the retort that sprang to my lips as I flattened my palm against the magazine.

Don't react. Dad's trying to get under your skin. Don't react. Don't react.

Oh, what the hell.

React.

"Seriously, Dad? Are you suggesting that I should ignore my customers? Is that what you do when your patients come to your office? Ignore them?"

"It's hardly the same thing. I'm a doctor. My patients come to see me. Your customers come to see your stock. You're entirely replaceable."

I looked around my pristine, well-organized shop showcasing comic books and graphic novels. My favorite Wonder Woman poster with its "be the hero of your own life" quote hung on the wall, and the remaining limited-edition figurines were proudly displayed in the small but alluring window exhibit. Rage coursed through me. "Thanks for the vote of confidence. I was foolish to think I brought anything distinctive to this place. You're brutally honest, I'll give you that."

"Sorry, pumpkin, but I'm just telling it like it is."

"There's a difference between being truthful and being mean.

Chance and I always dreamed of opening this store together. I wish you'd stop trashing it."

"That shop was your brother's dream, not yours."

Dad's comment hit like a physical slap to the face. I closed my eyes as I caught my breath."You know that's not true. Chance and I were working together to open this store." Though in truth, my role was limited to behind-the-scenes tasks such as orders and taxes, while Chance planned to oversee the day-to-day operations.

When I opened my eyes and looked down at my countertop, the face on the magazine cover in front of me finally registered. I stopped breathing. I knew those brown eyes. That dark skin and broad, endearing smile. I peeled the post-it off the photo to reveal Destiny, my former roommate and business partner, smiling at me from the cover of *Boston Business* like she had the world by the tail.

Destiny Woodworth in negotiations to sell Stel-Wood Game Studios.

I inhaled sharply. She'd actually done it. She'd become the hero of her own life. Something inside my chest seemed to deflate, like a flattened whoopee cushion that had just farted.

"What about the career you invested in?" Dad asked. "The one making video games? How could you let yourself get side-tracked? Seriously, Mara. You need to stop being so stubborn. I might not play video games, but even I could recognize the creativity of the game you and Destiny were developing. I can't believe you gave up on your own company for Chance's half-baked idea."

My heart clenched, and I suddenly had trouble breathing. Here it was... proof that I was a screw up, just like Dad always said. Was his timing impeccable, or what? Did he already know Destiny was working on a deal to sell Stel-Wood? But no. Definitely not. He would have led with that rather than dancing around it.

What would my life have been like if I hadn't turned my back on everything Destiny and I had built? Would we even be considering selling our nascent company? I paused for an instant. Stel-

Wood wasn't our baby anymore. When a personal crisis had hit, I had abandoned it.

Nothing about our company had turned out the way we'd planned. Certainly not for me. Not for Destiny either, I was sure of it since she was about to sell. But what other decision could I have made? "I didn't have the heart for it anymore. Not after…"

Dad only let the silence linger for an instant. "After Chance was killed?" His bald statement sliced into me.

Even a year later, those words still hit with the force of a physical blow. Right now, I just wanted to hurl the phone across the room to silence him. I tightened my grip as I resisted the impulse. "Exactly. I know you didn't approve of his career choices, but you could have been more supportive when he was still here. Hell, you could have—"

"He was my son, Mara," Dad interrupted, his tone harsh. "I know he was your twin. I know you were close. But sometimes you act like you're the only person in this family grieving."

There it was. According to him, I was wrong, and he was right… again. The last thing I wanted to do was listen to my father wrap himself in some contrived shroud of grief when no one understood what losing Chance meant more than I did. What the world had lost without him in it.

Dad's disdain for Chance's hopes and dreams had wounded him. Dad knew precisely how to undermine a person. He'd applied his well-chosen words with surgical precision, and he'd readily sliced into both me and Chance—into my other siblings too, but not as often.

Dad may be on board with my video game company now, but that wasn't always the case. He used to mock my career choices when Destiny and I were struggling to find investors for our game, yet he berated me for selling it to open Ghost of a Chance. No matter what I did, it was always wrong in his eyes.

"You should have been a supportive father while Chance was still alive—"

"Do we have to go through this again?" Dad snapped. "I

thought an art degree was a waste of money. I wanted him to choose a career where he could support himself. Is that a crime?"

"Seems like you've changed your mind since then. You didn't mind sending Rachael and Aubrey off to chase their dreams on stage," I said, frustrated at the unfairness of it all. He hadn't stood in the way of my younger sisters when they pursued careers in acting and dance. That still bothered me. I didn't resent them, I just wished Dad had been more supportive much sooner. "You're a hypocrite."

"I may be old and stubborn, but I can learn from my mistakes. Besides, your sisters are extremely talented."

"*Chance* was extremely talented!" I shouted back at him. "Are you saying he wasn't?" Did my father purposely try to infuriate me this way? Because he was damn good at it. "Never mind. Forget I asked. I don't want to hear your answer. At least you're finally admitting you treated him badly."

"I admit to treating each of my children exactly the way I think they need to be treated. Sometimes one of them needs a kick in the pants," he said, clearly irritated. I could hear that sentence echoing in my head as I curled up, despising how my father's words could still make me feel like I wasn't good enough, as though I wasn't trying hard enough. At least I'd managed to strike back this time. I just wished I could do it more often. "I still think he needed to be pushed. Your brother always performed better when he faced a challenge."

Typical. Dad always thrived on making each of us kids do whatever it was he wanted us to, even if it meant manipulating us. Like that time he'd had me transferred into a different classroom in fifth grade "for my own good." I found out later he'd wanted to separate me from my best friend Tina, who he'd deemed a distraction. Then, there was that time when I was a junior in high school and Dad called the police on my eighteen-year-old boyfriend when we crossed the state border to attend a concert. The guy had broken up with me over that fiasco. He'd said I "wasn't worth the potential jail time." Not that I blamed him. At least Dad had dropped the charges after that.

I dropped my head onto my folded arms. I was tired. So tired. Tired of fighting with Dad. Tired of trying to make this store a success. But mostly, I was tired of missing Chance.

Couldn't life be easier? If only a little bit? Maybe this was my fault, too. Did I really need to argue with my father every single time we talked? Chance had always been the one to go toe-to-toe with him, often defending me. Without him around, I was forced to take care of myself. I had to admit, it was my own fault as much as Dad's when we got into it. I should know better than to confront him. The man almost never backed down.

Trying to lighten the mood, I forced myself to sound cheerful. "Or maybe Rachael and Aubrey finally wore you down. I've heard the youngest kids have an advantage. By the time they come along, the parents have already been broken in."

"You and your brothers certainly did a number on me," he replied, his voice laced with irritation. A long silence followed before he spoke again. "You know, Marilyn, it's not too late for you to reconnect with Destiny and ask her to take you back. You could follow your own dreams instead of Chance's. Your mom and I would be happy to offer whatever financial support you need to buy back into Stel-Wood."

It was like a gut punch. My breath caught, and tears stung my eyes. A hollow feeling settled in my stomach. He had never made such a generous offer before. Why now? And why did he have to pair any kindness with a subtle insult?

I stashed Boston Business underneath a pile of comic books on the countertop as quickly as I pushed aside my father's alluring suggestion, then I stilled. "Is that why you called today? To convince me I gave up on my own dreams? That ship has sailed. I own Ghost of a Chance now. I'm happy. You need to let it go." I could never forgive myself if I let this store die. Why couldn't Dad understand that? Why didn't he ever actually *listen* to me?

"Don't turn me down immediately. Think about it for a while

and we can revisit it. You might believe you're content owning that store, but I know better. You're unhappy. Listen, I'm pulling into the hospital parking garage, so I'll lose the cell signal. I'll call you later so we can discuss this further, pumpkin. Maybe you can—"

The call disconnected.

I groaned in frustration and stuffed my phone into the back pocket of my jeans. Dad drove me insane.

I grabbed the *Boston Business* magazine back out from under the stack of comics. A small rectangle of paper came out with it and fluttered to the floor.

I picked it up.

Ford's business card. I'd placed it here the other night after book club, and I must have put that stack of comics on top of it. Great—yet another unresolved issue. I didn't want Ford to distract me, so I set his card on the counter.

I returned to the magazine and flipped to the article about Destiny. According to it, two major video game companies were competing to acquire Stel-Wood Game Studios, which was precisely what she and I had always envisioned. I sometimes missed those days of cranking out new code and guzzling coffee while trying to meet a deadline. It had been intense work, but I had found my niche in the world. I had adored my work. Our goal had been to release our kickass creation and use the revenue to develop our next fantastic game. Then... well, after that, the sky was the limit. At present, my sky felt like a suffocating bubble determined to suffocate me and quash every dream I had ever had. I feared that my brother's dream would be the ultimate casualty.

Befuddled and frustrated, I let out a heavy sigh. In my present sour mood, I might as well go back to figuring out how to rescue my store. I inserted Ford's business card inside Destiny's maga-zine to keep my place and put it aside. Back at my computer, those images of Ford and his slew of actresses confronted me. The man was dangerously alluring, and the women he dated were stunning. Scratch that—they were smokin' hot. My gaze drifted to the magazine, only to have my eye snag on Ford's business card protruding from the top.

Ford. I couldn't get away from him today. My chest tightened as I recalled his smile. The way it lit up his entire face did something to my insides—as did his amazing body. A wave of heat ran through me, heading directly to my sexy parts.

Shut that down, girl.

Ford might be sex on a stick, but getting involved with him was a terrible idea. He didn't plan to stay in town for long, and I wasn't interested in a casual relationship.

I glanced at that Wonder Woman poster behind my register. Ford had said I resembled her. A smile tugged at the corners of my mouth, then I read the caption again about being the hero of your own life. My smile fell, and I looked away. I should play it safe. Be smart. That fiasco with Doug had sent me scampering far from the dating scene. If I decided to try going out again—a big if —it certainly wouldn't be with a player like Ford—plus he wasn't planning to stay.

I didn't need another relationship filled with potholes in my life. I already got enough turmoil from Dad, thank you very much.

My self-confidence had been shattered. Would I ever regain it?

Could Dad be right?

That thought brought me up short. Dad's not-so-subtle digs were insidious. Doug's had been too. I needed to figure out how to protect myself from his negativity without Chance's help because I was failing at it.

I chucked *Boston Business* and the makeshift bookmark of Ford's business card in the trashcan under my counter. But I couldn't throw away the article about Destiny and Stel-Wood. I was proud of what we'd accomplished, even if that pride was tinged with regret.

I pulled the magazine from the waste bin. A piece of chewing gum stuck to Destiny's smooth, brown forehead, and I used a tissue to gently peel it away.

I couldn't trash the magazine, but I didn't want to obsess over it either.

With determination, I strode into my storage room and headed for a high shelf where I'd placed a box of comic-book-related mementos. I had to take out my stair-stepper to reach it. Being short was frustrating. Chase wouldn't have had this problem. I missed him being so tall and reaching the upper shelf in a cabinet.

I opened the box, ready to slip the magazine inside, and my gaze lingered on the stack of early panels Chance had inked for Ghost before switching to digital tools. I paused, feeling a little unsteady on the stair climber.

Tears pricked the backs of my eyes, and my heart pounded too hard. I touched the plastic sleeves protecting the panels, but then snatched my hand away as though I'd been burned.

I needed to keep a lid on that chapter of my life, or my grief and regret would overwhelm me. Sometimes, I felt as though I was holding onto this new life I'd forced into existence by a thin thread that could break at any moment. Where would I end up if I fell?

I placed the magazine in the box and snapped the lid shut.

As I settled back at my computer at the front of the store, I turned the screen back on and was immediately confronted by photos of Ford from "Here's the Scoop." There was something about his eyes that I couldn't seem to ignore. Even now, when I looked at them, I felt that snap of connection.

Rain pattered against the sidewalk outside, but the shop was silent, a vast change from two days ago when Ford had ducked in here. I hadn't had such a great conversation with anyone but him in ages. I hadn't felt that sort of connection with a man ever before.

7

SHOT DOWN

FORD

As I walked down the sidewalk in Sewickley, my shadow grew longer behind me. The recent rainstorm had left the sky a pale blue, and I took in the fresh scent of the damp earth. But my thoughts were interrupted by the sound of Sheila's angry voice blasting through my cell phone. I pulled the phone away from my ear, bracing myself for the onslaught of her anger.

"Sorry," I repeated. "I thought you said you had to be on location early this morning for filming. If I had known you were planning on sleeping in, I wouldn't have called at the crack of dawn." I pushed open the door of Ghost of a Chance as I spoke.

I spotted Mara and a rush of something—happiness? desire? simple contentment?—filled me. She was wrapped up with a customer, completely unaware of me. She looked as gorgeous as I remembered, maybe even better.

She slid a glossy graphic novel into a shopping bag. The skinny teenager nearly snatched it from her in his eagerness to hold his newest possession.

His Precious? I half expected the guy to cackle "me wants," in a Smeagol-like reenactment of Lord of the Rings.

"You deserve the earful you got. Asshat." Sheila's voice in my ear was as cold and bitter as yesterday's coffee. "Today's been shitty, and I blame you for starting it off that way. You woke me up an hour early. It rained all day, and I'm having problems with my lead actress. I swear, all I've wanted for the past hour is to go back to my hotel, pour myself a drink, and climb into bed."

I could hear the beep of a hotel room unlocking and the clunk of the door opening before Sheila's heavy sigh. "At least I've managed that first part. I'm back in my room."

If I didn't know her so well, I'd be intimidated. But based on a friendship that extended back to film school, I knew if I let her tirade roll, she'd purge it and then return to her normal self.

"Sounds shitty, all right." I could relate. Having a day when nothing goes right is bad enough, but during filming, the financial and social consequences could be amplified. If the wrong person took notice, my bad day could end up being described in detail in *Here's the Scoop*—the bane of my existence—and everyone could critique and lampoon me.

While I was talking to Sheila, Mara scowled at me from across the room. She sent a sharp glance towards a pair of boys browsing the racks.

I reviewed the last words I had spoken and grimaced in apology. I shouldn't have used the word "shitty" in front of her young customers.

I moved away from Mara and down one of the aisles. The vivid comic books were displayed on polished birchwood shelves. The bright overhead lights heated the top of my head and provided ample light in what might have been a dark and cramped space. As a director, I had developed an acute awareness of light and shadow, and I appreciated how Mara used it in her shop to keep the place bright and inviting rather than harsh and glaring.

"How'd you guess?" Sheila grumbled. "Everything was flat today. I had to fight to get anything usable on film. My lead actress is being a pain in the ass. Now she wants a day off to deal with some personal shit. I don't have time for this."

"Are you talking about Zoey?" I asked, surprised. "I've always found her to be a consummate professional. I doubt she'd ask for time off if she didn't need it. Besides, if you let her deal with her problem now, there's a good chance she'll be more focused. Grateful, too." I slid a comic book off the shelf, glanced through it, and decided it looked interesting. I grabbed a copy of the previous issue as well.

"Of course you'd side with her. You took her to the Oscars last year. Or did she take you? I can never keep track of your social calendar."

I let out a harsh laugh. "I haven't taken a real date to one of those industry events in years. I only go with work colleagues. You should know that since you and I have gone to so many openings together. Besides, Zoey has been with the same guy for a couple of years now. He hates the spotlight."

She blew out a sigh. "I'd have been more willing to give Zoey the time she asked for if she hadn't been distracted all week during filming. We've had to keep reshooting her scenes, and now we're behind schedule and over budget."

"In the long run, you'll be better off if you give her time to sort out her shi—" I remembered the two boys nearby and glanced at Mara over the tops of the shelves to find her watching at me with an irritated frown. "Uh—her life. That way, filming can start going smoothly again. Talk it over with Zoey and see what she says. Ask if the time off will make her less distracted."

Mara kept frowning at me today. Was something wrong?

"Fine. I'll try it your way, even though it means I'll have to rearrange my shooting schedule. Zoey had better appreciate it." She sighed. "You know, Ross, sometimes you come up with some decent ideas. I guess that's why I put up with you." The sound of rattling ice whispered across the satellites and cell towers as Sheila took a sip of something. "Mmm. That's better. Now, tell me. What was so important that you had to call me at five in the morning?"

And there it was. She had talked through her problems and was now relaxed. "It's McCormick," I said flatly. "He finally called and offered me the movie."

She let out a soft cackle. "You mean the superhero movie, not the superhero film."

She let out a soft cackle. "You mean the movie, right? It's called a superhero *movie*, not a superhero *film*."

That hit home. Would people view this shift in my career as selling out? All my other films had been small, artistic, and thought-provoking. They had focused on character development and nuance, but many of my artistic choices and creative workarounds had been due to my tight budgets. "You sound like a snob when you say sh—," I stopped myself, "things like that. You know that, right?"

Sheila snapped back a retort. "Go suck a duck, asshat. You called me for advice, remember? What gives you the right to call me a snob?" It was a good thing Mara couldn't hear the kind of language Sheila was using on the other end of this conversation. She'd go ballistic.

Mara was doing something on the computer now, her ponytail brushing against her neck. She kept flicking it, as though she didn't know that motion drove me wild. How would that ponytail feel wrapped around my hand? Silky, I bet. And soft.

She was such a strong, determined woman. Would she enjoy letting me control our fun together in that small way? Wrapping her ponytail around my palm, before I bent her back over the sofa and—

"Does everyone think I'm a snob?" Sheila asked.

I placed a hand on top of a nearby rack to ground myself. "Undoubtedly. Face it, Sheila. You're a snob. Own it." At this moment, I wanted nothing more than to end this call and focus all my attention on the bewitching Mara, but instead, I turned my back on her and all that—distraction. "I wanted to run my thoughts on the project past you, but since you insist on taking your bad mood out on me, maybe we should talk some other time. McCormick wants my answer in a week."

"Call me after you've read the script."

"Will do." I ended the call.

Since Mara was alone now, I sauntered over to her, taking in all that gorgeous nerdiness.

She raised an inquiring eyebrow. "Urgent call?" she asked playfully. I couldn't quite make out her mood. She'd seemed irritated with me a moment ago, but now I saw a spark of curiosity.

I leaned onto the counter and lowered my voice so no one else in the store could overhear. "I was talking to a friend to get some advice. I got an offer last night to direct a Superman movie."

She stiffened. "That's big." The faint spark of playful interest disappeared. Her smile didn't reach her eyes and barely infused her cheeks. "Congratulations."

I watched her closely, trying to decipher her reaction. "I need to read the script and decide if I want to take it on."

Avoiding my eyes, she glanced down at the computer and clicked something on the screen. "You'd head back to L.A. to film it, right? Why wouldn't you jump at the chance to direct a big movie?"

She wouldn't look at me. Did the idea of me filming out in Los Angeles bother her? Was she starting to care about whether or not I planned to stick around?

"Rumor has it that McCormick is attached to the script exactly as is," I explained. "If the storyline and writing are subpar, I won't be allowed to do much to fix it. Starting a project by fighting with the producer over the script sets a bad tone."

She lifted her hand to her face. The sunlight streaming in through the window glinted off her shiny cuff-style bracelet as she scratched her jaw. The moment my gaze fell to her mouth, she dropped her hand, as though suddenly self-conscious. "So, it's all about the script?" Something about her question sounded forlorn —and faintly heartbroken.

A sudden sense of loss pierced me. Of longing. Was that what was bothering Mara? She didn't want to develop feelings for someone who'd only leave her. "At this stage, it's key," I admitted. "But to answer your question, I'm not sure." I stared down at the counter, about to reveal something I hadn't talked about to anyone. "I'm at a turning point in my career, and choosing the right project is critical. Doing something like this Superman movie with a big studio could be a great opportunity for me... but only if I can make something truly amazing. I have a lot riding on this decision."

"And he's giving you a week to make it?" She pressed her lips together in a frown.

So, she *had* been eavesdropping. I kind of liked that, since it meant she was as fixated on me as I was on her.

"A week to respond," I clarified. "If I like the script, it will come down to negotiating details with the producer. I'm a control freak when it comes to my films. I admit it. It's what makes me a good director. But that also means I'll need a solid contract that gives me complete creative control." I also needed to weigh what I'd get regarding my career with what I'd be giving up personally. I was about to say as much when two boys who'd been shopping approached the counter, clutching their selections. I stepped back to let them make their purchases.

Mara flashed them a smile. That upturn of her lips did crazy things to my insides. Made me want to share my personal dreams rather than my career ones—dreams I was only beginning to comprehend. After that, I'd like to slide my hands through her hair, back her up against the wall and tease my tongue into her mouth—

"Did you find everything you were looking for?" she asked.

The boys stood like two deer in the headlights. All they could do was nod wide-eyed at Mara as they stared at her in pubescent awe. I couldn't blame them. She was a marvel.

These two looked like they were around twelve. At their age, I would've been tongue-tied too if I'd been facing Mara's feminine beauty. Damn, she was hot. She'd swapped yesterday's red, white, and blue Wonder Woman t-shirt for a black-and-gray version that fit her like a glove. Where did she stash her lasso of truth? She could try it out on me any time.

No glasses today, though. Maybe contact lenses? I liked having an unobstructed view of her face. Her features seemed more delicate without glasses. Or maybe it was because there was nothing between us—not even her glasses. Earlier, I'd caught a glimpse of something in those cognac-brown eyes of hers. Something she'd managed to hide from me when she'd worn her glasses. Interest. In me—and that was as hot as hell.

"Stop by next Tuesday." Mara held up flyers with an announcement emblazoned across the top and then shoved one into each bag. "I'm giving away free copies of a brand-new comic about a boy who can shape-shift. First come, first served."

Her two young customers looked suitably impressed. "Thanks. We'll be here," one of them said.

The door closed behind them with a jingle of bells that would forever make me think of her.

Mara stepped out from behind the counter, but she didn't meet my eyes. Was she afraid of what I'd see in them? That hint of interest?

"If you don't make the Superman movie, what'll you do instead?" she asked.

"That's the big question. There's a lot for me to consider. I've been focusing on my career these past ten years, but I've also lost touch with my family." It was easy for me to confess that to her. Something about Mara urged me to be open and honest. "I used to be an integral part of their lives, but not anymore. Hollywood might be the easiest place to be, career-wise, but it's not the only place where I can make movies."

She finally met my gaze. "That's a big part of why I'm here. Family." Her expression turned sad. "Don't wait too long. You never know what might happen. Lost opportunities can never be recaptured. All you can do is create new ones."

I moved closer to her, wishing I hadn't made her think of

whatever was making her sad. I reached out and cupped her soft cheek.

She closed her eyes and pressed her face into my hand, as though relishing the comfort and connection I offered.

I couldn't resist. I wanted to be even closer to her, and those gently parted lips beckoned me. I lowered my head and let my mouth hover scant millimeters from hers.

She sensed me there and closed the gap, pressing her lips against mine.

Her mouth was warm. Soft. Gentle. Then eager, pressing into me—but an instant later she pulled away, blinking her eyes as if waking from a dream.

Her open, expressive face immediately shuttered as she backed away from me and scurried back behind the counter. She erased every bit of evidence of our brief moment of passion—as if that kiss had never happened.

With the counter between us, Mara morphed into someone else—someone businesslike—and tucked a stray lock of hair neatly back into place behind her ear as easily as she'd tucked away her emotions. "It isn't raining, so I can't imagine what brings you here today," she said tightly. "Should I thank you for not driving away my customers?" She sat on her stool and turned her attention to her laptop.

Her cool tone chilled me, but the shield she raised cut me off from her. I needed to tease her back into a bantering mood. "I thought I made up for my bad behavior last time by buying all those comics and graphic novels."

I leaned my hip against the counter and edged closer to her, but she refused to even glance at me. Instead, she focused on her computer screen.

"The ones you recommended were excellent," I said, adjusting to this new, unsteady footing between us. "Thanks for adding me to your mailing list. I'm looking forward to reading the new releases. In the meantime, I was hoping I could find some back issues."

She stiffened. She looked embarrassed as she finally glanced at me and then away again. "Um. The new issues came out yesterday. Wednesday is the traditional release day."

My heart sank, and I watched as she ostentatiously busied herself organizing an already organized rack of *Magic the Gathering* card packs. Mara was easy to read. She'd intentionally left me off her email list, and now she was embarrassed at being caught. This woman would be crap at playing poker.

She was irritated with me. I was nothing more than an inconvenience.

I suddenly realized I wanted just the opposite. I wanted to be everything to this woman.

"You decided to leave me off your email list," I clarified.

She shrugged. She couldn't look much more uncomfortable as she avoided my eyes. Her tongue darted across those full lips. "I decided to keep my distance from you."

A streak of sensation shot straight down my spine to the pit of my stomach. Those were some mixed signals she was sending, simultaneously seductive and distancing.

I leaned in. "That seems like a rash decision. Don't you think we should have a date before you decide to cut my part from your life and leave me on the editing room floor?"

She leaned back, finally meeting my eyes and revealing a stunning flash of warm brown. Then she let loose a shaft into my heart. "A date with you? Thanks for asking, but no. You live in Los Angeles, and you don't *have* a part in my life. Not with *your* reputation."

I straightened, then tilted my head, flummoxed. At least she'd been direct, even if she'd left me confused. "What reputation?"

She let out a frustrated sigh and lowered her voice, even though we were completely alone. "I'm referring to all the different women you've dated. I've seen the photos in *Here's the Scoop*. You're always with someone new. I'm not interested in a disposable relationship."

My back went rigid. "I'm with a different *actress* in every photo," I corrected, emphasizing the point that I wasn't with numerous girlfriends, only actresses I'd worked with.

"Sure. Whatever," she said, clearly not understanding the distinction I was making. She reached up to push her nonexistent glasses back up onto the bridge of her nose, and her lips tightly pursed into a shape I desperately wanted to kiss.

Frustrated at not making myself clear, I snapped at her. "Did you happen to notice that all those pictures were taken at movie-related functions? The entertainment industry happens to be my business. Those events have nothing to do with my personal life. Don't make assumptions about me based on a handful of photos. I'm not romantically involved with the women I escort. We were together because it was easier than going alone. The arrangement was mutually beneficial. That's it. End of story."

"Mutually beneficial?" She arched an eyebrow as if she thought I was using a sly innuendo.

I sighed my frustration. "Each of us needed to attend an event and didn't want to go alone. I haven't been on a real date in over a year."

Her confused expression let me know I was getting through to her, but then her jaw tightened. She seemed determined to think the worst of me, even when I was offering her a perfectly plausible—and true—explanation.

"Please. A year? I can hardly believe someone who looks like you—" she stopped when the door chimed and someone walked in.

I glanced over my shoulder, glaring at the person who'd interrupted us. When I recognized the raven-haired woman in the doorway, I broke into a smile. "Scarlet Smith? How many years has it been?"

She darted over and wrapped me in a merciless hug. "Way too many, Ford Ross. Congratulations on your Sundance win." She glanced at Mara, read something in her expression, and then looked back at me again. "I hope you aren't causing trouble."

"Me? Trouble? Never. You were always the one living on the edge."

"Shh." She smacked me playfully against the chest. "That's supposed to be our secret."

Grinning, I glanced at Mara, but she wouldn't meet my eyes. My good mood faltered.

Mara forced an over-bright smile as she came out from behind the counter. "What brings you in today, Scarlet?"

"I need a copy of *Watchmen* for book club." As they hugged, Scarlet's eyes shot daggers at me over Mara's shoulder. I almost stumbled back. Did she blame me for Mara's mood?

"I'll give the two of you a minute to catch up," Mara said, oblivious to our silent exchange. "I was about to grab some new releases Ford wants. I'll get you a copy of *Watchmen* while I'm at it." Mara headed between her shelves, leaving me alone with Scarlet.

Scarlet moved closer to me. "What's going on in here?" she hissed. "What did you do to piss her off?"

I grimaced. "We were having a connection, and I kissed her. When I asked her out, she turned me down flat. Apparently, she thinks I sleep around. I'm pretty sure she just accused me of being a slut."

Scarlet grinned. "You? Seriously? She clearly doesn't know you very well."

I dragged my fingers through my hair. I still needed to get a haircut. "How could she? We've known each other less than a week. Is there any chance you could set her straight?"

That took her by surprise. "You're asking *me* for help?"

I wasn't beyond giving her a pleading look.

She put her hand on her hip and stared up at me, a calculating gleam in her eye. "Fine, but you'll owe me one. A *big* one."

Knowing Scarlet and the political ambitions that ran in her family—and in her veins—it could be a big favor indeed. "Anything."

A small smile ticked up the corner of her mouth, seeing how

desperate I was to be on Mara's good side. "I'll remind you of that promise when I hit you up for a campaign donation in a couple of years."

I let my head drop back as I stared up at the ceiling for a moment and wondered how much money I'd have to spend to satisfy her. Then I lowered my head and met her gaze, giving her a single nod.

Scarlet's eyes widened. "You really *are* desperate. I was only joking about the donation."

Mara came back, carrying the items she'd selected. "I had to go to my storeroom to find one of Ford's. Let me ring him up first." She shot me a coolly professional smile. "These are the most recent releases of the ones you bought last week. Will that be all?"

"For now." I gave her a level stare, with a hint of sultriness mixed in. She averted her eyes as her cheeks turned an interesting shade of pink. "I know you weren't open to my other suggestion, but I still hope we can talk. I want to learn more about your take on comics and the movie industry. I found the comments you made the other day... refreshing. Let's have coffee. My treat."

She glanced at Scarlet, then back at me again, then shrugged. "I work long hours. The only days I'm closed are Sunday and Monday, and then I'm usually busy getting all my laundry and shopping done for the week."

"Workaholic," Scarlet said.

"Think about it," I urged. "I could always bring coffee here to the store."

She replied with another noncommittal shrug.

My fingers brushed hers as she passed me the bag, and she snatched her hand back as if my touch had sent a blaze of fire up her arm. Her eyes widened in surprise and then locked with mine for an instant.

The attraction between us flared, undeniably. She couldn't hide it from anyone—except maybe herself.

8

ENDORSEMENT

Scarlet waited until the door closed behind Ford before she whirled to face me. "What was all that about?"

"What was all what about?" I deadpanned, hoping to buy some time while I tried to make sense of what had happened. Had Ford and I actually kissed? Had he really asked me out? And had I actually *turned him down*? The hottest guy I'd spoken with in —forever?

One part of me wanted to scream in protest, like a kid who just had a toy torn away, while another part of me was convinced I'd done the right thing.

Well, I'd done it. Besides, he'd probably take that movie deal and head back to Los Angeles where he could date gorgeous actresses and attend film openings.

A little voice in my head screamed that I'd made another horrible decision fueled by self-doubt, but I ignored it as I rang up Scarlet's order.

"Don't play dumb with me," Scarlet said. "The tension between the two of you was so thick I thought it would smother me."

I forced a false bravado as I slid *Watchmen* into a bag. She was

77

way too perceptive for my own good. "Chill. I shut down emotionally when I get nervous. Don't judge me."

"What's going on? Spill it."

I heaved a sigh. The last thing I wanted to do was explain myself when I didn't understand why the hell I'd just done what I'd done. Unfortunately, Scarlet could be as tenacious as a Dalek— minus the whole chasing down Dr. Who and all the humans while shrieking "exterminate" bit. I might as well tell her and get it over with. "Ford asked me out, and I turned him down. End of story."

Scarlet's jaw dropped. "Why the hell would you turn down Ford Ross? Are you insane? The man is gorgeous, talented, and a genuinely great guy."

I stilled, but I couldn't hide my grimace of dismay. Scarlet's 'genuinely great guy' comment made me doubt myself all the more, but then I gave myself a mental shake. Even if he was the nicest guy on the planet, the two of us would never work. He planned to go back to Los Angles.

I handed her the shopping bag.

"Why should I waste my time with him? He lives in L.A. I live in Pittsburgh. Besides, he's a player. I'm a one-man kind of woman. I'm not going to spend my precious free time with some guy who's only looking for something temporary. I'm too busy as it is." Even as I spoke, I realized I was ignoring his claim that all those "dates" had been work events. Why was I lying both to myself and to Scarlet?

"You're wrong about him," she insisted. Seeing my doubt and confusion, she offered, "Why not say yes? It's obvious you're into him. And he's clearly into you. Why not go out with him and see where things go? I'm not suggesting you marry him, for cripes sake. I'm just saying the two of you could have some fun together. He'd be a perfect antidote to that jerk you used to see. They're complete opposites. Besides," she leaned in and lowered her voice, even though we were alone, "a few sessions of amazingly hot sex would do you worlds of good."

Something unexpected zinged through my belly, but I shoved

it down—way down. I gave a derisive snort as I rounded the counter to stand next to her. "You make Ford sound like he's a pro at it, but I'm not interested in something temporary."

"It might be temporary, or it might not. You won't know if you don't try. You're in your prime. You should be knocking boots with someone hot. Someone like Ford."

"That's ridiculous," I rolled my eyes. "I'm not going out with some player—some temporary fuck boy—just because you think he's hot. I want more than that."

Zing. Apparently, my stupid libido disagreed, because it gave me another jolt at the thought of sleeping with Ford. I needed to focus harder on wrestling it into submission and locking it into a deep, cold sleep.

Scarlet stilled. *"Fuck boy?"* she repeated in a near whisper, scandalized. "Ford? I don't think so. That's definitely not the person I know. I can tell you have a low opinion of him, but you're wrong. Is it because of those red-carpet photos Rose mentioned?"

I shrugged halfheartedly. He'd already explained away the photos. Why was I clinging to my own version of what they indicated? Still, Scarlet deserved some sort of explanation. "I searched for him on *Here's the Scoop*. They have loads of photos of him, and he's with a different woman in every single one. That means he's a fuck boy, through and through."

Scarlet gave a small shudder and then shook her head emphatically. "I hate that term, and I really don't think it describes him. Back in high school, he was a really decent guy. I can't believe he would change that much."

Relief washed through me. I must still have doubted him. But —how could Scarlet be so certain he was a good person? "I thought you said you didn't know him that well."

Scarlet looked doubtful. "I don't think I said that. We went to different schools, so we might not have seen each other every day, but we were still friends." She seemed to consider something and then gave a nod as she came to a decision. "I have a story to tell you, but you'll have to promise to keep it between us."

"Of course." The promise was an easy one. I'd never repeat something a friend told me in confidence. Doing so was a surefire way to destroy trust along with that relationship.

"You probably heard that my parents died when their private plane crashed while my dad was running for Congress."

Rose had told me about the incident, but I'd never asked Scarlet about it since it's not the kind of thing you bring up in conversation. "I have. I'm so sorry," I said, feeling awkward.

Scarlet nodded, barely registering my words. "You also know my uncle is a senator. After the crash, my aunt moved in with me while I finished my senior year of high school here in Sewickley. My uncle stayed in DC. It was a tough time for me—well, it was tough for all of us, but I wasn't handling my parents' deaths well. Auntie Em did her best to be supportive, but I was spinning out of control."

Scarlet crossed her arms tightly and her unfocused gaze turned inward on what had to be painful memories. "I acted out a lot. Mostly, I got drunk. I don't know what would've happened to me if I'd moved to DC. I probably would've wrapped my car around a tree. As it was, I'm pretty lucky that didn't happen. I have my conversation with Ford to thank for turning me around."

I frowned as my image of a competent and pulled-together Scarlet Smith underwent a dramatic transformation. Now I pictured the lost and lonely teen, and my heart broke for her. "I think I can still see bits of that willful, heartbroken child in you, but these days you only unleash her in certain situations. You're meticulous about every detail in your life—always in control. Always image conscious."

"*Now* I am. I focus on being mindful. But back then, I partied every single weekend—weeknights, too, if I could get away with it. If I couldn't find a party at a friend's house in town, I'd meet up at Pitt with some older classmates I'd known in high school, and we'd find something to do in the city or on campus. I might have only been seventeen, but it was easy to get drunk whenever I wanted to, and I wanted to all the time."

I pictured Scarlet—wild—desperate—brokenhearted and out of control. "Your aunt didn't stop you?"

"She tried, but what could she do? The poor woman was beside herself and had no idea how to get through to me. I was grieving and lost, and I refused to talk to anyone about it."

I knew exactly how that felt, because losing Chance had had a similar effect on me. I'd been cast adrift. He'd been my defender—my anchor—and without him, I was lost. Scarlet and I had more in common than I'd realized. Grief had caused both of us to fall apart and lose our way.

Scarlet distractedly plucked a package of Magic the Gathering packs from my display stand, stared at it in consternation, and then shoved it haphazardly back onto the rack. "The Saturday after Thanksgiving, my friends and I went to a house party at a place some Pitt students were renting.

"I saw Ford there, but we just nodded and went our separate ways." She shivered. "It was a nasty night. Cold and blustery. I remember drinking something hot that was laced with alcohol and cinnamon. It warmed me up, but really did a number on me. Later that night, the police showed up, trying to break up the party. I was drunk, but not completely wasted. Since I was only seventeen and my uncle was a senator, I knew I needed to get out of there or the story could end up all over the news."

My chest tightened as I imagined how frightened she must have been. A mistake like hers could have happened to anyone in her situation, but her uncle's status would have made the fallout a million times worse.

"I lost track of my friends as everyone tried to get out of the house," Scarlet recalled with worry in her eyes. "I wasn't sure how I'd get home. I'd just found my coat where I'd left it in the kitchen when Ford came into the room behind me. He said he'd seen me zoom past him and came looking for me to make sure I was okay." She hesitated.

"What happened?" I asked, hanging on every word.

"When we heard heavy footsteps approaching, we hustled out the kitchen door and down the back steps. I think we barely avoided getting caught. We escaped down a snowy alley and headed down the street to his car.

"I still remember how lovely the police lights looked as they flashed across the snow—and how frightened I was to see the footprints we'd left coming out the door. They'd merged with all the other footprints on the slushy sidewalk though. As we drove away, I spotted the friends I'd come with climbing into their car, so I knew they'd gotten out as well. I sent them a text so they'd know I was safe.

"Ford and I were exhilarated by our near miss. Wired. We were laughing like crazy. We headed to an all-night diner and stayed there for a couple of hours, discussing all sorts of things—school, friends, holiday plans—eventually we got to the subject of what we wanted out of life. Our dreams. Our fears."

She finally turned to face me again, but when she looked into my eyes, I could tell a part of her was still caught up in that night.

"Ford already had his life planned out. He wanted to direct films." She laughed. "Movies were his favorite thing to talk about —probably still are. He loved to dissect each one he saw, analyzing plot points and camera angles and film techniques and lighting choices." Scarlet painted a vivid image of a young, enthusiastic Ford Ross that completely entranced me. "I'm sure a lot of that had to do with his father's influence.

"But he also mentioned things about the movie industry that turned him off. That's the part I wanted you to know about. He hated the way certain directors forced people to do things—like have sex—in order to advance their careers."

"The casting couch," I said with a grimace.

"Exactly. Ford was big on loyalty, even back then. He didn't see people as being disposable, or replaceable. I can't imagine he's changed so much that he's now the kind of guy who uses women and then tosses them aside. It isn't part of his moral code. Don't assume he's untrustworthy simply because you have trust issues."

Ouch. Is that the way she saw me? That I had trust issues? I pinned my flaky behavior on problems with my own self-confidence. Trust though... that was an interesting take.

SCARLET PICKED up her purchase and tucked it into her large purse.

What she'd said tracked with what Ford had told me earlier. At the time, I'd pretended to myself that he'd been lying—but even as I'd tried to fool myself, part of me had known he'd been telling the truth. A part I'd willfully ignored. Was I so messed up by my relationship with Doug that I couldn't trust anyone? How could I be that screwed up?

Scarlet slid her purse onto her shoulder. "There are moments in life that shape our futures. That night, Ford and I talked about my goals too. He helped me realize I wasn't only sabotaging myself, but also hurting my aunt and uncle, who were doing everything they could to help me. I could have destroyed my uncle's career that night. Plus, my parents would have been devastated if they'd known their deaths had made me throw away the opportunities they'd given me in life. I decided that night I needed to become a better version of myself."

"Because talking with Ford..."

"...changed me," she finished for me. "I wanted to make sure you didn't have the wrong idea about the man. I think you might not trust your own instincts after Doug betrayed you, so let me make this clear. Ford is a stand-up guy, not the sort who uses people and discards them. Don't believe the things you read in *Here's the Scoop*. That thing is nothing but a scandal rag."

My guilt for mischaracterizing him soured my stomach. "I get it," I said. "And I believe you when you say that he's not a player. He's a good person."

Every part of me screamed "take a chance," and I pressed my

lips together to hold back my words. But they still came out. "The man still has one fatal flaw. He isn't planning on sticking around."

As Scarlet looked into my eyes, her hopeful expression faded. With a sigh, she turned to the door, but then hesitated and turned back to look at me. "One last thing for you to think about, and then I'll drop it." Her clear blue eyes seemed to bore into me. "You'll never know what the two of you might have together if you don't even bother to take a chance."

9

MORE FATHER-SON TIME—OF A FASHION

FORD

As I headed toward my dad's place, Mara's rejection stung. It had been a long time since I invested so much emotional capital in a woman. Typically, I moved slowly where relationships were concerned, but with Mara, I had rushed in. And now, I was paying the price.

Women didn't stick around, that was the pattern of my life. My mom died when I was a kid, and the nannies Dad hired never lasted long. Girlfriends had come and gone in high school as well as college. And the trend continued into my adult life.

My marriage to Chelsea was no exception. We had divorced a year after tying the knot. Her career in marketing and my career in directing collided on Christmas when I couldn't attend her annual party. Despite explaining the consequences of missing a day of filming, she accused me of being selfish and not caring about her career. Her resentment towards me only grew, leaving me feeling guilty and frustrated.

Desperate to make it up to her, I bought her expensive gifts with the money I had earned from directing a film. She had seemed happy, but two days later, she cleared out half of our joint savings account and left me. Her new husband was her perfect match, always at her beck and call.

I wondered if it was too much to ask for a partner who understood the demands of my job and didn't blame me for things beyond my control. Was it too much to want someone who wouldn't abandon me when things got tough?

Just when I thought I had given up on finding someone, Mara had come along. But now, she had shot me down, accusing me of something I didn't do and refusing to believe my explanation. It raised red flags in my mind.

I hoped visiting my dad would help me clear my head. I couldn't keep dwelling on my conversation with Mara and wondering if I could have done things differently.

I drove up the long driveway of my dad's estate, with the sprawling golf course of the adjoining country club beside me. The golfers on the course were clad in an array of brightly colored shirts, each unique from the other.

As I crested the hill, the gray stone mansion with its slate-tile roof came into view, sprawling across the lush green lawn like a lolling beast. It had always been home, but now I was struck by its stunning beauty. The opulent house sat on five acres and was over a century old. Built by one of Pittsburgh's steel magnates, it resembled an enormous manor house from old England, complete with a round tower at the entrance. It had so many bedrooms that my dad could probably host twenty overnight guests and hardly bat an eye.

The grass was perfectly trimmed and edged, and a row of white phlox flowers bordered the immaculate beds. My mom had once instructed the gardeners to only use plants with white flowers, saying it made for a calming and orderly vista. To this day, the gardeners still followed those instructions.

The lawn guy who had worked for my dad for years waved at me as he drove the riding mower into one of the outbuildings.

I entered the front door into the round, stone foyer and spotted my dad's keys on the Italianate table—right where he always left them. A minute later, I found him in his opulent wood-paneled office.

"Hi, Dad," I said.

"I heard you come in," Dad replied, rubbing his hand across his chest before pressing a button on his smartwatch and frowning at the screen. He glanced at me, seeming annoyed that I had interrupted him. "I didn't expect you to stop by today."

The visit wasn't off to a great start. "I was hoping to catch you at home," I said, wanting his advice but hesitant to say so given his annoyance at my visit. "How are things?"

Dad's frown deepened into a grimace. "Could be better. I'm trying to put together a film, but nothing's gelling. I might end up having to table it for now." He glanced at his smartwatch again, seeming distracted.

Was he recording our conversation? That didn't make sense. Maybe he was checking his pulse. "What's are you—"

"I have to admit," he cut me off, "I'm not very enthusiastic about the project. Maybe that's why I can't get any traction."

"If you don't have enthusiasm at the start, you'll have a hard time forcing it later." It was the same advice he'd given me countless times before.

He waved my words away. "You don't have to tell me that. The problem is, I don't have any other projects I'm remotely interested in." He glanced at his smartwatch again before meeting my gaze. "You did a lot of work in the basement after I left, clearing things out."

I tensed, feeling uneasy. Had I overstepped? "Yeah. I wanted to finish the job in one day."

"Well, thanks for that," he said gruffly. "It needed to get done."

My unease eased slightly, but something still seemed off. What was bothering him?

Embarrassment briefly flashed across his face, disappearing before I could be certain I'd seen it. "Sorry I didn't stick around to help. I need to take care of some things. It looks good down there now that you got rid of all that junk." He swallowed and shifted his gaze to his computer screen on the desk, then glanced back up at me. "What did you do with everything?"

I couldn't seem to get a read on him today, which was strange since we typically were in sync. "I threw out anything that was broken and donated the stuff we hadn't used since we were kids. Did I get rid of too much?"

Dad shrugged. "Nah, I just didn't think you'd be able to do so much after I left." He coughed and then slid his hand over his chest as if it ached. He'd rubbed it like that yesterday, too.

"You feeling okay?" I asked.

He scowled and dropped his hand. "Of course, I am."

"It's just that you're rubbing your chest and Hailey mentioned you've been looking a little pale lately."

Dad let out a low laugh. "You know your sister. She's a worrier. I'm fine. My muscles are just a bit achy from lifting furniture yesterday. Nothing a Tylenol won't fix."

I hesitated. "Your heart's fine?"

He waved away my worry. "No more heart attacks, if that's what you're asking."

That was good news. He was healthy then. Which meant this could be a good time to bring up the subject near and dear to Hailey's heart—renovations. "Are you still against the idea of making any changes to the house?"

"What makes you think I'm against change?" Dad asked, looking genuinely surprised. "I'm a movie producer. A big part of the job is to manage change, and I happen to be great at it."

"That's at work, not in your personal space. Whenever any of us kids suggested changing anything in the house, you always refused. Hailey says she's been trying to get you to fix up the lower level for ages. She's dying to get rid of the old Laura Ashley stuff in the guest suite."

Dad let out a sudden laugh, his eyes crinkling at the corners in good humor. "It isn't change I'm against, it's the mess and the disruption. Your mom had some builders renovate the kitchen when we first bought this place, and it took months. Of course, she was trying to keep the style authentic to the time period—to the extent that was possible. It wasn't as if we actually wanted an 1880s kitchen. We just wanted something that felt authentic. Besides, in a house as old as this, you can't hire just anyone. It takes a skilled craftsman to do things right, and those guys need to be booked months in advance. They take their time. After they tore out the appliances, your mom set up a temporary kitchen in the dining room. It was like that for months. I hated it."

"We're just talking about the lower level though," I said. "That shouldn't interfere with your life much. Why not let Hailey handle everything? You know she'd love to."

I glanced around his only slightly outdated office with its golf-themed decor and hunter-green trim. At least the gorgeous antique furniture was built to last, as well as the oak-paneled walls and the mullioned windows. All of it was perfectly in style with the time period of the house.

Now that I thought about it, most of the upper floors were like this, too. Tasteful, but in need of a light facelift. It looked like Hailey had overstated what needed to be done around here. "You really only need fresh paint on the first floor," I said, with a little surprise. "Maybe update the bedrooms upstairs so they don't look like teenage hangouts. No big changes. I bet there's a way to keep the disruption to a minimum, but it's your decision."

Dad heaved a sigh. "You're probably right. I could set her loose on the basement and see what she can do to bring it into the current millennium. Nothing down there is original to the house. Someone renovated it not long before we bought it, and your mom had fun turning it into a kid hangout and guest space. If I let Hailey loose down there, it's unlikely it would impact my daily schedule."

I grinned. "That's great. I'll let her know. Don't be surprised if she ambushes you with paint and fabric samples."

He gave a grunt of resignation, but I caught a glint of fatherly indulgence in his expression. He liked making Hailey happy. "That's what I'm afraid of."

Dad rolled his shoulders and rubbed his hand across his chest again. When he saw my questioning look, he said, "I think I pulled a muscle when I helped you move that bookcase."

I winced. I shouldn't have asked him to help me, knowing how much Hailey worried about him.

I rubbed the back of my neck. How do you ask someone about their health without sounding pushy? I couldn't figure out how to be subtle about it, so I went with the direct approach. "This is hard for me to bring up, but Hailey is worried. About you, I mean. We all have been," I added, so he wouldn't blame Hailey. "You've refused most of Hailey's dinner invitations lately... not just hers, but from your closest friends as well. She says you've been spending more and more time alone. We're all afraid you have a health problem and you're hiding it."

Dad's eyes narrowed with irritation, but then he sat back in his chair. "t's been a long time since someone's asked me to explain my personal decisions...not since your mom passed, but I'll answer you... this once." His mouth was so tight it seemed hard for him to get the words out. "People change," he said. "I've changed. Your mom was the one who liked chitchatting with the neighbors at their cocktail parties and dinners. I went along to keep her company, but I never really connected with those people. Besides, it's mostly couples. I'm always the odd man out." He held up his hand as if to keep me from interrupting. "Don't get me wrong. It's no big deal. I can hold my own in those situations. But the question is, why should I? What do I get out of socializing with my neighbors? I have nothing in common with them. My closest friends are all in the film industry, and they're scattered all around the globe. I see them whenever we happen to be in the same town, and that's fine with me. You and your sister and brothers need to stop being so nebby. I'm fine." He cleared his throat and sat forward in his chair as if he was about to stand. "Is there anything else you think you need to quiz me about?"

I winced. Nebby—one of those Pittsburgh words that I only heard when I was in this part of the country. Dad had just accused me of being nosy. "Sorry for being so direct. I asked because I worry about you."

He waved me away as he rose to his feet. I watched as he steadied himself. He looked stiff and awkward, but he tried hard to hide it.

Maybe he was just getting older. I couldn't expect him to move around like a thirty-year-old. He'd explained why he wasn't spending time with his old friends here in town, but that didn't explain why he'd been avoiding Hailey's invitations. I wasn't completely convinced everything with him was fine.

Was he telling me the truth?

I needed to see things for myself, and the only way that would happen was if I spent more time with him. The cooking class could be the perfect opportunity.

"Do you remember my friend Dante Bastiano from Middle-bridge Academy?"

Dad looked down and to one side as he searched his memory, then his expression brightened, and he nodded. "Sure. Tall kid. Good sense of humor. I remember his mom was a great cook. She'd send over pans of lasagna from time to time after your mom…"

We both glanced away. Dad and I never really talked about mom's passing. No one in my family did. This was as close as any of us ever got to discussing the taboo subject. "That's him. I had dinner at the Not a Yacht Club and found out he's a co-owner and the chef." I hesitated. "He's putting together a cooking class for men. You interested in joining it with me and Max?"

Dad's face contorted as though I'd suggested he take up competitive cat bathing as a hobby. "Hell, no. I'm decent at the grill, and that's good enough for me. Besides, I'd rather eat out than try to keep a refrigerator stocked. Do you have any idea how much spoiled food I've thrown out over the years? Stuff goes bad when you have to rush out of town at a moment's notice. Nope. I'll just have meals delivered or grab something at the country club. It's just across the golf course." He tapped his smartwatch, flicked his finger around on the screen, and then lifted it to show it to me. "Speaking of which—I have to cut this short. I have a tee time in twenty-five minutes, and I need to make a phone call first."

He was golfing with someone? That was good news. Maybe he wasn't as isolated as I'd thought. "So, you *do* have a social life. Who's your golf partner?"

Dad's expression turned flat as he lifted his cell phone to his ear. I could hear it ringing on the other end as he waited for someone to pick up. "No one. If I play alone at this time of day, I can finish up pretty quickly." He seemed pleased with the prospect. "I regularly squeeze in nine holes in the afternoon. Good exercise. When I'm done, I'll grab dinner at the club."

My worries about his isolation sprang back in full force. "Sounds lonely. Want me to join you?"

"Nah. You hate golf. Besides, you'll only slow me down." The person on the other end of the call must have answered because Dad suddenly plastered a broad smile onto his face and said, "Hey, Jim. Glad I caught you. We need to talk about this film I'm putting together." He shooed me toward the door and then turned his back on me. I took the hint and left.

Dad hadn't always been so isolated. After Mom died, he'd often gone out in the evening. He'd leave us kids with the nanny, or when we were between nannies, my sister would be in charge. Dad had even continued to host parties at the house, which had seemed weird since he hadn't seemed to enjoy them very much. When I'd asked why he did it, he'd said that Mom would have wanted it that way.

When had all that stopped? Before or after his heart attack? I had the feeling it was after, but I was ashamed I didn't know. Just more proof I'd abandoned my family. Maybe his heart attack had made him reexamine his priorities.

After Mom died, I'd sensed that Dad kept going through sheer force of will. He hadn't slowed down at all. I think he was afraid to. Had his heart attack changed that?

I'd only just turned nine when Mom died. Despite the fact that she'd had breast cancer, we'd thought she was going to beat it. She'd promised us she'd be okay, but she'd been wrong. Following her last round of chemo, she'd caught pneumonia and had been gone within days. I'd been devastated to lose her. We all had.

Hailey had been thirteen and had done her best to step in and mother me, Max, and Sean, but she'd been half-orphaned too and was barely able to cope. Even worse, Dad kept firing our nannies and bringing in new ones. I don't think he realized how confusing those constant turnovers were. I'd learned never to get too attached to them.

With Dad burying himself in his work, we'd each had to figure out how to handle our grief separately. My method had been to do what Dad had done: push through the pain and loss through sheer force of will. Hailey had mothered us. Sean had acted out. Max? He'd been the mediator—always trying to make sure everyone was getting along.

Dad dropping his old Sewickley friends worried me. Should I dig deeper? I hesitated. Was Dad's social life any of my business? The man deserved his privacy. He'd already let me know I'd overstepped when I'd asked him about it. How much angrier would he get if I kept pressing the issue?

This was a big part of why I'd come home, though—to help Hailey and Max get to the bottom of these changes. They sensed something was wrong, and now I was beginning to see why. If I wanted to learn more, I'd need to go about it more subtly. It was time for some sleuthing.

I did some poking around on the first floor but came up with nothing. The enormous mansion was perfectly clean. Pristine even. Then it dawned on me that Dad's weekly cleaning crew kept it that way. How was I going to learn more about his social life if there were no clues lying around?

What would even constitute a clue?

I considered the question for a moment and then headed into the enormous pantry. If he had people over, he'd keep supplies on hand, right?

The room looked empty and forlorn. When I'd been younger, it had always been filled with snacks. Not anymore--just paper towels, cleaning supplies, Keurig K-cups, and cans of soup.

The refrigerator was nearly empty too. I could almost be convinced this place had been turned into a museum. Then again, he'd already told me he never kept food on hand.

I checked in on Dad. He was still on the phone, so I slipped upstairs to continue my snooping.

The bedroom doors upstairs were open. My old room looked exactly the way it had when I'd left for college. So did my brothers' and sister's bedrooms. They were like time capsules. Hailey's room had Nirvana posters, Sean's had Chinese action-movie stars, Max's had posters of rock and roll icons, and mine had Stanley Kubrick posters.

When I made it to the master bedroom and saw my dad's messily made bed, I hesitated. I was crossing a line by coming in here, and I knew it. Wasn't this the entire reason I'd come home, though? To figure out why Dad had changed?

I pushed down my guilt and headed into the master bathroom where I spotted three prescription pill bottles next to the sink.

What the hell?

Maybe they were meds he'd started taking after his heart attack. In fact, that was probably it. He'd mentioned something about blood pressure medicine.

But—what if I was wrong? What if they were for something else? With Mom's sudden death, the specter of cancer always seemed to lurk just out of sight.

I glanced at the labels but didn't recognize them—not that I would. I took photos of them so I could do internet searches.

When I glanced at myself in the mirror, the person I saw looked embarrassed and furtive. Like a kid who'd been caught stealing. Shame and guilt flooded me as I looked away from my reflection. For an instant, my thumb hovered over the delete button—Dad deserved his privacy—but finding out the truth was for his own good. Instead, I jammed the phone into my pocket and headed for the stairs.

I should have been around more. If I had been here, I'd have picked up on the clues myself. All of these changes in Dad had occurred while I'd been off making movies.

I wasn't fair of me to leave everything to Hailey, Max, and Sean to deal with. Well, mostly Hailey and Max. Sean traveled all the time as a stunt man, but at least he kept a home base here in Sewickley and came back between jobs.

Not like me. I'd been nothing more than an occasional visitor for years now.

Back downstairs, I checked on Dad, but he wasn't in his office anymore. I headed toward the kitchen to look for him there.

It was time to make a change in my life. The signs were there. I'd screwed up by abandoning my family for so long. I needed to get more involved with them. With their lives. Be a real part of this family again. Try to encourage Dad to engage with people.

A nagging thought returned. Could Dad be suffering from depression? Wasn't isolating oneself a sign? Or maybe he was hiding a problem with his heart.

I headed toward the great room at the front of the house—the one with the three-story cathedral-style ceiling and the fireplace so enormous I could walk into it without stooping. I'd always loved the ostentatious room, and it was Dad's favorite hangout. At the far end, he'd even installed a gorgeous hand-carved bar that mom had purchased from an antique dealer years ago. It had come from an old estate outside Chicago that had been torn down.

Dad wasn't in here, either.

I heard an engine turn over out front. Glancing through the mullioned windows that alternated with the long row of stained-glass ones, I caught sight of Dad's car pulling away in a hurry.

I bet he was hurrying to make his tee time. He hadn't even bothered to say goodbye. Is that what happened when you lived alone for too long? You forgot when other people were in your house? Was he that wrapped up in himself and his insular life?

Mara had accused me of pretty much the same thing—of being wrapped up in my own life and unaware of the people around me, and she'd been right. I was surrounded by yes-men despite my attempts to foster an open environment. Her refreshing ideas and ability to ground me were just what I needed. She saw me clearly, without being swayed by my success.

As I headed for my car, a thought brought me to a standstill. Could it be possible that I was unconsciously following in my dad's footsteps?

I'd been completely unaware the other day when I blabbered about a murder scene in front of her customers. Not to mention, I'd unintentionally offended Mara for her love of comic books. I'd even been avoiding dates lately because I felt like most women were self-centered.

It got me thinking, did my dad go through a similar phase of just focusing on work after Mom passed away? This thought was unsettling, and I can't help but wonder if I could still change course before it's too late.

Dad once said that after finding the love of his life, it was hard to settle for second best.

This was the wakeup call I needed... not just about Dad isolating himself, but about my own lack of a personal life. I sure as hell didn't want to end up solitary and lonely, rattling around in a huge, empty house.

At least Dad had found someone to love and build a life with. That was more than I could say for myself.

The love part—that was key.

An image of Mara with her blue-tipped hair and her never-ending array of Wonder Woman t-shirts flashed into my mind.

I didn't want just anyone in my life. I wanted someone like Mara. No. Not someone *like* her. *Her.*

All that attitude. All that mouthiness. All that intelligence and honesty. Not to mention that body. What would it be like to have her pressed against me? To have her legs wrapped around my hips? That smart mouth of hers nibbling away at my neck? Even more—what would it be like to have her by my side? To build a life with her?

I had the feeling it would be bliss.

Only, there was one big problem.

I'd asked her out, and she'd said no.

Scarlet might come through for me. I'd seen her work magic before when she'd needed to convince one of her uncle's donors to write a bigger campaign check. She'd talked him into an additional ten-thousand dollars.

My phone vibrated with an incoming call, and I scrambled to answer it, convinced it had to be Mara. Scarlet must have worked her magic.

My heart thumped a rhythm of hope as I looked at the screen.

Disappointment hit me, sharp and intense. Not a local number. Not Mara. The call was from California.

McCormick Studios.

I answered. "McCormick. How are things in L.A.?"

"You can decide for yourself when you fly out to discuss my movie. We need to talk in person. Can you get here by tomorrow?"

10

MAYBE

MARA

After Scarlet left, I went upstairs to my apartment to check on Zephyr. I'd taken him upstairs to rest after lunch, but now he bounced with joy at seeing me.

"Want to join me in the store?"

His enormous ears perked up as he cocked his head to one side and then ran to the door and sat down. He glanced over his shoulder at me and wriggled his butt, giving me a broad doggy-grin. That dog could be perfectly obedient—when he wanted something.

Laughing, I opened the door. He darted down the rear staircase ahead of me, into the storeroom.

After I settled myself in front of my laptop, I read through the email regarding the project I was supposed to be coding. I couldn't concentrate, though. I kept thinking about Scarlet. It was a good thing she hadn't been with them on her parents' flight to D.C.

How had she found out they'd died? Oh, no—my breath caught in my throat—what if she'd learned via the internet? Had she been alone? She was an only child. It had to have been devastating to lose her entire family.

I turned off my computer screen. Since I couldn't settle down to do any coding, I grabbed a broom from my storeroom and started sweeping.

I moved around the store sweeping and straightening, and then opened the front door and swept the bits of dirt and dust outside with a practiced flick of the broom. The sun was out, and the bits of dust caught the light for an instant before disappearing.

I closed the door. Scarlet and I had both lost people close to us, but I hadn't faced it alone. I'd grown up in the heart of a large family with two brothers and two sisters. Without a doubt, losing my twin had been the most wrenching experience of my life. Even now, I still ached from the loss, but at least I'd had my family to share my grief.

I put away the broom and dustpan. Scarlet's story about Ford rescuing her so many years ago made me feel even guiltier about the way I'd blown him off. My actions didn't make sense.

As I made my way back to the front of the store, it hit me like a truth beam - the root of all my romantic troubles. It wasn't Ford's string of girlfriends or his tendency to spout curse words in my store. No, it was my dad and Doug, those two male masterminds who had been tinkering with my confidence like a couple of evil villains.

I realized with a pang of regret that I'd been afraid to give Ford a chance, all because of my ex, Doug. That guy was a walking, talking pile of bantha poo-doo - and I had unfairly associated Ford with him. How could I have been so blind?

When I first met Doug, I thought I'd hit the jackpot. He was interested in everything I said and did, and he even helped me through a difficult time. But then he started criticizing my every move, like he was the King of Decisions or something. I didn't notice at first because he sounded so much like my dad. And don't get me started on the time he left the door unlocked, even though he swore he locked it - that's why I upgraded the security system.

On top of that, he kept trying to push me into closing the

physical store and focusing on online sales, even though he knew I hated the idea. He'd even tried to drive a wedge between me and my friends. When I would push back or complain, he pretended I was being difficult or imagining things, claiming he'd never do anything to hurt me or my store.

"You're imagining things," he'd said. "This isn't the first time you've misremembered things. Maybe the stress is getting to you. After all, it hasn't been that long since Chance died. I can't imagine what you must be going through. Losing a twin must be devastating. You're doing your best, but I noticed you had two glasses of wine last night. Did you have more when I wasn't looking? Maybe you don't remember things clearly."

Doug made me doubt myself. *Could* I have been mistaken? Later I realized the jerk had been gaslighting me every step of the way, and it had taken me way too long to recognize it. On top of everything else, he'd been only too happy to fall into bed with the first woman who offered. At least when that happened, I'd finally wised up and broken things off with him. After that, his subtle attempts to hurt me became overt. He'd gone out of his way to try to ruin my business.

Ford was nothing like him.

My problem was that, after Doug, I wasn't sure if I should trust my own judgement. I'd learned that self-doubt is a lingering after-effect of gaslighting, but knowing it didn't make it go away. I could trust Scarlet, though, and according to her, Ford was a genuinely good guy.

I let out a sigh of frustration. I'd been thinking about this for too long and I wasn't getting anywhere. All I was doing was spinning in circles.

I should focus on the here and now and get some work done on that coding project I'd picked up to help make ends meet.

I opened my laptop and logged into GitHub to locate the software package I was supposed to develop. It took a couple of minutes to complete the download and unpack it, so my mind drifted again while I waited, but this time I tried to focus on finding a solution.

I needed to put Doug and all his bullshit behind me, and that couldn't happen if I didn't start moving forward. A good way to do that would be to fix things with Ford. Scarlet had convinced me I'd been wrong about him, so why not have coffee with him?

I'd need to redeem myself first for jumping to conclusions based on nothing more than those gossipy headlines and photos in *Here's the Scoop*. When I recalled accusing him of bed-hopping, my cheeks heated. I squirmed, embarrassed at my behavior. He deserved an apology.

I headed back to my storage room, lifted the box containing all my souvenirs from the top shelf, and pulled Ford's business card from the magazine. As I stared down at it, I slid my thumb across the slightly raised lettering.

I should call him today.

Could I?

Of course I could. But—was I ready?

The door chime jingled, and I headed back to the front of my store. Zephyr trotted ahead of me as I tucked Ford's card into my pocket. The next two hours passed quickly as I rang up purchases between bouts of intense Java coding.

Late in the day, one of my customers purchased one of my last remaining statues. Sales were always a good thing. Only now my eye kept catching on the empty spot in my display window. I wished I had something else to put there, but my storeroom was empty. Mother Hubbard's shelves were bare; I desperately needed money to buy more collectibles.

Right around closing time, my new Java code was slick, elegant, and functional. Success. I uploaded it and notified the client that it was ready, then flipped the sign on the front door to "Closed" and locked up.

Zephyr did a happy dance at my feet, recognizing the cues that I was done for the day.

I took a moment to check my email. Yes, I was stalling.

Was I really so nervous about calling Ford?

As I scanned my inbox, my eye caught on a reply from one of the vendors I'd contacted about reinstating my credit.

I couldn't help it. A small bubble of hope began to rise within me. I squelched it. It was always easier to kill a tiny hope than one that had grown over time.

As I opened the email, I had only the tiniest flicker of curiosity. It would only be another rejection, I was sure of it.

"All of my credit problems could be laid entirely at Doug's feet. Doug, the steaming pile of poo. What made it worse were his connections to so many advertisers and influencers in the city of Pittsburgh. Connections he'd used to try to ruin me. The bastard.

He'd pulled off a masterclass in sabotage, using his position at the local TV station to pull a fast one on me, the sneaky little weasel. The station had decided to do a story on failing businesses in the area, and Doug's conniving friend had lured me into an interview under false pretenses. I thought it was about my successful business, but nope - it was a hit piece designed to make me look like a total failure.

After the report aired, the world seemed to crumble around me. My suppliers all panicked and stopped extending me credit because they thought I was about to go belly up. I tried to explain that it was a setup by my conniving ex, but they wouldn't believe me. I was about as trustworthy as a used car salesman with a fake mustache. I couldn't even blame them.

Doug was a Machiavellian genius. A manipulative asshat.

Because of his calculated attacks on me and my store, all my vendors began insisting I pay for everything in advance before they'd ship. That had made it nearly impossible to keep enough stock on hand.

The suppliers who'd previously been happy to give me sixty- or ninety-day credit while I established my business suddenly demanded payment in advance. It didn't matter that I'd never missed a payment or defaulted on a loan. They knew about the news report, and that was all that mattered.

I'd already been short on cash, so paying up front wiped out my savings. Covering all my print items as well as the high-profit, low-turnover collectible items I hadn't sold yet had taken every cent I owned. To make things worse, I'd ordered extra stock because I'd placed orders for the booth at the comic convention that I'd planned to attend... the one Doug had canceled behind my back.

Seriously. The guy was toxic in every possible way. No, beyond toxic, he was nuclear-spill level wastewater sludge. But instead of turning me into a superhero like in a comic book, that sludge had nearly destroyed me.

I'd been forced to take out a short-term loan with lousy interest rates. Covering that additional debt each month cut deep into my profits, and now I was in bad shape. If only Chance hadn't started off with so much debt with all the renovations.

I quickly skimmed the email, and then stilled.

I had to go back to the beginning and start reading it again. From what I could tell, I'd finally gotten through to a real person at this company—one who seemed sympathetic.

I let out a squeal of joy that made Zephyr start prancing with excitement.

The supplier was offering me a sixty-day credit cycle! This was exactly the break I had been begging for!

"We did it, Zephyr," I said, dropping to one knee to cup Zephyr's chin and kiss the top of his head. When I stood up and did a jig, he let out a yip and started dancing with me.

I whirled back to my computer and shot off a thank-you message before immediately logging into the company's website and placing an order. With luck, my nearly-depleted store would be filled by the end of the week.

With that delicious dose of success, I felt invigorated enough to face another challenge.

Ford.

Before I could lose my courage, I pulled out my phone along with his business card, entered the number, and then—

I hesitated.

My thumb inched toward the cancel button.

Was I really this scared?

"Do it. Just do it," I muttered.

I did it. I pressed the call button and then waited for him to answer.

"Hello?" Ford's rich voice rumbled into my ear and down into my belly.

"Hi. It's Mara."

He didn't say anything for a heartbeat, and I panicked. This proved it. Calling him was a mistake. A huge one.

"I was hoping I'd hear from you," he said.

My heart fluttered. Those were the perfect words. Hearing them turned my insides out.

He pitched his voice lower—softer. The intimacy made my stomach do a flip. "To what do I owe the pleasure?"

I grabbed a strand of my hair and twirled it around my finger. "I wanted to apologize for the things I said to you earlier. The way I behaved. I jumped to conclusions."

"I appreciate that. You get bonus points for calling me. Was it hard to do?"

I wilted under the Wonder Woman poster. "You have no idea."

"You aren't the person first to assume the worst of me. You probably won't be the last."

I bit my bottom lip. I didn't like that other people misjudged him. It was embarrassing to be lumped in with that group. "I was wondering if your offer for coffee was still open?"

"Coffee?" He hesitated. "Sure."

Did he sound slightly disappointed? Should I have asked him on a real date? I suddenly felt embarrassed. Every bit of self-confidence I'd been able to accumulate was spent in a flash. It was like being in a video game and having your endurance bar drop to zero after using your big attack. I didn't have enough oomph left in me to let Ford know I wanted more than just coffee.

"If we need to meet on a Sunday when you're closed, it'll have to wait until next week," he said. "I just got off the phone with the producer I mentioned, and he wants me to fly to L.A. for a meeting. I'm leaving tomorrow."

My self-confidence started dropping into the red zone, and I pulled on my ponytail, twisting it around the end of my hand. I'd blown it. "Are congratulations in order?"

"Not yet. I haven't officially agreed to anything. I think he's convinced I'll say yes if he meets with me in person."

I stopped tugging at my hair and my hand fell limply to my side. Maybe I'd made the right decision in turning him down for a date. After all, I wanted someone who'd stick around. "How long will you be gone?"

"Just a few days. I plan to fly back on Monday. I need to close up my house there."

My heart started to beat double-time as I stood up straight. "Wait. I'm confused. You're moving here? Does that mean you aren't planning to make that Superman film? Then why are you flying to Los Angeles? How long will you be gone?"

He laughed. "Which question should I answer first?"

I rolled my eyes at myself. I was such a smooth talker. "Your choice."

"Even if I end up doing McCormick's movie, I intend to do all the pre-production work from here. That'll have to be part of the deal I negotiate with him. I need to spend more time with my dad. I haven't been here enough since I moved away. Time keeps slipping away."

I knew exactly what he meant. I often wished I could go back and recapture some of my lost time so I could have spent more of it with Chance.

Maybe that's why I was so focused on the store now—our store—because I hadn't been involved enough before.

The path that had brought me here to Sewickley had been paved with shattered ambitions. Ones I'd willingly sacrificed. It was the price I'd paid in order to turn our shared dream of owning a comic book shop into a reality.

I stilled. Sacrifice? Shattered dreams? Where were these thoughts coming from? I'd gladly made the decision to move forward with opening the store over a year ago. Why doubt myself now?

Zephyr let out a whine of impatience, pulling me to the present moment. He knew our evening routine, and by now we were usually out on a well-deserved ramble around town. "I have to go. Zephyr is begging for a walk. Pretty soon he's going to start crossing his legs. Next step is peeing on the floor."

Ford let out a low laugh. "I won't keep you then. Let's plan to meet a week from Sunday at Loco Mocha Cafe. Does noon work for you?"

"Sounds great. See you then," I said, riding high on a new bubble of hope. Maybe by then, I'd be able to adjust to some of this newly found self-awareness and be in the right state of mind.

No, not maybe. I'd do it.

11

1ST COOKING CLASS

FORD

Los Angeles had drained me, but at least I'd managed to get a haircut. McCormick had summoned me to meet him on location, and upon my arrival, a hair stylist had taken one look at me and dragged me into a chair, insisting on a trim before I even had a chance to locate McCormick.

During my free time there, I'd researched my dad's medication. It seemed standard for someone who had experienced a heart attack: blood thinners, blood pressure and cholesterol-lowering drugs. Nothing out of the ordinary.

I wasn't really in the mood to attend Dante's first cooking class tonight. I knew it would wipe out the rest of my reserves, but a promise was a promise. Besides, it would give me a chance to catch up with my brother, and we really needed to talk.

Dante had told us that even though Not a Yacht Club was closed, the door would be unlocked, so when Max and I arrived, we walked on in. The bar was empty, but the restaurant's sweeping view of the Ohio River glittered in the evening sunlight.

Conner stood with his hands braced against the bartop, glaring down at it. When he glanced up and spotted me and Max, some of his tension eased. "I'm glad you're both here," he said as he ambled over to us. "I was afraid I'd be the only one. I tried to talk my way out of it, but Dante wouldn't budge." Conner smoothed his hand over his brown, close-cropped hair. "Like I told him, it seems like only one of us needs to know how to cook. He didn't buy it."

"Not surprised," I said. "You remember my brother Max, right?"

"Sure, I do. He's a regular here." Conner shook his hand. "Thanks for coming, man."

"No problem," Max said. "I like to cook. This class will be a great way to pick up some tips from a real chef. Besides, it gives me a reason to drive to Sewickley and hang out with Ford before he heads back to California."

"Do you ever think about moving here? To Sewickley?" I asked. "I know Dad keeps you busy with the business end of things."

Max shook his head. "Nah. It's not that long of a drive… just twenty-five minutes or so. I suppose I might move here someday, but a lot of my meetings happen in Pittsburgh, so living there is convenient. Besides, Sewickley is for families. They roll up the sidewalks at ten. I want more nightlife than that."

It dawned on me that since arriving here I'd been so focused on choosing a new movie to make, reconnecting with my dad, and learning more about the distractingly sexy Mara Stellar, I hadn't even noticed the lack of nightlife. However, the Not a Yacht Club was lively enough for me most nights.

Admittedly, I rarely went out in the evening. When was the last time I'd hung out with any of my L.A. friends? We'd celebrated when I'd won that Sundance, but that had been with the people who'd worked on the film. Sure, they were my friends, but not the sort you could count on when you needed help moving your sofa, or coping with a rough breakup. Come to think of it, who would I even ask back in L.A.? Maybe Sheila, but she wasn't the couch-lifting sort of friend. She was more likely to text me the phone number for a moving company.

I looked at the two men in front of me. Max would definitely help me move a sofa. I bet Conner and Dante would too.

When I'd been eighteen, I'd run away from this life. This town. My family. From everything I'd believed was holding me down—but maybe I'd been wrong. Maybe they'd given me the solid foundation I'd built my success upon.

Of course, that foundation had a huge void in it. My mom.

Losing her had unmoored me. Sure, we'd known she had cancer, but she'd been fighting it. If she hadn't caught pneumonia, she'd probably have beaten it. It had taken me years to find my feet.

When I'd left for college, I'd found a new tribe—the creative types who made music and art and movies. I'd met my ex-wife Chelsea back then, too. She was different from my other friends since she was studying marketing instead of something in the creative arts. We'd fallen in love. Taken a chance. She'd been my home—my heart—my future—until she'd abandoned me. I'd thought we'd had each other's backs, but I'd been wrong. She'd bailed on me the moment I put my career over hers—not over her —over her career. That distinction didn't matter to her.

The consequence was that someone I depended on left me again.

When I hadn't attended that office party with her, she'd taken it as a betrayal. I'd pointed out that by leaving, she was choosing to betray me. She'd cried a little at that, and then finally admitted that she'd thought I'd give up on becoming a director and settle down—whatever that meant. She'd said she didn't want the kind of life I'd offer her if I was constantly on location directing movies. She wanted to be with someone totally devoted to her in every way.

Devoted and in love—that I could handle as long as it was reciprocal. But being taken for granted? That wasn't me, and it never could be.

Looking back, I see now how needy she'd always been, always testing me with little demands to prove my love. Like filling her car with gas after she drove home with it on fumes, or blaming me for running out of shampoo, even though we didn't use the same brand. They were all signs of her underlying lack of self-confidence, and it was exhausting to constantly prove my devotion to her.

And then came her final confession. She wanted me to put her job ahead of my mine. It put our entire relationship in a new light. All the subtle ways she'd undermined my career by steering me away from big opportunities, all because she felt threatened. I couldn't believe how manipulative she'd been. It was like I was finally seeing the real her, and it wasn't pretty.

Mara had her life together. She didn't seem to care what other people thought about her. She was intelligent and direct, and I found that sexy as hell.

Of course, there was the problem that, after I'd asked her out, she'd put me squarely in the friend zone. This Sunday's coffee date gave me a glimmer of hope, and I focused on that spark of light like a spelunker lost in a cave. There was something about Mara Stellar that told me she was worth waiting for. She saw straight into me in a way other people couldn't.

"You can go on back to the kitchen," Conner said, silencing my thoughts as he pointed toward the door behind the bar. "Dante's waiting. I'll join you after Kincaid gets here."

I walked into the kitchen and came to a standstill. The place was pristine. From the stainless-steel ventilation system and gleaming countertops to the white floor, the space was as spotless as an operating room. I noted the neatly stocked shelves through an open doorway that served as a pantry, as well as the two pairs of stools positioned next to a couple of the stoves.

Dante exited one of the enormous stainless-steel walk-in freezers and closed the door behind him. He beamed at us, then schooled his face. "Welcome, Padawans," he intoned with mock solemnity, bowing at the waist.

I grinned as I faced him and bowed in return. "Thank you, Master Jedi."

"*Star Wars?*" Max asked, then shook his head in mock dismay. "You're both closet nerds." He held out his hand to Dante. "It's good to see you. What are we cooking tonight?"

Dante shook his hand, his eyes dancing with humor. "I'm starting things off with something easy. Chili. My version is rich and robust because of my secret ingredients." He gave a sly wink, then leaned closer. "I use coffee and dark chocolate for added depth and complexity."

I nodded in agreement, though I had no idea how the hell coffee or chocolate could make chili great.

Dante lifted the lid off a pot on the nearby stove, and the fragrant steam wafted up from it. "Besides, who doesn't like chili?"

The tantalizing aroma made my mouth start watering. "That smells amazing."

"Yours will too, I promise. Once Kincaid gets here, I'll serve everyone so you'll know how it'll turn out. It'd be great with a margarita or a beer, but I'm limiting you each to one drink tonight. I don't want any injuries."

"Something smells great," Kincaid said as he strolled into the kitchen, followed by Conner.

"Thanks," Dante said. "I'm glad you're here. It looks like we're all here." He frowned as he surveyed us. "I'd still like to get a couple more guys in the class."

I scratched my elbow as I turned to Max and said quietly, "I tried to get Dad to come, but he said no. What about Baris? I don't think he knows how to cook."

Max shook his head. "Hailey wouldn't let him set foot in her kitchen. She loves to cook, but our sister can't share worth a damn. I doubt her husband would want to fight that battle."

Conner sniffed the air. "Are we making chili tonight? Kincaid's right. It smells great."

Dante beamed with pleasure. "We are. I'll serve you some, and you can grab a stool at one of the workstations while you eat." Dante dished out the chili into a line of bowls with easy, competent movements. I took one and carried it to one of the worksta-tions. Max joined me there.

"This is excellent." Max wiped his mouth with a napkin and turned to me. "How was your trip to L.A.? Did you meet with McCormick?"

I gave a single nod. "He's pushing hard for me to direct that Superman film. I have to admit, I don't like the script. It's a rehash of every Superman origin story I've ever seen. I'm not convinced I'm the right person to turn it into something special."

Max paused, his spoon hovering partway to his mouth. "Does that mean you'd consider something else?" he asked as he lowered his spoon to the bowl.

I shot him a sharp glance. "What are you talking about?"

"Partnering with Ross Film Productions." Max sounded indif-ferent, but I spotted the tension in his jaw. This was important to him.

"Dad's company?" I only asked to buy myself time.

A flash of irritation crossed his face. "*Our* company. I know working with family can be challenging, but you'd have complete creative control. That best-director win of yours would make my job easy. Finding investors would be a breeze—as long as you don't try to make something that's too offbeat." Max hesitated, then met my gaze. "This could really help us."

I sat back. Was Ross Film Productions having problems? Instead of asking directly, I decided to see what Max decided to tell me. "I didn't realize you were directly involved in making deals like this."

My brother gave a jerky shrug, revealing the tension in his shoulders. "I keep a low profile, but yeah. I'm pretty heavily involved. Ever since Dad's heart attack, he hasn't had as much interest in running the business." Max hesitated. "He distances himself from everyone. I've been picking up his slack more and more."

And there it was. Evidence that Dad was having problems—the trouble I knew, deep down, had to be there.

Guilt swept through me. "I didn't know." I should have, though. I should have been here.

Max's jaw tightened. "You weren't supposed to."

Surprised, I curled in on myself. "What do you mean by that? Have you been hiding things from me?"

Max glanced at me as he finished his chili. I waited impatiently. Finally, he said, "Nothing concrete. I'm just concerned about him. I didn't want to influence you, but now that you've spent time with him, you've probably noticed some things. As far as I can tell, he's healthy enough—not that he'd tell anyone if he wasn't. He seems to keep pulling away from everyone—everything. I'm no doctor, but I think he could be suffering from depression."

"The same thing crossed my mind," I said slowly. But still, I hesitated. "I think that's part of it, but I'm worried there's something else going on." I told Max about the way he'd abandoned me after moving that bookcase and how pale he'd been.

Max's worried gaze met mine. "Investors are starting to comment that he's less involved. I'm having a harder time getting funding for our films."

I stared at him, shocked. Dad's company was everything to him. I'd had no idea things had gotten so bad. "What do we do?"

"*We?*" Max repeated back to me, his expression easing as if a load of weight had suddenly dropped from his shoulders. He looked hopeful.

He started to say more, but Dante cut him off. With a broad sweep of his arm, he beckoned us all over. "Let's get started."

"We'll talk more," I promised Max. "Between the two of us, we can come up with a plan to fix this."

Relief filled Max's face.

That did me in. Conviction hardened in my chest. This was up to me. I had to find a solution.

"Thanks again for coming tonight," Dante said, his thousand-watt smile lighting up his face. "I've wanted to teach a class like this for a long time. Over the next few weeks, I plan to instill in you some basic cooking techniques. Things you can build on."

Dante rubbed his hands together in anticipation. "Now, let's get started on tonight's chili recipe, and I'll introduce you to proper onion-cutting techniques."

Cutting onions didn't look like rocket science. Maybe solving the problems in my life wasn't rocket science either. It could be like peeling away the layers of an onion to see what was really going on. My film. My future. Ross Film Productions. It was all connected.

Max's idea that I make a film with Dad's production company was the perfect solution to all my problems. Of course, it would mean passing on McCormick's film. Opportunities like that didn't drop into your lap every day. A big budget movie like that could really launch my career into the stratosphere. I'd be a fool to turn it down. Why was I even considering it?

Because—it might be exactly the right move for me. Staying here meant I'd be able to spend time with my family. I was needed here.

"Let's start cooking," Dante said. "Head to your workstations and get to chopping those onions."

Max motioned me ahead of him. "I've chopped my share of onions over the years. You can do these."

"No problem." I held the onion the way I'd seen Dante do it, slicing the sharp knife through it. "I didn't realize how much you'd been covering for Dad. Knowing that puts everything in a different light." A moment later, my eyes started prickling.

I blinked. I sniffed loudly and wiped my eyes with my sleeve.

Max let out a hoot of laughter. "Don't cry, Ford. It'll be okay."

Dante came over. "Breathe through your mouth so the onion vapors don't go directly into your eyes, and don't put your face right over the cutting board. Weren't you listening when I told you to lay a damp towel next to the onion? The vapor will be drawn toward it instead of your eyes."

I felt like an idiot. He must have offered that gem of wisdom while I'd been tuning him out. I scowled at my gloating brother as I started to wipe my cheek with the back of my hand, but it stank of onion, so I stopped.

Max snorted out a laugh.

My control over my irritation snapped. "Is this the kind of crap I'll get from you if I decide to make a movie with Ross Film Productions? It's not a selling point."

Max shrugged, still grinning. "I'm not involved with filming. You'll never see me. I just handle the money and the contracts up front, and the marketing and PR afterward."

I wiped my face against my shoulder again. "That's good because you're annoying as hell." I headed over to the sink and washed up with some lemon-scented soap. When I splashed water on my face, the burning finally eased.

I headed back to the prep station and glared at the bell peppers, poblano, and tomatoes. Had I missed some pro-tip about cutting those as well? Wary, I shoved the chopping board over to my brother. "Your turn."

Max pressed the knife into the tomato, and the pulp squirted out, covering the cutting board with a gelatinous mess.

"Amateur," I said. At least I knew how to slice a tomato.

"How's the chopping coming along?" Dante asked as he stopped to peer over Max's shoulder. He grimaced at the tomato massacre. "It works better if you slide the knife across the tomato to slice it rather than pressing straight down."

Max tried again, with more success.

"Bravo. Excellent." Dante slapped Max on the back. "Time to start cooking." He gestured toward our skillet. "All you have to do is follow the recipe. First, brown the beef and onions, and then add the other ingredients."

I clicked on the gas burner at our cooking station, feeling confident about this step. Browning the beef would take a few minutes. If our chili was any good, maybe I'd take some to the comic book shop tomorrow in a subtle attempt to win over its prickly owner. Wasn't food supposed to be a gateway to the heart?

Maybe not, though. I didn't want to push her. It might be a better idea to wait until our coffee date this weekend. Was it even a date?

"Do you know Mara Stellar?" I asked, acting all nonchalant. "She owns a comic book shop in town—Ghost of a Chance."

Max raised his eyebrows. "She has blue hair, right?" He glanced at the skillet and then elbowed me in the ribs. "Stir the meat or you'll burn it."

"Shit. Sorry. She distracts me. What can I say?" I stirred. "What do you know about her?"

"Pretty. I like the hair. She doesn't seem like your type though. You tend to go for glitzy movie stars."

I scowled. "How would you know what type of woman I go for?"

"You mean since you never brought any of them home?" Max's tone seemed offhanded, but I sensed there was something deeper there. Some long-held complaint that was just now being voiced.

"Any of who?" I pressed.

"Any of the starlets you date."

"Not you, too. Why does everyone rely on Here's the Scoop for info about my dating life? That rag never fact-checks anything."

"Tons of bloggers and entertainment sites write about you too."

I shrugged. "True, but Here's the Scoop loves to jump to conclusions."

"It's not like you're an open book," Max pointed out. "It's bad when your family only knows you have a new girlfriend when we read about it. You never talk about the women you date."

"That's because I'm not dating anyone."

"Not now."

"I haven't dated anyone seriously for a couple of years," I protested.

"Not since you broke up with what's-her-face? The blonde?" He seemed genuinely surprised. "Was the breakup that bad?"

I shrugged. "Her name was Cindy," I said. "Things fizzled out with her. All we ever talked about was our work and the movie industry. You know, dating is a real pain in the ass. Especially in Hollywood. It's all pretense. Everyone acts like a perfect version of themselves, so getting to know someone deep down takes time — and lots of energy. Energy that was better spent directing a movie or doing something productive. I hate wasting it in some pit of emotional quicksand."

Max raised one eyebrow. "Not that you're jaded or anything."

I let out a chuckle. "You're one to talk, considering you're not dating anyone either."

"Not after what Raven did to Essie. That primadonna rock star destroyed Essie, and her fans were downright rabid. I can't risk having a relationship until I know Raven won't lash out again."

"*Help!*" Kincaid's shout rang out from across the kitchen.

I whirled to see smoke billowing from Kincaid's skillet. Dante bolted over, grabbed the skillet, and pulled it off the burner.

"Damn, dude," Conner said, scowling at his brother. "You burned dinner." He shoved Kincaid hard in the shoulder, but the guy barely rocked to one side.

Resigned, Conner shook his head as he turned his back on the smoking ruin and came to join us. "I should have known cooking with Kincaid would turn out this way," he said as he approached. "The two of us can't work together. I'm hungry, dammit."

"Have some more of Dante's chili," I suggested.

"Pay attention!" Dante yelled as he pointed at something behind me. "Your pan is smoking."

I caught a faint, acrid scent of burning meat and whirled to discover our food was ruined, too. Max grabbed the handle and yanked it off the burner, then yowled with pain. He'd forgotten to grab a potholder before touching the metal handle.

I shook my head in disbelief. "Hell. I can't believe I let that happen. Why didn't any of us smell it?" I looked up at the enormous silver vent above the stove. "I guess your industrial grade vents really work."

"Both meals ruined," Dante said, shaking his head like a disappointed dad. "I suppose it wasn't a complete disaster. You didn't set the place on fire."

12

TROUBLEMAKER

MARA

On Friday, as the clock edged toward closing time, I took a step back to look at my carefully arranged display of collectibles. My foot bumped one of the empty boxes littering the floor, so I nudged it aside. Normally, I restocked my display window after I closed, but between after-work plans and an achingly empty window, I decided to unpack all that eye candy right away.

With all the boxes and paper littering the floor, and the shiny, new, superhero figures, I felt like a kid on Christmas morning.

I stashed the boxes and swept away the packing peanuts. I even had to brush bits of Styrofoam off my jeans. Zephyr would have loved playing in the mess—which was why I'd left him upstairs in the apartment. I didn't want him to end up eating something he shouldn't.

My ponytail drooped to one side and my back ached. I pulled out the elastic hairband and then stretched my arms overhead to release the knots that came from leaning over the display shelves.

The bell on my door jingled to announce a customer, and I grinned as I turned to face the door. For some reason, I expected to see Ford. He hadn't been around all week, which was exactly what I'd thought I'd wanted when I'd turned down his invitation. Had he dropped by to surprise me?

My grin turned into a frown when I spotted Doug Aspin—the absolute last person I ever wanted to lay eyes on again.

A year's worth of suppressed emotion roiled up inside me. Frustration, fury, and, most of all, disgust. With myself, for letting that relationship last as long as it did when I knew I should've left after a month. No, make that after the first date. The man didn't know how to be a decent human being. Then again, narcissists never take the blame for anything. In their minds, they're always right.

I wished I had the superpower to make him go away by pure force of will. On the off-chance it would work, I tried, but he didn't budge. Instead, he strode toward me like he owned *my* store.

Whatever words were about to come out of his mouth, I didn't want to hear them. I began inching toward the counter, but then stopped and stood my ground. There was no way I'd back down to this manipulative jerk. Not in my own store. Not again. I needed to stand up to him.

I turned to face him square on and stared him down. "You know, up until right now, I was having a good week... I read the new Deadpool comic... I ordered some new stock... everything was coming up *me*. Now you're here, ruining it all. Turn around and go away. I don't want you here."

"Don't be like that," Doug said in an irritating, wheedling tone. "I came to check on you. I've missed you."

Dumbstruck, all I could do was shake my head in disbelief. This guy couldn't take a hint. Hell. It hadn't been a hint. I'd clearly said, "*go away!*"

"I'm taking you out to dinner tonight." Those were the same words he'd used the first time he'd asked me out. Judging by the smirk on that face I'd once thought of as handsome, he expected me to swoon at his invitation. Had I done that the first time? If so, I'd been an idiot.

Instead, I gave him a hard blink of disbelief. "In your dreams."

He stepped closer, crowding me toward my display window. "I know you're about to close. We can leave now and grab a bite to eat."

The man never listened. "I'm not interested. I have plans with Courtney and Scarlet."

He scowled. Seriously—the man had the nerve to scowl at me. "Why are you spending time with those two? They're always trying to push their ideas onto you. You're better off without them."

Anger hit me like a punch from a supervillain. Instead of staggering back from the blow, I steeled myself, doubling down on the emotion to fuel my strength. "No Doug, *you're* the one I'm better off without. *You're* the one who was always trying to push your ideas on me. To manipulate me and keep me away from my friends. *They've* been nothing but supportive."

"That isn't true," he stated, his tone frustratingly mild as he met my gaze with those arresting, deep blue eyes. They were eyes you'd trust. Eyes that could reel you in. Eyes that were just as deceitful as the man. "I was trying to protect you from them."

"Revisionist history. I'm not buying your retcon crap."

He stared at me blankly. "Retcon?"

Not again. He loved to pretend he didn't understand terms I'd explained to him over and over. This time, I didn't let it bother me, recognizing it as the petty manipulation it really was. "I'm sorry you can't seem to remember the word," I said sweetly. "That must be frustrating for you when I've explained it to you so many times before. You're usually so smart."

His patronizing smile wavered, and the corners of my lips curved up in satisfaction.

"I'll explain it to you again. The word retcon is short for retroactive continuity. It's when a show or comic book series tries to pretend something in the storyline never took place or when it provides some bogus logic to explain it away. Like you're trying to do with me right now." I snapped my mouth shut. Time for me to *kick him out*.

Doug shook his head at me just like my dad would do when I'd disappointed him. "Honey, we need to talk."

My bile rose at being called honey by this guy. I shuddered as I pressed my lips together.

"I miss you, Marilyn. I miss us."

"Mara," I snapped, irritated that he'd used my full name, like a parent scolding a child. He was way too much like my dad with his superior attitude and manipulative behavior.

I stilled. Epiphany alert. My obnoxious ex reminded me of my dad. Gah! That was completely gag-worthy. I'd put a bookmark in that and think about it later.

Or maybe never. *Ugh.* Who wanted to think they had daddy issues? Gross.

"We need to move beyond what happened," he said. "Things can be good between us again. You just need to try."

Anger, sharp and hot, blasted through me, and I let out a bark of laughter. If I tried to write down a list of his offenses with a black Sharpie on Superman's red cape, I'd have had to use both sides. As if I'd ever do something so heinous to Superman.

"You've got to be kidding me. There's way too much to *move beyond*," I snapped back. "The cherry on top was when you had sex with another woman, lied to me about it, and then blamed *me* for it when I found out."

"It was just the one time, I promise. I made a mistake. It meant nothing."

"It meant everything. You cheated. I caught you in the act. End of story." I kept my tone cool. I refused to let this man get under my skin. His cheating wasn't the only reason I'd left him, but it was the simplest one to explain. The less time I spent dealing with Doug, the better. Besides, screwing around was something he could never justify.

"You have to admit, we were lucky to see each other once a week." He gave me that accusing look I'd come to know so well.

He'd used it whenever he was disappointed in me—I'd seen it daily toward the end. "You were working late all the time. I had problems with my boss, and you weren't there for me."

I stared at him. I guess I'd been wrong. He really *could* try to justify it. "We've been over this. That doesn't excuse you." Doug didn't even know how to grovel. In his mind, he was always in the right.

"Mara, honey—"

I needed him to go away. "Sleeping with someone else was only one of your betrayals. What about my booth reservation you canceled for the Pittsburgh Comic Convention? You knew how much I was depending on the exposure I would get for Ghost of a Chance. Not to mention the income it would have generated."

He held his hands up as if surrendering to me. "I'm the one who paid the booth fee. I needed the cash."

I stared at him in disbelief before my eyes narrowed. "Every word out of your mouth is a lie. I have the check I wrote to prove it. They sent it back to me after you canceled."

"Huh." He quickly covered his satisfied smirk, but not before I spotted it. "I was wondering why I never got the money back."

Was he for real? "And then there was the news crew you sent here to do that exposé."

He shrugged with only one shoulder. It was as if my accusation was beneath his notice. "I already told you, I have no idea how your name got on that list."

I couldn't help it. I rolled my eyes. "Right. Just like you had no idea how your cock got inside that woman."

His mouth dropped open. "Jesus, girl. I can't believe you said that."

"Jesus, Doug," I mimicked. "I can't believe you *did* that." I pointed toward the door. "I'm finished with you, and it's closing time. *Go*. I need to lock up."

When he didn't budge, I swept past him and pulled open the door.

He let out an exasperated huff and spun to face me, his elbow hitting one of my new superhero figures and knocking it to the floor.

I let out a yelp as one of Superman's legs snapped off and landed at my feet. "Seriously? You're breaking things now? Stop wrecking my store and my life!" I snatched up the pieces, stormed past him, set them on the counter, and pointed at the open door. "Get. Out."

He crossed his arms over his chest. "I'm not moving until you agree to have dinner with me."

Cool anger descended. He wanted to play that game with me? Fine. I swept past him and flipped off the light switch. "Then you can stand in the dark in my locked shop all night, because I'm not going anywhere with you. Just don't burn the place down."

I stormed out the door. After I slammed it shut, I heard the idiot let out a muffled curse of frustration.

An instant later, he yanked it open, making it bounce against the wall. "You were really going to leave me in there, weren't you?" He had the nerve to look offended.

"I told you I was." Not that I would have. I wasn't *that* stupid. I was trying to make a point.

"What's going on?" Scarlet demanded.

I whirled to see her and Courtney. They both glowered at Doug with nearly identical looks of loathing. My team was here.

"Doug was just leaving," I told them.

He stepped onto the sidewalk and I locked my front door.

"You can be completely unreasonable sometimes, woman," Doug snapped.

"Yes, I can." I gave him a self-satisfied smile.

Scarlet pulled out her phone and started texting someone. "You should go, Doug." She sounded distracted. "Mara is leaving with us."

"I don't know why I bothered coming here today." Doug sounded like a petulant child.

"Neither do I." I went to stand between my friends. With Scarlet in her business suit, Courtney in her heels and pencil skirt, and me in my t-shirt and jeans, we made an interesting trio. A powerful one.

I could imagine cartoon puffs of smoke billowing from Doug's ears as he tromped over to his Camaro, flung open the door, and threw himself into the driver's seat. He backed out of his spot without even bothering to look, punched the gas, and with a squeal of tires he tore off.

I put my hands on my hips. "Well, look at that. Poof. He's gone. Scarlet, you're like magic."

She gave a perturbed frown. "Well, shoot. I didn't want him to leave quite that fast."

I shot her an *are you crazy* look. "Not fast enough for me."

A police car turned onto the street and Chief Brown pulled to a stop next to us. "Hey, Madam Mayor," said the gray-haired man.

"Hey, Mister Police Chief. You just missed him."

He grimaced and shot Scarlet an apologetic look. "Sorry about that. I got here as fast as I could. I'll have my guys keep an eye out for him."

"Thanks. I'll let you know if he comes back." She gave him a wave as he pulled away.

I faced Scarlet squarely, my hands on my hips. Something was going on. "Spill it," I said. "What was all that about?"

"I alerted our police chief that Doug was in town. Did you know there's a bench warrant out for his arrest for unpaid speeding tickets?" She wiggled her eyebrows up and down like an old-time villain as she grinned in delight.

My mouth dropped open. She'd checked up on him? Scarlet's mind was even more devious than I'd realized. "You're kidding me."

Her grin widened. "If he comes back to town and our police chief catches up with him, he'll end up spending a night in jail."

Courtney let out a peel of laughter. "Scarlet, I love the way your mind works."

A gray Volvo sedan pulled into the spot Doug had vacated,

and Lianna sprang out. She looked worried. "I'm pretty sure I just passed Doug, and he looked mega-angry. Was he *here*?"

As Lianna hugged me, I said, "He was, but everything's okay now. Scarlet scared him off. We're heading to dinner. Join us?"

"Sounds like fun, but I can't," Lianna said. "I'm going home early to cook a celebratory dinner for Paul. He just got a promotion!"

"Tell him I said gratz," I told her.

She looked at me blankly.

"*Con-grat-u-la-tions*," I clarified. "Gratz."

Comprehension dawned. "Will do. I'm welcoming him back from his trip with my hand-rolled sushi."

Courtney gave a wicked grin. "You could have him eat it off of your stomach. That could be fun."

Scarlet scrunched her nose. "Fish? On her stomach? That's just gross."

Courtney bobbed her head from side to side. "Yeah. Probably. I was thinking of that scene from *Sex and the City*."

"Not so sexy in real life," Scarlet said.

"I need to hurry if I want to finish before Paul gets home. His flight arrives soon, and he should be home an hour after that." Lianna checked her watch. "That doesn't give me a lot of time." She waved goodbye, climbed into her Volvo, and pulled away.

Scarlet thrust one arm in front of us, looking like a general leading a charge. "Onward! To the Not a Yacht Club," she said.

Courtney linked arms with us and all but dragged us down the sidewalk toward the Ohio River.

"Now—what can we gossip about?" Scarlet asked in a singsong voice. She tapped her forefinger against her lips as she gazed skyward, pretending to think. "Oh, I know. Mara can tell us all about her upcoming *date* with Ford Ross."

I gaped at her. "I—what—how—?" I sputtered. Finally, I managed to form a cohesive sentence. "How did you know? And it isn't a date. We're just meeting for coffee to discuss movies." That was it, I reminded myself. Nothing more. I'd already turned

Ford down, and if I wanted our coffee-time to turn into anything more than a meeting of minds, it was up to me. Right now, I wasn't sure what I wanted.

I had to hand it to Doug. Today's well-timed visit had been an excellent reminder for me to be careful. The last thing I needed in my life was a man.

"Yeah. Right. Keep telling yourself that," Scarlet said with a smirk. "And for the record, I didn't know. I guessed. I'm glad you changed your mind." She looked me in the eye. "Don't fool yourself. The man asked you out. He clearly has more than talking movies in mind."

I latched onto that glimmer of hope. Could she be right? Could I still have a chance at something more with Ford? And did I actually *want* more? My stomach knotted up with anxiety, so I broke contact with Scarlet's perceptive gaze.

Part of me wanted the man, but a bigger part was panicking. I couldn't juggle another failure right now. What if Ford ended up being as horrible as Doug? Maybe I should accept the fact that I wasn't a very good judge of character.

But—was that true? What about my friends? Courtney and Scarlet. Lianna and Rose. They'd all been kind and supportive this past year. Not manipulative in the least. They were amazing women, every one of them. Maybe I wasn't such a bad judge of character after all. I simply needed to hold the men in my life to a much higher standard.

13

COFFEE DATE

MARA

Typically, when I made it to Sunday, I could take a break from work and tackle all my chores. Grocery shopping and laundry were high on my to-do list since I liked eating and not looking like a homeless person. I also visited my parents twice a month. In fact, I was having lunch with them today at one.

But right now, I could only think about meeting Ford for coffee. The man seriously distracted me. I should focus on a plan instead of standing next to my dryer and staring dreamily into space.

I needed to frame my expectations. This was *not a date*. It was a meeting between colleagues. Nothing more—at least, not yet. It would be up to me to turn things around. My stomach churned at the thought. I wasn't outgoing when it came to men and relationships. If I wanted to get us out of the friend-zone, I needed to walk into the coffee shop with that goal firmly in mind, otherwise I'd lose my nerve.

Scarlet's words wriggled their way back into my mind. *"The man asked you out. He clearly has more than talking movies in mind."*

I hoped she was right.

I put my folded clothes away and then stared into my closet, hoping inspiration would strike. I wore jeans and superhero t-shirts every day to work. Today I wanted to wear something different. Something pretty.

I plucked a cream-colored, open-weave, bohemian summer dress from my closet, along with the lightweight sheath that went under it. I'd bought it as a pick-me-up a few weeks ago, but hadn't worn it yet. It was the perfect not-too-dressy, not-too-formal outfit for meeting a sexy director for coffee.

As I turned to set it on the bed, I nearly tripped over Zephyr. The little stumbling-block stared up at me, grinning his doggy grin.

I leaned over and scratched his head. "You're too quiet. I didn't know you were in here."

I padded into the bathroom where I put in my contact lenses and then styled my hair into a bun, letting a single, blue-tipped strand fall loose to frame my face.

I dressed, then adjusted my bedroom door so I could look in the full-length mirror mounted on the back of it. I stared at my reflection, surprised. This outfit looked *good*. Would Ford think so too?

The mirror wobbled, then swung to one side as Zephyr nosed the door open and came back into my bedroom.

"What do you think? Do I look okay?"

He cocked his head to one side and then sat, grinning up at me.

I adjusted the door and reexamined myself in the mirror. "You don't think it's too much, do you? Do I look like I'm trying too hard?"

He stood and wagged his tail.

I glanced at the clock. I needed to leave now, or I'd be late.

"Want to go for a walk?"

We trotted down the staircase and stepped out onto the front sidewalk. I gave the entrance to Ghost of a Chance only a brief glance before striding off.

Living in an apartment directly above my store meant my

morning commute was a breeze, but the location also made it challenging when it came to separating my work from my personal life. After all, why not unbox an order of comics while I waited for that load of laundry to finish?

Which reminded me, I still needed to move my laundry to the dryer. Plus, go grocery shopping. All those weekly chores weren't going to do themselves.

Today was gorgeous—mild and clear. Perfect for being out and about. I didn't see many people on the short walk to Loco Mocha.

I spotted Ford sitting at one of the sidewalk tables. Behind him, the huge garage-door-sized windows were open and the delicious scent of fresh brewed coffee greeted me.

He sipped coffee as he thumbed through his phone. When he spotted us, he immediately set his phone aside and rose to greet me.

"Mara." Those gorgeous eyes that matched the blue of his shirt gleamed with pleasure. "Thanks for meeting up today." He leaned over to give Zephyr a scratch behind the ears before straightening. "What would you like to drink? My treat."

My heart gave a hard thump. "Th-thanks, but you don't need to do that." I rejected the offer automatically. Why did this man make my brain freeze up?

"But I do," he said. "You're here because I asked you to talk with me about superheroes. It's the least I can do."

With those words, I realized putting our relationship on a more intimate footing wouldn't be easy. Inside, I wilted, but I hid my reaction. I could make things right between us. I had to.

I gave a small shrug. "Your treat, then. Thanks. I'll have an iced caramel latte."

He nodded and came back a couple of minutes later with my latte as well as a small cup of whipped cream for Zephyr.

"No glasses today," he commented as he set our cups on the table. "Your glasses are cute, but I like this look too."

His grin made my toes curl. Stupid toes. Stupid grin.

Then I froze. He definitely knew how to charm someone. What

if I was wrong about him? What if he really was a player? I avoided his gaze and sipped my drink. This man seemed to overload all my circuits. I was blowing it.

Ford cleared his throat and then sat across from me. "I have lots of questions about the comic book industry and superhero tropes." His voice sounded entirely businesslike.

I smiled tightly, knowing I'd blown a perfect opportunity. "Everyone likes to be needed." I was the one who'd made it clear I wanted to keep our relationship professional, and he was abiding by my wishes.

Be careful what you ask for, and all that.

Irritation with myself twisted my stomach. I nearly smacked myself in the forehead for being so bipolar. I couldn't keep swinging back and forth between wanting this man and trying to convince myself that I was better off without him. I needed to make a decision and stick with it. *Move forward, Mara! Stop being a nutcase. He isn't Doug!*

I lifted the little cup of whipped cream in a toast. "Thanks for this. It's one of Zephyr's favorite treats." I leaned over and held it out to Zephyr. He licked it clean and then settled in underneath the table to watch passersby.

"How was your trip to L.A.?" I asked Ford.

"Good. I ended up leasing my house to some friends for the next few months. They're filming a movie and need a place to stay while they decide if they want to relocate to L.A. or just rent. The timing worked out for everyone. They get a furnished place, and I get people I trust living there."

That sounded promising. "Does that mean you plan to stick around Sewickley?"

His jaw flexed. "For a while. I need to be here to take care of some family stuff." He rested his forearm on the table. "My Sewickley house is empty right now. I could either rent it to someone again or live there. After spending the past couple of weeks in my sister's place while she prepares for renovations, the decision was easy. People are constantly stopping by to take measurements or drop off samples." He rubbed his chin. "I have a few items in storage, but I need new living room furniture."

"I heard you hired Kincaid Gillette to do some painting and repairs. Good choice. He does great work."

His eyes glinted with curiosity. "You seem to know everyone around town. You've only lived here for a year, and you're already wired in. I'm impressed."

A flush of warmth filled me. If he knows I'd only lived here a year, he must have asked about me. "Kincaid is Courtney's brother. She's one of my closest friends. She mentioned something about it."

The connection clicked for him. "Now I get it. His brother Conner and I used to be friends. Still are."

I poked at the ice in my latte with my straw. "You met with a producer when you were in L.A., right? How did it go? Are you going to direct his movie?"

Ford frowned. "I haven't made a decision yet. It's a great opportunity, but I still have doubts. We're negotiating, but I'm not sure there's much McCormick will let me change. I need to start exploring my other options."

That caught my attention. "Such as?"

He shrugged. "Things that would keep me here."

I raised one eyebrow. "In Pittsburgh?"

"Maybe."

"Enigmatic man."

He chuckled. "There are several factors to consider. I don't want to talk about it too soon, but—" he paused and considered me for a moment, "what the hell." He shot me a conspiratorial grin. "The conversation you and I had the day we first met got me reexamining everything I believed about superhero movies."

A rush of pleasure thrilled me. He'd really listened to me instead of dismissing whatever didn't align with his worldview. I respected him all the more for admitting it. "You mean the one where I called you out about your moldy old ideas?" I teased, just to confirm.

"Thanks for that. You were right." He tilted his head, his eyes filled with respect and admiration—for me. "Even if McCormick's movie doesn't pan out, I've decided to make a superhero movie." His eyes glowed with enthusiasm. "I owe it all to you. Your comments about the movie industry and comics got me thinking, and now ideas keep pinging around in my head." As he spoke, his face became more and more animated.

Had I really triggered this change in him? Opened him up to something new? The thought invigorated me. "Glad I could help."

Was this how a movie was born? Was I at the birth of an idea that could become great? Huge, even?

Ford set his coffee on the table. "There's one thing I've been wondering about. Why do you think Deadpool has been so successful? The way I see it, the movie goes out of its way to poke fun at comic books, and the main character is more of an anti-hero. I'd have thought superhero die-hard fans would've hated it."

I grinned with delight that he'd brought up that particular character. "Oh, contraire, *Deadpool* is one of my favorites for precisely those reasons. The story works because the writer knows the standard tropes of the superhero genre and how to poke fun at them without alienating his audience."

He focused on me intently. "I was thinking the same thing."

"To make a story like that work, it comes down to connecting with the main character. Understanding what motivates him. Showing how he was wounded, profoundly, and how it changed him. In the beginning, Deadpool just wants to be with his girl-friend—the love of his life—and when he discovers he has cancer, he does everything he can do to treat his illness so they can be together. Showing their love makes you root for Deadpool even when he turns into a bitter jerk later in the movie. Their relation-ship makes you want him to succeed. When the secret govern-ment organization eventually takes advantage of him, you care. You want him to defeat them."

"The director did a great job of conveying that in the movie," Ford said.

"The opening scene was exciting, but he wasn't likable," I said. "He came across as snarky, not superhero material. It isn't until you learn how he got there—what brought him to that point—that you start to root for him."

"Movies are great at action scenes," Ford said. "Anything you can see, they can show—but when it comes to conveying emotions—internal thoughts—movies aren't so good. It's hard to show internal conflict onscreen."

"Why don't you just do it with dialogue?" I asked.

"No one likes listening to someone complain," he pointed out. "It's a turnoff, just like in real life. We like to see our heroes act heroically."

I thought about that. About how Deadpool complained to his friend in the bar, which went counter to what Ford had just said. "But in the movie—"

Ford held up his hand to stop me. "In Deadpool, they hooked you in with the action scene, unveiled his backstory explaining how he ended up where he was, and then made you care by showing you why he and Vanessa were perfect for each other. The director did a great job showing their evolving relationship with those short romantic vignettes as the calendar flipped by. By the time she's kidnapped, you know those two misfits are perfect for each other."

This was fun. I hadn't dissected the plot of a comic like this in ages. Not since Chance—

A sharp pain of loss pierced me. Moments like this hurt the most, when, just for an instant, I forgot he was gone. The bleak realization came pouring back into my heart—and nearly undid me.

"Are you okay?" Ford asked.

My eyes met his. He'd noticed? "I'm fine. I was just thinking about my brother." I didn't want to talk about this. Not now. "I can see how romance can be hard to show on screen, since a love story isn't exactly action-packed."

Ford's eyes betrayed his concern for me, but he went along with my subject change. "Movies need to either *say* or *show* what a character is thinking, and that can be challenging. It takes a great script and great acting."

He started peppering me with questions about various popular superheroes, as well as some of the lesser-known ones. "What about the indie comics in your store—do you read those as well?" he asked.

I nodded enthusiastically. "Absolutely. It's hard for an indie creator to get established. I like to help whenever I can."

"I picked up one called *Ghost* at your store. I really liked it. Do you have some other indies you'd recommend?"

The mention of *Ghost* brought me up short. It took some effort, but after a moment, I was able to think of a couple. "There's *The Dregs*. It's a bit dark, but I really like it. Then there's *Faith*. She's one of my favs. She's not your traditional superhero since she's a heavy woman, but she's funny and kicks butt. It's penned by a woman and promotes positive body image."

Ford's eyebrow quirked. "I like that. That one has possibilities. Any others?"

I mentioned a few more. Ford's decisiveness, curiosity, and enthusiasm intrigued me. Brainstorming with him like this felt invigorating. I hadn't felt this alive in months. His excitement tugged at me, pulling me closer to him.

As we talked, my world shifted. The solid resistance inside me finally softened where he was concerned.

Wait. Slow down. We were still in the friend-zone. I didn't want to get ahead of myself.

I abruptly sat back in my chair and put my hands in my lap. Ford was keeping things professional, just like I'd asked.

We were worlds apart. He was Superman, and I was... What? Lois Lane? Yeah, right. Not likely. While he traveled the world and used his creative superpowers to make award-winning films,

I drudged away stocking shelves, watching out for potential shoplifters, and keeping my business afloat. The only things that ramped me up these days were my freelance code gigs. Especially the ones Destiny sent my way. What could Ford and I possibly have in common besides superhero movies?

As I mentally shut down the possibility of anything romantic between us, he went and flashed that damned smile at me.

Shazam. Check out those dimples. The man had me hooked.

I stared at that full, delectable mouth. What would it be like to kiss him again? This time I could slide my tongue along the bottom edge of his lip—along that border where it met the line of stubble just beginning to emerge.

Ford abruptly stopped talking. "I hope I haven't bored you. I tend to get carried away."

He'd caught me daydreaming—about him! My cheeks prickled with heat and I brushed my hair away from my suddenly hot neck. Good thing he didn't have a mind-reading super-ability. "Not at all. I like talking with you. It's fascinating—listening as ideas ricochet through your brain. It reminds me of the way Destiny and I brainstormed our video game. Destiny focused more on the storyline, and I loved solving the graphics problems and tightening the code to make it nimble. I loved testing new ideas. Finding innovative ways to look at problems."

I missed it.

Wait. No!

I *loved* my store. Loved it with every fiber of my being. Yes, I used to own an indie video game company, but there were plenty of things about it I'd hated. The organizational end of things. The lawyers. The financing. All that stuff had driven me bonkers.

"You come alive when you talk about it," Ford said. "It must have been hard to give up."

"It seemed like a no-brainer at the time," I said with a shrug. "Ghost of a Chance was my dream."

Ford rose to his feet. "I like it when everything clicks and you know the perfect decision to make. I'm not there yet. I have too many ideas bouncing around in my brain right now. I need to narrow things down." He glanced at my cup. "Can I get you another coffee?"

I picked up my drink and realized it was empty. "Thanks. That would be great."

Zephyr stood and looked longingly at Ford.

"Should I get something for Zephyr?"

"Water?"

"Sure thing." He headed to the counter. His snug tan shorts hung perfectly from his hips. I forced myself not to gawk.

If I wanted things between us to change, it would be up to me. Clearly, Ford wasn't going to press the point.

I snuck another look at him at the counter.

At that moment, he glanced back at me.

My cheeks immediately warmed with acute awareness.

His grin broadened, and all I could do was suck on the straw of my empty iced latte and look away like some witless nerf-herder fresh off the farm. Why did I freak out whenever he flirted with me?

What was wrong with me? Where had all my confidence disappeared to? Maybe Dad was right. Maybe I should have stuck with my own passion—my gaming company—rather than pursuing a dream Chance and I had once been enthralled with as children.

Wait—was I actually wavering? This was ridiculous. I *wanted* my store. I'd wanted it for years. The dream might have started when I'd been a kid, but it continued into adulthood. That's why my brother and I had been opening the store together.

Chance's comic books and this shop were all I had left of him. I might not have the ability to turn one of his graphic novels into a bestseller, but I had no doubt I could keep our comic book store going. Everyone else might have written off his ambitions, but *I* hadn't. And I never would.

Keeping our store alive felt like keeping Chance's dreams alive.

Ford approached me warily. His brow furrowed as he sat down. "Is something wrong?" He handed me my coffee and set Zephyr's water next to him.

"No, no. I was just—" I blinked, and the sting of unshed tears made me realize I was on the verge of crying. "I started thinking about my brother again. It's been over a year since he died, but every now and then, the loss still hits me hard."

His eyes deepened with sympathy. "That must have been devastating."

"He was my twin. We were close, as you can imagine." I rolled my lips together, pressing them tightly so they wouldn't tremble. "It's weird. Even now, I sometimes think, 'Chance will love this. I can't wait to tell him.' And then I remember I can't. It hurts, you know?"

He nodded. "I think I do. It's painful to lose someone you love. That's the simple truth. My mom died when I was young. Nothing is ever the same after a loss like that."

I gave a jerky nod and then took a big swig of my iced latte. The cold made my teeth ache, which was good. It gave me a new pain to focus on and helped to push down my grief. "Those things shape us. They're our origin stories, just like in the comics."

He cocked his head to one side. "Do you see losing your brother as a turning point for you?" He sounded genuinely curious.

"Absolutely," I said immediately. "It sent me in a new direction. What about you? What was your turning point?"

He shrugged. "Probably losing my mom. I was in elementary school when she died. We thought she'd beat breast cancer, so losing her to pneumonia took everyone by surprise. Dad didn't remarry. We didn't move. He kept everything at home pretty much the same, but it was all different without Mom, if you know what I mean."

I did. Nothing would ever be the same without Chance. "Did your dad start dating?"

"Nah. He kept Mom's memory almost sacred. The two of them

were crazy in love. Now I know that having a relationship like that is rare, but at the time I took it for granted. Dad found *the* woman he wanted to spend his life with, and when she was gone he wasn't willing to settle for anything less. I respect that—I do—but it's sort of intimidating, too. Maybe it's why I've never dated anyone for long." He was silent for a moment, then cleared his throat.

Maybe that's why he was photographed with so many different women he never actually dated. "Weren't you married?" I asked, recalling reading about her when I'd cyber-stalked him.

"I was," Ford said, "for a hot minute. Our careers both took off and our relationship couldn't weather it, so we called it quits." He shrugged. "I was crazy about her at the beginning, but was she the love of my life? No. Maybe I was looking for what my parents had. If I was, I didn't find it. She's a good person, just not the *right* person. Not for me, anyway."

As his words sank in, my heart quickened. Had I found a man who was a romantic at heart? "What made you decide to be a director?"

"That's easy," he said with a relaxed smile. "My dad. The movie industry was always my backdrop growing up. It was Dad's main topic of conversation. Still is. Back in middle school, I made a video for extra credit in my English class, but when my dad found out, he went overboard and tried to take over. Let's just say we had 'creative differences'. He wanted costumes and lighting, some sort of soundtrack. I wanted a handheld video camera and a grainy, minimal look. I had to learn to stand up to him if I wanted to make the video I really wanted. That lesson has stuck with me. Maintaining creative control is essential."

I imagined a plucky little Ford Ross going toe to toe with his dad. "Did the two of you end up in a big fight?"

"How did you guess?"

My mouth quirked. "To me, that sounds like *your* origin story."

He tossed his head back and let out a laugh. "With my dad as the evil villain? You know, I think you might be right. I bet Dad would laugh his ass off if I told him."

I gaped at him. "Would he? Not my dad. He'd be offended." I could picture his face turning bright red.

"Tell me about him," Ford said, intrigued.

"He's a doctor. A cardiac surgeon. A great one with an excellent reputation." Saying so gave me that same flash of pride I'd always felt. "But he's a perfectionist too. Nothing's ever good enough for him."

"And your mom?"

"She's great." My heart gave a squeeze. "Best mom ever. She's my dad's polar opposite in most ways. Similar in others. When they met, she was a dancer and a choreographer. Now she teaches ballet and tap classes. She's really laid back unless you don't try hard enough in one of her classes."

His eyes gleamed with amusement. "They sound like quite a pair."

"I think it's one of those opposites-attract things. He was always pushing us kids toward STEM careers, and Mom would undermine him at every chance to get us to focus on the arts."

The bells in the clock tower in the center of Sewickley chimed one o'clock. I was surprised we'd been talking so long. "It's later than I realized. I'm supposed to be at my parents' house." I scrambled to my feet.

He stood as well. "Thanks for talking with me today. You have to let me know if there's anything I can do to repay the favor."

My stupid libido kicked in right then, flooding me with images of all the things I could imagine him doing for me. To me. Deliciously wicked things.

I could feel the clock ticking, pressing on me to *do* something. *Take action.* How was I going to bridge this romantic gap with Ford in the next few seconds?

Pursuing men might be completely out of character for me, but when what you kept doing wasn't working, sometimes you had to make a change. Especially with someone as perfect as Ford Ross standing in front of you.

I looked into his eyes. "You're welcome to drop by Ghost of a Chance whenever you want. I'm not very busy in the early afternoon during the week. I'd love to spend more time with you." After a brief moment of hesitation, I added, "I've really enjoyed being here today."

At my comment, Ford's expression changed. "So have I." He locked gazes with me, and the blue of his eyes seemed to intensify, making my heart thump hard against my ribs. Suddenly, his smile seemed much more personal than the one he'd given me only a few minutes ago. "Since you're closed on Monday, I'll see you on Tuesday."

14

THE SCRIPT'S THE THING

FORD

I tossed our cups into the trash and then slid on my sunglasses. I watched as Mara ate up the sidewalk with her smooth, graceful stride. The woman looked like a slice of summer in that dress.

A man turned to watch, his gaze sweeping up and down her body. A wave of possessiveness swept through me, and it lingered even after he entered the dry-cleaning shop.

I hadn't been able to read Mara very well. At first, she'd seemed happy to see me. She'd even worn that amazing dress, which had given me hope that she was feeling flirtatious, but then she'd pulled away.

Since she'd already turned me down, it was important that she make the first move if she wanted to put things on a different footing. I didn't want any more misunderstandings between us. Throughout our conversation, she kept holding something back—some essential part of herself. I'm a patient guy, so I waited. Finally, she made that overture. A small one—just enough to keep me on the hook.

I bit. Hard.

The woman definitely sent mixed signals, but that last offer was meant as an opening.

She left me confused, though. She came across as self-confident at work and when dealing with customers, but when it was just the two of us, that confidence faded.

She turned a corner and disappeared from view. I dragged my gaze away from the empty sidewalk, already missing her as I headed toward my house. I glanced down in time to avoid an uneven area in the pavement.

Sewickley was an old town with old trees and old sidewalks. Back in L.A., people rarely walked. Cars were king. It was different here though. All around Pittsburgh you'd find sections of brick roads—like the one I lived on.

I turned onto my street, flanked by graceful houses that were built over a century ago when Teddy Roosevelt had been president.

I'd never seen Mara's gorgeous bare legs before today. She always wore jeans at her shop, and in my opinion, that was a damned shame. They were long and toned and perfect. The straps on her sandals didn't seem like they'd be strong enough to keep them on her feet, but clearly, they did the job. Those coral-pink toenails left me wanting to strip off her sandals right there in the coffee shop and give her a foot massage. She stood most of the day, so her feet probably ached by the time she went home.

Wait—was I fixating on her toes? Damn, but I had it bad for that sexy little nerd.

I pulled out my phone and sent her a quick text.

Me: Thanks for joining me for coffee and conversation. It was fun. See you Tuesday.

Her reply came almost immediately.

Mara: I'd love that. I had a great time too! Thanks again!

Not a sonnet, but it gave me hope.

Time to get to work. I had some decisions to make about that Superman movie, and I knew the best person to talk them over with. Sheila.

When I called, she picked up immediately. "Hey, Ford." She sounded happy. Relaxed. Much better than the last time we talked.

"Hey, yourself. What has you in such a good mood?"

"I finally had a day off. No filming. I kicked around Amsterdam for a while, playing tourist."

"I filmed there a few years ago. Gorgeous city. What places did you visit?" The bright sun bounced off the white sidewalks in front of me. The afternoon was warm and humid, but still pleasant.

"I wandered through Vondelpark and then headed over to Rijksmuseum," she said. "The park is great. Reminds me a lot of Central Park."

"I remember thinking the same thing. Especially that big pond."

"Did you visit the Rijksmuseum?" she asked.

"Nope. Never made it there. Was it packed with paintings by Dutch masters?"

Sheila let out a throaty huff of laughter. "How'd you guess? I even visited the museum's research library. No surprise, right? I love libraries. I think the artist who drew the Beast's library in the animated Beauty and the Beast must have seen this one. The place actually has spiral staircases in the corners that lead all the way up to the third-floor gallery."

A spring breeze shook the leaves in boughs that arched overhead, causing the dappled bits of sunlight and shadow to swirl around me in a miniature snowstorm of light.

"Did you go with anyone?" I asked.

"Absolutely not! I'm sick of people right now. I needed some alone time."

I chuckled. "I'd forgotten that about you. Your need your solitude so you can recharge."

"It's the best medicine after ten straight days of shooting. Humans drive me nuts after a while."

"Not me." I came to the corner of my street and turned right. "Being alone gets to me."

"Yeah. You're weird that way."

"Loner." I used the word like an accusation. "I like Amsterdam. It's a gorgeous city." But the quiet street right in front of me held its own charms. The perfectly manicured lawns. The stately hundred-year-old homes. The enormous trees lining the brick street.

A sense of belonging overtook me. This was *my* street. *My* town. That was *my* house just up ahead.

I took in the slate tiles on my roof. The mullioned windows. The newly trimmed shrubs with the rough, pungent scent of freshly laid mulch. The flowering rhododendrons. The perfectly trimmed grass along the driveway and the planters overflowing with multicolored pansies flanking the front door.

Totally charming.

Amsterdam might be an amazing city, but right now I was exactly where I wanted to be. In Sewickley. I'd missed this place more than I'd realized.

Coming home after being gone for so long allowed me to see everything in a different light. Years ago, I'd been desperate to get away—to find my path and make a name for myself. Now, I could appreciate everything from a more seasoned perspective without being swayed by youthful wanderlust. My detached point of view would fade, but maybe I could use it right now to go through my house as though seeing it for the first time.

Keeping that perspective firmly in place, I pulled the key from my pocket as I approached the door. A moment later, I stood in my empty foyer.

"I'm still on the fence about directing McCormick's film," I told Sheila. My voice surprised me as it echoed in the vacant foyer, bouncing through the nearby empty rooms. I continued, more quietly, "I've been trying to figure out how to fix the script, but all my ideas would require a significant rewrite."

"What's wrong with the script?"

I strode into the spacious, echoing family room, sunlight pouring in through the towering windows. Above the fireplace, a hidden TV panel was designed to lift away, revealing a stunning Russian landscape painting. But my mind was elsewhere.

"It's just another Superman origin story," I said. "Planet Krypton explodes, he gets sent off in a spaceship, lands on Earth, gets raised by a couple. It's been done to death."

"Does that mean you don't think it's time for another remake?" Sheila teased.

I shook my head, my frustration mounting. "I mean, am I the only one who can't get past Christopher Reeve? He was the perfect Superman. And this script? It's the same old story, with slightly different words."

Walking into the kitchen, I admired the stainless-steel appliances and the mosaic stone tiles on the backsplash. Maybe I should give cooking Dante's chili another try.

"There's nothing new about this version," I explained to Sheila. "It's just another repeat. Even the first date with Lois Lane is identical."

Passing through the grand family room with its stone fireplace, the sunroom with its tall windows, and the dining room with yet another oversized fireplace, I headed toward the main staircase. My hand slid possessively over the decorative newel post shaped like a pineapple. This place was even more impressive than I remembered.

"I'm not interested in making just any movie," I told her. "I'm looking for the perfect one."

Sheila clucked her tongue sympathetically. "That's a tough one, Ford. Have you talked to McCormick about your concerns?"

"Not in any detail. I don't want to offend him. He's in love with the script." I climbed the stairs, sliding my hand along the solid, smooth wood of the banister. "Maybe the problem is with me. I don't think I'm the right director for this project. I want to do something different. Unique."

She sighed. "That *is* a problem."

I glanced into the three empty bedrooms off the hall as I headed toward the master suite. Along the hallway, the built-in cabinets would be perfect for storing my enormous collection of DVDs and Blu-rays. "How do you think McCormick will react if I turn down the movie? I don't want to piss him off."

"You can be diplomatic. You're a lot better at it than I am."

I laughed to myself as I stepped into the master bedroom. "That's not hard."

I'd forgotten how big this room was. This really was an amazing house. I stood next to the large windows overlooking the emerald-green back yard rimmed with scalding yellow daffodils and electrifying pink and orange tulips. Thank god my dad's landscaper was able to maintain everything at my house as well.

"Whatever. I gave up on bothering with diplomacy years ago. I suck at it. Besides, it never got me anywhere. If you're a woman and you're in charge, they either call you bossy or a bitch. Might as well live up to either name. But when it comes to McCormick, maybe you'll piss him off, maybe you won't. He wants the right person for the job, and he knows it's important to get a director who is enthusiastic. If that person isn't you, then you're both better off parting ways."

She made a good point. Enthusiasm couldn't be faked long-term. Hadn't I said essentially the same thing to my dad?

We rang off. Without Sheila's outsized personality on the other end of the line, the house suddenly felt lonelier. Emptier.

This place had good bones. I still hadn't decided what to do with the area on the third floor that used to be the servants' quarters. Maybe it could be my home office.

This place was a gem.

An empty, echoing gem. As empty as my personal life.

I needed to work on that. To fill my life and my house with people who mattered to me. I refused to let myself end up as closed off as my dad.

15

WHY DIDN'T YOU TELL ME IT SOLD?

MARA

I was carrying an armful of comics out of my storeroom on Tuesday afternoon when my phone rang. I pulled my phone out of my pocket and checked the caller I.D.

Dad.

I sighed, but I answered it. "Hi."

I set the stack of comics on the counter.

"A friend just sent me a link to an article announcing that Destiny is selling Stel-Wood." My dad's voice seethed with anger. "The news floored me, Mara. Absolutely floored me. The worst part is, he assumed I already knew since it was announced a week ago. Why didn't you bother to tell me at lunch on Sunday?"

"I—I—" I sat down hard on the stool behind the counter. She'd actually sold Stel-Wood? I thought she was still shopping it around. How had I missed hearing about the sale?

I was happy for her, of course, but the news left me feeling hollow. I should have been celebrating with Destiny rather than sitting here listening to my dad berate me. In another life, that's exactly what I'd be doing right now.

"All you talked about was that ridiculous movie director you met. Why can't you spend as much mental energy thinking about your career as you do about some man you hardly know? This is your future, young woman! Get your priorities straight!"

Anger flared through me and I pulled my phone away from my ear to stare at it. I'd only mentioned Ford once, when Mom asked why I wasn't wearing jeans. But it always came back to this with my dad. He thought I'd screwed up by opening Ghost of a Chance and he wouldn't stop harassing me about it. Why didn't I mention I knew Destiny wanted to sell? Because I knew this was the reaction I'd get!

Instead of letting him berate me some more, I gave him the contrite-sounding, "Sorry," I knew he wanted. Maybe it would shut him down.

He let out a huff of frustration. "What's worse is that there wasn't a single mention of you in the entire article. It called her the sole owner of the business. How could you throw away your partnership like that? You flushed years of sweat equity down the drain. All you have to show for it is a failing store. I knew you'd left Stel-Wood, but I never dreamed you'd been stupid enough to turn over your share of the company."

As I reached out to flip the sign on the door from "back in five minutes" to "open," his choice of words smacked into me and I froze. I knew he'd be upset about the sale, but that didn't make his evisceration any easier to bear. He always attacked me and my sibs when we failed to meet his impossible standards of perfection.

Inhaling deeply, I squeezed my eyes shut and tried to shake off his hurtful words. But with just a few well-chosen jabs, he had me feeling like a helpless twelve-year-old again, showing him the B+ I'd gotten on my history quiz. In his eyes, that grade was proof of pure laziness.

"I can't believe you just called me stupid," I said as I stomped back toward the counter.

"Someone has to. If you'd stayed the course, you'd be cashing in on that deal. Instead, you're killing yourself working sixty-hour weeks at that store."

My stride hitched slightly at that accurate hit. More like eighty when you counted my freelance coding work, but that still didn't match the ninety-hour weeks I used to pull. "You're mistaken if you think I wouldn't have been working crazy long hours with Destiny. We poured everything into Stel-Wood."

"The difference being, when you were with Destiny, you loved what you were doing. Now you don't."

His words punched into me, making my chest tighten. The man was on a roll with these well-placed blows. He was right, and each fact he rattled off struck right to the heart. I'd loved working with Destiny. Loved starting our own company. Loved it so much that it had never felt like work. Even now, my favorite parts of the day were when I wrote code to help make ends meet. Still, it hurts to hear *I told you so.* "You know, as my dad, you're supposed to be supportive. Gloating doesn't fit the job description."

"I'm also supposed to let you know when you're screwing up, and you happen to be doing it on a world-class level. If they had an Olympic event in screwing up, you'd take the gold."

My throat tightened. I couldn't speak a word as tears welled. Finally, I was able to squeeze the air out of my lungs. "Thanks, Dad. I'll treasure your words forever." I shut my eyes and covered them with my hand. "I have to go. I have a customer," I lied.

"I didn't hear the chimes," he said, calling me out.

Frak.

I strode back to the door and reached up to smack the chimes, sending them into an angry frenzy. "Was that loud enough for you?" I snapped. "Bye."

I ended the call and marched back to my register as I dashed my hand against my cheek to wipe away my tears. I leaned against the counter with my back to the door and stared at the *Wonder Woman* poster directly in front of me without really seeing it. Instead, I mentally replayed my father's words.

He'd gone for the jugular today. He hadn't been this angry with me since the day I'd told him I was leaving Stel-Wood

Gaming Studios to open Ghost of a Chance. Stel-Wood had been heavily in debt at that point. Dad had railed against my decision, telling me I was making a huge mistake by leaving my business and my career. I'd told him it would be a financial strain, but that I had to do it to keep Chance's dream alive.

He'd said I was on my own. Where the hell had he thought I'd gotten the money from, if not by giving up my half of Stel-Wood?

Why did I still let him get to me this way? He'd said hurtful things like that to me often enough in the past that I should be immune to them by now.

Apparently, I wasn't.

Having my dad harangue me was at the top of my list of perfectly terrible ways to start my work week. At least things could only improve, right? Although, with my luck, I'd check my social media and discover some cyber stalker had a vendetta against me.

Maybe I'd even get my own supervillain who'd try to bring me down. "My own Lex Luther. Or maybe the Borg," I muttered. Then again, I already had my dad and Doug vying for the role.

Zephyr glanced up at me. When he realized that I wasn't talking to him, he returned to staring at the front door. Clearly, he was eager for a customer to arrive. My dog loved each and every one of them.

Dad's call left me stunned. Conceptually speaking, I'd known what I'd be giving up when I'd left Stel-Wood. Destiny and I had developed a great game. I knew it would be a hit. Even so, witnessing her success felt more like a blow than a cause for celebration. Destiny was a millionaire, and I was struggling to keep afloat. It hurt a lot more than I'd expected.

"Let it go," I said. I'd made this decision over a year ago. I had to live with my choices. If I had regrets, then it was up to me to make new decisions to improve my life. I couldn't simply obsess about the past. That kind of thinking was destructive. I needed to focus on the present and look to the future.

Pep talk time. There were loads of good things in my life. I hadn't hit rock bottom. I had my health, right? And a great dog. And my own business. Things could be worse. I had a roof over my head, there were currently no natural disasters here in Pittsburgh, and although Doug was an ass, he wasn't a supervillain set on destroying me. He was nothing more than an annoying ex-boyfriend my friends and I had outmaneuvered.

"Mischief managed." I let out a snort of laughter as I groaned at myself. I was such a nerd.

The door chimed, and I whirled around to see Ford bathed in sunlight as he strode into my shop.

When he shot me a sexy grin, little bubbles of happiness effervesced in my chest, and my smirk turned into a smile. My dismal day had suddenly taken an about-face.

Ford clutched a large, brown paper bag bearing the logo of the local mom-and-pop grocery store, and my gaze lingered on his flexed bicep peeking out from the sleeve of his pale-blue shirt. Ford Ross was one fine-looking man. Even better, he was great to talk to. The perfect pick-me-up for a seriously crappy day.

Stuffing down those lingering tendrils of devastation, I put on my game-face and cocked my head to one side. "On your way home from doing some grocery shopping?"

"Nope. I wanted to surprise you with lunch. Don't let the grocery bag fool you. I didn't buy you a premade sandwich. I actually made something for you myself."

I stared at him, flummoxed. "You made me lunch?"

"I was inspired by an excellent roast beef and basil panini I ate while I was in L.A." He opened the bag, and my eyes widened as he pulled out plates and foil-wrapped packages that he neatly arranged on my counter. "I did my best to recreate it. Dante even loaned me his panini press. By the way, I moved out of my sister's guest room and into my house. It's still mostly empty, but I'm having some furniture delivered tomorrow."

I could only stare at him with a mixture of awe and relief. The man swept through my door and, with the flick of a hand—or a grocery bag—changed my awful day into something much better.

Ford set out two bottles of water and then fixed me with an uncertain gaze. "I hope you haven't already eaten. You mentioned you eat lunch late because afternoons are quiet."

My heart swelled. He'd planned all this just for me. I tried to contain the broad smile that wanted to split my face but only succeeded in tamping it down a degree or two. Everything about me softened in response to him... my mood, my tense jaw —my heart... It all seemed to melt. "I'm starving. You making me lunch is so...unreal." Warmth blossomed in my chest. "These sorts of things don't happen to me. This isn't my type of life."

He quirked an eyebrow. "Then we need to change that. I wanted to do something nice for you. You've been a huge help to me. Besides, you never take any time off. As far as I can tell, the only days your store is closed are Sunday and Monday."

My eyes welled with tears, the happy kind, which was ridiculous. I gave myself a brutal mental shake, not wanting an over-the-top reaction to his kindness freaking him out. I cleared my throat as I tried to regain my composure. "And that's when I get all my chores done. You know. Laundry. Dishes. Groceries. That sort of thing." Babbling. I was babbling. I snapped my mouth shut.

"Then I'm glad I brought you lunch. That's one less thing for you to worry about." He nudged one of the plates toward me.

With fumbling fingers, I unwrapped the warm, foil bundle. The delicious scents of garlic, basil, cheese, and roast beef hit me full force, making my mouth water. "This smells like heaven."

"Tell me how it tastes."

I bit into it.

He watched me as I chewed, as though trying to gauge my reaction. It made me self-conscious, so I closed my eyes and focused my sandwich.

Perfectly toasted bread. Warm, flavorful cheese. And that basil —so awesome. This panini was delicious. The moment I swallowed, my eyes opened and I found him still staring at me. "I do declare, Mr. Ross," I said, using my best southern belle imitation, "this is one of the best sandwiches I've ever tasted."

"Shucks, ma'am." He glanced away as he faked a bashful response.

I was still grinning as I took a swig of water. I casually leaned against the counter, trying to look a little less overwhelmed than I felt. "Sorry to make you stand while you eat. We can't go to the back room because I need to keep an eye on the store in case someone comes in. If you want, I can grab you a stool from back there."

"No need. But if you want customers to come in, you might want to flip over your sign so it reads, 'Open.'"

I gave a yelp and darted to the door to change the sign. So much for looking cool. Dad must have rattled me so much I'd forgotten to do it.

I headed back to the counter and picked up my panini. "This sandwich is delicious. Is this the kind of thing you're learning how to make in Dante's class?"

"I picked up some techniques from him. Now that I have a couple of classes under my belt, I'm starting to get confident enough to try new things." His slow smile warmed me, and I felt a flush rise up my neck. "Thanks for being my guinea pig—and for inspiring me to make the effort."

I playfully fluttered my hand as though trying to fan my face and put on my southern belle voice again. "I do declare, I bet you say that to all the girls."

"No. Only you."

My eyes snapped to his, and I suddenly found myself trapped by his gaze. I seemed to be falling into his eyes. I'd already noticed how blue they were, but I'd never let myself stare into them this way. It was a heady experience. His irises were rimmed with a darker blue, but flecks of lighter blue lightened them toward the center, like twin vortexes. I felt those tiny whirlpools pulling me in... sweeping away all my resistance.

Resistance is futile.

I was such a ridiculous nerd.

I yanked my eyes away. I wasn't sure where to look instead. All I knew was that continuing to gaze into Ford Ross's mesmerizing blue eyes was far too risky.

Besides, I was probably reading too much into this surprise lunch.

The lunch that he'd made.

And delivered to me.

On second thought, maybe I wasn't reading too much into this. Maybe I had this exactly right.

I glanced at Ford again and found him watching me. He took a step closer and set his panini next to mine on the counter. "Now that you know I won't kill you with my cooking, I was hoping you'd agree to join me for dinner tomorrow night. At my place. I want to cook for you. I mean, an actual meal. Not just a sandwich."

I stared at him, incredulous. "Dinner? You want to cook me dinner? For reals?" God. Did my voice have to go all squeaky like that? I must sound like I was twelve.

He cocked one eyebrow and the corners of his mouth turned up. "I'm pretty sure that's what I said."

I was momentarily dumbfounded, not quite able to absorb the idea. Ford Ross wanted to cook for me.

Me. The town super nerd. The opposite of a Hollywood starlet.

I hesitated, needing clarification. "Will it be a business-date or a date-date?"

His smile deepened, making my face grow warm. "I'm glad you asked. I'll leave that choice up to you. I was hoping for a date-date, but it's your call."

Was it? That was a lot of responsibility. I swallowed. "A date-date, then," I said, before I could censor myself.

Gah! Shut up, mouth.

I panicked. Why had I said that? Clearly, my mouth knew what it wanted, even if my brain didn't. Why was I so afraid of taking this step?

Ford stared at me, an odd, confused sort of expression on his face. That's when I realized I was nodding like one of those stupid bobble-head dolls. Apparently, not only my voice, but also my body was on board with saying yes to this guy. And they were dragging the rest of me right along with them, whether my brain thought dating anyone—let alone Ford—was smart or not.

"Let's do Friday night," he said. "Come by after you close." He scribbled the address on my napkin.

I swallowed, still nodding.

Stupid nod. Stop it.

I stopped.

Was I really going to do this? "I—I can be there at seven thirty."

Apparently, I was.

"Sounds perfect." He tapped his water bottle against mine in a toast. "Here's to our first real date."

"Our first date." I took a long drink of water.

What had I just done?

16

LIANNA'S NEWS

MARA

As I walked upstairs to my apartment that evening, I was still in a state of stunned euphoria. I had a real date with Ford. My anticipation shoved the sale of Stel-Wood from the forefront of my mind.

Stel-Wood was my past. I needed to focus on the here and now.

This was my life, and it was a good one. I had a great store, my family lived nearby, I had an amazing group of friends, and I'd just agreed to a first date with an amazing man. Life was good. All I had to do was keep reminding myself of that fact instead of dwelling on the past, and I'd be fine.

My book club would be here shortly. As I lit the candles on my dining table, my first guest knocked.

Zephyr let out a yip of delight.

"Zephyr, sit," I said, as I shoved the lighter into a drawer.

He ignored me and scampered ahead of me as I crossed the hardwood floor. He danced with excitement as he stared up at the doorknob, overjoyed at the prospect of having a visitor.

"Zephyr, sit," I repeated more forcefully.

He continued to ignore me, wriggling with anticipation.

I sighed and scooped up the fur ball. I tucked him under one arm like a warm, furry, football. He gave my cheek a lick before turning his attention back to the door. The dog literally vibrated with excitement.

I opened my door to Courtney. She wore a black business dress, so she must have come straight from work.

"Hi, sweetie." I gave her a one-armed hug as Zephyr tried to sneak in a quick lick to Courtney's ear.

"Thanks for leaving the downstairs entrance unlocked." Courtney set her purse on the hall table.

"No problem. It saves me from buzzing each person in." I closed the door and set Zephyr down. He immediately sat—finally—and squirmed as he stared up at Courtney. "I think he wants you to pet him."

"He's so sweet." Courtney crouched down and scratched the little beggar behind one of his enormous ears. His eyes closed in bliss.

"Only when he gets his way. The bossy little monster likes to be in charge."

At another knock, Zephyr immediately looked up at me with those bright black eyes, gave a short bark that I interpreted as "answer that!"

"See what I mean?" I pulled the door open.

Scarlet strolled in wearing white capris and a red summer top with spaghetti straps.

My timer went off and I headed toward the kitchen. "I just need to pull the appetizers out of the oven."

Scarlet followed me. "Smells good. What is it?"

"Mini-quiches from Costco. I knew I'd be short on time, so I picked some up yesterday while I was stocking up on supplies for the store."

Courtney came in with Zephyr in her arms, grinning as the little dog licked her ear. "He's quite the lover, today."

"That dog has a freaky ear fetish." I gave him a stern look that he completely ignored as he continued to give Courtney's ear a tongue-bath. Gross.

"Can I help?" Scarlet offered.

"Sure. You can put these on that serving plate." I indicated the multicolored glass plate next to me.

"This is gorgeous," she commented, turning it over and letting the light dance across the green, orange, and red surface.

"Thanks. I picked it up at an art show in Boston when I lived there. Back when I had money to spend on things like that."

"You work so hard," Scarlet said. "Your store is bound to start turning a profit soon."

A pang of longing mixed with regret pierced me. I'd worked just as hard at my other job—the one that would have made me a millionaire if I'd stuck with it. I shoved that thought aside as I opened a package of frozen spanakopita appetizers while Scarlet wrapped one of my aprons around her waist. "Not hard enough, apparently. I hope you're right about the store though." It had to, or I was in big trouble.

I glanced over my shoulder and found Courtney still loving on Zephyr. "Why are you so dressed up today?" I asked her.

"I had to present our findings to our board of directors," Courtney said. "I'm not sure which is more important to them—content or style. Whenever we meet, I need to make sure I wow them."

Scarlet clipped a sprig of basil from the plant over my sink and added it to the plate of appetizers. Nice touch.

"Lianna texted me she's on the fence about coming tonight," Courtney said.

"I bet she didn't finish reading the book again and doesn't want to face me," Scarlet said. "I told her I'd give her a hard time if she couldn't. It isn't even all that long."

"I hope that's not it," I said. "I even picked *Watchmen* so she could watch the movie in a pinch."

Courtney's face tightened. "That isn't the problem. She's going through a rough time."

Both Scarlet and I stopped what we were doing and swiveled to face Courtney. "What's wrong?" Scarlet asked. "Did something happen?"

Courtney gave an angry huff. "Yep."

Another knock sounded on the front door, and I called out, "Come on in," without taking my eyes off Courtney, but she didn't say anything else.

"We're here," Rose called out.

A moment later, she and Gertrude stood in the doorway of my small kitchen, but I kept my attention focused on Courtney. "Spill. What happened?"

"She might still come." Courtney crouched down to give Zephyr another scratch behind his ear as she avoided meeting my eyes. "I think she wants to tell everyone herself."

At Rose's confused expression, I murmured, "Lianna."

"What's going on with Lianna?" Rose asked.

The room fell silent as we all exchanged worried glances.

Courtney poured herself some water. "So, Mara... has Doug bothered you again?"

My chest tightened, and I scowled at her, annoyed to be used as a distraction. "I haven't seen him since the night he showed up at my shop." Between Destiny announcing the sale of Stel-Wood and my upcoming date with Ford, I'd completely forgotten about Doug.

"Smart of him to stay away." Scarlet set the plate of mini-quiches on my round copper-topped table in the adjoining dining room. "The police are keeping an eye out for him. If he comes into town, they'll arrest him on that bench warrant."

My tension eased a bit. "That's on him since he should have paid his tickets. I'm not sure how I feel about the situation being used as some sort of punishment to keep him away from me though. It isn't as if he's ever actually done anything to hurt me. He's just a jerk."

Scarlet's mouth pressed into a thin line. "It really worries me that he showed up at your store at closing time."

"Doug isn't dangerous. Just obnoxious." I grabbed the wine bottles and headed for the dining room.

Scarlet sidled to one side to let me squeeze by and ended up colliding with Courtney. "Sorry," she said. "You're probably right, but I'm not taking any chances. Unless he pays off those unpaid tickets, he'll be arrested the next time he sets foot in my town."

After I pulled the corks from a bottle of red and a bottle of white, I turned to reenter the kitchen only to find my path blocked once again. "It's getting crowded in here," I said as I squeezed past Rose. "Why don't you all pour yourselves some wine and head to the living room?"

At a sharp knock on the front door, I hurried to open it and came face-to-face with Lianna.

Even if I hadn't already known there was a problem, Lianna's drawn expression and wrinkled clothes would have told me something was seriously wrong. I'd never once seen her wear an oversized t-shirt and leggings to one of our book club meetings. The woman was always completely put together.

Not today.

I immediately swept her into a hug.

At first, Lianna kept her back ramrod straight, but a moment later, she melted in my arms. "You heard?" Her chest caved against me as she spoke.

"Not any details, but I know you're having trouble."

Lianna let out a snort in my ear. "Trouble? That's one way to put it."

I pulled back and locked gazes with her. "What happened?"

"It's Paul." Lianna's chin quivered. When she turned toward the living room and found everyone watching her, she gathered herself and lifted her chin.

"I came home early the other night to make that sushi dinner for him. It was supposed to be a surprise." Lianna let out a harsh bark of laughter. "It turns out I'm the one who was surprised. He'd taken an earlier flight home and was in bed. With a woman."

We gaped at her.

"That rat fink son of a runt." Gertrude's words cracked through the silent room like a whip snap. "Where does he get off treating you that way?"

Lianna's face crumpled, and her chin began to tremble.

Scarlet pulled her into the living room where she pointed to a chair. "Sit. I'll get you some wine."

Lianna collapsed onto the comfy red wingback. That chair had seen me through more than one rough night. It enveloped whoever sat in it, like a hug.

"You caught him in the act?" Rose's voice trembled, along with her wine glass. "Did he see you too?" She took a deep gulp of wine.

Lianna let out a sharp bark of laughter that sounded too much like a sob. "Oh, yeah, he saw me. He moved off her so fast the woman he was on top of squealed in shock even before she saw me standing in the doorway." Lianna shook her head in disgust. "When she finally spotted me, she said, 'What's she doing here? You said you were getting a divorce!'"

Scarlet's mouth dropped open before snapping closed with a click. "Oh. My. God. Paul is a complete lowlife."

Rose's nostrils flared. "What are you going to do? What can we do to help?"

Lianna bit at the corner of one of her nails. "I don't know yet. I'm still in shock. He screwed another woman in our bed! I can't wrap my head around it. I keep wondering how many times he's done it before. I haven't spoken to him since then. I've been too angry. How long has this been going on? How can I ever trust anything he says? How could he betray me on such a fundamental level?"

Gertrude looked defiant. "Kick the jerk to the curb. You're young. There's no reason to stick with someone who lies. Especially since he's never around."

Rose frowned. "He's a jerk, yes, but you two seemed perfect together. Does it make sense to throw it all away and uproot your life?"

Courtney scowled. "She isn't the one throwing anything away. That was all him."

Rose held up her hands. "I agree entirely. I'm just trying to make sense of the fact that the idiot didn't appreciate how great he had it. Seriously, Lianna... You're amazing. Kind. Gorgeous. Successful. What's wrong with him?"

Lianna held up her hands to quiet us. "There's nothing he can say that can explain this away. I guess we'll have to talk at some point, but I'm too pissed right now. If he were to walk in that door right now, I'd lose it."

"I'd want to even the score," Rose said.

Lianna shook her head. "How, though? Sleep with someone? That isn't my style. Besides, Paul would probably roll with it and say we were even. I don't want to live that way. Tit for tat. I can't." Her lower lip trembled. "I want to be with someone I can trust, not someone I need to keep score with."

Love. Sex. Relationships. Marriage. That part of life was full of risk. Scary stuff. Was the good part worth it? This was exactly the sort of thing I could be letting myself in for if I started dating again—but with the right person, it was worth it.

Wasn't it?

Lianna tipped back her head and drained her wine glass. "I really want to take my mind off this. It's been consuming me."

Scarlet plucked Lianna's empty glass from her hand. "One break, coming up." She poured more wine and handed it back, then turned to face everyone else. "Why don't we all talk about the book? Did everyone finish reading *Watchmen*?"

Lianna let out a snort. "Not me. Like that's news to anyone."

"This time you have an excellent reason." Scarlet sounded like a mother soothing an overwrought child.

"It's still sitting on the nightstand next to my bed." Lianna's face darkened. "I completely forgot I'd left it there until an hour ago."

"Whether you leave him or stay, you'll need to burn that mattress," Courtney muttered.

"I'll host a bonfire," Lianna said, her tone flat. "Roast marshmallows. Make it a party."

My mouth twitched at the dark humor, but I wasn't sure if I wanted to laugh or cry.

Scarlet set the wine bottle on the end table next to Lianna and then claimed a spot on the sofa. "What did everyone think of it?"

Lianna cleared her throat. "I liked what I read of it," she said, her voice stronger now. "The story was more complex and darker than I'd expected. It wasn't for kids, that's for sure."

"No happy ending," I said. "No heroic characters. They were all deeply flawed, but they kept trying."

Scarlet's eyebrows drew together. "All the characters seemed frenetic. As if they were trying too hard—especially considering how everything ended."

Lianna let out a groan of irritation and glanced up at the ceiling. "I really want to finish this one. Maybe I should plug my ears while you talk about it."

"You aren't living at your house!" Gertrude interjected in a startled tone, as if suddenly coming to this realization. "Where on Earth are you staying?"

I froze. Why hadn't the rest of us asked that question?

"I'm at a hotel on Neville Island. I left with nothing but the clothes on my back and the gym bag in my car. Thank God I had a toothbrush and deodorant in there. I had to go Target the next morning before I could go to work. The last thing I wanted was to show up in the same outfit two days in a row and have someone ask about it."

"I'll stop by your place tomorrow and pack a bag for you," Rose offered.

"Thanks, Rose," Lianna said. "That would really help."

"I'm sorry if I sounded like I was defending Paul earlier." Rose winced. "That isn't where I was coming from. You know I was in the foster system. I have an almost pathological resistance to moving or changing homes. The idea that your entire life imploded when you walked into your bedroom freaked me out.

All I could think about was how you could hold onto what you had."

"I get it," Lianna said gently. "Don't worry. I didn't feel like you were defending him."

"You're going to move into my carriage house," Gertrude announced, her tone as crisp and authoritative as a drill sergeant. "It's furnished and set up as an apartment. I just renovated it a year ago. You can stay as long as you like."

Lianna's mouth fell open before snapping shut. "That's so generous," she said. "Are you sure? I don't want to impose."

Gertrude waved her hand dismissively. "It's no imposition. Someone might as well use it."

"You have to let me pay you something. I insist."

"You can cook, right?" Gertrude said. "If you insist on some sort of payment, then invite me over for a home-cooked meal once a week. We'll call it even."

Lianna's eyes welled with tears. "It's a deal," she managed to croak out.

"Perfect. It's settled," Gertrude said, folding her arms. She turned her gaze on me. "Did you prepare questions for us?"

My hands a little shaky, I picked up my list of *Watchmen* questions. We all needed to process this news. It was hard to come up with the enthusiasm I'd had when I'd written them down, but I knew, deep in my gut, that this was the sort of break we all needed.

I forced a cheerful tone as I said, "Get comfortable, everyone. This should be fun." At least, I hoped it would. I glanced down the list. "Let's start with this one. What did you think of the social dynamics and the abuses of power in the book? Did the characters behave in heroic ways, or were they antiheroes?"

"Ooh. Excellent question." Rose gave a little bounce of excitement. "I loved how real and complex the characters were. Rorschach was a real mess, wasn't he? He was such a rigid thinker. He tried to protect things that were good and pure, but he went about it in despicable ways by killing the bad guys without feeling a shred of sympathy for them."

"That Doctor Manhattan character was utterly lacking in compassion," Lianna said. "He had real superpowers, but he was completely inhuman compared to the others. I think he scared me the most, but honestly, I wouldn't want to meet any of them in real life. They were all pretty messed up."

Over the next hour, we finished off all the wine and most of the food I'd set out. Since this was the first time I'd ever hosted, I was surprised by the amount of alcohol we'd consumed.

Mental note for next time I host — buy more wine.

"You know, that was one of the most stimulating conversations we've had about a book in a while." Scarlet sounded genuinely surprised.

"I thoroughly enjoyed it," Gertrude said. "It's exciting to discover an entirely new form of entertainment at my age. Last month I rediscovered romance novels, and this month it's graphic novels. I'm loving this book club. Do you have any other graphic novels you can recommend?"

A sense of satisfaction filled me. "I can't tell you how happy I am to hear you say that. I'm surprised, though. I didn't think you'd embrace them so readily."

"Don't underestimate me." The delight in Gertrude's eyes softened the sharpness of her tone. "Now, tell me which ones to read next. Maybe something a bit more female-focused? I'm feeling empowered."

Growing satisfaction filled me. This was exactly what I'd needed to hear right now. I'd poured my heart into Ghost of a Chance, and knowing its existence had influenced Gertrude and the others was its own vindication. "Try the Alias Investigation series. It's about a woman named Jessica Jones. Based on how much you liked Watchmen and its themes, I think you'll enjoy it. You also might like Faith." That was the second time I'd recommended that graphic novel in the past few days.

Gertrude squeezed my forearm. "I'll stop by and pick them up tomorrow. You're a real peach, Mara. I hope you know that. Your parents must be so proud of you."

My chest pinched as I heard my Dad's words ringing in my ears again. *"If they had an Olympic event in screwing up, you'd take the gold."*

I lifted my chin, refusing to let Dad's words define me. He was wrong. I'd had my reasons for the decisions I'd made, and they were good ones—even if he didn't agree with them.

17

DINNER FOR TWO?

FORD

On Friday evening, I was running late. I rushed into my kitchen carrying two canvas grocery bags and dumped them on the counter. Mara would be here in less than a half hour, and I needed to hurry to get dinner started.

To make matters worse, I still needed to unwrap my new furniture. The delivery men had dropped it off earlier today. The leather sofa, loveseat, and chairs sat in my huge family room, encased in plastic wrap. I hoped nothing had been damaged since I'd already signed off on the delivery. I'd shoved the men out the door because I had a call scheduled with McCormick.

They would have unwrapped everything, but they'd arrived two hours behind schedule, making me late. The last thing I wanted was to give McCormick the impression that I was blowing him off. Even if this project didn't work out, I might want to partner with him in the future.

I imagined Mara's eyes lighting up as she savored her first bite of my mushroom chicken. With the clock ticking, I wasted no time pouring olive oil into two large nonstick skillets and getting them heated up. Working quickly, I browned the chicken in one skillet while dicing onions, garlic, and mushrooms in the other.

Glancing at the recipe card, I flipped over the chicken and tossed the veggies into the other pan. I double-checked the recipe once more, making sure I had everything just right. As soon as the chicken was cooked through, I combined it with the veggies, adding a pinch of dried thyme and a splash of wine before covering the pan with a clear glass lid.

Done.

I was really getting the hang of this cooking thing. Dante had been right. It wasn't all that hard once you learned some basic skills.

Time for "the great furniture unwrapping."

I stood at the room's threshold, momentarily stymied by the shiny, plastic-wrapped blobs. They didn't look like much. I yanked at the wrapping but the stuff was sturdier than it looked. I needed scissors, so I headed back to the kitchen and grabbed a pair from the junk drawer.

Dinner smelled delicious. At least that part of the evening was on track.

I glanced at my watch. Ten minutes to go. I carefully cut through the plastic wrap and threw it in a heap near the window. The whiskey-brown leather furniture was exactly what I'd wanted.

I stepped back to assess everything, only to discover I had a new problem. Lengths of plastic wrap littered the floor.

I shoved everything into the two enormous bags that had covered the chairs, then tied the ends of each bag shut. It was just like bagging autumn leaves.

The doorbell rang, and I took a sharp inhale. This was it. Showtime.

I glanced around. The room wasn't perfect, but it was presentable.

I shoved the trash bags into the corner, strode to the door, and pulled it open.

Mara stood smiling on my front porch, wearing a slim-fitting blue dress that matched her blue-tipped hair. She cradled a bottle of wine in the crook of her arm.

Stunned, I managed to say, "You look gorgeous." Simply looking at her made my heart beat faster.

"Thanks. This is for you." She held out the bottle, blushing slightly.

I fumbled to take it as I leaned in and kissed her cheek. She pulled away too quickly, and the brief caress only left me wanting more. "Thanks," I said, lifting up the bottle. "You didn't have to do that."

"My mom would be furious if she found out I showed up to someone's house for dinner and didn't bring anything. She's like the eye of Sauron, making me behave."

"Lord of the Rings," I said, recognizing the reference. I stepped back from the doorway to let her come inside.

She paused, took one sniff, and said, "Is that dinner I smell burning?"

18

TAKE TWO

MARA

"My chicken!" Ford said as he dashed toward the kitchen.

I followed. As I entered the room, I spotted smoke seeping out from under the lid of a skillet. Ford turned off the burner, grabbed the pan, and then dropped it into the sink with a loud clatter. A hiss of steam erupted as the hot metal came into contact with some water.

"I can't believe I forgot to turn down the burner," he said, shaking his head.

"That would do it," I said, glancing around in the enormous kitchen with its granite countertops, caramel-colored cabinets, and white mosaic tile backsplash. That walk-in pantry was bigger than my entire bathroom. "But who cares about perfection when you get to cook in this gorgeous kitchen?"

He sent me a sanguine look, then removed the lid to assess the damage. A dark puff of smoke emerged, and he quickly replaced it. "Dinner's ruined. Rookie mistake. I had some furniture delivered today, and I wanted to get everything ready before you got here." He inhaled deeply, and as he exhaled, he visibly calmed down. "Live and learn. Can you recommend a good place that delivers?"

His composure surprised me. Doug would have flipped out, and the night would have been ruined. But Ford had transitioned from being upset to finding a solution within seconds. It showed resilience, and I liked that. "Even though it didn't work out, thanks for cooking dinner. It means a lot to me."

He shrugged. "Thanks. It's more fun to cook when I know I'm not the only one who will eat it. Where should we order from?"

"That depends. What are you in the mood for?"

"I'm easygoing." He rubbed his stomach as though he was starving. "Something quick?"

"Chinese," I said immediately. "The local restaurant is great and the food's usually ready within twenty minutes."

"Sounds good to me," he said, flashing a grin.

I felt relieved that he wasn't upset about ruining dinner. "I'll call them," I said, pulling out my phone.

As I dialed, Ford came over to stand next to me, and I caught a whiff of his cologne. It was spicy and masculine, and I liked it. He met my gaze and grinned again. "What would I do without you, Mara?" he asked, making my name sound like a caress.

My heart started beating like one of those anime characters where you can see the heart-shaped emoji thumping outside of her chest. I felt a blush creep up my cheeks. "You'd be eating burnt chicken alone."

While I ordered, Ford carried the pan outside and dumped the ruined food in the trash. The charred scent still lingered, making me appreciate his efforts all the more. Even if it hadn't been a success, he'd doubled his charisma points with that move.

"Come here," he said, taking my hand. He looked at me like he wanted to devour me instead of dinner. "You look amazing."

My pulse quickened at the intensity of his stare. "Thank you," I said, trying to ignore the flutter in my stomach.

He led me out of the kitchen and into a spacious family room. "Here's my new furniture," he announced. "I got distracted unwrapping it, which is why I ended up burning dinner."

The room was sparsely furnished, but the few pieces he had

were stunning. I couldn't take my eyes off the gorgeous painting on the wall. The sunset depicted in the landscape was so vivid, it looked like you could step into it.

"Wow, where on Earth was there a sunset like that?" I asked, admiring the painting.

He chuckled. "It's a little place called imagination."

I grinned at him. "Well, it's beautiful."

He gestured to the other painting on the wall. "And that one?"

I studied the whimsical image of a woman's profile. The colors were rich and vibrant, and the objects floating inside her head were intriguing. "It's amazing. I love how it conveys her thoughts."

"I'm glad you like it. It's one of my favorites. Should I open some wine?" he asked, his gaze lingering on me.

"Sure," I said, trying to ignore the way my heart was racing.

I grabbed the bottle of wine I'd brought from the table in the foyer and handed it to him. "Beware of geeks bearing gifts."

He laughed. "Your mom guilted you into bringing it, didn't she?"

I rolled my eyes. "Yeah, but it's good wine."

He grinned. "You're the cutest geek I know. I'm a geek too when it comes to movies." He quickly opened the bottle and poured it. "Sorry again about dinner. Let's toast to lessons learned." Handing me a glass, he continued, "My dad always had us toast our mistakes. He liked to celebrate them because they proved we were trying something new and taking chances."

As I tightened my grip on my glass, tension rippled through my body. Had he immediately bounced back after burning the chicken because he wasn't risk-averse? For him, it was a learning experience.

I needed to do the same with the news of the Stel-Wood sale—learn from it and move on. I made my decision a year ago, and I knew what I was giving up. Would I have made the same decision if I knew where I'd be now?

A resounding "yes" came from deep within me. I'd do

anything to keep Chance's legacy alive. Even give up a million dollars. It was a small price to pay. I couldn't forget this when I started doubting myself. "Your attitude is great. My dad is terrified of mistakes. Then again, in his line of work, they're deadly. He's a heart surgeon."

"A demanding job that requires a lot of hours perfecting skills. But in the movie business, mistakes can lead to something spontaneous and creative. Great actors can do amazing things."

"What about with action scenes and stunts?"

Ford frowned. "No, not there. I'm more like your dad in that respect. I like having everything planned out to avoid accidents."

"I used to plan out every detail of my life," I said, my thoughts turning inward. "But after Chance died, it seemed pointless. Why bother when everything can get derailed in an instant? All my brother's plans turned to ash when he died. That was part of the reason I left Stel-Wood and went all-in with Ghost of a Chance. I needed to make sure his dreams became a reality. I chucked it all and decided to take each day as it came."

Ford gestured for us to sit on the couch. "I understand that. It's hard to make long-term plans when life can be so unpredictable."

I sank into the leather upholstery and nodded, feeling understood. "I'm glad I moved here, but sometimes I wonder if I went overboard with that whole 'seize the moment' mentality. I mean, there's no reason for me to simply react to life, right? It's possible for me to take charge of my future again. Plans can get derailed, obviously, but that's no reason not to try."

Ford sat down next to me, and our thighs barely touched. I shifted slightly, inching closer to him.

"It sounds like you're trying to find a balance," Ford said, his attention focused intently on me.

"Your dad and mine sound like polar opposites." I glanced up at that painting of the woman in profile again, with all those thoughts pinging around in her head. The way my thoughts were racing, I could certainly identify with her. "Mine always expected perfection. It was a lot of pressure growing up. Still is."

"I bet," Ford said, nodding sympathetically. "It had to make it hard to try new things. You have to be bad at something before you can become great at it."

"Exactly," I said, relieved that he understood. "He always wanted us kids to be perfect. It was exhausting. Mom was good at redirecting him when he got obsessed, but we had to learn how to stand up to him. We've all learned how to fight our own battles with him. Chance and I always had each other's backs, though. I really miss him."

Ford took a sip of his wine, considering me for a moment. "It takes a lot of strength to stand up to someone like that," he said. "You should be proud of yourself."

Little did he know how intensely my self-doubt chipped away at me. "Thanks. I'm glad I have you fooled. Half the time I feel like an imposter, trying to convince the world that I'm good enough. I try, but it hasn't been easy. I'm proud of my two outright rebellions, though. One was getting a software degree instead of going into the medical field like Dad wanted, and the other was opening Ghost of a Chance. I went head-to-head with him both times. He didn't make it easy."

"I'm serious," Ford said, his gaze steady. "It takes courage to go against someone's expectations, especially when they're as high as your father's are. But it sounds like you've found your own path, and that's something to be proud of."

"Maybe that's why I gravitated toward computers," I said, swirling the wine in my glass. "Even ugly code works. From the outside, most people can't tell the difference between code that's beautifully crafted and code that's shoddy. Both will still perform the same task. Only another expert would be able to spot the differences. That made it a lot easier for me to learn how to become a software developer without my dad telling me I was doing everything wrong."

Ford gave a wry smile. "I guess software code and people have a lot in common when it comes to the whole inner beauty thing. It's like you said, people may look perfect on the outside, but you never know what's going on inside. I've met so many people who look great on the outside but are a mess inside. It's kind of like ugly code that seems to work fine until you dig a little deeper."

I nodded in agreement. "Exactly. And sometimes people are just like that—a mess on the inside, but they put on a good front. It's hard to know who's genuine and who's not."

Ford looked into my eyes. "But I think you're different. There's nothing ugly about you. You have a beautiful soul. I'm sure anything you create is beautiful both inside and out, just like you."

I felt my cheeks warm as I slid my hand across my chest, over my heart. Ford saw me, really saw me, and I found it both novel and exhilarating."Thank you. That's really sweet of you to say." I took a deep breath and then changed the subject. "Speaking of creating beautiful things, how's your week been? Any progress on the movie front?"

His eyes drifted to my mouth, and then he glanced away. "I'm probably going to turn down McCormick's Superman movie. I haven't told him yet, but I've started searching for a script."

"I guess McCormick won't budge on changing the script. Is it killing you to pass up the chance to make a big-budget movie?" I asked.

"Yes, and no. I'm getting a bad feeling about the project, and I've learned to trust my gut. Even if I don't do McCormick's movie, I'm sticking with superheroes."

A wave of satisfaction washed over me, and I couldn't help smiling. "I'm glad to hear you weren't just using a line to get me to have coffee with you." I teased."How do you go about finding a script?"

"My assistant Wendy is a genius at finding ones I like. She's having trouble sifting through the screenplays, though. She doesn't know the superhero genre well."

His answer still left me confused. "I guess I don't under-stand how the whole screenplay thing works. I know books get turned into films all the time, so why not make a movie based on one of the graphic novels I sold you? One of the ones you liked?"

He stilled for a moment and then smacked himself on the fore-head with the flat of his palm. "I can't believe I didn't think of that myself. I bought one at your store that I couldn't put down. It had a great plot, great characters..." He trailed off as he became lost in thought.

A moment later, he pulled his phone from his pocket. "I need to text Wendy and have her look for a screenplay for *Ghost*."

I stopped breathing. Every muscle in my body froze. Had he just said what I thought he'd said?

Ford's thumbs flew over his phone screen, and then he grinned at me. "Done. Wendy will work her magic. If a screenplay doesn't exist, she'll find the author's agent to acquire the rights so I can hire a screenwriter to develop it."

With a satisfied sigh, Ford grabbed a small remote off the coffee table and pointed it toward the painting above the fireplace.

A motor whirred as the bottom edge of the painting started moving forward and the entire thing cantilevered up to reveal a television.

Ford managed to temporarily derail my freakout with that display of Star Trek-style technology.

I blinked rapidly as I thought about Ford's new plan. My mind was racing with thoughts and emotions, and I struggled to find the right words to express myself.

I should tell him, shouldn't I? Of course, I should. This was something he needed to know.

Right now.

"Ford," I said, touching him lightly on his forearm as he scrolled through what looked like an on-screen digital film library.

He turned to me, giving me all his attention.

"There's something I need to tell you." I ran a hand nervously through my hair.

He picked up on my tension and set aside the remote. "What's up?"

"That comic. *Ghost*?" I bit my lower lip.

He watched me as I took a long breath.

"That's the one my twin brother wrote." My voice caught in my throat as I spoke, and I felt a lump form there. "It was his passion project."

He just stared at me for a moment, his face slack, then his eyes widened in astonishment. "You've got to be kidding me."

"It's the genesis of the name of our store. Ghost of a Chance."

He took my hand in his and squeezed it, stunned. "This is unbelievable. Your brother wrote that?"

"Wrote it, lettered it, penciled it, inked it. Every detail," I said, my eyes brimming with tears of joy as I recounted my brother's creative process. Ford's eyes widened in amazement. "I only helped when he needed to bounce ideas off me."

Ford grinned in a cute, enthusiastic way. "That means you're the expert on all things *Ghost* related. That's fantastic."

I pulled my hand from Ford's grasp and brushed the tears from my cheeks. "There's no screenplay. I'm pretty sure no one ever bought the film rights, either. Chance was a creative genius, but when it came to selling his work—not so much."

"That's no problem. In fact, it's even better. I know some great screenwriters. Did your brother have an agent representing him?" Ford leaned forward eagerly, his eyes shining with excitement.

I blinked a few times. This was all moving so fast. "Amy Tate. He designated me as his literary trustee, so I've been working with her. She handles all his foreign rights." I shook my head in disbelief. "This is huge. Holy freakout, Ford."

He watched me with a mixture of amusement and affection, taking in my deer-in-the-headlights expression. "Do you want me to explain how this works, or would you rather have his agent handle everything?"

I blinked at him, trying to process everything. The room felt like it was spinning. "Could you give me an overview?" I said, my voice trembling with exhilaration.

He shifted to face me, excitement vibrating off him. "Sure thing. So first, we'll need to secure the film rights from your brother's estate. I'll contact his agent, and she'll work with you on crafting a deal. Then, we can hire a screenwriter to develop the script. From there, we'll find investors and get to work on casting, production, and all the fun stuff that goes into making a movie. That means my first step is to have Wendy contact Amy Tate."

I took a deep breath, my head reeling with possibilities. "Wow. I can't believe this is happening."

Ford reached out and took my hand again, his grip warm and reassuring. "Believe it, Gorgeous. This is going to be amazing. We can dive into the details after I find out about the rights," he continued. "There's always a chance someone has already optioned it, which complicates things."

I tried to contain my excitement, clasping my hands together. "This is incredible. Just knowing you want to turn *Ghost* into a movie is—" I paused, searching for the right word, "mind-blowing. I always believed that *Ghost* was something special. Dad never saw it, but if you make it into a movie, it will prove that Chance had talent others recognized."

Tears started to flow down my face, and I couldn't help but embrace Ford. "Thank you so much," I said, my voice cracking.

Ford hugged me back, but his forehead creased with concern when he pulled away. "Don't tell anyone yet. I don't want news that I'm interested in the film to leak. It could complicate things if I have to buy the film rights from someone else."

I nodded, trying to keep my composure. "Can I tell my parents?"

He hesitated. "They'll need to keep it a secret too."

"Absolutely," I replied, taking a deep breath to steady myself. "This is the best news I've had all year. This could change everything."

He took my hand, his fingers interlacing with mine and

cupping it with his other hand. "This is only the first step. Thousands of books get optioned every year and never get made into movies. If Chance sold his film rights and the owner won't budge, my plans could grind to a halt."

My heart gave a wary thump. "Reality check," I said with a laugh. "I can be a wee bit obsessive when it comes to counting my chickens... and by a wee bit, I mean completely. Let's change the subject. This is supposed to be a date. You said you wanted us to watch something, right?"

"Are you sure? I promised my brother Sean I'd check out some stunt work."

"Your plans need to ferment in my brain. I could use a distraction." I frowned at the title of the movie he highlighted on the screen. "I just saw that in the theater with Courtney last month. Is it already out on video?"

He relaxed back on the sofa. "This is an advance copy." The film started, and text appeared at the bottom of the screen. "'For your consideration,'" I read aloud as I shifted closer to him.

"It's for the academy awards. I get advance copies of films so I can vote on them."

"Lucky you," I said.

He held my hand as he fast-forwarded through the movie. "My youngest brother Sean is in this one, and he's been harassing me because I haven't seen it yet. He's a stuntman. Has been for a few years now, but for this film, he was also the stunt coordinator."

"I knew about Max and Hailey, but I didn't know you had another brother."

"That's it. Hailey, Max, and Sean. What about you? Any other siblings you haven't mentioned?

"I have an older brother Grayson who's a professor at Pitt, and younger twin sisters, Rachael does musical theater in New York City, and Aubrey is with a ballet company in Texas."

He arched his eyebrows. "Two sets of twins? Impressive. Do they visit often?"

"Sometimes, but never over holidays because of performances."

"It's hard when work keeps you apart like that. I was filming in the Philippines when Dad had his heart attack. He was home from the hospital by the time I was able to get here. It was a brutal trip. Thirty-three hours and four connections."

"Ugh, that sounds awful. But just think, if they filmed movies in Pittsburgh, you could have been home in time for dinner." I batted my eyelashes at him, trying to hide my grin.

He chuckled. "You know, Pittsburgh actually gets plenty of screen time. You just haven't been paying attention."

"Oh, really? Pittsburgh hardly seems like a movie Mecca." I raised an eyebrow skeptically.

"Really." He leaned in closer, his lips almost brushing against my ear. "You make me see my world from a new perspective, and I like it."

I felt my cheeks flush as I pulled away to look at him. "Happy to help."

"Stories can take you anywhere," he said, enthusiasm deepening his voice. "From the icy wilderness of Iceland to the romance of Paris, and even the scorching sands of the Sahara Desert. And don't forget about science fiction and fantasy, where the possibilities are endless. Time periods are no limit either. The historic architecture of Pittsburgh makes it the perfect setting for films set in the 1800s and 1900s, surrounded by towns straight out of the groovy 60s and 70s. And then there's charming little Sewickley."

"Sewickley? It's hard to imagine a movie being made here."

"You'd be surprised. Sewickley has actually been featured in quite a few films."

I arched an eyebrow skeptically. "Name one."

He grinned, undeterred. "Houseguest."

I wracked my brain. "Houseguest? Wasn't that a movie from the 90s with Sinbad?"

"Yep. It may be a bit of a throwback, but Sewickley played a prominent role in that one."

"Seriously?" I was intrigued. "I might have to check that out, see if I recognize any local spots. Anything more recent?"

"Definitely. Loads of movies have been filmed both in and around Sewickley. Happiest Season, Foxcatcher, One for the Money, Love the Coopers, Mindhunter, The Chair, and even a Hallmark movie whose name escapes me at the moment. Plus, August Wilson is a native Pittsburgher, and Denzel Washington is filming his stories here, too."

"I loved The Chair—I had a feeling some of the scenes were filmed in Pittsburgh." I paused. "You know, Chance set his Ghost comics here."

"It's one of the many things I liked about it." He shifted to face me. "Speaking of which, how about a movie tour of Pittsburgh? I'll show you all the sights this Sunday."

A delighted smile spread across my face. "You'll be my own personal tour guide?"

"You got it. And dinner's on me," he added with a wink.

My heart skipped a beat at the prospect of a second date with Ford. "I'd love that."

Brain explosion. I was dating a movie director.

His gaze fixed on my lips and he leaned closer.

Closer.

My grin evaporated, and my smile softened as I tilted my head into the kiss.

His lips were soft against mine. Gentle. Just the hint of a kiss. Lips grazing against lips. A kiss that was more like a tease.

A temptation.

A seduction.

A shudder of awareness washed through me as I closed my eyes and focused on my senses. His gentle touch. The scent of new leather mingling with his cologne. The heat between us.

I gave in to my simmering passion.

Ford's kiss was amazing. Erotic. Consuming. Instead of deepening the kiss, I let myself enjoy his uniquely tender touch. His whisper of a kiss. I trembled, releasing my breath in a soft sigh. I never imagined that the light graze of someone's lips on mine could affect me so profoundly.

Was I reacting this way because I was with Ford? Because I wanted him so much?

Just when I didn't think I could bear the delicious torment of his tantalizing, ghostly lips on mine an instant longer, the doorbell rang, shattering the moment.

Ford broke away, and my entire body tried to cling to that sensation as I leaned forward and my lips followed him, but he continued backing away.

My eyes flew open, and I scowled at the front door. Damned, prompt, delivery driver!

Ford stood and let out a slow breath. "I hope I didn't rush it with that kiss. I want to take things slowly. I know you have your doubts about me, and with the movie, you need to be sure this is what you want." He licked his lips—his full, sexy lips that had been on mine seconds ago—damn him.

My befuddled mind tried to process his words, and I latched onto the one thing that could complicate everything: *Ghost*, Chance's legacy that Ford wanted to turn into a movie. I couldn't let my emotions jeopardize this opportunity.

"Maybe we should take things slow," I said, my voice barely above a whisper.

Ford's eyes met mine, and I could see the disappointment in them. "I understand your concerns, but I don't want to lose the chance to get to know you better."

My heart ached at the thought of backing away . But I couldn't ignore my doubts. "I need some time to think about this. Can we just enjoy the rest of the evening and see where things go?"

The doorbell rang again, and Ford's attention shifted. He walked toward the door, leaving me alone with my thoughts.

Ford was refreshingly direct. No games. No manipulations. He simply told me how he felt. I stared after him as I ran through my reasons for keeping him at a distance. The only one that mattered anymore was *Ghost*. What if Ford really did make it into a movie? Could a new relationship withstand all those complications?

But life was complicated. Relationships were complicated. Did that mean I should hide away?

What was I willing to risk? My heart? Chance's dreams?

I exhaled slowly. One step at a time. Maybe this was enough for tonight.

After all, we'd already scheduled a second date.

19

NIGHT GARDEN

FORD

After dinner, Mara didn't linger. She seemed preoccupied, lost in thought. She had a lot to process now that she knew I wanted to turn *Ghost* into a movie. If it panned out, we'd have plenty of time together. I watched her car's taillights as she turned the corner, wishing she could stay a little longer.

Our kiss replayed in my mind, and I couldn't help but smile. It had been amazing, and I wanted more. But I also wanted to take things slow with her. I didn't want to scare her off with my intensity.

I paced around the living room, trying to shake off my restlessness. Mara was different from anyone I'd ever met. She wasn't just a challenge to conquer, but someone I wanted to know on a deeper level. Her intelligence, loyalty, and unique quirks had captivated me.

But I needed to be patient. Mara had her own life and her own dreams, and I didn't want to interfere with them. I thought about the doorbell interrupting our kiss, and how it had cut the tension in the air.

Maybe it was a sign to slow down, to savor every moment *

instead of rushing to the finish line. I smiled to myself, feeling a sense of calm wash over me.

Yes, Mara was worth the wait. And I was willing to take all the time she needed.

As I dumped the empty containers into the trash, memories of my parents flooded my mind. They had a rare kind of love, the kind that made other parents seem cold and distant by comparison. They'd always held hands and kissed, and as a kid, it had embarrassed me. But now, I realized how lucky they'd been to find each other. Maybe that's why I'd become so jaded about my own love life. I'd expected to have the same kind of relationship with Chelsea, but we hadn't. And so, I'd given up.

I flicked off the kitchen lights and stepped outside into the darkness. The sky was cloudy, and I couldn't see the stars, but that didn't matter. All I could see was Mara's face, and I knew she was something special. Despite everything she'd been through, she was still fighting. And the more I got to know her, the more I admired her.

She'd done everything she could to make sure her brother's talent and dreams weren't forgotten, even at the price of setting aside her own goals. She'd never give up on him.

If that doorbell hadn't interrupted us—well—my imagination could predict the rest. Once our tongues had touched, the fiery connection would have ignited our pent-up passion. Lips, tongues, hands—we'd have been obsessed with one another. I'd have run my fingers through that gorgeous dark hair, trailed kisses down her neck, unbuttoned her dress, and kissed those amazing breasts. Would we have made it upstairs, or would we have thrown caution out the window—the one with no curtains, I suddenly realized—and made love right there on the sofa?

I stopped the film reel running through my mind. I wanted to savor the moment when it truly happened rather than fantasize about it.

Besides, I needed curtains, even in my fantasies. No way would I put Mara at risk.

Take it slow. I sensed it would be a mistake to rush things. Mara had plans for the future that didn't include me. I'd need to prove to her I wouldn't derail them.

As the wind rustled the leaves and the cool night air brushed against my skin, I couldn't help but reflect on what I'd learned about Mara tonight. She was a woman of contradictions - ballsy and hard-hitting on the surface, yet harboring immense pain underneath. I'd always admired women like that, but the fragility she'd revealed to me was unexpected.

She trusted me enough to share some of her deepest insecurities, and the realization humbled me. I would never betray that trust. I'd go to the ends of the Earth to protect her.

As I thought about her, I realized that my feelings for Mara had taken on a life of their own. She'd made her way deeper into my heart than I'd ever realized.

Then, it hit me - the reason why *Ghost* meant so much to her. She'd suffered a deep wound when she lost her brother, and *Ghost* was her way of keeping his memory alive. Her tearful joy at the news that I wanted to turn it into a movie was all the proof I needed. It gave me a glimpse of the passion and drive that lay beneath her tough exterior.

Ghost of a Chance. The name resonated with me, and I wondered how I hadn't picked up on it sooner. But I knew that Mara wouldn't give up on it - not in a million years.

With a newfound sense of clarity, I pulled out my phone and sent a text to my assistant.

> **Me:** Any luck yet chasing down those screen rights?

> **Wendy:** I haven't heard back from his agent yet. Since she's in New York, I probably won't hear back from her until tomorrow at the earliest.

> **Me:** Let me know as soon as you do.

Turning away from Mara and that deliciously tempting kiss had been damned hard. I'd had to keep reminding myself that I wanted more from her. Much, much more.

Was I falling for this woman?

Slow down. Don't get ahead of yourself.

Good advice. Too bad I wasn't going to follow it. I was already way ahead of myself when it came to Mara Stellar.

With a sigh, I turned my back on the night and headed back inside.

I'd do some research now. I wanted to create an academy award-winning sort of outing for Mara. An amazing day. One she wouldn't soon forget. One that would leave her wanting even more. Wanting me.

Wanting *us*.

MOM AND DAD

MARA

All day Saturday at my store, I kept hoping to see Ford breeze in, wearing that special smile he seemed to reserve just for me. It was a busy day, but every time the door chimed, I turned to look, hoping to see him.

No such luck.

Early that afternoon, I received a text from Chance's agent saying she'd been contacted about a movie option for *Ghost*.

Ford had been busy.

Around closing time Ford finally texted me. A smile spread across my lips as I read his message.

> Ford: Hey, beautiful. How was your day?

> Me: Great! Busy.

> Ford: Me too. I'm looking forward to tomorrow. I was tied up with work all day, but I've made some special plans for us. Can I pick you up at 9:00 A.M.? Wear something comfortable, but dressy enough for a nice dinner at the end of the day.

> Me: Sounds like fun! I can't wait! See you at 9.

As I locked up my store, my heart swelled with satisfaction. Business was finally good, and the prospect of tomorrow's date filled me with excitement.

Knowing I'd be busy all day, Zephyr and I dropped by my parents' house for a visit. The little goofball adored them, especially when Mom slipped him some cheese or chicken.

I knocked briefly and entered the family room next to the spotless kitchen. Dad sat reading in his leather chair, and Mom was on the sofa with her laptop. Something garlicky and delicious lingered in the air.

"Hey, guys," I said, plopping down next to Mom.

"Zephyr, sweetie!" she said, ignoring me as she placed her computer on the coffee table and patted her lap.

He jumped up next to her and greeted her in his own special way—his signature ear bath. Mom pulled him close and peppered the top of his head with kisses. "How's my grandbaby doggie today?"

Dad never let us have a pet, so Mom doted on Zephyr.

"Hi. I'm here too," I teased.

Mom gave me a playfully dismissive wave and kept loving on Zephyr.

"Hi," Dad said as he tucked in a bookmark to save his place. "We don't usually see you on a Saturday night."

"I have plans for tomorrow, so I won't be able to stop as usual."

That finally drew Mom's attention. She raised her eyebrows, looking hopeful. "Tell me you have a date."

"Actually, I do. With Ford Ross. I mentioned him to you last weekend. He's in town visiting family."

Mom's hopeful expression disappeared. "You didn't tell me his name was Ford Ross!"

"The one and only," I confirmed, confused by her reaction.

Dad frowned. "Am I supposed to know who that is?"

Mom tut-tutted. "Only if you ever watch movies or pay attention to the local news. He's from Sewickley and just won best director at Sundance." She glanced at me. "Is he a relationship kind of guy? He always seems to be dating someone new."

Dad grimaced. "And you're next on his list?"

I tensed. "Relax. It's just a date."

"He sounds like a waste of your time. Why date someone who's just visiting?" Dad insisted.

I narrowed my eyes, hearing him voice my own reservations. This was where I got it from—this need to avoid risk and predict the future. "You need to stop worrying," I told him, but the words were for me as much as him.

"Have you eaten dinner yet?" Mom asked, changing the subject. "I just put leftovers in the fridge. I can heat them up for you. Lasagna and garlic bread."

My mouth watered. "Sounds delicious. I love your lasagna."

While Mom prepared my plate, Dad opened a bottle of wine. Five minutes later, I was sitting at the kitchen island next to my dad, enjoying a delicious meal, while Mom rinsed out the plastic food container.

"I have exciting news to share," I told them.

Dad's expression brightened. "You're going back to Stel-Wood?"

I ignored him and shook my head, grinning. "Nope. Ford wants to turn *Ghost* into a movie."

Mom turned from the sink to face me. "What? Say that again?" She reached back and turned off the running water, then cupped her hand to her ear as though she couldn't believe what she'd just heard.

"Ford wants to turn *Ghost* into a movie," I enunciated.

"That's amazing!" Mom said, her face lit up with excitement. "You've poured so much of yourself into keeping his dream alive. I'm proud of you." She rounded the kitchen island and threw her arms around me.

"It isn't a done deal," I said, laughing as I hugged her back.

"He's working with Amy, Chance's agent. It's a secret, so don't tell anyone. If word gets out, he might not be able to buy the rights."

"Likely story." Dad set down his wine glass with a clatter.

I closed my eyes, exasperated with the man. Of course, he had to throw a wet blanket on everything. It was his modus operandi. "What do you mean?"

"I mean, he wants it kept secret because it's all a lie. He's trying to get you into bed. Why else?"

I certainly hoped so, but Dad didn't mean it as a compliment. My temper flared. "Don't be so cynical. You haven't even met the man. Why would you accuse him of something so deceitful?"

Dad shot me a scornful look. "Those Hollywood types are all alike. Out for what they can get."

Mom scowled at him. "Don't be hurtful, Thad. Of course, the man doesn't want news to get out and ruin his deal. People could use the information to their advantage."

Dad just shook his head. "Stop being naive, you two. If Chance's comic books were any good, he wouldn't have had to self-publish them."

I sprang from the barstool to face him. "We've been through this before," I said furiously. "He self-published by choice. Dammit, Dad, *Ghost* won awards. Stop saying Chance wasn't any good."

Dad just shook his head, letting me know how disappointed he was in me.

"She's right," Mom said, "and you know it. I have his award framed and hanging on the wall of your office. Don't be so dismissive."

"I just want to watch out for her. Is that wrong?"

"It is when you say such hurtful things," Mom said.

I didn't need this. I didn't need his constant disapproval. His condescending manner. His predictions of failure. Mom could deal with him. I'd had enough.

"I'm heading out," I said, sliding off the kitchen stool. "You've made up your mind about Chance, and there's no changing it, but that doesn't mean I have to stay and listen to you say such hurtful things." I lifted Zephyr into my arms and headed for the door. "Thanks for dinner, Mom. It was delicious."

21

SIGHTSEEING

MARA

The next morning, I rushed to drop off Zephyr and get ready for sightseeing. Since Ford had suggested I wear something comfortable but dressy, I chose a summer dress and a pair of pretty wedge sandals.

At 9 A.M. sharp, just as I finished buckling my sandals, the doorbell rang. My footsteps echoed in my quiet apartment as I hurried to the intercom and pressed the button.

"Hello?"

"Hey, gorgeous." The tiny speaker didn't do justice to Ford's deep, rich voice, but a shiver still raced down my spine. He'd called me "gorgeous."

I smiled. "Hey, handsome. Come on up." I pressed the button to unlock the exterior door. I was so eager to see him that I stepped onto the landing to watch him climb the stairs.

He bounded up the steps, two at a time, carrying a pair of iced drinks. When he reached me, he brushed soft lips against my cheek and then stepped back.

"Your favorite," he said, handing me a Loco Mocha cup. "I remembered from our coffee date."

My heart skipped a beat. He was sweet and thoughtful. Points for him.

He glanced down. I thought he was going to compliment my sandals, but then he surprised me by pulling a dog biscuit out of his pocket. "Where's Zephyr? I have something for him, too. I got it for him at the pet shop in town."

Aw! He even wants to win over my dog? More bonus points! "He would have loved it, but I left him with my friend Gertrude, since we'll be gone all day."

"You can give it to him when you pick him up." He set the elaborate treat on the table by the door.

Once we were downstairs, Ford directed me toward a black BMW with 850I imprinted on the back in chrome lettering. He opened my door, and I slid onto the white leather seat

His gaze lingered on me, and a grin tugged at the corner of his lips. "You know, I read somewhere that green is the color of luck. Looks like I hit the jackpot with you in that dress," he said, winking at me.

I chuckled. "Well, you'll certainly look like a winner in this convertible. You sure you're not compensating for something?"

Ford raised an eyebrow, pretending to look offended. "Hey now, what are you trying to say about my car?"

I grinned back at him. "I'm just saying, you can't buy happiness...but a sweet ride like this comes pretty close."

He laughed and pressed a button to open the convertible top. It moved back like a transformer toy, stowing everything in a compartment in the back. I used the hair tie I always kept around my wrist to pull my hair into a ponytail.

Ford revved the engine as we took off down the road. "You know, I once read that driving a convertible makes you feel ten years younger. So you better buckle up, because we're about to turn back the clock."

As we cruised down the road, I couldn't help but enjoy the wind whipping my ponytail against my neck. "You know what they say. Life is too short to drive with the top up."

He chuckled. "I like the way you think, but let's hope we don't regret that decision when we're caught in a sudden downpour."

I shrugged. "We'll suffer through it together. Misery loves company."

Ford shot me a sly grin. "I think I can live with that."

On Beaver Street, he slowed to a crawl in front of a Victorian house from the late 1800s. "This is where a lot of *Houseguest* was filmed."

"It's beautiful, especially the rhododendrons. I love these older houses. They have so much character and history."

"They've done a great job renovating it while still keeping the look authentic," he said. "It's a shame more builders don't take the same care. From a filmmaker's point of view, new buildings just don't have the same charm and personality."

As we continued down the road, stately houses dotting the land gently sloping toward the Ohio River made a picturesque view. The lush trees blocked my view of the waterway even though it was only a half-mile away.

My ponytail fluttered against my neck. "This is such a lovely drive. The scenery is like something out of a painting. It's amazing how nature can create such breathtaking beauty."

A few twists and turns later, we came upon a narrow lane that led to a gorgeous stone bridge.

"Wow, this is stunning. It looks like something out of a fairy tale. I can imagine a prince and princess riding their horses across it."

Ford slowed to a crawl. "This is stop number two on our movie tour. It was another location for *Houseguest*. Isn't it picturesque?"

"It's gorgeous. It's amazing how different locations can add so much to a movie. It makes me appreciate all the work that goes into making a film." I tilted my head back and gazed up at the canopy of trees. "Zephyr and I sometimes take walks down here. There's something magical about this spot. It seeps into you."

"So, you do get out," he said, his voice deadpan.

I shot him a glance and caught him grinning. "A girl's got to get her exercise. Besides, Zephyr loves long walks."

"I'd like to join you sometime." He shifted the car into gear.

"Absolutely."

He smiled his mega-watt Hollywood grin. That smile made my toes curl.

Our next stop was near a beautiful low stone wall. It ran alongside the road and seemed to go on forever. "This is where they filmed some scenes from *Foxcatcher*." Ford pointed at an enormous house set a fair distance away. "They used that as a stand-in for the DuPont residence."

"This wall looks like it's been here forever."

"At least a hundred years. It took Italian stone masons years to build it," he said as he started the car moving again. A couple of minutes later, we were back in Sewickley.

"It's hard to believe that grand old estate is right outside town," I said.

"That's Sewickley for you," he said, as we turned onto Beaver Street. "Lots of old money around here. The steel barons used to build summer homes out here in the nineteenth century."

"Sounds like a place for some serious wealth," I said, nervously drumming my fingers against my leg.

"Definitely," he replied. "In fact, lots of scenes from *A Man Called Otto* were filmed nearby in Ambridge."

"Ooh, I'll have to add it to my list of movies to watch," I said, trying to take my mind off my nerves.

"Speaking of movies, how did your parents react to the news about *Ghost*?" he asked.

"My mom was ecstatic, but my dad..." I trailed off, unsure of how to finish the sentence.

"He wasn't as thrilled, I take it?"

"No," I said, wincing. "He thinks you're just trying to get into my pants."

He let out a hoot of laughter, "I won't deny that I find you incredibly attractive," he said, shooting me a sexy grin that made my heart skip a beat. "But I also think *Ghost* is amazing. Just like you."

"Thanks," I said, smiling shyly. "I know you're not like that. It's just...my dad. He never liked Chance's comics, and he's not a fan of anything that's not grounded in reality. He's more of a documentary kind of guy. No magic. No superpowers. Only cold hard facts. Since he never liked *Ghost*, he can't understand how anyone else could."

Ford sped down the highway, my ponytail whipping my neck. I felt like a Hollywood superstar in his car, wearing my big diva sunglasses. This car was the bomb. People in other cars gawked, but I knew I could never go incognito with the blue tips in my hair.

As we stopped at a traffic light, Ford pointed toward the train tracks. "Those tracks run parallel to the river all the way into the city. One of the railroad presidents who lived in Sewickley had his own private train stop for commuting."

"Must be nice to have that kind of power," I said with a grin.

He nodded. "You know all about that, running your own store."

I hesitated. "True, but it also means I'm accountable for everything, from customer satisfaction to preventing shoplifting. I'm trying to learn more about marketing and advertising, but it's not my strong suit. Owning my own company definitely has its drawbacks."

"I'm lousy at the marketing side of things, but you and Max should talk. He's great at it. He might be able to help you."

"Maybe. It might be nice to bounce ideas off someone. Thanks."

Ford rubbed his neck. "I'll need to develop new skills. I've never made an action flick before. I'll have to pick Sean's brain about complex action sequences. All my previous movies were psychological thrillers that relied on tension, with smaller action sequences."

The light turned green, and Ford accelerated. "I almost forgot to mention another movie made here in Eastern Pennsylvania. *Unstoppable*. It's about a runaway train heading into a city and the two men who stay on board to try to stop it."

"Are they the heroes?" I asked.

"Reluctant heroes," Ford replied, smiling. "My favorite kind."

"I love stories about ordinary people facing extraordinary situations," I said, excited. "Seeing them make difficult choices and dig deep to tap inner resources they didn't know they had is inspiring."

He glanced at me. "That's not exactly the superhero model."

"It depends on the story," I said. "*Deadpool*, for instance. He's certainly not your typical superhero. Or Will Smith in *I Am Legend*, an everyday man facing overwhelming odds after a zombie apocalypse."

I glanced at Ford. His delicious lips were curved in a relaxed smile. He looked perfectly at ease as we breezed down the highway.

As we approached downtown Pittsburgh, Ford filled me in on more than just the city's moviemaking past. Apparently, George Washington fought in the French and Indian War near here. He gestured toward Point State Park. "Check out the fountain."

I'd seen it before. Even at a distance, it was hard to miss. "That thing is enormous."

"One-hundred and fifty feet wide. The Allegheny and the Monongahela come together here to form the Ohio River. Fort Pitt was right here, at the confluence of the three rivers. The entire fort all but disappeared until an archeology team unearthed its foundation. A museum is there now, and part of the fort has been rebuilt. The only original building that's still standing is a blockhouse."

"You really know this city."

"I've always been a history nut. I can't help it. Stories get to me. Always have. I guess that's why I like to make movies. My eighth-grade history teacher had our entire class walk down to the Ohio River one day to emphasize the impact the waterway had on Pittsburgh and the entire region. He talked about how history affects our everyday lives. All we have to do is look around, take notice, and see the connections."

"It sounds like he hooked you."

Ford took the next exit. "He did. A good teacher at the right moment can have a lasting impact."

"I know what you mean," I said. "I took a robotics summer camp in fifth grade. The teacher was a riot. She kept talking about all the amazing things computer programmers could do. It really opened my eyes to the possibilities. She's the reason I became a code-slinger."

He glanced at me. "You seem to miss it."

"Sometimes," I said with a shrug. "But I keep my hand in by picking up coding jobs here and there." It was the only way I could keep up with the loan payments on the store and the apartment above it after Chance had made all the renovations.

As we drove, Ford pointed out where a Batman movie had been filmed, as well as *Fences* with Denzel Washington.

"How is it I never knew all these movies were filmed here?"

He shrugged. "You've only lived here for a year. Plus, you've been busy. Have you seen *The Perks of Being a Wallflower*?" Ford asked.

"Of course!" I exclaimed, swiveling in my seat to face him. "It's one of my all-time favorites. Especially that scene with Emma Watson where they drive through the tunnel."

"The tunnel isn't far from here," he said, sliding his hand over mine. "Do you want to drive through it now?"

My heart gave a hard thump. "That'd be freaking amazing. I could reenact the scene. Your convertible is perfect for it."

"Whoa. No way. No standing up in my car. Safety first," he said firmly.

"Wimp," I teased. His concern for my wellbeing did odd things to my heart.

"Maybe," he said, giving me a side eye. "Or just sane."

Before long, we approached the entrance to a white-tiled tunnel, and I gave a startled gasp. "That was quick."

Suddenly, an idea hit me. "Wait... Aren't we supposed to be listening to a certain soundtrack? What was the song that was playing in that scene?"

"*Heroes*. By David Bowie." He gave a wry smile. "That seems surprisingly appropriate for you."

"That's the one!" I did a quick search on my phone and started playing the song.

As we entered the tunnel, I couldn't help but gasp in awe. I tipped my head back to stare up at the white subway tiles flashing by. The rush of noise and wind filled my senses, and I found myself lost in the beauty of the moment.

Without thinking, I released my seatbelt and stood up. The wind whipping at my face—the bright white tiles—the tips of my ponytail flicking riotously and stinging my cheeks and neck—the lights lining the tunnel—it overwhelmed me. Ford's voice barely registered over the din as I reveled in the overwhelming sensation of it all.

I shouted in pure joy, wanting this moment to last forever, but as we burst out of the tunnel into the clear blue sky, Ford's hand tugged at my elbow.

"Please," Ford insisted. His voice finally penetrated as the bubble of sound and fury and nothingness surrounding me suddenly collapsed.

22

RISK AND REWARD

FORD

"Sit," I repeated. "I don't want you to get hurt."

Memories of my brother Sean taking similar risks flashed through my mind—especially that time he'd jumped some steps on his skateboard, landed wrong, and broken his wrist.

Mara dropped into the seat and buckled her seatbelt. She swiveled to face me, a huge grin on her face. "That was amazing."

I inhaled deeply, trying to control my frustration. "I'm glad you loved it, but you nearly gave me a heart attack." I reached out and grabbed her hand, not wanting to let go.

Her smile dimmed a notch or two when she realized how much she'd freaked me out. She stroked my tense forearm.

"I'm sorry I scared you," she said. "I didn't mean to. The impulse swept over me and I couldn't stop myself. I think it's part of the whole seize the day kick I've been on." She hesitated, then said, "I'm glad I did it though. I think it must feel something like that to go hang gliding or skydiving."

I forced a laugh. "I wouldn't know. I have a healthy fear of heights."

"Really?" She squeezed my hand. "I would have pegged you

for a daredevil. Did all those genes end up in your youngest brother?"

I glanced over at her. "Watching Sean take stupid chances with his life stopped me. He was reckless when he was a kid. At least he has some common sense now. Even so, being a stuntman is risky. What sane person puts themselves in danger?"

She swiveled in her seat, adjusting her seatbelt as she studied me. "Are you ever worried you'll look back on your life and regret the things you *didn't* try? The chances you *didn't* take?"

I sensed there was more behind her question. This wasn't just about standing up in the car.

"It's good to take risks and push boundaries—I do it all the time—but not every boundary needs to be tested. I'm more interested in looking back on a very, very long life filled with things I achieved rather than risks I took. I have to accept some blame though. My entire industry glorifies that sort of behavior. Plus, there are millions of videos and memes floating around of people doing stupid stunts."

She shook her head. "People can be pretty reckless."

I gave a wry smile. "Like jumping off bridges and posting videos about it? Or walking on the parapets of buildings?"

"Parapets?"

"The wall around the top of a building," I explained.

"A parapet sounds like something you'd find on a castle."

I grinned, enjoying the banter. "That too. Are you into architecture?"

She swiveled to face forward again, pulling the seatbelt firmly against her hips. "Not really. I never really thought much about it. I take it you are?"

"You'd be surprised at the things you pick up as a director. Architecture, labor laws, building codes, stunt mechanics. Not to mention more obvious areas of expertise like writing, cinematography, acting, sound, and so forth."

She shot me a wry smile. "I've noticed you can be a little detail oriented."

"You got me there," I admitted. "About certain things."

"A control freak, too."

The corner of my mouth twitched as I unsuccessfully tried to hide my smile. "Does it show?"

"Occasionally, Mr. Director. It's in the job title." She cast me a sidelong glance. "Did it drive you nuts that I didn't sit down the moment you told me to?"

I stopped trying to suppress my smile and let it spread across my face. "Maybe," I glanced at her, "but I also liked seeing you let go. Moments of pure release are good for the soul."

She grinned as my words sank in and relaxed into her seat.

I took a sharp turn onto a road that hugged a steep hill, and Mara let out a squeal.

"Serves you right." I revved the engine. We climbed up the hillside and the landscape whipped past us in a blur.

Just ahead, the trees thinned and then disappeared on the downhill side of Mount Washington. I caught a fleeting view of the spot where the three rivers converged far below us. Water from the enormous fountain in Point State Park sparkled in the sunlight.

At the top of the hill, I turned onto a narrow, brick-paved side street and found a parking spot.

I opened Mara's door, and she stepped out onto the uneven pavement. "The bricks are gorgeous, but can you imagine trying to walk on them in stilettos?" she asked. "I'm glad I wore my wedge-heels. The Chuck Taylors would have been even better though."

At the top of the hill, we crossed to the far side of Grandview Avenue. Mt. Washington dropped off below us, offering a breathtaking view of the city. Pittsburgh sat nestled in the triangle where the three rivers converged. The fountain sparkling in the sunlight at the tip of Point Park punctuated the city like a period at the end of a sentence.

Mara let out a sigh. "What a fabulous view."

A little farther down the street, I pointed out the unusual

building that sat cantilevered above the steep slope. As we watched, the strange-looking angled train came trundling up the slope and disappeared into a chute extending from the bottom of the building.

"This has to be the Duquesne Incline." Mara picked up the pace in her excitement. "I've been meaning to visit, but I never seem to get around to it."

I wrapped my arm around her and pulled her closer. "You really need to get out more," I murmured in her ear.

Mara came to a halt and turned in my arms to face me. She looked troubled. "Until I met you, I didn't realize how much I'd withdrawn from everything. I chalked it up to pouring myself into my new business, but I think it's more than that. I think I cut myself off because I lost Chance."

MOUNT WASHINGTON

Mara

Ford's arm tightened around my waist, and he pulled me to a stop as he turned to face me. "Grief does that—makes us retreat." His gaze pierced me, seeing straight into my pain. "I withdrew too, after my mom died," he said. "It took a while, but I eventually made my way back from it." He stroked my back. "You'll make it back, too. You've worked hard to keep your brother's dreams alive. Just don't give up on *your* dreams. They're equally important."

"Ghost of a Chance was always *our* dream," I said, the words coming automatically, almost defensively.

"Absolutely, but it's not your *only* dream. You're an amazing woman. Smart. Talented. Hardworking. You can do anything you set your mind to." His thumb grazed my cheek as he brushed back my hair. "I know you can."

A smile tugged at the corners of my mouth. "I guess."

"No more gloom and doom," he said with a grin. "We're going to focus on the positives."

I raised an eyebrow, intrigued. "And what are those?"

"Well, for starters, you're an amazing woman," he said, his

gaze warm and appreciative. "Smart. Talented. Hardworking. And, might I add, extremely good-looking."

I laughed, feeling a warm blush rise to my cheeks. "Flattery will get you everywhere."

"Good to know," he said with a wink. "But seriously, Mara, you've accomplished so much with Ghost of a Chance. It's impressive. But don't forget that you have other dreams too. You can do anything you set your mind to."

I felt a surge of energy at his words, as if he'd ignited a spark within me. "You're right," I said. "I've been so focused on the store that I haven't given much thought to anything else."

"Time to change that," he said firmly. "Let's make a list of all the other things you want to do in life. You mentioned skydiving." He pretended to shudder. "What about learning to play the guitar? Traveling to exotic locales?"

I grinned, feeling the weight of my worries lifting. "I like the sound of that."

I needed to be present in the moment. Be here, now.

I owed it all to Ford. His charming personality, quick wit, and thoughtful insights had made this day possible. He had left me feeling seen, valued, and appreciated, and I hadn't felt this connected to someone in a long time.

The better I got to know Ford, the more I valued him. He wasn't someone who could fill in my missing pieces, but he was like a frame that enhanced the image or the oil that made the gears run smoothly. Being with him made me see myself more clearly, a better and more capable version of Mara.

We strolled until we came to a sloping lawn where people lingered, taking in the view of the city. "I was going to suggest we sit on the grass, but you're wearing a dress. Should we find somewhere else to sit?" Ford asked.

In reply, I grabbed his hand and led him down the hillside to a flat area where we sat down. He braced his arm behind my back, and I leaned against it, nestling into him. As we watched boats motor around Point Park far below us, we let out simultaneous contented sighs. When we realized what we'd done, we broke into laughter.

An uninhibited smile curved my lips. "Thank you for today," I said, an uninhibited smile curving my lips. "I used to go exploring all the time when I lived in Boston, but these days, I rarely venture far from home. I'm in a rut."

I gazed at the spot where Pittsburgh's three rivers met, far below.

"When I came out for Chance's funeral a year ago, I faced a tough decision about the comic book shop. We had taken on debt in both our names to renovate the store and the apartment above it. But when I walked in, everything was ready to go - the shelves were stocked, and Chance had worked hard to get it ready to open. I couldn't bear the thought of shutting it down. So, I decided to give it a shot and open it on my own. All I needed was a great name, and after tossing around a few ideas, I settled on 'Ghost of a Chance' - I'm pretty sure Chance would have loved it too."

I plucked a flat blade of grass and wrapped it around my fingertip.

"Ghost of a Chance is a clever name," Ford said.

"Thanks." I carefully split the strand of grass lengthwise. "I turned over my half of Stel-Wood to my partner, Destiny. She gave me a little money, but we had huge startup loans. Then I started running the comic book shop on my own."

"Starting a business is never easy, especially with all the expenses," Ford said, leaning his head closer so it touched mine.

I nodded, grateful for the physical connection. "Yeah, especially with video games. Lots of employee expenses with no product until the game is finished."

"I left Destiny in a tough spot, abandoning my career goals, realizing how quickly everything can disappear." I sighed and wrapped the split blades of grass around my finger again.

Ford didn't lift his head from mine, and I leaned closer to him. "It seemed fundamentally wrong that the light of life that had shined so brightly in Chance could be snuffed out in an instant, and that everything he'd accomplished would disappear too."

My fingers fumbled, and one of the blades fell, disappearing in the sea of green around us. Ford felt so solid and comforting. I lowered my head and rested it on his shoulder.

"It turned my understanding of the world on end. That's why I decided to devote myself to making sure his comic book shop didn't die along with him—to making sure his graphic novels still had an audience."

I tossed aside the other blade of grass, lifted my head from Ford's shoulder, and wrapped my arms around my bent knees.

He held me close, sitting patiently, giving me his support.

"We'd planned for Chance to focus on writing more Ghost graphic novels and handling the day-to-day aspects of the shop. I was supposed to take care of the stuff he hated. We'd done tons of work, so it made sense to move forward with the opening even after he was gone."

"Do you miss working on games?"

Regret hit me hard, making me tense. "Often. It's frustrating, you know? To want two completely different things simultaneously? But I can't pursue one without setting aside the other."

Ford held me closer. "Couldn't you hire someone to run the store and go back to Stel-Wood full-time?"

I let out a huff of bitter laughter. "Until my shop gets on a financially stable footing, I can't afford to pay someone... or more likely two or even three someones... to do what I do. The shop is barely breaking even with all the debt it's carrying." My shoulders slumped. "Besides, Destiny just sold Stel-Wood to a major company."

Ford's eyebrows lifted. "Whoa, that's huge." Then he frowned. "Are you okay with that?"

"I'm happy for her," I said quickly. "Don't get me wrong. Only

—I feel like she took first place in a race I quit. I can't help wondering how things would be different if I'd stuck with it. Maybe we could have taken the game directly to market instead of selling the entire company."

As I gave voice to the deep, guilt-filled regrets I hadn't even wanted to admit to myself, my chest seemed to break open. The pain came pouring out.

He kissed the top of my head and then rested his cheek there. "You're an amazing woman, Mara. Try to be kinder to yourself. Your brother's death was an unfathomable blow. If the situations were reversed, I'm sure you would've been understanding if Destiny had done the same thing."

"You're probably right." I sighed. "I'm not sure where that leaves me now. I don't know if I'm doing the right things with my life, but I also don't see any other choices open to me." I couldn't shake the feeling that I was stuck between a rock and a hard place, with no way out.

Ford leaned in closer, his expression serious. "Start by taking one step at a time. And remember, happiness and fulfillment aren't always found in the most obvious places. Sometimes you have to go looking for them, or even create them for yourself."
"Easier said than done," I muttered. "I have some mutually exclusive dreams."

"Maybe you should go in a completely new direction. Figure out a way to realize both goals."

I stared at him. "How am I supposed to manage that?"

He kissed the tip of my nose. "You're a clever woman. I'm sure you can come up with a solution."

"Clever?" I grinned at him. "Is that how you see me?"

His eyes seemed to glow with some inner warmth. "It is."

"You give good advice," I told him.

"Hard-won advice," Ford admitted. "I was married before. Chelsea hated my career. She signed a lease for a new apartment a month before she left me. She opened her own marketing firm a couple of months after our divorce. I found out later that she'd been planning it ever since we'd moved to Los Angeles."

"Wait, she signed the lease before you missed the Christmas party? That's pretty manipulative."

"Turns out she was good at keeping secrets. She never talked about important things. Only about coordinating our schedules or stories about people she knew from work. I don't think I ever knew the real Chelsea. She hid too much of herself from me."

It must have been hard to accept that the person you'd married wasn't the person you thought you knew. "You must have felt deceived. What a huge betrayal."

"It was like she'd been playing a role the entire time we'd known each other. I fell in love with the person she pretended to be, not who she really was. She never let me see the real Chelsea."

I leaned into him. "I promise you'll always get the real me. Warts and all."

He wrapped an arm around me and placed a gentle kiss at my temple. "I bet even your warts are cute."

I stared at him blankly. "I'm trying to come up with a comeback about cute warts, but I can't think of a single thing to say."

He rose to his feet. "That's a tough one." He looked down at me with such sweet affection that I caught my breath. "Let's head back to the Duquesne Incline and check it out. They have a museum there I think you'll like. We can even buy tickets and take a ride down the mountain."

I rose to my feet and brushed off the back of my dress. "Wild guess. The Incline was a movie location, right? Which one?"

"Ever hear of *Flashdance*?"

I raised one eyebrow. "The iconic eighties movie? Of course, I've heard of it."

"It took place here in Pittsburgh, and there's a scene at the incline." He paused and shot me a devilish glance. "There's another movie too... but you probably haven't seen it."

"Try me."

"*Zach and Miri Make a Porno.*"

My jaw dropped. "I haven't seen that one in like... forever. I totally forgot it was filmed in Pittsburgh." I nudged him in the ribs. "Just don't get any ideas. No pornos, Mr. Movie Director."

"Scout's honor." He grinned, grabbed my hand, and led me toward the famous cliffside.

DINNER AND SOME MOVIE TALK

MARA

We drove all over Pittsburgh, and by the time we drove away from a location where scenes from *The Fault in Our Stars* had been filmed, my energy level was dipping into the red zone.

As we climbed back into Ford's car, I slumped in my seat. "I think you've worn me out. I can't squeeze another bit of movie trivia in my head.."

Ford gave me a quick look, then asked, "Hungry?"

"Famished." My stomach grumbled in agreement.

"Let's head back to Mt. Washington. I made reservations at a restaurant there with a spectacular view of the city."

As we arrived at the restaurant, a valet took Ford's keys and he escorted me inside. The interior was tastefully decorated in black and cream, with large windows that offered an amazing view of the city.

The hostess led the way to a table alongside the window. I barely noticed anyone around us because I kept my gaze firmly fixed on the startling view. Below us, Pittsburgh was drenched in sunlight. The world seemed to fall away as we gazed out at the city together.

"This has to be one of the most beautiful city views in the

world," I murmured, unable to tear my eyes away from the skyline.

Ford's eyes were fixed on the view as well, but when he finally turned to me, his gaze was intense. "I need to include this in my movie," he said, his voice low and rich.

I couldn't help but feel a thrill of excitement at the thought of being a Ford turning *Ghost* into a movie. "You know, you said you wanted to show me around the city today," I teased, "but I suspect you were actually working. Admit it. You were scouting film locations."

Those blue eyes flickered with worry. "Would that bother you?"

The corners of my mouth quirked up. "I feel dirty. Used."

His lips curved in a matching smile. "I can see I've traumatized you. I'll have to think of some way to make it up to you."

"I expect nothing less," I replied, wiggling my eyebrows at him. The chemistry between us was undeniable, and I knew I wanted more than just a paltry kiss this time. If he was up for it, I was ready to collect.

Ford picked up the menu, his eyes smoldering briefly before he glanced away, and said, "Maybe if I feed you, you'll forgive me." I felt his leg slide against mine under the table.

I let out a long exhale, feeling way too good—the kind of good that makes you worry because you wonder when the other shoe is going to drop.

Quickly scanning the menu, I ordered an appetizer before focusing all my attention on Ford. The restaurant faded away as we talked, and I found myself more interested in him than the food. Being with Ford was like being swept away in a tidal wave of long-buried dreams. His passion and energy radiated from him, infusing me with new life and energy.

Ford was an immersive experience.

All his passion. All his energy. It radiated off him, and I'd spent the day absorbing every bit of it, like a pale plant that had spent too long in the dark. I hadn't even been aware of my pervasive lack of energy until it came flowing back into me. Ford's passion and creativity had infused me and made me ready to take on the world.

The realization filled me with gratitude, and I knew I wanted more of this feeling, more of him. When the waiter brought the bay scallops appetizer, I watched as Ford spread butter onto a slice of rosemary bread. My mind drifted to what it would feel like to have those hands on me, savoring every inch of my body. I hadn't felt that kind of touch in far too long, and I knew Ford would drive me wild.

As he took a bite of the bread, I imagined his lips grazing my neck, sending a shiver down my spine. Our gazes met, and I saw a dark intensity in his eyes that made me think he had read my thoughts or the flush on my skin.

I glanced down and focused my attention on the... scallops? Yes. That was what they were. I even remembered ordering them, barely. They were delicious, but my attention was entirely consumed by the man sitting across from me—

—and visions of how the rest of tonight would unfold.

I knew I had to invite him up to my apartment and really kiss him, not just the teasing butterfly kisses we'd shared the other night.

I needed to touch him.

Explore him.

Have sex with him.

Plain and simple.

Or hot and kinky. Heat slashed through me at the thought. I bet that man's imagination could take us to some extremely interesting places.

But right now, I just wanted him.

"Dessert?" Ford asked.

I glanced at my empty plate, realizing with some surprise that I'd not only finished my appetizer but my main course as well. When had it arrived? What the heck had it even been?

I shook my head. "I couldn't eat another bite..." *because I'm dying to bring you home with me. I want your warm hands on my skin. I want your tongue tracing my lips before you dive in and make me yours. I want you to take me completely.*

When the waiter brought the check, Ford tucked cash into the leather holder and rose to his feet. "Ready?"

As I stood up, he pulled out my chair and our bodies were suddenly close. I could feel the heat emanating from him, and it took all my willpower to resist the urge to lean in and kiss him. But the eyes of the other diners made me feel exposed, and I craved privacy.

Once outside, a valet brought Ford's car and he opened the door for me. We drove home in comfortable silence, the lack of conversation feeling natural rather than awkward. I let myself relax into the moment, enjoying the warmth and comfort of being with him.

As the sun set, its glare blinding us, we pulled up at a stoplight on Ohio River Boulevard. Ford gestured toward a flower vendor and we pulled over. He selected a bouquet of pink roses, and as he handed them to me, he said, "These will look perfect with your green dress."

"Are you sure you're not secretly a color theorist?" I joked. "You sound like Chance. He was always going on about the color wheel and complementary colors, But seriously, thank you. They're so romantic." I inhaled the sweet scent of the flowers and smiled like a love-struck teenager. "I can't believe you just did that."

His eyes seemed to drink me in. "I like doing things that make you look this happy. Your smile, your eyes, they're like sunshine to me. You just have this way of making me feel alive."

I saw my own infatuation and desire reflected back at me in his gaze. Our hands connected and we interlaced our fingers.

This.

This was perfect, in every way.

Twilight enfolded us as Ford pulled into a parking spot in front of my store and we got out. Other than a mother and daughter I spied on the sidewalk in the distance, my street was nearly vacant, which was fairly typical for a Sunday night.

"I had a wonderful time with you today," I told him.

"So did I. More than you know." We stopped at my door. He leaned toward me and barely grazed my lips with his. His mouth was soft and seductive. Then he repeated that gentle kiss a second time, leaving me trembling. My breath hitched in my throat.

This kiss.

This kiss that was barely a kiss... this subtle, devious kiss that set my body trembling with desire. Why did it drive me wild for him? I was a direct and forthright woman. Why did his astonishingly soft touch set me on fire, ablaze like the orange light of the setting sun that surrounded us?

I let him set the pace as he grazed his lips across mine a third time...teasing me. His butterfly softness set my entire body ablaze. I wanted him. Wanted him like I wanted air to breathe after diving into the deep end of the pool and staying underwater so long my lungs were starved of oxygen.

His hand caressed the side of my hip in exactly the way I had imagined when he'd buttered that roll in the restaurant, and I leaned into him, needing his touch. Needing him.

"You're a dangerously seductive man," I managed to murmur as all logic spun away from me. I didn't want to retrieve it.

He inhaled sharply, his breath hitching as he leaned closer. "You bring out the devil in me, Mara Stellar," he murmured. "You drive me absolutely wild."

Before I could respond, a young girl's voice shattered the moment. "Uncle Ford!" she shouted, her footsteps pounding toward us. "Where have you *been* all day?"

I stilled. I actually stopped breathing. The girl might as well have screamed, "Cut!"

The last thing I wanted was to stop. All I really wanted was for Ford to fulfill the promise he'd been making with his lips.

He froze and then pulled away, turning to face a girl of around nine with the remains of a mostly eaten ice cream cone in one hand.

"Emma," Ford said, smiling down at her. "How's my favorite niece?"

"I'm your only niece," she said, for the millionth time judging by the eye roll. "You have to see my movie," Emma said, skewering him with pleading eyes. "Mom wouldn't let me call you because she said you had plans all day. You're back now though, so that's good. I want you to come and see it."

"I'm so sorry we're interrupting your date. I'm Hailey, Ford's sister," the mother said. "We were just on our way home from the ice cream shop."

"Nice to meet you," I murmured.

Hailey nodded her head toward her daughter. "It's been an exciting day. Emma and her friend filmed a short movie and she's been dying to show it to Ford. I told her not to bother him since I knew you had plans together."

"But you can come over now," Emma said, bouncing up and down on her toes and swinging Ford's hand back and forth. "You're done, right? We can show the movie on the big television in our living room. We'll pop popcorn. It will be just like watching it in a real movie theater."

Ford looked from me to Emma and back again, reading my mood and clearly unsure how to reply.

I took in Emma's excited face and realized that tonight was a bust. I might want Ford all to myself, but that clearly couldn't happen right now. "It's okay. You should go," I said, giving a wobbly smile. Fortunately, my phone chimed with an incoming text, so I used reading it as an excuse to break away.

"Sure thing, Emma," Ford said. "I'd love to come over."

"Awesome!" Emma crowed.

I glanced at my phone and tapped out a quick message. "It's Gertrude," I told Ford. "She wants to know when I'm picking up Zephyr. I told her I was on my way."

"Zephyr?" Hailey asked, her eyes lighting up. "Your dog?"

I nodded. "Yeah, my friend's been watching him all day."

"You're welcome to join us," Hailey offered. "The more the merrier."

I hesitated, considering her offer. "Thanks, but no. He'll be all squirrelly after being away from me all day. I should take him straight home."

"Understood," Ford said, turning to his sister. "I'll head over to your place in a few minutes."

Hailey took Emma's hand. "Come on kiddo. Let Uncle Ford say good night to his friend."

As they walked away, Ford closed the distance between us, and my heart skipped a beat. "I'm sorry to end our night so abruptly," he said, his voice low and regretful.

I shrugged under the weigh of my disappointment. "Me too, but what else could we do under the circumstances?"

Ford reached out and brushed a strand of hair away from my face. "Thanks for being understanding. Oh, and don't forget to give Zephyr the treat I brought him this morning. He deserves it," he said, a gentle smile tugging at the corners of his lips. "You deserve something special too." His tone was soft. Teasing. It sent a shiver of desire down my spine.

Stupid shivers.

My heart raced at the playful note in his voice, and I couldn't help but feel a sudden surge of desire. "Can we try this again tomorrow?" I asked, my voice laced with hope.

He cupped my cheek. "That's a promise." He leaned in—

I closed my eyes, savoring the moment, and then I felt him lean in, his breath hot against my skin. I prepared myself for the feel of his lips on mine, but then he whispered in my ear, "I can't kiss you right now. If I do, I'll never be able to leave. You're a wicked, dangerous woman, Mara Stellar, like a siren tempting Odysseus to his doom."

I pulled back, surprised by his words, and the absence of the kiss I so desperately craved. "You're the one doing all the tempting and teasing right now," I softly accused. "And if you'll recall, Odysseus resisted the sirens. Just like you're resisting me right now."

Ford shook his head as he exhaled softly. "He only managed to hold out because he lashed himself to the mast. In this scenario, I think Emma is my mast." He hesitated, then wrapped his arms around me and pulled me close, his body solid against mine. "Even so, if I stay here any longer, I won't be able to tear myself away."

My heart racing, I leaned in, my forehead resting against his. "You're stretching the metaphor a bit thin," I said, trying to keep my voice steady. "Honestly, though, I think you should go. If you stay any longer, I won't be able to let you leave."

Ford sighed, his breath warm against my cheek. "You're right," he said, reluctantly stepping away.

My heart sank, but then I remembered something. "You have to make me two promises though," I said, a small smile playing at the corners of my lips.

"Anything."

"First, promise you'll take me someplace amazing tomorrow. Pick me up at one." A spark of excitement coursed through me at the thought of spending another day with him.

"As you wish. And the second promise?"

I leaned in, my lips brushing against his ear. "That our day together will have a much happier ending."

Ford's eyes flickered with desire, and for a moment, I thought he might give in to temptation. But then he stepped back, his eyes dark with longing. "I promise," he said, his voice low and husky. "I'll pick you up at one."

2 5

EMMA'S MOVIE

FORD

As I drove to Hailey's house, I tried to reconcile myself to my derailed plans. All day long, I'd been anticipating being with Mara tonight. I'd intentionally built up the tension between us to a slow simmer. All that passion had been about to boil over. Having that snatched away from me at the last instant left me aching with pent-up frustration.

I hate it when people let me down at the last minute. Doing it to Mara ripped a hole in my heart. I resented the situation, but I also recognized no one was to blame. Sometimes, shit happens, and you had to deal with it. I searched for that quiet place of inner peace within me. It was harder to get to than usual, but I finally centered myself.

I turned my attention to creating another perfect day for Mara. Today I'd gone all-in with movie trivia. Tomorrow, I'd need to change things up. I wanted something relaxing that would still impress her.

As I sorted through my options, I tossed each aside. Nothing seemed quite right. To complicate matters, lots of places were closed on Mondays.

Scheduling a third date in only four days came with a lot of pressure. I didn't want to overwhelm her, but even though we'd barely started seeing each other, I already wanted to spend more time with her. A lot more time.

As I headed up the sidewalk toward Hailey's front door, lost in thought, my dad's voice startled me.

"You look like you can't decide if you want to go in or not," Dad said, frowning. "Not sure if you want to be here?"

"It's not that," I said. *Well, not exactly.* "I was thinking. I need to come up with a great place to take Mara on a date tomorrow."

"Mara?" Dad raised one eyebrow.

"She's the woman I'm seeing." Stating it in that simple way felt like claiming her. I liked that. "She owns the comic book shop in town. She's new to the area. Any suggestions on where I could take her?"

Dad's eyes lit up, a sharp contrast to how expressionless he'd been lately. "You're asking me for advice? I like that. What kind of place are you thinking of? Crowded? Private? Cultural? Food oriented? There are tons of options."

"I drove her all over Pittsburgh today, showing her the sights. Tomorrow I want to do something more peaceful, but still show off the city."

He gave a decisive nod. "In that case, my number one pick would be the Phipps Conservatory. It's gorgeous there. Relaxing. Romantic, too."

"Brilliant." I grinned, picturing us wandering hand-in-hand through the botanical garden with all its curving paths. "That's perfect."

Pleasure filled Dad's eyes. "Glad to help." He glanced toward Hailey's front door. "Here for Emma's grand premier?"

"Absolutely," I said. "It looks like we have another filmmaker in the family."

Dad rapped sharply on the door, then pushed it open and walked inside. "We're here," he called out.

"I'm in the kitchen," Hailey called back.

We headed toward her voice, and when we stepped into the

kitchen, the changes there took me by surprise. I'd only moved out a week ago. Now, the countertops were stripped bare, some cabinet doors were gone, and paint swatches of various colors dotted the walls.

"What's going on?" I asked Hailey as she pulled a bag of popcorn from the microwave.

"We're moving on to the next stage of our renovations," she said as she dumped the popcorn into a big bowl. "We're expanding the kitchen and the second floor. I'm getting a walk-in closet, a soaking tub, and a new shower with jets." She wiggled her eyebrows. "Bliss. As for this kitchen, we're bumping out that wall. You can say goodbye to these dark cabinets. The new ones were just delivered. They're in the garage. I wanted to wait to start the demolition until everything arrived."

"Good idea to wait," Dad said. "The kitchen's the heart of the house."

"I remember what it was like when Mom renovated," Hailey said. "What a nightmare."

"It wasn't all that bad," I said. "Mom let us eat in front of the TV. I loved it."

"You say that because you were only five," Hailey said. "Pizza and fast food were haute cuisine to you." She picked up a tray of fruit and cheese. "Carry that for me," she said, indicating the popcorn. She headed into the family room, so I followed.

Hailey's husband, Baris, had his hand behind the television, plugging in a cable that led to the laptop. The two of them had met in Turkey when Hailey had been working on a film. They'd become inseparable almost immediately, and he'd happily relocated to Sewickley after they'd married. Baris's youngest brother —a doctor—had even moved here. Baris was some sort of petrochemical industry guru. Whenever he talked about work, I felt like I was in a college chemistry class—one I was failing.

"Uncle Ford! Grampa! You're here!" Emma said, darting over to us. "We're almost ready. Dad's setting things up so we can watch my movie."

Max walked in carrying some beers and handed them out to us, and then handed a soft drink to Emma.

The only family member missing was Sean.

"Looking forward to your movie, Emma my love," Max said. He glanced at Hailey. "Emma took me upstairs to describe what her bedroom will look like after you renovate."

"Framing for the addition starts in a few days, but we won't get to the second-floor renovations until this fall, after the kitchen is done."

"Sit with me, Grampa Don," Emma said, taking him by the hand and pulling him down next to her.

Dad wrapped an arm around her and pulled her close. He looked around the room with a satisfied smile. "It's great to have us all here. Too bad Sean's missing."

"He's in Mexico, right?" I asked, double-checking.

"Filming," Max said. "He isn't due back for another week."

"I'll give him a private screening when he gets back," Emma said.

"That's a wonderful idea," Hailey said. "I bet he'll love it."

"Ford, how long do you think you'll be in town?" Dad asked with a frown. "Will you be leaving after you sign with McCormick?"

Baris shot us a curious glance, then turned his attention back to the laptop. Hailey grabbed a handful of popcorn as she watched me.

I cleared my throat. Whether or not I was ready to share my plans with my family, I couldn't avoid the question without misleading them, and I didn't want to do that. "Actually, I'm pretty sure I'm going to turn him down. I'm searching for a different project now."

Suddenly, everyone's attention focused on me.

Dad drew his eyebrows together in confusion. "I thought you said the McCormick deal was your big break."

"I'm not satisfied with the script, and McCormick is

stonewalling all my suggestions for improvements. It won't be much of a break if my first big-budget movie is a flop."

Dad nodded slowly. "Makes sense. What other films are you considering?"

I shrugged. "I'm chasing down one excellent possibility now, but it's too soon to say more."

The wrinkles in Dad's forehead smoothed out. "I know you'll pick something great. You always do." He lifted his beer toward me. "Here's to family."

His words of praise rang in my ears as I clinked my bottle against his. Baris chimed in with, "Cheers to that," and lifted his bottle. Then he picked up the remote, pointed it at the television, and Emma's opening credits appeared there, on pause.

"It's movie time," Emma announced.

Baris pressed play.

Emma's five-minute production was surprisingly good. During the closing credits, I applauded enthusiastically along with everyone else.

"Great job, Emma," I told her. "Well done. Who did all your camera work?"

"Sometimes me, sometimes my friend Marley, and sometimes we used a tripod and a remote," she explained.

"I like the way you framed your shots and your use of close-ups," I told her. "You did all the editing, right? You did a great job with those transitions and establishing shots."

Emma grinned, delighted. "You think so? Really? Thanks. I'll let Marley know. She's the one who wrote the script. We filmed it together and I edited it."

"Keep it up and I'll hire you when you get older," Dad said, giving her a hug.

Emma squeezed him back. "Would you really, Grampa Don? That'd be awesome."

An instant later, she threw herself onto my lap and wrapped me in a hug. "Thanks for coming over, Uncle Ford. You're the best."

Surprised by her unexpected display of affection, I froze for an instant before hugging her back. "I'm glad I could be here," I told her, realizing it was true. Even though the timing couldn't have been much worse, my family made it clear they really wanted me here, and that made all the difference. I'd been wrong to assume no one had missed me all these years.

Where would my career be if I hadn't grown up in a supportive family? Like I'd told Mara, Dad always encouraged us to try new things. To make mistakes and learn from them. I owed him so much. Not just him, but my sister and brothers too. Mom would have been proud of the way we'd turned out.

Mara should have had this sort of encouragement growing up, too. She deserved to have someone who believed in her and supported her dreams. Everyone did. At least she had her mom in her corner to offset her dad's constant criticism. Even with him holding her back, she'd managed to start two companies.

"We need to get together like this more often," Hailey said. "Things are a bit hectic right now with all the renovations, but once we're finished, I'll have a huge party and invite everyone over."

"You should bring Mara next time," Dad said, grinning, clearly hoping to get some sort of response from me. "I'd like to meet her."

"I will. You'll like her," I said, realizing how well she'd fit in.

He raised his eyebrows in surprise at my reply. "I already do. She lives here, after all. That's a huge plus in my book."

THIRD TIME'S THE CHARM

Ford

When I pulled up in front of Mara's place the following afternoon, I spotted four preteens—a girl and three boys—standing in front of her store. They held dripping ice cream cones as they stared into the display window filled with comic book figurines.

Despite the heat of the afternoon, they seemed more interested in the store than in eating their ice cream. A boy pointed at one of the statuettes. When he touched the window, he left a smudge of ice cream.

I sat in my car and closed my eyes, savoring this perfectly vibrant moment. Anticipation filled me with warmth and light.

Waiting like this was the best part—well, not quite, but close. Suspense always intensified pleasure or excitement when it finally arrived. Although at this point—the suspense might kill me.

For me, anticipation was like a drug. I strove to ratchet it up in my movies. Sexual attraction stretched between me and Mara as tight as a bowstring. At any moment, it could explode. As I imagined how tonight would unfold with her when we were finally alone together, my imagination ran wild.

I pulled myself out of the reverie. Now was the time for action, not fantasy. I catapulted from the car, startling the kids by the store window. Their gazes followed me as I strode to Mara's front door and pushed the bell.

Her reply came an instant later via the intercom. "Be right down."

Feet clattered on the interior staircase with her rapid descent. I stepped back just in time to avoid a collision as she burst through the door.

She beamed at me. "Let's do this," she said, linking her arm through mine and pulling me toward my car.

I laughed as I playfully dragged my feet. "Not even a hello?"

She grinned as she whirled to face me. The woman absolutely glowed with vitality. I wanted to pull her into my arms and kiss her, but the group of kids openly gaping at us made me hesitate.

She followed my gaze and then grinned up at me. "Careful. Preteens are preeminent passion-killers," she said in a husky sotto voce.

"No risk there. My passion is quite healthy and at no risk of imminent death," I murmured back to her. "But, what about your reputation with the middle-school crowd? Would kissing their comic book purveyor gross them out so much that they stop coming to your store?"

She glanced at them. "Possible. Hard to tell. My supply of comics might not be a big enough enticement to overcome their horror at seeing us in a lip-lock." She grabbed my hand and tugged again. "Come with me if you want to live," she said, loud enough for our audience to hear. She shot me a saucy grin.

I ran alongside her, and we threw ourselves into my car. I revved the engine and took off, making my tires squeal for effect and drawing cheers from the little passion-killers.

Mara tossed her head back and let out a throaty laugh. "That was fun." She slouched into her seat, completely relaxed. "I've always wanted to say that. I bet they'd be disappointed if they found out we weren't running from killer robots."

"How about you? Is the Phipps an acceptable alternative?" I'd texted her earlier in the day suggesting it, and she'd seemed enthusiastic in her reply, but text messages could be deceiving.

"Abso-tively, poso-lutely. I've been wanting to go there for ages, but every time I make plans, something happens, and I have to cancel."

"Nothing's stopping us now," I said. The day seemed full of possibilities.

We chatted about nothing and everything for the next twenty minutes. I liked this easygoing version of Mara. It was as though she'd let go of some heavy weight. She was lighter now.

Effervescent.

Alive.

Had yesterday's outing helped her relax? She'd mentioned things had improved with her store recently. If I could do anything to keep her looking and feeling this way, I would in a heartbeat.

Soon, Mara and I were stepping into the lush green world of the Palm Court. Various palm trees filled the room and smaller, variegated plants dotted the garden with splashes of color. Low brick serpentine walls delineated the pathways. A rich, loamy scent infused the glass-domed room, and Mara hummed her satisfaction. "Just smell all that fresh air. I swear I can feel my brain cells jumping for joy."

"I bet this place has a high oxygen content with all these plants busily photosynthesizing."

"Nerd," she shot at me.

I flashed a smile. "Pot, meet kettle."

She took my hand as we wandered around a bend in the path. With a gasp, she came to an abrupt halt. "Sweet Ada Lovelace. Is that glass sculpture by Dale Chihuly?"

Confused, I glanced at the sinuous, plant-like tendrils of glass and then back at Mara again. "That sentence requires translation. Sweet who?"

"Ada Lovelace. Daughter of Lord Byron. She was a mathematician and was widely considered to be the first computer programmer because she wrote the first algorithm." Mara spouted this off as though everyone already knew it, and I was just a bit slow on the uptake.

I looked at her skeptically. "Lord Byron? From the 1800s? If she was his daughter, how could she be a computer programmer? Computers were invented back in—what? The 1950s?"

"Actually, Ada Lovelace worked with Charles Babbage on his Difference Engine back in 1822," she said pertly. "Unfortunately, they weren't able to finish building it. The first one that worked was built in Germany in the 1930s, although that one was soon surpassed by Alan Turing's work on the Turing machine."

I gaped at her, amazed by the profusion of information she'd just spouted. This girl was hot! "And you called *me* a nerd? You outclass me by lightyears."

Her cheeks turned a bit pink, recognizing my words as the compliment I'd intended them to be. "What-ev's," she said, not bothering to hide her grin. She stepped closer to the nearest piece of Chihuly glass and peered at it.

"If you're a fan of Dale Chihuly, you're in for a treat. They have a lot of his artwork here." I swept my arm, taking in the large domed space.

She turned in a slow circle, searching for more pieces hidden among the greenery. "This place is amazing." Her eye caught on something, and she pointed toward a disk embedded in the wall. "1893. Is that when they built the conservatory?"

"Sounds right. It was built when steel was king, and the big magnates were all trying to outdo each other with philanthropic gifts. Carnegie had his libraries and Phipps had this conservatory."

"And Pittsburgh was the beneficiary."

"Pittsburgh and the rest of the world. Carnegie's free libraries are everywhere. Europe, South Africa, New Zealand. It was a pretty impressive feat."

The formal low brick walls transitioned to more rustic stacked stone ones, and Mara made appreciative sounds as she discovered more Chihuly pieces. When we finally moved on to the next room, her eyes widened with delight at the waves of tulips.

"They change the plantings with the season in here," I told her. "In a couple of months, everything will be different."

"I like the repeated patterns and the colors. The combination of order and variation reminds me of an elegant, well-written piece of software." She moved through the space a bit more quickly than the previous room since this section of the conservatory served more as a connecting corridor. She paused at the far end and looked back at where we'd been a moment ago. "We need to come back in a few months to see the new display."

Exhilaration filled me, tinged with hopeful expectation because she was making plans for us.

I took her hand, and she didn't let go as we entered the next room. We eventually made our way to the South Conservatory, where an enormous display with a miniature train took up the center of the large room. The three-inch-tall train trundled its way through a scaled-down version of Pittsburgh.

She slowly approached it. "This is impressive."

"Somehow, I knew you'd love it. This shows Pittsburgh's history. As you move around the train track, you'll see the city go from its founding days to the present."

Mara marveled aloud over the lights inside the buildings, the miniature version of the Phipps Conservatory, and a little trolley in front of Mr. Roger's castle from the Neighborhood of Make-Believe. "I loved that show when I was a kid," she said. "I'd forgotten it was from Pittsburgh."

Toward the end of the display, we came to a spot where the three rivers converged at Point Park.

"This is just like the view we saw from the restaurant last night," she said. "Except there's one minor flaw. Last night I didn't see an enormous rubber ducky floating in the Ohio River." Her eyes danced with delight.

I laughed as I wrapped an arm around her waist and pulled

her against my side. "Didn't you hear? Pittsburgh was invaded by a giant rubber duck back in 2013."

Her arm snaked around me and she nuzzled closer. "You're such a goof. Some poor kid is going to be upset when he remembers he left his duck there."

"No." I smiled down at her as I looked into her eyes. This woman was a delight. "Really. Pittsburgh was invaded by a giant rubber ducky. It was part of an art exhibit that traveled around the world. Pittsburgh was its first stop in the U.S. I flew out to see it."

"Seriously?" She frowned at me, her tone dripping with disbelief. "Do I look that gullible?"

"You have a smartphone. Look it up."

She slid away from me and flourished her device like a weapon as she raised an eyebrow in a playful challenge.

A moment later, her eyes went wide. She held up the screen to show me a crowd of people gathered on the shore of the Ohio River gazing up at an enormous yellow rubber ducky. "That's totally flipping awesome. I wish I'd seen it in person."

"Everyone was sad to see it leave."

She stared at the display, a look of consternation on her face. Then she shook her head, obviously confused. "I'm sort of identifying with my dad right now, which is something I never expected to have happen today. I've always judged him harshly because he's never appreciated Chance's graphic novels. He said he didn't understand them and couldn't connect with them. Right now, though, I don't get how a giant rubber-ducky even qualifies as art. What am I missing?" She looked at me as though she honestly wanted an explanation.

"That's a really good question." I laced fingers with her and headed toward the conservatory's cafe. "In my opinion, it's art because of the way it shaped the mood of an entire city in a shared experience. The duck was evocative of childhood and innocence and joy. That's something special, don't you think? I love it when the entire country is talking about a movie. Being part of creating a piece of art that shapes the conversation of an entire nation? Of the world? It's heady stuff."

She pursed her lips, pulling them to one side. "I never thought of it that way." She seemed to consider the idea for a moment. "I suppose comic books and movies do the same sort of thing, but on different scales."

"I like where you're coming from. There's definitely a similarity. Movies are different from books or comics because they're a communal experience. You read a book alone, but a movie is typically first shown in a theater to a group. After it ends, you immediately discuss it—share your opinions and impressions. Even if you see a new movie alone, you become part of an ongoing wider conversation about the film, and it gives you a way to connect."

"Books don't do that?"

"They aren't as widely consumed all at once. I'm sure you've met lots of people who claim not to read, but I doubt you've met more than a handful of people who don't watch movies. Take *The Handmaid's Tale*, for example. It was a highly acclaimed book, but the country didn't talk about it until it was made into a series. Same with *Game of Thrones*." I gestured toward the cafe. "Want to grab a bite to eat? This place has great food."

Mara examined the cafe's display board. "That's an impressive menu. No burgers and fries. No boring salads."

"During the summer months, they grow a lot of their food on their rooftop garden. The menu changes regularly, and they locally source as much as they can."

"Plus, they have wine," she said. "Nice touch."

We placed our orders and carried our food to a nearby table.

Mara took a bite, and her eyes went wide. "This is amazing. The menu calls it a Congo stew. Want to try it?"

"Sure."

She lifted a spoonful, so I opened my mouth and let her feed me. "Peanut butter?" I asked, surprised. "It's savory with a hint of sweetness. I like it." I lifted one of my sliders, suddenly wishing

I'd ordered something other than some little sandwiches so I could feed her too. "Want a bite?"

At her nod, I handed her one of my pulled pork sliders.

"Mmm." Her soft hum of approval echoed through me. "Delicious. Toasted buns. My favorite."

I bit my tongue to stop myself from asking if she was trying to talk dirty to me. "Nice touch," was all I managed to say. All this pent-up anticipation was going to get me in trouble.

"Have you made a final decision about McCormick's movie?" she asked.

I met her gaze. "Not yet. I need to speak with him in person first. I owe him that much." I still hadn't decided which choice was better for my career, but knowing Mara's brother had written *Ghost* was a huge point in its favor—as was the fact that the story was set in Pittsburgh.

"How about you? How's business? Those kids out front were glued to your window display."

"I was closed yesterday and today, so no big changes. Fingers crossed tomorrow will be a good day." She looked down at her plate, moved her food around with her fork, and let out a heavy sigh. "I've been frustrated by some ongoing problems. I think I mentioned I started having trouble getting stock a few months ago. Not having the newest comics and collectibles for sale hurt business." She glanced up at me. "I had a breakthrough a few days ago, though. One of my vendors decided to extend me credit again. I was finally able to place a big order, which is why my display window is full."

I wished I could help, but I wasn't sure what I could do. At least she'd opened up to me. "That sounds like a difficult position to be in. What caused all your trouble?"

She tossed back the rest of her wine and then looked down into her empty glass, avoiding my eyes. "Not what. Who. The guy I started dating after I moved back here. I trusted him and he betrayed me. I was totally gullible, and I'm really trying to move beyond it. I try not to think about him. I hate rehashing past mistakes. I guess it goes back to the whole perfection thing we were talking about."

Anger against this faceless, nameless guy flared in me. How could he betray such an amazing woman?

She finally met my eyes. "Let's not talk about him right now. We're having fun, and I refuse to let him spoil things. Give me a moment while I clear him out of my headspace." She picked up her tray and headed toward the recycling area. This was clearly a difficult subject for her.

I hated the idea of some jerk taking advantage of her. It brought all my protective instincts to the surface—ones I hadn't even realized I had.

I could tell there was more she wasn't telling me, and after all of Chelsea's secrets, knowing Mara was withholding information would normally get to me. I let it go, though. Getting to know someone took time. Mara was so open—I knew she wasn't hiding who she really was.

I headed over to where she stood, all crossed arms and tight shoulders. I wanted to comfort her. Wash away her hurts and pains. Make her feel appreciated and valued.

"I know something that will make you feel better," I said.

Her shoulders tightened even more, and she shot me a side-long glance. "What? Talking things over with someone?"

I shook my head. "Although that probably would help, I was thinking more along the lines of offering you a massage. I bet I could make you forget all your troubles."

She let out a surprised laugh. "A massage?" She sounded intrigued as she relaxed a bit. "I haven't had one of those in ages. Are you any good?"

I gave a shrug. "You'll have to be the judge."

Arousal flared deep in her eyes, igniting it in me as well. "You're on." She grabbed hold of my hand and pulled me toward the exit. Sparks of excitement fired between us.

I had to force myself not to speed as I drove to her place. The sexual tension between us took on a physical presence in the car. Hot. Pressing. Imperative.

The moment I pulled into the spot in front of her apartment, Mara unbuckled her seatbelt. She turned to me with that playful come-with-me-if-you-want-to-live gleam in her eyes from earlier today. This time she said, "Massage time?"

"As you wish," I replied, my voice husky. Would she recognize the line from *The Princess Bride*?

An odd expression crossed her face as she opened her mouth, but then she apparently decided not to say whatever had been on the tip of her tongue. Instead, she glanced down and bit her lip. Then she seemed to gather herself, and she met my gaze with her determined one. "Just to be clear… 'massage' is code for 'sex,' right? I wouldn't want any misunderstandings between us."

I was out of the car in a flash. She stood as well, and we stared each other down from across the too-vast expanse of my car's roof. "As you wish," I repeated. "Which do you want first?"

"Take one guess." She gave me a devilish grin. "Race you!"

We both darted to her door, arriving at the same time. She fumbled while punching in the code and had to start over, but that was probably because I couldn't keep my hands off her. Trembling, she muttered a frustrated curse before the code finally worked and she shoved the door open.

The instant we stepped into the stairwell, she pulled me to her, pressing her body against mine. I reached around her and slammed the door, plunging us into relative darkness with only faint light illuminating us from the transom window.

Our breathing filled the silence. I could barely make out her eyes, her pupils large in the low light. I held her close, our bodies pressed together, and savored her, slowly lowering my mouth to hers, teasing her with one of those soft kisses that seemed to drive her wild.

Her entire body began to tremble. "Ford," she managed to gasp out, "you're killing me. I can't take another moment of this."

THE PAYOFF

MARA

Waves of passion rocked me from the top of my head to the tips of my toes. How did Ford do this to me? How did he make my entire body light up like a Christmas tree with nothing but those tiny, chaste kisses that barely grazed my lips?

I was beginning to like this though. Each tantalizing touch had me anticipating the next. I'd heard about teasing someone with a feather during lovemaking, and Ford's featherlight kisses finally made me understand why that could be arousing.

I had a moment of clear-headedness as I opened my eyes to look at him, but then his thumb grazed the tip of my breast through the fabric of my dress. I trembled, forgetting everything.

I wrapped my arms around him, pulling him closer. There was no way I could possibly let him go. Not now. God, I wanted this man.

I attempted to take control and deepen the kiss, but trying to move Ford Ross was like trying to move a boulder.

He wouldn't let me take over. Instead, he maintained that soft, gentle pressure. That tender torment.

Finally, I gave up on wresting control from him and instead

gave in to the perfect agony of those exquisite kisses. So far, I'd let him lead us to this point. Let him set the pace. After all, he'd gotten me into my current state of overwhelming arousal with just those soft brushes of his mouth. What came next might be even better.

His lips trailed along my jaw. Kissing me gently. Skin against skin. Lips against neck.

I shivered.

I dropped my hands to my sides as I let him lead the way, surrendering. A moment later, the fingertips of both his hands grazed my palms, sending jolts of awareness and electricity coursing up my arms and through my body. I hadn't been touched in such a gentle way during a seduction since high school, but my former teenage body had never reacted this intensely.

He dragged his lips down my neck—gently—tenderly, then grazed the juncture between my legs with his hand—lightly —delicately.

My entire body reacted, and I immediately trembled with need. My mind gave way as my body took over. My arms flew around his shoulders, and I kissed him with every iota of the need and urgency burning through me.

Finally, he responded with equal intensity, his mouth devouring mine. I melted. Tasting, thrusting, retreating, exploring. I shuddered in his arms, barely able to remain standing.

He shifted his weight, turning us both toward the stairs.

"Let's go up to your apartment." He put his hand on the base of my spine and guided me in front of him.

My body felt uncoordinated as I took the first two steps. I stumbled slightly, grabbing the stair rail to keep from falling. Then I turned abruptly and sat on the third step from the bottom. I reached up, enveloped Ford in my arms and legs and pulled him close. We weren't going to make it to my apartment—not if I had anything to say about it. I wanted him right here, right now.

He chuckled as he braced his hands against the step behind my head and lowered himself to kiss me. His kiss wasn't purely teasing or tantalizing. It was slow, deep, and thoroughly breathtaking. He shifted his body so that the length of him grazed against every part of me, making millions of my nerve endings vibrate with joy. His erection pressed against me in exactly, perfectly, precisely the right spot to drive me wild with want.

"Let's go to your apartment," he said again. His breath teased my neck as he spoke.

I was suddenly aware of the hard edges of the steps digging into my lower back and shoulders. A soft bed definitely sounded appealing. He helped me to my feet, and then took hold of my hand and all but dragged me up the staircase. I loved this combination of rough and tender from him. Clearly, there was a part of him that couldn't wait to get more of me—just like I couldn't wait to get all of him.

On my landing, we only let go of each other long enough for me to unlock the door and push it open.

I grabbed his shirt, yanked him inside, and then wrapped my arms around him again.

I was immediately brought up short by a sharp, insistent bark.

Zephyr.

He needed to go out.

I slumped, collapsing against the wall, frustrated beyond endurance. "Zephyr needs to go out." My heart wailed against the interruption as I gestured toward the leash on the table next to us. "It's our routine."

Ford exhaled. "I'll take him."

He began to loosen his grip on my hand, but I couldn't seem to let him go. Instead, I tightened my hold.

One more kiss. That's all I needed. Famous last words? Or thoughts? Or whatever...

I leaned into him, pressing my mouth against his.

His other arm wrapped around my waist. He backed me up

against the wall and pressed his entire body deliciously against mine. When he released his hand this time, he slid it down my waist, over my rear, and grabbed hold of my thigh, pulling my leg up to wrap around his waist.

This. Yes. This.

I let out a shuddering breath as I took hold of his shoulders with both hands and pulled him to me like a drowning woman grabbing hold of a lifeline.

In this position, my skirt was conveniently hiked up around my waist. He grazed his fingers against the thin fabric of my thong as I unbuttoned and unzipped his jeans. I wanted him closer. In me. All of this teasing had my body on overdrive. All I knew was that I needed him. Now.

I reached inside his boxer briefs and found what I was looking for. My eyes widened. Holy wow. His length was solid in my palm. I slid my thumb across the tip of his erection and found a slippery droplet there.

He took hold of my wrist, stilling my hand. "I have a condom."

I'd nearly forgotten. Thank god he hadn't. "Put it on. Now."

He backed away, pulled the foil packet from his pocket, lowered his pants, and rolled on the protection. He was back in my arms an instant later.

I hitched my leg around his waist again as he backed me against the wall and pressed against my entrance. I was so wet and ready for him that he was able to slide right inside me. I let out a groan of instant pleasure—of exquisite relief.

He echoed it with a deep-throated moan.

Having him enter me was... transcendent. The man fit perfectly. As if our bodies had been made for each other. He began moving. Small thrusts at first, then stronger ones.

His breath came softly against my neck. "Grab hold of me."

I wrapped my arms around him, and he lifted my other leg and wrapped it around his waist as he gripped my bottom to hold me up. He pressed me against the wall, thrusting deep into me.

His slick length glided inside me, and each thrust lifted me to heights of pleasure I'd never experienced before—at least not in this way—not so suddenly and in such an all-consuming way. The buildup of the last two days amplified my body's every response until, with surprising speed, an orgasm swept through me, surprising me.

I let out a deep, keening moan of pleasure. My orgasm was intense. Earth-shattering. Waves of pleasure rocked me, and for moment, I thought my heart might stop.

I'd never experienced such an intense orgasm. How could this have happened on our first try? Where was the bad sex that improved over time? If it was this great starting out—that meant...

My brain short-circuited as I tried to imagine how much better this could get between us.

Is this what two days of pent-up sexual frustration did to me? No, this wasn't about waiting two days. I'd waited a lifetime for this man's touch. His impact. I'd never had an orgasm like this.

Still shuddering, spirals of passion flickered outward through my limbs. I felt boneless.

Ford kept moving. Thrusting. Yes. This was perfect. He was perfect.

Almost immediately, my body began quickening again. Was I about to have a second orgasm? For the first time in my life?

Ford slowed and then did some amazing swirling motion with his hips that sent my head spinning as another intense wave of pleasure built up and then slammed into me. My head fell back against the wall as another orgasm pummeled through me. I was completely shaken to my core.

My eyes squeezed tight as my entire body began to tremble. My mouth opened in a scream, but nothing came out... at first. Finally, the sound I made was inarticulate and animalistic. I'd never uttered a noise like that before. That came from me?

Ford. What had he done to me?

He moved his hand down to stroke my clit, but it was too

much. I couldn't stand it—hell, I couldn't even stand *up*. I was slick beneath his touch, and soon I sensed a third orgasm welling within me.

He continued to thrust, but then his entire body stiffened, and he arched, trembling. Mind blown, my third orgasm hit its peak, and I clung to him as he pressed so deep into me I felt the pulse of his release.

Just as my weak legs began to give out, he let go of one of my thighs and carefully lowered my foot to the floor.

He steadied me, which was good since I felt wobbly. Transformed. And completely, utterly satisfied.

Even so, I knew I wanted to do that again.

Soon. In fact, almost immediately.

"That—that was amazing." Greedy. That's what I was. A greedy, greedy girl.

He leaned his forehead against mine. "Amazing is right."

"*You're* amazing." I lifted my lips to his and he pulled me close as we shared a long, lingering kiss.

A moment later, Ford sighed and stepped back, withdrawing from me. He removed the condom, wrapped it in a tissue from the nearby box on the hallway table, then padded into the bathroom to dispose of it.

I couldn't move from the spot where he'd left me propped against the wall. My head was spinning as I stared down at the floor. I glanced up when he came back in. He grinned when he saw the state I was in, then kissed me on the bridge of my nose. Before I realized what was happening, he was buttoning his jeans.

I could only stare at him in confusion. "You're leaving?"

"Not on your life," he said, his eyes filled with a promise of things to come. "You won't get rid of me that easily. We'll be right back." He grabbed Zephyr's leash from the table and gave a sharp whistle. "Come on, boy. Let's take a walk."

Zephyr obediently trotted over from his pillow next to the sofa where he'd apparently been waiting patiently.

I slid open the drawer of my hall table and handed him my spare key. "It works on both doors."

After he left, I managed to peel myself off the wall and wash up in the bathroom. I caught a glimpse of my riotous hair in the mirror. When had that happened to my cute ponytail? It must have been when we were on the stairs. My reflection grinned with satisfaction. The version of me in the mirror looked much more relaxed and... um... well-shagged than she had in a very, very long time.

The front door opened and closed. Ford hadn't been gone long, so Zephyr must have done his business in record time. I heard water running in the kitchen sink as Ford washed up.

Zephyr nudged the bathroom door open to check on me and greeted me with a broad doggy grin and a tail wag that shook his entire body.

"Were you a good boy for Ford?" I ruffled his head and he followed me out of the bathroom.

As I sauntered into the foyer, Ford entered from the kitchen. He couldn't seem to take his eyes off me.

"Thanks for taking Zephyr out," I told him. The sexy spark in his eyes made my heart go thump.

"Glad to help." He closed the distance between us in a flash. "Now, where were we?"

My body responded to the huskiness of his tone.

Greedy body.

Greedy me.

"Um... I don't recall." I inched closer. "Maybe you could remind me."

"Maybe I can." He slid his hands down my back, caressing me.

"Ah... It's all coming back to me," I managed to say. A sigh left my lips.

"Is it now?"

"Maybe this time we can manage to make it into my bedroom," I suggested. "With an emphasis on the word 'bed.'"

"I still need to give you that massage."

I grabbed hold of his hand and dragged him down the hall. "Massage-smassage," I said, sending him a naughty glance over my shoulder. "I have other plans for you."

THE NEXT MORNING

MARA

When my cell phone alarm went off the next morning, I reflexively reached out to my nightstand and turned it off, and then immediately turned to face Ford.

I hesitated before I lifted my lashes to look at him.

My whole body softened. I felt more relaxed than I had in a decade. Maybe longer? The last thing I wanted was to leave this bed.

Last night had been phenomenal.

With his face all relaxed and smooth in sleep, he looked younger than his thirty-one years. His dark, wavy hair was a bit tousled, looking sexy as hell. Mine had to be a tangled mess. His soft lips looked kissable, tempting me.

I raised myself onto one arm and moved closer, but his eyes snapped open, and I froze. It only took a moment for those sexy, morning-softened eyes of his to focus on me. A satisfied smile spread across those gorgeous lips.

This was nice. Verra-verra nice. A girl could get used to this.

I glanced at the clock on the wall across from my bed. Unfortunately, I didn't have time to revel in Ford and all his sexiness right now. If I didn't get moving, I'd be late opening Ghost of a Chance.

I leaned closer for a kiss. At the last minute, I changed my target and kissed his forehead instead of his mouth. He gave a moan of disappointment and reached for me, but I dodged his hand and made a quick exit from the bed. "Sorry, but I have to hustle. I have a store to open in thirty minutes."

He raised his eyebrows. "That's not much time."

"You forget." I grinned, sitting up in bed as the sheet puddled around my hips and I stretched, arching my back. "My morning commute is a walk down the back staircase to my storage room."

His eyes raked over my naked body, then he closed them. "Do you have any idea how much self-control I'm using right now not to pull you into my arms?"

At that, I nearly rolled back into bed. Could I be a little late today? I mentally checked my calendar and let out a groan. "Don't tempt me. I have a call scheduled with one of my suppliers and I can't be late this morning."

As I forced myself to stand, Ford opened his eyes and sent me a sexy look that made my toes curl.

Heading out the door toward the bathroom took a monumental amount of self-control. When I glanced back, I could see him climbing out of bed. Swoon! The man looked amazing. All the sexiness on display almost had me running back to him, but I forced myself to make the responsible choice and take a shower.

As I stood under the water, I kept thinking about last night's spectacular sex. I'd never had such an immediate physical connection with someone before. It always took time for two people to figure out how to please one another. Not so with me and Ford. Being with him felt miraculous. We fit together in bed like two pieces of a puzzle.

Good sex was its own sort of magic.

Contentment welled within me, warming me. I smiled.

I wanted more. More Ford. More sex. More fun outings. More happiness. More joy. All of it.

I brushed my teeth and hurriedly dried my hair and tugged it into a smooth ponytail. When I left the bathroom, I followed my nose into the kitchen.

Ford flashed me a smile. "I found bacon and eggs in the fridge." He held out a delicious smelling plate of food. When I moved to take it, he wrapped an arm around my waist, pulled me close, and kissed me. Somehow, he tasted minty. Toothpaste? How had he managed to brush his teeth?

"Why do you taste so good?"

He flashed a grin. "I found a pack of chewing gum in the kitchen drawer when I was looking for the spatula."

"Smart man. And a good cook. You must be Dante's star pupil," I said, inhaling the delicious scents.

He grinned. "Breakfast is one of the few things I knew how to make before I started taking his classes. Now, eat, so you can last the morning before you break for lunch."

He gestured toward my small café table. As I sat down, he placed a cup of coffee in front of me. Then he grabbed his own plate of food and joined me.

I marveled at how natural this felt. I stared at him pensively. "I was thinking…" I said, then bit into my eggs and got momentarily distracted.

His eyes seemed to sparkle with humor. "You're good at that."

"Thinking? What can I say? I have a brain. I use it. What do you think about me cooking for you? I'll warn you now not to expect anything Earth-shattering."

His eyes took on a pleased gleam as he smiled. "I'd like that."

"Tomorrow night? I need to pick up some groceries."

"Sounds great." He glanced down at my plate. "You should hurry if you don't want to be late."

I checked the time and gave a start. "I guess my shower lasted longer than I realized." But we both knew my delay had nothing to do with my shower, and everything to do with how much I loved him cooking breakfast for me—and how much I really wanted to linger here with him.

I shot Ford a sorrowful smile, quickly finished eating, and then gave him a peck on the cheek. "Thanks for making me breakfast. I'll clean up after work."

Zephyr stood next to the door, and when I grabbed his leash so he could come with me, he danced with joy.

"Don't worry. I'll rinse the dishes." Ford immediately started clearing the table. "See you soon."

I opened my mouth to protest, but Ford held up one hand to stop me. "Go. It's all good. I'll head home and shower as soon as I'm done here."

I checked the clock and then headed for the door, a smile tugging at my lips. Being with a man who cooked, respected me and my work, and was a veritable sex-god in bed was definitely something I could get used to.

A CALL

Mara

Memorial Day weekend rolled around a couple of weeks later. I came home on Sunday evening after spending most of the day with Ford. He had an important phone call scheduled for tonight, otherwise we'd probably be together right now.

The store was doing better, too. Having all those new superhero figures in the window had brought in more customers. My bottom line looked much better these days.

Zephyr greeted me the moment I walked in my door, eager for dinner.

As I headed into the kitchen, my phone chirped and Lianna's image appeared on the screen. "Hi, I just walked in the door," I said. I turned on the speakerphone so I could open a can of dog food while we talked.

"Hi. I had to drop by the office. Small catastrophe with a client. What time should I be at your place tomorrow?"

"Does nine work for you? You're still at Gertrude's, right? My place is a short walk from there. We can head to my parents' place together."

"Excellent! Tomorrow should be fun. See you then."

I tucked my phone into my pocket and set Zephyr's bowl in front of him. He immediately started eating.

Today, Ford had taken me to Pamela's Diner for brunch, and then we'd attended an art festival in Shadyside. Pamela's crepe-style hotcakes stuffed with blueberries and sour cream might be the best breakfast food I've ever eaten.

Last weekend, he surprised me with a trip to the Nemacolin resort. Between the champagne welcome, the couples massage, and breakfast delivered to our room, I'd felt more relaxed and pampered than I'd been in ages.

I picked up Zephyr's empty bowl and rinsed it out. "Ready for a walk?" I asked. He replied by darting to the door and staring at the knob.

We headed out the door, my thoughts still on Ford, but the moment Zephyr and I hit the sidewalk, my phone rang. I assumed it must be Ford, but when I glanced at the screen, I came to a halt.

It was Destiny Woodworth.

I hesitated to answer. What could she possibly want? To crow about the sale? Probably not. She wasn't the gloating type—at least, she hadn't been when we'd been roommates and business partners, but people can change.

I'd never know if I didn't talk to her.

Finally, I pressed the green button to answer the call. "Hi, Destiny. How are you?"

Zephyr took the lead and we headed toward the library.

"Mara, it's great to hear your voice. How's Ghost of a Chance doing?"

"Great!" I forced a broad smile. "Couldn't be better."

Destiny was silent for a moment. Had she picked up on the lie in my voice? She'd always been perceptive. "I'm glad to hear it," she finally said.

"Congratulations on selling Stel-Wood," I told her as Zephyr and I crossed the street.

"They made me an offer I couldn't refuse," she said. "It wiped out all the company debt and left me with enough money to give me lots of options for the future."

"Does that mean you're thinking about launching a new company?" I asked, keeping my voice light through the pang of jealousy that skewered me.

Zephyr slowed down and started doing what I think of as his poopy-walk.

"I am. In fact, that's why I called. I'd like to develop an idea we kicked around a couple of years ago. I wanted to discuss it with you first."

I let out a soft laugh. "You'll have to refresh my memory. We talked over millions of ideas. As I recall, that was one of our favorite things to do… brainstorm."

Destiny sighed. "I miss that."

My throat tightened as loss and longing overwhelmed me. "Me too." I reached down with one of the plastic bags covering my hand to scoop up what Zephyr had deposited. It seemed a bit metaphorical to be cleaning up a pile of crap right now. Destiny had that amazing deal, and I was left holding a handful of dog poop.

"This was the one about having the game read facial expressions and having the characters react to the players' emotions," Destiny said.

I grinned as I tied off the bag. "That was a good one."

"I want to develop it, and I want us to be partners again."

I froze, stunned, not quite sure I'd heard her correctly. "Us?" I repeated in disbelief. "As in, you and me?"

"Together again. I hate not working with you. It's boring and tedious without you to bounce ideas around. I need you back. I miss you."

Quick tears sprang to my eyes. "I miss you too."

"Oh, thank God," she said, sounding relieved. "Then let's make this happen."

I inhaled sharply, wishing things were different, then let out a sigh. "It isn't that easy. I have my store."

"But you said things are going great. I bet you could hire a manager to run it now that it's on its feet."

I dropped the bag in a nearby trashcan. The manager idea again. It kept popping up. "I might have exaggerated. I'm getting by, but it's been a challenge."

"Aw, honey. I'm sorry. This has been a rough year for you. Losing Chance must have been devastating. It'll take some time to get your feet back under you."

Her kindness and understanding pierced me, releasing some of the pain and guilt I'd been holding in. "Thanks. I think business is finally starting to improve."

"I tell you what—give yourself some time to think about my proposal. If you're interested, we can talk through the details. I really want you as my partner again, but only if that's what you want too."

"I do," I admitted, "I just don't know how to make it happen."

"Call me back in a couple of weeks and let me know if we can figure out a way," she said. "If you decide you can't, I'll be disappointed, but I'll understand. In that case, I'll have to move on to one of the other ideas I have percolating."

DON'T LET YOUR DAD DRAG
YOU DOWN

FORD

On Sunday evening after I got home from spending the day with Mara, I headed up to my sparsely furnished home office. I kept an eye on the clock, and at 7 P.M., I called McCormick.

"Good to hear from you, Ford," McCormick said. "It's too quiet here. I hate holidays. No filming."

My low laugh rumbled. "Maybe you should've taken a short vacation. You know… relax a little. I hear Iceland is great this time of year."

"I am relaxed," McCormick insisted. "I hate it. I *like* working." He inhaled, and I could tell he was dragging on a cigarette. "Where are we with *Superman*? You ready to sign?"

I waited a beat. "That's why I wanted to talk to you. I'm going to have to pass on this one. I don't think I'm the right person for it. You need someone who loves the project, and that's not me."

"Well, shit, Ford," McCormick groused. "That's what I was afraid you were going to say. Anything I can do to change your mind?"

"Sorry. No. It's simply not the right project for me."

"What are you gonna do instead, if you don't mind me asking?"

I hesitated, but I decided I owed him something. "I'm considering making a movie with Ross Film Productions."

"Going with your dad." He didn't sound surprised. "Makes sense. He could use a win."

I picked up on the subtext behind that comment. "You hearing things? About Dad?"

"Eh. Just some gossip. Might be true, might not." He drew on his cigarette again. "He's canceling appointments. Refusing to take meetings. Rumor has it he's sick again and trying to hide it."

I closed my eyes. Well, shit. That was a bad rumor. "Not sick. Not from what I've seen." At least, I hoped not. "I've been here for a couple of months now, and he's busy working all the time. No sign of a problem." At least, nothing I could put my finger on.

"That's good to hear, and all," McCormick said, "but it's not as if you'd tell me if there was one, right?"

"I wouldn't lie to you," I insisted.

"Let me give you some unsolicited advice. Even if you don't make this movie with me, you need to do something big. I know you want to help your dad, but don't blow this golden opportunity. This is a breakout moment for you. With that Sundance win, you're a hot commodity. Everyone expects something big from you. If you blow this, you'll just be a flash in the pan, like so many others. Nothing but unfulfilled potential. Be careful. Don't let your dad drag you down."

MEMORIAL DAY

Mara

Lianna and I headed toward my parents' house on Memorial Day. My brother Grayson would be there too, but my sisters couldn't make it back. Ever since that last face-off with Dad about Ford's movie, things had become even more tense between us, so I wasn't exactly looking forward to seeing him. I was counting on Lianna's presence to keep him in check.

I took us down Main Street to check out the crowds gathering for the parade. There were dogs on leashes everywhere. Last year I'd brought Zephyr, but the bagpipes and little snapper firecrackers had stressed him out. This year, I'd left him at home in the relative peace of my second-floor apartment.

A gray-haired man in an Army uniform thrust a small American flag into my hand with a cheerful, "Happy Memorial Day." His polished brass buttons glinted in the bright sunlight.

"Thank you for your service," I told him.

As I continued down the street, I spun the wooden stick between my fingers, sending the little flag spinning back and forth, wondering if I should have reminded my parents not to mention anything about the Ford turning *Ghost* into a movie. I pulled out my phone and sent a group text:

> Me: Remember not to mention the movie possibility to anyone until I tell you we've finalized the deal.

> Mom: <thumbs up>

> Dad: So, never? Easy enough.

I rolled my eyes. Dad could be such an ass.

As we left the business district and approached my parents' street, the crowd thinned out, making it easier to speed up.

I was a bit nervous. This would be our first Memorial Day celebration since we'd lost Chance. Sadly, we've had a lot of similar firsts in the past year. First Thanksgiving. First Christmas. They'd all been rough.

I spotted my parents in front of their house, setting up five matching red lawn chairs in the grass bordering the street. The parade would pass by before looping back through the town's business district.

Mom and Dad always hosted brunch following the parade. They'd started the tradition the year they'd moved in, when my twin sisters Rachael and Audrey were still in high school, and I'd been attending college in Boston. I'd come to visit for the weekend and had found the entire experience so charming that I hadn't missed it since.

Mom, relaxed and completely chill in her tan capris and white short-sleeved top, smiled when she spotted us. Her entire outfit was understated... except for those Prada sunglasses. Dad stood ramrod straight in his habitual khaki shorts and golf shirt.

"Hi." I kissed Mom's cheek.

"Don't you look adorable in your red, white, and blue Wonder Woman t-shirt!" Mom exclaimed as she pulled me into a hug.

My heart squeezed and my face fell when she misidentified my shirt. It made my twin's absence strike home. Chance would have chided Mom, reminding her he'd given me the shirt on our last birthday together.

"Actually, it's a Captain America shirt," I pointed out. "I thought the flag theme was perfect for Memorial Day." I glanced down at the shirt with its white star centered on the blue background above the wide vertical red and white stripes as I tried to corral my emotions. "Chance—"

"Po-tay-to, po-tah-to," Dad said with a frown, interrupting me before I could explain why the t-shirt mattered so much to me.

My sudden flash of irritation with the way he casually dismissed my pain eased it—for the moment.

"That's nice, dear." Mom patted my arm. Clearly, she didn't pick up on the tension between me and Dad.

"Heard anything from Destiny about Stel-Wood?" Dad asked.

I stiffened. He couldn't possibly know Destiny had called me last night, and there was no way I'd mention it to him right now. Maybe a subject change would do the trick. "Is Grayson here yet?" I asked, casually tossing my habitually late brother under the bus. Since Grayson was Dad's favorite, I knew he could take the heat.

"Not yet," Dad said, frowning in irritation. "He got a late start." He turned to Lianna and held out his hand. "Good to see you, Lianna."

"Thanks for having me," she replied, shaking it.

Too bad there weren't any shade trees nearby because today was already a scorcher. I put on my sunglasses and plopped down on the red lawn chair at the end of the row. Lianna claimed the one next to me. This time last year, Chance had been sitting there instead of her.

A wave of sadness hit me. I pushed my sunglasses up my nose. Was I the only one thinking of Chance today?

"Thanks for inviting me, Monica," Lianna said as Mom sat down next to her. "This is a great place to watch the parade. Will you be choreographing the musical at summer camp again this year?"

"You bet." Mom beamed. "We start in three weeks. I love working there. Those kids always impress me."

"Too bad I wasn't still in high school when you and Dad moved here. I could have gone to that camp too," I said, attempting to join the conversation. "The kids look like they're having a blast."

"You and Chance would have loved it." She glanced down at her hands.

"I used to attend that camp," Lianna said. "How long have you been the choreographer there?"

"Ever since we moved here seven years ago." Mom folded her hands in her lap, and her hot pink nail polish flashed in the sunlight. "Our realtor mentioned it, so I enrolled Rachael and Aubrey. When the camp's regular choreographer had a family emergency, they were scrambling to find a replacement and asked me to help." She lifted her hands in a ta-da sort of gesture. "I've been doing it ever since."

"I loved being in those shows," Lianna said. "It was my favorite camp, ever."

Dad came up behind us. "Monica, is there anything else we need to do to get ready?"

Mom gave a start. "I almost forgot. Can you carry the cooler down here? It's too heavy for me."

That was normally Chance's job during the Memorial Day parade.

Dad frowned. "I'll get it right now. You stay here. You've been running around preparing things all morning."

"That's okay," Mom said as she stood. "I need to put the casserole in the oven for brunch. It'll only take a minute."

Dad shot me a glance. "If I know your mom, her 'minute' will take at least ten."

"Is it my fault I always think of more things that need to be done?" Mom teased.

I watched them head off. Dad reached over and took Mom's hand in his. Was it just affection, or did he sense she needed some comfort today? I suddenly wished Ford was next to me right now.

Having him with me would have made today easier. I missed him.

Lianna watched my parents walking hand-in-hand. "They're cute together."

"They are," I said. "He knows how to keep her organized, and she knows how to handle him when he gets cranky."

Lianna cocked her head as she examined me. "And look at you. I could swear you're positively glowing these days. I think you might have found yourself a keeper in Ford. Even seeing your dad didn't dull your shine."

"You can tell?" I could feel my cheeks warm, and it wasn't from the sun. "I have to admit, Ford is pretty amazing. He took me to the Nemacolin Resort last Saturday night. It was fabulous. Massages. Breakfast in bed—"

In the distance, a marching band began playing. The parade would arrive soon.

The corners of Lianna's lips drew down. "Paul and I went there a couple of years ago for our anniversary." Her gaze became unfocused, her expression distant. A moment later, she seemed to come back to herself as she glanced back at me again. "I bet you had a wonderful time." Her tight smile didn't reach her eyes. "What did you do while you were there?"

Witnessing Lianna's battle between carrying on with normal life and the heartbreak of her recent separation made my heart ache. My own struggle with trying to move on after losing Chance was similar in many ways. If I spotted Lianna's husband Paul right now, I'd want to rail at him for all the pain and heartache he'd caused.

I tamped down my anger, not wanting to burden Lianna with it. "We visited Falling Waters. It's amazing. Have you been there?"

"The Frank Lloyd Wright house?" Lianna asked. "I've been meaning to go."

"I loved it. The entire building is a work of art. It melds

perfectly with the landscape. Did you know every piece of furniture in it was created specifically for the house?"

"I keep meaning to take a day trip there." Lianna gave me a sidelong look. "I've hardly seen you in the past few weeks. Are you spending all your free time with Ford?"

I was so happy that I couldn't help grinning. "It's been a whirlwind. Have I been neglecting you?"

Lianna waved her hand dismissively and gave a half-hearted smile. "Nah. I'm fine. I think it's great that you're finally into someone. And Ford Ross—how amazing is that? He's totally hot."

"Talented, too. He's the whole package." I glanced down at my hands and shrugged. "Am I getting too attached, too fast? I can't keep spending all my free time with him. I've been neglecting my friends and my business. If I'm not careful, I'll put the stu—" I bit off the word stupid, shocked that I'd nearly used it, and instead said— "st-store at risk."

Did I really think Ghost of a Chance was stupid?

No, not stupid... of course not, but my feelings about the place had been changing lately, and Destiny's phone call last night had left me feeling conflicted. I could almost see Chance frowning at me with concern.

Lianna gave me a strange look. "Is there anything going on you want to talk about? Yes, you're happy with Ford, but I think something else is going on with you."

My eyes pinched at the corners as I shrugged. "Mind reader."

Lianna arched an eyebrow.

"It's the store. It's doing a bit better now, but I could never forgive myself if it failed. Dad's been on the phone with me nearly every day harassing me about selling it." I hesitated, then spoke before I changed my mind. "Destiny called me last night about a project. She wants to start another new company."

Lianna turned to face me with undisguised curiosity. "She's the one you started your video game company with, right?"

"She wants us to work together to develop a concept for a game we brainstormed a while back. The idea would be to allow the gamer to use an image of themselves to customize their avatar and then use hand gestures along with an emotion detection component of facial recognition to control gameplay. Your every smile or grimace would show up on screen, and the NPCs—non-player-characters—would react to you based on how you interact with them. I mean—holy awesome! That would be so much fun to develop."

Lianna's eyes went wide. "Now, that's a great idea. Unique, too. What do you think? Will you do it? Will you partner with her again?"

I heard a thump behind us as Dad set down the cooler. How long had he been there?

"She should," he said, "but she's too stubborn." He took a seat on the cooler and loomed over my shoulder.

"Thanks, Dad, but you've already made your opinion abundantly clear."

"Obviously not clear enough, if you're considering turning down Destiny's offer."

Crap. He'd heard too much. "It's not an offer!" I protested. Yes, I was mincing words, but we hadn't gotten to that point yet. "She simply wants to discuss a game idea we'd tossed around. Jeez, Dad. Eavesdrop much?"

His phone rang, and he immediately pulled it from his pocket. "She'll make an offer. Don't be naive. You and Destiny built Stel-Wood out of nothing, and that's not easy to do. You were the creative force behind everything. Clearly, Destiny needs you. Too bad you threw everything away on your brother's half-baked idea to open a comic book shop." He glanced down at his phone screen and his expression changed to one of concern. "It's the hospital. I need to take this. I'm on-call."

I was stunned by what sounded like praise sandwiched between two hurtful digs. A moment later, Dad's comment about the hospital registered, and my stomach dropped. Concern warred with disappointment, but concern quickly won out. The hospital would only have called if there was an emergency.

Apparently, shreds of my childhood resentment still lingered. I might admire Dad for the way he rushed to help his patients, but that ethic also meant there'd been too many times when he'd bailed on the family.

A horn honked, and I turned toward the street to see a white convertible with its top down leading the parade.

The mayor's car.

Scarlet sat in the passenger seat, waving at everyone, and tossing handfuls of candy to the kids. When she caught sight of us, her smile morphed into a devilish grin. She grabbed a fistful of candy, but instead of using her gentle underhand candy-toss technique, she switched to a fierce overhand throw and bombarded us with sweets.

As the hard pellets smacked us, Lianna and I let out startled shrieks. One piece bounced off my sunglasses and landed in my lap along with other pieces of candy shrapnel.

"I'm leaving now," Dad said to the person on the phone. "Send me the test results as soon as you have them. I'll be there as fast as I can." He ended the call.

"What happened?" I asked.

"One of my cardiac patients collapsed while preparing to march in the parade today. He's an Air Force veteran. He's in the E.R. now. I need to tell your mom, and then I'll head to the hospital."

"I hope he's okay," I said. I knew better than to ask who it was. The guy's family might not even know yet, and Dad was uber-careful when it came to privacy issues.

Dad tossed me a wave as he trotted back to the house.

"That was intense." Lianna's eyes were wide as she watched Dad leave.

"That's my dad in a nutshell. Intense."

"He really wants you to go back to creating video games. If Destiny makes an offer, do you think you'll take it?"

"How can I?" I slumped back in my chair again and opened a little box of Chiclets gum Scarlet had thrown at me. "If I step away from Ghost of a Chance, it'll fold. I can't do that. I've invested too much of myself to abandon it now." I crunched into the hard shell. Wintergreen chilled my tastebuds. The marching band got closer, so I had to raise my voice. "With either decision, I have to turn my back on one of my dreams. Plus, if I give up on the store, I'll also be giving up on Chance's dream. In a way, I'd be giving up on Chance. There's no good solution."

Lianna waited until the band had moved on before she spoke. "What does Ford think you should do?"

"I haven't told him yet."

Lianna cocked her head to one side and furrowed her brow like a confused puppy. "Why not?"

I shrugged. "I'll tell him later today. I just found out last night."

When a pair of Cub Scouts marching past in the parade spotted me, their eyes lit up and they began waving excitedly.

"Look," one of them said. "It's Wonder Woman."

"Go, Scouts!" I shouted. I glanced at Lianna. "Regular customers."

"Even *they* thought you were wearing a Wonder Woman t-shirt," Lianna commented.

I rolled my eyes. "They weren't talking about my t-shirt. They call me Wonder Woman because I wear Wonder Woman t-shirts all the time. It's a nickname."

"In a rut much?"

"It's part of my comic-book-shop-owner persona. I need to look the part."

A group of juggling unicyclists wearing matching t-shirts came next in the parade.

Lianna settled back into her lawn chair, staring at me rather than the jugglers. "I'm glad you plan to tell Ford about Destiny's offer. He'll have some good insight. Besides, keeping him in the loop will ensure there aren't any misunderstandings later. Back when Paul and I were first trying to get pregnant and I would end up disappointed each month, I shared what I was feeling with him. Every time my period came, I took it as a personal failure. It was depressing as hell, and he hated hearing me talk about it."

My chest tightened. "Oh, sweetie. That had to be rough. He should have been supportive, not selfish."

She shrugged without meeting my eyes. "It is what it is."

One of the unicyclists dropped a beanbag he'd been juggling. A young man wearing a matching t-shirt trotted over to the lost beanbag and snatched it up from the ground, deftly tossing it up to the man.

Lianna leaned closer to me. "I used to take my temperature every morning to track my ovulation. During the week when I was most fertile, our lovemaking wasn't about being together. It was entirely about making a baby. I could feel Paul distancing himself as months went by and I got more and more depressed about not being able to conceive. I wanted to protect him, so I started hiding my disappointment each time my period inevitably started again like clockwork. Looking back now, I realize it was a mistake. Hiding my feelings created a rift between us. Keeping secrets, even for the best of intentions, is a bad idea. I think he must have decided I'd accepted the fact that I couldn't have kids, and he was relieved."

"That has to hurt."

She let out a sigh that broke my heart.

"I've been thinking about me an Paul. Trying to figure out how things went so horribly wrong. I think a rift formed as all those monthly failures piled up and I pretended each one didn't kill me." She picked at a hangnail. "Maybe if I'd gotten pregnant, he wouldn't have strayed."

I gave her a stern look. "Strayed? The man isn't a lost dog. He's a cheater. He *chose* to be a cheater. That's his fault, not yours. Cheating is never a solution. It only creates more problems. Let me ask you this. Did he come to you to discuss his concerns about your relationship?"

She shrugged. "Sort of. He asked if I thought we could," she crooked her fingers in air quotes, "'make things work' with him traveling all the time. I thought he was asking about my level of commitment to our marriage and how much I missed him. I never guessed it was *his* commitment that was in question."

I stared at her with my mouth hanging open before I snapped it closed. "He never told you he was feeling disconnected? That he thought your marriage was in real trouble?"

"Never. In fact, I now realize he was hiding a lot of things from me."

"There you go. Despite what comic book writers include in their stories, no one can actually read minds. You have to actually *tell* people what's going on with you." I grabbed a bottle of water from the cooler and cracked open the lid.

"Hey, sis," Grayson said, startling me as he moved one of the red chairs to sit next to me. "It looks like I'm late for the parade." His snug button-front navy shirt with white stars looked appropriately festive.

"You missed the high school marching band and the unicycles," I told him.

Grayson dropped into the chair. "Damn. I'm usually here in time for the unicycles. Did anyone fall?"

I gave him the side-eye. "Is that the only reason you like that part? You know, if you showed up a half-hour earlier, you'd get to see the whole thing."

He pulled off his dark blue Pitt ball cap, ran his hand through his hair, and then settled it back in place, adjusting the brim to shade his eyes. "That would mean waking up earlier on a Saturday morning than I do on weekdays, and that's not happening."

"Poor baby," I commiserated. "The trials and tribulations of being a university professor sound grueling."

"Hey, I resemble that remark." He shot me a wink. "I'll have you know, I normally work until one in the morning. I deserve to sleep in with that sort of schedule."

With a pang of perverse longing, I recalled keeping a similar timetable when Destiny and I were trying to hit deadlines. These days, I was usually asleep by ten so I could get up early and walk Zephyr before I opened the store.

"Do you remember Lianna?" I asked.

"Sure." Grayson tossed a friendly wave in her direction. "Good to see you." He tipped his chin toward the two other empty lawn chairs. "Where are the parents?"

"Inside. Mom's busy perfecting brunch and Dad got a call from the hospital."

Grayson's smile faded. "Does he have to go in?"

"Yeah. It sounds like it's someone who lives in Sewickley."

"Heart attack?"

"I think so."

"I'll try to catch him before he leaves." Grayson stood. "Save my seat." He ruffled my hair, and I knocked his hand away. He wore a grin as he jogged toward the front door.

"Your brother is cute," Lianna said, watching him.

"Don't worry. He knows it." I dragged my fingers through my hair to smooth it back in place. The sun was really beating down and made my dark hair hot to the touch. "Enough about him, back to you. How are things going? Are you and Paul on speaking terms?"

"Not hardly. He hasn't even apologized. I don't think he cares that he hurt me. Did I ever really know the man?"

That stunned me. Unfortunately, it also fed directly into my own fears about ever being in a relationship again. "What will you do?"

"Divorce him. I've already contacted a lawyer."

That took me by surprise. "So soon?"

Her lips thinned. I could see her pain clearly. "I can never trust him again. Not after he lied to me for so long."

That made perfect sense to me. Lies were the worst sort of poison. They infiltrated all your memories, making you doubt everything that had ever happened in your relationship. Making you feel like a fool. "What about Paul? Is he on board with that?"

"When I mentioned divorce, he acted like it was a foregone conclusion." Pain shimmered in her eyes.

"Ouch. That must have hurt. No pushback at all?"

Lianna shook her head decisively. "Nope. *Nada*. He gave up. Simple as that."

I stared at her, stunned. "That sucks in all kinds of ways."

"Yeah." Lianna watched a guy in the parade wearing black leather gloves do a series of backflips and cartwheels down the center of the street. "It would have been nice if he'd fought for us, but I guess it was too much to ask, considering he threw everything away so easily."

"He's an idiot."

A wavering smile flitted across Lianna's face. "That he is."

A group of bagpipers approached with their pipes blaring. Men in kilts were always a treat.

"Mara!" A middle-school girl in a tartan skirt—one of my regulars—broke away from the marchers and handed me a Tootsie Pop.

"Thanks!" I shouted back to be heard over the bagpipes.

Lianna plucked the red Tootsie Pop out of my hand and unwrapped it. "Tell me more about you and Ford. I want to believe in romance again."

I scowled at her for snagging my treat. "He's amazing. Sometimes I wonder if he's too amazing. His accomplishments are pretty impressive."

Lianna sucked on my lollipop—her lollipop now—for a moment as she considered the question, then she pulled it from her cherry red lips with a smacking sound to speak. "Interesting. What about him makes you feel... intimidated?" Her breath smelled like cherries.

I threw up my hands in frustration. "His fame? His lifestyle? That fact that he could have any Hollywood starlet he wants, but he's with me?" The knot in my stomach started to tighten again. "The two of us together doesn't make any sense."

"Mara…. Why can't you see what's special about you? You're

an amazing woman. Kind. Funny. Intelligent. Beautiful. Level-headed. A great friend. Compassionate. He's lucky he found you. You should judge him based on the way he makes you feel when you're with him. Does he make you feel as though you could conquer the world? Does he give you confidence? Are you your best self when you're with him?"

I could only stare at her. "Yes. I think I am."

"Then you have your answer. He's a good guy."

A tight band of tension that had been stifling me the past few days suddenly eased. Until that moment, I hadn't even realized it had been there.

Grayson came back with Mom. He grabbed a bottle of water from the cooler and sat next to me. Mom took the spot next to Lianna.

"I hear Ghost of a Chance is a great place to buy Indie comics," Grayson commented. "Your reputation is spreading with the college crowd. Congrats."

I rotated in my chair to face my brother. "Say that again?"

He grinned. "I overheard some students raving about your store. I thought you'd want to know."

"See?" Lianna said. "You're growing your reputation. You just need to give it time."

"With you running it, that place is bound to be a success," Mom said.

Her praise felt good, but still I muttered, "Not according to Dad."

Mom rolled her eyes. "Your father worries about you. The only way he knows how to show his love is by helping you avoid problems before they happen. Unfortunately, that means he's constantly second-guessing every decision you kids make. He's coming from a place of love. He only wants to keep you safe."

Grayson gave a snort of disbelief. "By undermining us?"

"By watching out for you. He's trying to make sure you kids don't fail." Mom held up her hand. "I know, I know—he goes about it the wrong way. Try to remember his heart is in the right place."

"I didn't know he had a heart," Grayson muttered under his breath so Mom couldn't hear.

I grinned and bumped shoulders with him.

"I'm proud of you, Mara," Mom told me. "You've done an amazing job. Chance would have been thrilled."

Overwhelmed, I soaked up her kudos. I needed those positive words from her like a parched field needed rain. I'd made sacrifices to keep Chance's dreams alive, and it was good to know at least one of my parents acknowledged that fact.

"Besides," Mom continued, "I can't even begin to tell you how happy I am that you moved here from Boston. It means the world to me that you live nearby."

Grayson slung his arm around my shoulders and planted a loud kiss on my cheek. "Me too, sis. It's great having you around."

I glanced at him, surprised by his show of support, but something about the glint in his eye and his broad grin seemed incongruous.

A moment later, frigid water spilled down my back. I let out a shriek as I shoved him off me. I jumped to my feet and whirled on him as my chair toppled back. "You can be such a jerk sometimes!"

His grin deepened. "But you still love me, don't you, Captain America?"

I glanced down at my t-shirt, and all my anger evaporated. Finally, one of my family members had correctly identified my t-shirt. It was as though Chance was right here with us.

I tried to scowl at Grayson for the prank but failed. Instead, I righted my chair, sat back down, and grabbed the water bottle from his hand. "You're just lucky it's a hot day," I grumbled, hiding my smile behind the raised water bottle, "or I'd have had to kick your ass for that."

Where had all my stress and angst about today gotten me?

Nowhere.

I should stop emulating Dad's habit of predicting bad news and learn to roll with things, like Ford did. After all, the worst thing in my life had been losing Chance, and I never could have predicted it.

3 2

REVELATIONS

After I left Hailey's house on Memorial Day, I headed straight over to Mara's place. The sun glared off the hot pavement as I pressed her doorbell. When she buzzed me in, I entered the cool, dark staircase, and trotted upstairs to find her waiting for me on the landing.

"We need to talk," I said as soon as I saw her.

Mara's eyebrows drew together. "That sounds ominous." She glanced down at Zephyr, who was bouncing up and down at her feet as if his legs were springs. With a sigh, she picked him up and tucked him under her arm in a football hold.

"Sorry, I guess that came out wrong," I said as I shifted the canvas grocery bags to one hand and wrapped my arm around her waist. I pulled her in for a kiss, being careful not to squash the squirming bundle of fur intent on licking my ear. "It's nothing bad."

Her lips were soft and warm, and she smelled of flowers and new comic books. I'd never again be able to walk into a comic book shop without thinking of her.

As I broke the kiss, Zephyr made one more valiant squirm and managed to lick the bottom of my earlobe. I grinned as I wiped dog spit away.

Mara looked worried as she stepped out of dog-licking range. "I've never had a good conversation that started with the words 'We need to talk.'" She set Zephyr on the floor.

"Then this will be a first," I said.

She held out her hand toward me, and it took a moment for me to register that she was holding out a keychain. "What's that?" I asked.

"Your key. To my apartment." She said it simply.

I exhaled in a whoosh of relief. Her timing couldn't have been more perfect.

"Thank you. This is a big step, but it's one I want to take, too." I pulled a key to my house from my pocket and held it out to her. "I brought this for you. Great minds think alike, and all that."

She wrapped her arms around me and kissed me. "I'm glad we're on the same page."

In the kitchen, I gently set my bags on the table, and one sounded the chime of clinking glasses.

I reached in and pulled out a bottle of chilled champagne along with two flutes.

She raised her eyebrows. "I'm amazed they didn't break."

"I'm resourceful." Grinning, I pulled the empty beer carton from the bag.

"You put the champagne glasses in there? Clever."

Familiar with her kitchen, I plucked a large pot from her cabinet and filled it with water. I set it to boil and then tore the foil from the champagne bottle.

She watched me with a look of nervous excitement. "Champagne is a good sign, right? No one celebrates bad news with champagne."

"Not unless they're really twisted." I shot her a playful grin. I have to admit, I liked seeing her this way—filled with anticipation. It reminded me of those kisses I'd teased her with when we'd first started dating.

With a pop, the cork came out and ricocheted off the ceiling.

Mara let out a yelp of surprise and then started laughing. When the stopper came to a rest near her feet, she set it on the counter. "What are we celebrating?"

"I spoke with McCormick last night." I handed her a glass.

Her mouth tightened and turned down at the corners. She met my gaze, and I could read her trepidation. "Does that mean you made a decision?"

I couldn't stand teasing her any longer, so I said it straight out. "I turned down his movie."

Her eyes went wide. "You did?" She gulped her champagne, then coughed, almost choking.

"He took better than I'd expected." Except for his parting shot about Dad. I'd write it off as petty resentment if not for the fact that I'd also noticed similar problems.

"That sounds great." She clenched the stem of her glass so hard that her knuckles showed white. "Where does that leave *Ghost*?"

"I tracked down the film rights. Your brother sold them."

Her face fell. She looked devastated. "Oh, no."

"It's okay," I immediately reassured her. "I was able to purchase them back."

Her expression transformed to stunned amazement. "That's... good?" Her voice squeaked with uncertainty.

"Wait. It gets better." I paused for effect. "I met with Dad and Max. Ross Film Productions is going to make *Ghost* right here in Pittsburgh. Dad's excited. He borrowed your brother's comic books, and he's reading them now. He wants us to come over for dinner on Friday to discuss everything."

"What?" Mara paused. When she read the truth on my face, she let out a shriek of delight. "Pinch me! Is this really happening?"

I set down my champagne glass and kissed her, my lips bumping against her teeth because she was grinning so hard. "It is."

"Are you sure about this?" She tipped her head back to look into my eyes. "I thought McCormick was your big break. What about your dream of making a blockbuster movie for a major studio?"

I shrugged. "Big breaks can come in many forms. It dawned on me that having the freedom to choose my next project, and film it in Pittsburgh with my family, also constitutes a big break, and one I shouldn't ignore. By making my own movie on my own terms, I get everything that's important to me. No one will try to fight with me over creative control, I can make exactly the film I want, and I can spend more time with my family."

I started unpacking the second grocery bag.

"What's for dinner?" she asked.

"Something special. A new recipe." I unpacked it and set chicken breasts, tomato sauce, onions, and rice on her counter.

When I pulled a jar of peanut butter from the canvas bag, a huge grin broke over her face. "You're making Chicken Moambe!"

"Right on the first guess. After I saw how much you liked it at the Phipps Conservatory, I found this recipe. It cooks for a long time, but it's pretty easy." I kissed her and then started cutting the chicken breasts into smaller pieces to boil.

"Do I finally get to tell everyone about your plans for *Ghost*?" She bounced excitedly on her toes, reminding me of the way Zephyr would jump up and down when he was excited.

"Not yet," I said, smiling at her antics. "Keep it under wraps until I make a press release. Just a few more days." I kissed her cheek. She was adorable. "You know, I owe it all to you." I shook my head in bemusement as I turned to the sink and scrubbed my hands. "What if I hadn't ducked into your shop during that rainstorm?"

She mock-scowled at me. "Well, for one, you wouldn't have chased off two regular customers. They still haven't returned. But seriously," she added, relenting, "this is a dream come true. I always thought *Ghost* would be perfect for the screen."

"With your help, it will be. I'm counting on you to be a script consultant."

She looked intrigued. "What's that?"

"You'll review the script and provide feedback—make sure we stay true to your brother's vision."

"Sounds doable." She held up her champagne flute in a toast, her joy as bright and effervescent as the bubbles rising in her glass. "Here's to *Ghost*."

"To *Ghost*," I said, clinking my glass to hers.

"I don't want to take away from the moment," she said, "but I have news to share, too."

I raised my eyebrows, encouraging her to continue.

She took a breath. "It's about my former partner, Destiny. We started Stel-Wood after we graduated. She called me last night to tell me she's starting a new company." She hesitated.

Intrigued, I waited.

"She was hinting that she wanted us to be partners again." Her words came out in a rush, but she didn't look excited about the news.

I frowned, confused. "You don't look happy. That's... a good thing, right?" I raised my eyebrows and offered a smile as I lifted my glass to toast her. "Congratulations! You must be thrilled." Her expression told me otherwise, like she was conflicted about something.

"I am... along with terrified, confused, torn, and overwhelmed. I don't know what I'll do if she officially asks." Glancing away, she swallowed hard. "What about Ghost of a Chance? Shutting it down would feel like giving up on my brother." Tears pooled along her lower lashes, and I hated that this was causing her pain. "I'd be turning my back on our dream. I don't think I can do that."

Even if it meant I might ruin dinner again, I turned away from the stove and folded her into my arms. "How long do you have until you need to make a decision?"

Mara shrugged. "Destiny said a couple of weeks, but she still needs to find investors. Based on how slowly things moved when we tried to get Stel-Wood off the ground, I'm guessing all that will take at least a couple of months or longer."

"You have a little breathing room. A lot of things can change in two weeks." I used the back of the knife to scrape the diced chicken to the pot, and then added some salt and black pepper.

She took a deep breath and let it out. "Good point. I don't need to decide today."

I turned on the water and lathered up my hands, carefully cleaning them. "A solution might fall in your lap... or maybe you'll be able to use that logical brain of yours to come up with something out-of-the-box."

Her eyes widened, then her nose wrinkled. "Logical? Is that how you see me? As someone cold and rational?"

"Logical is a good thing," I said. "You're logical *and* inventive. You're the best of both worlds. I love how your mind works. I know that if a solution exists, you'll find it—and I'm sure there *is* a solution." I topped off our champagne glasses. "Use all that logic and creativity, and you'll find it. Start by exploring your assumptions about your goals, so they're clear in your mind. You owe it to yourself to find a solution that makes you happy." The pot was boiling now, so I turned it down to a simmer.

She cocked her head to one side, as though seeing me in a new light. "Thank you. That was some really good advice wrapped up in a pep-talk."

"I do what I can." I set the timer so I wouldn't ruin dinner again. "We need to let this cook for a while." I stepped closer to her, nuzzling my lips against the spot just below her ear. "We have an hour. What would you like to do while we wait?"

A slow, seductive smile spread across her face, and she grabbed the waist of my jeans, pulling me to her. "I might have an idea or two in my logical, yet inventive mind." She snagged the champagne bottle and pulled me to her bedroom.

I groaned, enjoying this take-charge attitude. I was all hers, and loving every minute of it.

I took the bottle of champagne from her hand, set it on the nightstand, and stripped her bare.

She sank down onto her bed, eyes dark with passion as she stared up at me, completely naked.

God, but she looked amazing. Good enough to eat.

"Aren't you a bit overdressed?" she asked in a sultry voice.

"Not for what I have in mind." I grabbed the champagne bottle and took a swallow, and then handed it to her. "Want some?"

She shot me a quizzical look, but drank before handing it back.

I pressed my palm against her chest to urge her to lie down, then drizzled some champagne onto her belly. She gasped in surprise.

"What are you doing?"

I drank in her body as I leaned over her, bracing my arms on either side of her on the bed, and then dipped my head toward her navel. "I plan to sip champagne off your stomach." I dipped my tongue into her bellybutton and licked champagne. "Does that meet with your approval?"

She let out a shaky sigh, and the pool of champagne quivered. "It does, Mr. Director."

As I sucked at her stomach, she shivered from head to toe.

I pressed my lips against the small pool of champagne on her belly and found it warm on her skin. "Delicious."

I gazed down, drinking in the image of her with her belly glistening with champagne. She looked perfect.

"You like looking at me," she commented.

I met the dark pools of her eyes. "You look like a siren. A temptress. One I can't resist." I grabbed the champagne again and took another swig before setting it aside. Then I dropped down between her thighs and kissed her in that most private spot.

She let out a gasp of delight.

Mara tasted even better than the champagne.

"Your lips are cool," she said in a breathy voice.

I flicked my tongue against that sensitive bundle of nerves, and she let out a whimper.

"Your tongue is, too."

"Is that bad?" I asked.

"It's amazing."

As my tongue teased her once again, she let out a sigh that ended in a sultry moan of pleasure. "Yes. That. Do that."

I kept going while gently sliding a finger inside her opening. She squirmed under me as though she couldn't stay still. Then I added a second finger. I steadily and rhythmically moved them in and out of her, listening to her quickening breath, feeling the slickness of her inner walls against my hand. She tasted deliciously sweet against my tongue.

"Oh, Ford. Ford," came her urgent cry.

She was close. I could feel the tension and heat building within her.

An instant later she arched her back and shuddered. She seemed to be *trying* to cry out, but she didn't make a sound as an orgasm crashed through her.

Knowing I'd done this to her drove me wild with wanting.

As her tremors began to ease, I stripped away my clothes. I wanted to feel her body pressed against mine. Skin-to-skin. Heartbeat-to-heartbeat. I wanted to savor her.

As I moved to join her on the bed, she watched me, her eyes fixed on my erection. Her voracious desire made me grow even harder.

"I need you inside me," she said as she sat up. She reached over and pulled open her nightstand drawer, revealing a few condoms.

Happy to comply, I grabbed one and sheathed myself.

I stared down at her, trying to draw out this moment of anticipation, but I couldn't hold back another second. I had to be inside her. Now.

I grabbed her beautiful hips and lifted her to meet me. I slid into her smoothly. She was wet and ready for me, welcoming me inside her with a deep sigh.

I stared into her eyes as we clung together. She revealed everything in her gaze. Her passion. Her joy. Her fascination with me... with the pleasure I gave her... with my desire for her.

This all felt so good. So right.

I loved taking my time with her. Savoring her body and her reactions.

I lifted her ankles to my shoulders and then grabbed hold of her hands. With her legs braced against my chest and her feet tucked slightly behind my neck, she was able to push into me, and we moved in rhythm. The sensations built on one another and finally edged us both toward a crescendo of erotic overload.

I stared down into her spellbound eyes, entranced by her. That blue-tipped hair cascading around her on the coverlet—I slid my fingers closer to the strands, barely able to reach them, the soft blue bits of hair sliding through my fingers.

I repositioned us, lowering her legs and pulling her up against my chest. I glided my hand up her spine, her smooth skin soft to my touch. With her wild hair right in front of me, I grabbed hold of a handful.

She inhaled sharply, and then let out a moan.

"You like that?"

She hummed her agreement.

I needed more of her. More of this. More of every delicious, sweet, sensation. Being careful not to pull too hard, I kept my fist wrapped in her hair—exactly as I'd once imagined—and drove into her. It wasn't long before her body tightened around my cock.

She felt so good. So amazing.

As my pleasure reached its peak, I gave in and embraced the delirious joy. "Mara," I cried out, even as she called, "Ford," in that throaty, sexy voice that made me cum even harder.

A moment later, I collapsed around her.

This was perfect. We stayed that way for a while. Wrapped in each other's arms.

She closed her eyes and sighed as I pulled out, then she curled on her side. I disposed of the condom and returned to her side as fast as I could. We spooned, Mara snuggling her back against me.

After a few minutes passed, the oven timer went off. Zephyr gave a warning bark from outside the bedroom door to make sure we'd heard it.

"It's been an hour?" Mara asked, sounding surprised.

Even though I wanted to stay exactly where I was, I forced myself to my feet. "I just need to toss a few more things into the pot. I'll be back in a minute."

She looked perfectly relaxed and sated. "I'll miss you," she said. "I have to admit though..." She raised herself onto her elbows with a cute grin on her sexy lips. "I'm starving."

Clasping my hand around one breast, I swirled my tongue around her nipple and sucked until she gasped. "I'll always be starving for you."

She groaned with half-pleasure, half-dismay at my wordplay, but it put a smile on her lips, and that's what mattered. I kissed her hard before I dragged myself away from her. "I'll be right back, baby."

FAMILY MATTERS

FORD

Late the next day, I stopped by the restaurant around closing time to see Dante and Conner, but Conner wasn't there. Only a few guests lingered at the tables scattered around the room.

The bartender took my order and let Dante know I was there.

Last night with Mara had been spectacular. Our connection kept growing and deepening the more time we spent together.

I found the flashes of self-confidence I'd seen in her from the very first day sexy as hell. She'd been rocked by the blows life had landed on her over the past year, but she was finding her way back to normal. As hard as it was to see her battle self-doubt, I loved watching her confidence grow stronger.

Pretty soon, that woman would set the world on fire.

I pulled up photos of her on my phone, thumbing through them. My favorite was the one of her standing at the top of Mount Washington with a view of Pittsburgh far below. In it, the breeze lifted her hair and her smiling brown eyes gazed directly into the camera. We'd had an amazing day together. The first of many.

"What has you in such a good mood?" Dante asked, startling me.

Even though I was a little embarrassed to be caught mooning

over a photo, I tilted my phone so he could see it. "Mara," I admitted.

His quick grin appeared. "Are things going well with her?"

I nodded. "Excellent. I couldn't be happier." Which was true. I hadn't been this content in—I couldn't even remember how long. Ever?

Dante raised his eyebrows, beaming. "That's great to hear."

With surprise, it struck me that Mara had become an essential part of my life, and that left me confused. So much of my happiness right now was tied to her. I tamped down my sudden anxiety. I needed to roll with this and see how things evolved, not overanalyze.

"Here for dinner?" Dante asked. "You haven't been stopping by as often since you started taking my cooking classes." He slid a menu closer to me.

I waved it away. "I had some of the leftover Chicken Moambe I made for Mara yesterday." At his questioning eyebrow, I explained, "It's an African stew with chicken and peanut butter."

Dante's face split into a huge grin. "Damn. Am I happy to hear that. You're taking the cooking techniques you learned and finding new recipes on your own. That's exactly what I hoped for."

"Thanks for talking me into taking your class."

He shrugged. "Couldn't have you eating takeout and frozen dinners the rest of your life."

Coming back to my hometown reconnected me to the world. Los Angeles was great, but there was something about the pace of life here that drew me in. Made me feel more connected. Maybe it was because I was spending more time with family and old friends. The cooking lessons. The family get-togethers. The plans for my movie.

And, of course, Mara was quickly becoming the center of my contentment.

I didn't want this to end. This life I was building. These connections I was forging.

And... if I wanted this to last—if I wanted to build a future here—*Ghost* had to be a success. Everything depended on it.

Dante came around the bar and sat on the stool next to mine. "How's your dad doing?" he asked.

I paused, trying to come up with an answer. It was complicated. At the Memorial Day parade yesterday, Dad had seemed happy, but he left my sister's place early, saying he had to make a business call. As he turned to leave, he'd dragged his palm across his chest. I saw a flicker of deep loneliness in his eyes. Was he thinking about Mom? Missing her?

I cleared my throat. "That's one of the reasons I want to stay in Sewickley. Dad's become more detached than I remember. He hides it well, but I'm starting to think he never really got over Mom's death."

Dante scratched his cheek. "Didn't she die over twenty-five years ago? Why is he depressed now?"

"I don't think it's a recent thing. It's been getting worse for a long time. I just didn't notice it before," I replied. But was that all there was to it? Dante had a point. Why now? Was there something I was missing?

Dante put his hand on my shoulder and gave it a gentle shake. "Don't blame yourself. People keep things hidden all the time. You're not a mind reader."

His words struck a chord. Chelsea had kept plenty of things from me. Was Dad doing the same? "I hear you," I said as Dante's hand fell away. "But he's my dad. It's my responsibility. I'm hoping I can help him now that I'm around more. I should have done it sooner." The guilt washed over me, and I looked away. "McCormick told me that people in the industry are starting to notice Dad's problems, and it's affecting Ross Film Productions."

Dante looked concerned. "That's not good."

"I'm hoping that making my movie with him will turn things around.... as long as we make something great, that is."

Dante caught my eye with his gaze. "It's a done deal then?

You're filming here? That's great. Sounds like the perfect solution for all your problems. If anyone can do it, you can."

His words steadied me, and I nodded, hoping he was right. "This movie has to be a success. Everything's riding on it."

"No pressure," Dante deadpanned.

"None," I said with a forced laugh. "Only all my hopes for the future."

No pressure.

Mara was becoming integral to my future happiness, both personally and professionally. What if she disappeared from my life right now? Would everything come crashing down?

When it happened to Dad... when Mom had died... he'd managed to hold everything together and make Ross Film Productions a success, even though he'd been ravaged by grief. He'd kept going. Losing her hadn't completely destroyed him, but —it had gutted him. I could recognize it now, as an adult.

I finished off my beer. I'd take my cue from Mara. From that burgeoning self-confidence of hers I admired so much. I could do this—make my movie a success and rescue Dad's floundering company. Could I solve his personal problems too? Maybe. At the very least, I could be here to help him figure them out for himself.

3 4

AN ESTATE?

FORD

"Is this dress okay?" Mara asked when I picked her up at her apartment on Friday. "I can change."

I took in her simple dress, with its image of Spiderman swinging on his web, and thought she looked adorable. "It's perfect. *You're* perfect. My dad will love you."

She waved her hand dismissively. "Don't BS a BSer. You can't know that."

"I can. You're a shoe-in. He'll like you because you live in Sewickley."

"Why does where I live make a difference?" She licked her lips, and the sight of her tongue drew my attention.

It took a moment for me to regain the thread of the conversation. "Since you live here, he'll think dating you will make me stay here."

Her eyes flashed with a knowing gleam. She knew exactly what the sight of her tongue always did to me, and she was pleased with herself. "Interesting. That will score me extra points?" At least she didn't seem nervous anymore.

"Absolutely. Double bonus."

"That feels like using a cheat code—up, up, down, down, left, right, left, right, B, A, start—but who am I to argue? I'll take it."

I smiled indulgently at hearing her rattle off that old Nintendo cheat code. Her adorable nerditude was endearing as hell.

As we drove towards my dad's house in Sewickley Heights, I couldn't help but admire the stunning scenery that surrounded us. Rolling hills and lush greenery surrounded us, while the occasional grand estate punctuated the landscape. "The magnates who built their estates up here in the 1800s knew what they were doing," I commented.

Mara tilted her head back and shielded her eyes to peer skyward. "I can't believe how blue the sky is today. Not a cloud in sight. And the air smells so fresh."

I couldn't agree more. "Yeah, it's amazing up here."

As we turned onto a street lined with grand houses, Mara pointed out a large property on the corner. "Did you see the hockey rink the owners built behind that place? They must really love winter."

"A pro hockey player lives there. My dad knows him," I said, trying to sound nonchalant.

Mara's eyes sparkled with interest. "Wow, that's impressive."I shrugged. "A pro hockey player lives there. My dad knows him."

"Of course, he does." Mara let out a nervous sigh as she smoothed her palms down her skirt.

"You okay?" I asked.

"Just a little nervous about meeting the fam. It'll pass."

I glanced at her as I drove up dad's long driveway. "Like I said, he'll love you." We rounded a bend and crested a hill, and the enormous gray stone estate rose before us. As usual, the rolling green grass surrounding it was perfectly manicured, and I spotted the groundskeeper trimming a dead branch from a tree.

I continued along the looping driveway and stopped so Mara's door lined up next to the path to the front door.

I walked around the front of the car, but Mara didn't move to open her door. She simply sat, staring up at the house with her eyes wide and eyebrows raised in exaggerated surprise.

"You grew up *here*? Holy mother of pearl! This house is flipping huge!" She held up her pointer finger. "Wait. That's not the right word. This isn't a house. It's an estate."

I never thought about it much, but Mara was right. Dad's place was pretty damned opulent. I'd forgotten the kind of effect it could have on people when they saw it for the first time.

I opened the passenger door and stepped to one side as she unfolded those gorgeous legs and exited the car. "A steel baron built this as a summer place."

"Steel baron. Right," she said. Her legs were wobbly, so she grabbed hold of my arm. "This is a far cry from the suburban house where I grew up. I thought we were well off, but this is a completely different level of wealth. I wasn't expecting it."

I shrugged. "You'll get used to it. This was a great place to grow up. Lots of woods to explore. The country club is nearby, so Hailey and my brothers and I could walk to the pool, grab lunch, or play duckpin bowling. There's even a creek at the bottom of that hill where I used to hunt salamanders."

She cocked one eyebrow, the hint of a smile on her lips. "Country clubs and salamanders? I caught salamanders when I was growing up, too, but lunch was usually a peanut butter sandwich."

"We'll always share our love of amphibians," I intoned wistfully.

She ran her hands down her dress, then started smoothing her hair. "There's that." She glanced at her clothes. "You're sure this dress is okay? Not too nerdy?"

"It's perfect. You're perfect."

"Thanks, but I don't feel perfect. I feel like I'm about to be judged."

I captured one of her fluttering hands to calm it and pressed a quick kiss to the back of it. "He'll love you. I promise."

The front door suddenly swung open, and Dad stood there, beaming at us.

"You're here." His eyes locked on Mara, and he held out his hand to her. "It's great to meet you, Mara. I'm Don Ross. Call me Don."

"Pleased to meet you, Don." Her eyes were wide as she shook his hand.

Dad gave her an approving nod. "Your dress is perfect. Very fitting. But as much as I love Spiderman, we really need to get you a Ghost version."

"Thanks," she said, brightening. "I love that idea." The tension in her shoulders eased. "Ford speaks of you often. I can see where he inherited those amazing blue eyes." Her brow furrowed slightly. "Yours might even be bluer than his."

Dad clapped me on the back. "I like her already."

"Dibs," I told him.

Dad chuckled. "Possessive much?" He grinned at Mara. "Thanks for coming to celebrate starting a new project together. If not for your brother, none of this would be happening. You must be proud of him."

Mara blinked rapidly. "I am. Thank you."

"Let's go to the kitchen," Dad said. "I have a surprise."

As he led us down a central hallway to the back of the house, Mara's eyes grew wider and wider as she took in everything. The enormous great room with its stained-glass windows and the fireplace big enough for a horse to stand in seemed to almost push her over the edge.

I took her hand and squeezed it. She held it in a death grip.

"Your house is amazing," Mara said as she looked around the kitchen. "Your kitchen alone is bigger than my apartment."

"Thanks. Lots of space to rattle around in," Dad said. "It was great when all the kids still lived here, but it's a bit much just for me."

"It must hold lots of great memories," she said, meeting Dad's gaze.

"Absolutely. Some of the best." Dad glanced away uncomfortably and then gestured toward the champagne and glasses sitting on the island with a flourish. "I bought a bottle of Ice Impérial to celebrate our new partnership."

I raised one eyebrow, intrigued. "Ice Impérial? I've never tried it."

"You'll love it. You serve it over ice... can you believe it? Your grandfather would turn over in his grave. The idea of serving wine over ice would kill him all over again. He was a real wine snob," he explained to Mara.

Dad snatched up the white bottle and tore off the foil wrapper. "Do me a favor and put one ice cube in each of the wine glasses."

I did as he asked and put one cube in each glass.

"See those bowls with raspberries, mint, and orange peels?" Dad asked. "Choose which one you'd like to have in your champagne."

Mara looked intrigued, finally beginning to relax. "For reals? That's different. I'll try raspberry."

Dad dropped a couple of berries onto the ice cubes in her glass.

As I reached for a raspberry to pop into my mouth, my hand grazed against Mara's, so I paused to stroke the side of her hand with my fingertip before snatching the berry.

Mara stopped breathing and then moved closer to me so that our arms were now touching.

God, she was perfect.

"I'll try mint in mine," I said.

"Let me do the honors with the mint," Dad said. "Check this out." He selected a large mint leaf, placed it on the palm of his hand, and then slapped his other hand against it. "Here." He held it out. "Smell."

The pungent aroma of mint filled the air.

"Bruising it releases the oil." Dad dropped the leaf into a second glass, added a couple of raspberries to a third one, and then added champagne. He handed us our drinks, then raised his own in a toast.

"Mara, your brother's comics are gonna look great on the big screen," Dad said. "That young man had a cinematic eye. Here's to the three of us making an amazing movie together." He tipped his head toward Mara. "Ross, Ross, and Stellar."

We clinked glasses and drank.

"What do you think?" Dad asked. "Like it?"

Mara blinked. "I love it. It's light and crisp."

"Delicious," I said. Grandad would have approved, even with the ice."

"I like to think so," Dad said.

As Mara's gaze took in the huge kitchen once again, Dad and I exchanged glances, and he let me know he realized Mara was nervous.

"Dinner should be ready in about a half hour," Dad said.

"Is it okay if we talk about the film?" I asked. "We need to work on casting. Chris Pitt is in town shooting a film. I want him as the lead, so I'm trying to arrange a meeting with him later this week. I want to bounce some ideas off you for the role of his love interest."

Both Dad and Mara frowned, but Mara was the first to speak. "I thought Chris Pitt was more of a comic actor."

Dad cleared his throat. "I'm not convinced Pitt's the right choice."

Dad's comment took me by surprise. I have to admit, it set me on edge a bit too. "No? Why not?"

"Like Mara said, he's more of a comic actor."

"I like comic actors," I said. "They have excellent timing and delivery."

"But they also have to overcome audience expectations," Dad said. "I'm not sure Pitt's up to it."

I hesitated, surprised to have him resist one of my first big decisions. This was only the first of a million I'd be making. Would I have to fight him every step of the way? My reaction now would set the tone. I didn't want to be combative, but I wasn't about to give in on this point. I decided to make a small compromise to appease him. "I'll bring him in so you can see him in a screen-test if that will help you feel more comfortable with my decision. Something informal."

Dad beamed. "That's an excellent idea."

I gave a tight nod. "I'll tell him I want to see how he and the co-star interact on screen. Which brings us back to my original question. Any thoughts about co-stars?"

Dad rubbed his chin, but just shook his head.

Mara cleared her throat.

I glanced at her. "Did you have someone in mind?"

She licked her lips nervously. "My brother used to talk about making *Ghost* into a movie. Daydreaming, I guess. Anyway, he always thought Kim Curry would be perfect as Ghost's nemesis and love interest."

I stared at her blankly for a moment, then grinned broadly. I could definitely see Kim in that role. "Excellent suggestion. She'd be perfect."

She grinned with pleasure.

I turned to Dad. "You have a good relationship with Kim. Can you approach her about it?"

He tilted his head from side to side like a clock pendulum. "I bet Chris and Kim would have great chemistry. She could even carry him if his acting isn't up to par. I wonder if she can keep from overshadowing him...she's a powerful actress. I'll tell you what. Let's see how they do in a screen test, and we'll go from there."

I gave a tight smile. "Sounds like a plan." Dad's skepticism was getting to me. He really didn't think much of Chris. "We'll have to work around his current shooting schedule. After I get him to agree, I'll send you his available dates and times. I'd like to get the test done within the next week. Two at the most. Let's keep my casting choices between the three of us for now. I don't want any of this getting out."

Dad nodded and made a quick note on his phone.

Mara raised her champagne glass. "May I offer another toast? To new connections, new ventures, and new friends."

"Hear, hear," Dad said as we clinked glasses. "You know, your brother Max took on a lot of responsibility after my heart attack. I've really enjoyed having him as my right-hand man. His official title is Executive VP of Marketing and Development, but he does more than that. He's involved in all my films. We've worked closely these past few years, and now I get to work with you too. Wouldn't it be great if Sean could do some of the stunt work on the film? Just imagine it. We could have the entire family working on this movie. I bet we could even convince Hailey to help."

"We're on the same page," I said. "Sean and I have already started bouncing around ideas for the action scenes."

"Excellent," Dad said, rubbing his hands together. "There's a great location up on Mount Washington we should use to film that kiss scene. It has a spectacular view of the city. I also have some ideas about how we can orchestrate filming the tunnel scene."

I let out a low chuckle. "I can tell you've studied the script."

"Did you expect anything less?" Dad asked.

"Never." I popped another raspberry into my mouth, biting gently as I released its sweet, tart, summery tang. "You and the screenwriter have a lot of ideas in common."

"I made some script notes," Dad said. "I want to discuss a few changes with you."

Mara frowned. "Changes?" Her entire body grew tense.

I arched my brows at my dad as I stroked my hand down Mara's back. "I'm happy to discuss things," I told him, "but you need to remember whose movie this is. I don't want a repeat of my seventh grade English project."

Dad hesitated for a moment as he seemed to try to recall what I was talking about, and then he cracked a wry smile. "What? You didn't like the professional musicians and the backup dancers?"

"It was an extra credit project for English class. Even you have to admit you went too far. I'm lucky the video didn't get out on YouTube or something. What if the whole thing had gone viral?"

"I might have let things get a little out of hand," Dad replied, "but the band was working on another project with me. When they found out about your project, they wanted to help. You have to admit you learned a lot."

"I did. I learned not to let anyone take over my project."

"A lesson that's served you well over the years," Dad said with a wink.

Mara touched my arm and I glanced at her.

"Where can I find a bathroom?"

"Head straight back down that hallway," I said, pointing to the ornate wooden archway we'd entered. "Go past those double doors leading to Dad's office. You can't miss it."

I kept my gaze on her as she walked away. It was something I'd become fond of over these past few weeks—watching her walk away. That woman had a knack for it. Something about her graceful yet unselfconscious way of moving made it impossible not to look. When she disappeared from sight, I was finally able to drag my attention away from her.

I found Dad watching me. He shot me a "gotcha" sort of grin as he set an antipasto tray on the counter. "You're smitten with her."

"I guess so. She's nothing like the other women I've met."

"Those Hollywood types? I know what you mean. Hollywood is a different world. It's why I prefer living here." Dad's phone let out a chirp indicating that someone was calling. "Pittsburgh people are more genuine. Like I always say—" he broke off as he glanced at the phone screen. "Sorry, but I need to take this. It's an investor for *Ghost*. He's new to the industry and needs some hand holding. I need to reassure him that just because my son is the director, that doesn't mean I'll let you get away with budget over-runs." He shot me a wink and then strode toward the door. "Nepotism can be scary. I'll take this in my office, so you don't have to listen to me talk about you."

EAVESDROPPING

MARA

As I headed out of Don's kitchen, I had an excellent view of the enormous living room.

For serious? This room is as big as a bowling alley.

The fireplace was tall enough to walk into. The carved stone mantel alone was probably worth more than my car.

This kind of opulence was mind-boggling.

As I twisted the lever on the antique gold faucet in the guest bathroom, my hand trembled. The opulence of this room was mind-boggling. Mahogany paneled walls, a crystal chandelier, and leaded glass windows were just a few of the extravagant features. I'd only seen decor like this in high-end hotels, not in private homes. It was a completely different world.

Growing up, my family was comfortable, but nothing like this. Even though my dad was a successful cardiac surgeon, we were paupers compared to the people who lived in this house. I'd been around people in the top one percent, but this was the top point zero one percent. These were the movers and shakers who owned private jets, yachts, and multiple residences around the world.

Ford's childhood was worlds away from mine, despite some surface similarities. He'd grown up around the Hollywood elite, but I never would have guessed he came from this sort of wealth. I felt like a fraud being here, sipping champagne and casually discussing casting actors like Kim Curry and Chris Pitt.

But really—what did I think I was doing? I was nothing more than a stand-in. Who was I to try to turn my brother's graphic novel into a movie? I barely had a creative bone in my body. I wasn't qualified for this! I was a coder and a nerd, riding on Chance's coattails. He was the one who should be here. Not me. I'd bailed on my software company, and my comic book shop was floundering. I should face it... I was a failure. This movie thing was bound to be a disaster as well.

That couldn't happen, though. I couldn't *let* it be a disaster. That wasn't acceptable. No matter what, Ghost had to be a success. I had to make this work.

Pull yourself together, Mara. Breathe. Don't get intimidated by this display of money and power.

I turned off the water and dried my hands on the thick white hand towel, then carefully adjusted it so it hung squarely on the towel bar.

One step at a time. Focus on the moment.

When I spotted a pretty ceramic bottle with the word "lotion" baked into the glaze, I pumped some into my hand more as a delaying tactic than because I really needed it. The delicate floral scent seemed to break through my panic, soothing my frayed nerves. I rubbed it into my hands and forearms as I descended from my momentary freakout.

"You got this," I told my reflection. Damn, if I didn't look determined.

If nothing else, I could fake it.

I could do this. I had a job to do here as Chance's representative. That meant I needed to voice my concerns about Chris Pitt. Chance would have hated having him cast as Ghost, I was certain of it.

But—I'd wait to talk to Ford until after we left this house. Its display of power cowed me. I'd be able to make a stronger argument once we were away from here.

Ford and his dad seemed to have a really good relationship. It reminded me of the way my own dad treated Grayson—as the golden child. Lucky him. Must be nice. Ever since I'd chucked it all and opened Ghost of a Chance, I'd become my dad's least favorite. Sucked to be me.

I sighed. What was it with me and parental displeasure?

Too deep. I'd end up back in a funk if I kept this up. I needed to stay focused here.

"You can do this," I told my reflection.

As I finally headed back to the kitchen, I heard Don's voice emanating from behind the partially open double doors of his office. As I passed, I heard him say, "I can handle my own son."

Well, of course, I stopped in my tracks. Who wouldn't?

"Give the guy some credit," Don continued. "It isn't as though this is his first film. He's an award-winning director. Besides, I'll be there to make sure everything goes smoothly. That's my job, and I'm good at it."

I shouldn't be eavesdropping, so I forced myself to turn to leave.

There was a moment of silence as the person on the other side said something, then Don said, "Don't worry. Just because he and Pitt are friends doesn't mean I'll let him cast the man as the lead. Like I said, I know how to handle my own son. I can promise you, I won't let him ruin the film by making a bad casting choice."

My breath hitched. Who on Earth was Don talking to, and why would he discuss Ford's casting choices when he'd specifically asked us not to? I might have my own doubts about having Pitt play the part of Ghost, but Don had agreed to give him a screen test. He shouldn't be promising someone he'd keep him out of the film.

I backed away from the door and hurried back to the kitchen.

Ford smiled the moment he saw me. He pulled me into his

arms for a kiss. Heady stuff. In an instant, the man made every thought disappear from my brain.

"Dad will be right back. He had to take a call. Are you getting hungry? We have snacks." He gestured toward a tray of appetizers as he bit into a bright-green pepperoncini.

I glanced at the arched opening of the doorway, then grabbed hold of Ford's arm. "Listen, I don't eavesdrop as a general rule, but I happened to overhear something just now that you should know about."

Ford glanced over my shoulder and tensed, then touched my arm as if to silence me.

I turned to see Don sweep into the kitchen. It was a good thing I hadn't lingered outside his door, because he would definitely have caught me.

I shot him a smile and hoped it didn't look strained. "Your home is spectacular."

"Thanks. Not my doing though. Most of it was like this when I bought the place. My late wife picked out the furnishings. I haven't changed a thing since then. I guess I'm a bit set in my ways." He cleared our empty champagne glasses. "You're probably getting hungry. Help yourself to the antipasto tray while I finish getting dinner ready."

Ford continued to chat with his dad about the film as Don pulled a bowl of ceviche from the refrigerator and then emptied his rice-cooker into a serving bowl.

Listening to their easygoing conversation, my tension layered on like the soft cheese I was spreading on my slice of twelve-grain bread. Soon, my stomach roiled with anxiety. Ford had no idea his own father was plotting to undermine his film. I'd clearly pegged Don wrong. I'd seen the supportive side of him and had bought into it, but maybe he and my dad had way too much in common. They both wanted to manipulate their kids.

Ford reached out and snagged a shrimp from the serving bowl of ceviche. "I know you didn't prepare this yourself."

"I picked it up earlier today at Carribbia's. The owner's a friend."

I knew of the Caribbean style restaurant by reputation only. It was supposed to be amazing.

"Why doesn't that surprise me?" Ford said. "You've always loved good food. Why won't you take those cooking classes with me and Max? It'd be fun."

"Not for me." Don set the serving bowls on a large tray and lifted it. "I like to have someone else do most of the cooking. I'd rather socialize with my guests." He tilted his head toward the door. "Let's head to the dining room."

I followed, wondering how Ford would act right now, if he knew what his dad had said. Chance had always felt betrayed when Dad had tried to manipulate him. Would Ford feel the same way? My stomach knotted.

The last thing I ever wanted to do was hurt Ford.

A realization struck me suddenly.

Anything that hurt him would also hurt me.

And that meant... I'd fallen for Ford Ross.

Warmth washed through me at this realization, but that sensation was quickly followed by a tightening in my chest. I glanced at him. What if he didn't feel the same way?

A moment later, his eyes met mine and our fingers interlaced. It was right there, in those amazing blue eyes of his. I mattered to him.

Most of my anxiety evaporated—because after all, maybe he was falling for me too.

YOU ARE RUBBER, I AM GLUE

MARA

Later, I twisted in my seat to watch Don Ross's estate disappear behind some trees as we descended the driveway toward the main road. The home's intimidating effect eased once I couldn't see it anymore, but I still couldn't relax. Not yet.

I took a breath, then yanked off the metaphorical Band-aid. "I mentioned I accidentally eavesdropped. It was when your dad was on the phone in his office. I didn't mean to listen in, but his door was open, and I heard him mention your name."

Ford rolled to a halt at the end of the driveway and glanced at me. "He got a call from an investor who is nervous about whether or not our father-son relationship will cause problems. Nepotism and all that. He had to reassure the guy. It's no big deal."

My hand felt clammy in his. "Actually, it sounded like it really *was* a big deal. I overheard your dad promise not to let you use Chris Pitt."

There. I'd said it. Now it was out there, and we could talk about it.

"You heard him mention Chris by name?" Ford's jaw tensed as he pulled onto the road.

I nodded as I scraped my teeth against my bottom lip. "Whoever he was talking to seemed dead-set against casting him."

Ford squinted and then adjusted the car's visor to block the glare of the setting sun. "He wasn't supposed to tell anyone about my casting plans."

"Well, this guy definitely knew." My entire body tensed as I waited for his reaction—for the shock and betrayal I knew would come.

He sighed, frustrated. "I'll have a word with him. No big deal." He shrugged. "Thanks for the heads up. I'll take care of it."

What? That was it? I stared at him in surprise, but he didn't glance over at me. Was he for real? I mean, sure, he's good at bouncing back from a setback, but this nonchalant reaction didn't even make sense. How could he be so blasé?

My anxiety spiked. In the same type of situation, Chance would have been terribly hurt, and Doug would have been outraged. Then again, Doug was a man of extremes. Calm one moment, furious the next. In love with me one day and screwing another woman the following night. Demanding I take him back, then trying to destroy my business.

That man was broken in some fundamental way.

I glanced at Ford and noted his faint frown. He didn't speak for the rest of the drive, so maybe hearing about Don bothered him more than he let on.

Ford parked in front of Ghost of a Chance. As we headed to my front door, I couldn't get a read on him. He seemed preoccupied, which was understandable. I kicked a small stone, sending it clattering across the sidewalk and into my long shadow. "Your dad's a man of strong opinions."

Ford finally glanced at me. "That's for sure. He's always been that way. He's already pushing his ideas about who to cast and where to shoot."

I opened the street-level door. "Are you worried that your vision for the movie will clash with Don's? What about those script changes he mentioned? What if he insists on a change that isn't true to Chance's vision? You know I won't be okay with that." I pushed open the door and flipped on the staircase light.

"Won't happen. I'd never let him mess with the story. Besides, he won't get involved with that aspect of things. Producers and directors have different roles. I'm in charge of the creative end of things. He handles all the nuts and bolts. Dad has people who will schedule the location shots, pay the cast and crew, arrange for food service, hire a casting company for extras, hire lighting crews... his plate will be full."

But if his dad held the purse-strings, didn't that give him ultimate control? Is that why I was still so uneasy about this—because of the way my own dad always tried to manipulate me and Chance? Money had always been one of Dad's favorite weapons. He loved to give us things and then threaten to withhold them to keep us in check.

With a flash of comprehension, it dawned on me that I'd be sharing control of my brother's creation not only with Ford, but also with scores of people I'd never even met.

A band of anxiety clamped around my chest.

I tried to stomp down my fears like stomping on an ant hill. After all, Ford was an award-winning director. He obviously knew what he was doing, and he loved *Ghost*. Even so, new little worries kept cropping up like ants crawling up my legs.

When we reached the landing, Ford wrapped an arm around my waist and gave me a quick kiss on top of my head. "Thanks for telling me what you overheard. It's probably nothing, but I'll make sure it doesn't turn into something bigger."

That band of tension eased a bit. At least he was taking my worries seriously, but something was still bothering me. Making me feel restless. I needed to figure out what it was so it didn't gnaw away at me.

TRAINING TIME

MARA

I pushed open my door and Zephyr greeted me, jumping up and down on spring-loaded legs.

"Hi, sweetie. Miss me?" I grabbed his leash and a small pouch from the table. "I need to take him out," I told Ford. "It won't take long. Want to join me?"

"Sure. Do you still want to watch Sean's movie together?" he asked, glancing at the Blu-ray sitting on my table.

"Absolutely," I said. I lifted the pouch to eye level. "Training treats. I'm teaching Zephie to stop when we come to a crosswalk. He has the habit of darting onto the road, which terrifies me."

Ford leaned over and scratched Zephyr on the top of his furry head. "Hear that, little guy? Mara wants you to learn to look both ways before you cross the street."

"Exactly." A sensation of lightness swelled in my chest. Ford was so easygoing. Doug would have been irritated if I'd wanted to train my dog while he was around. He'd never liked Zephyr, and the feeling had been mutual. That should have clued me in.

Stop it.

I'd successfully banished Doug from my mind for several days, but here he was, popping up again in my brain-space.

When we reached the bottom of the stairs, I turned toward the nearest crosswalk.

Ford held my hand. "I can tell something's on your mind. Want to talk about it?"

I shot him a sidelong glance. "There's a lot of stuff tumbling around in my head right now. Are you sure you want to hear it?"

He kept his gaze fixed on me, making me believe he really wanted to know what I was thinking. "Always."

Maybe talking would help. "I think this situation with your dad is bringing back echoes from my past. Maybe I'm projecting my own family dynamics onto your relationship with your dad."

Ford stopped, wrapped his arm around my waist, and pulled me against him. "My dad can be a lot to take in. He wanted to impress you tonight, and he works in a world where first impressions matter. A lot. When you get to know the real man behind the persona, I know you'll like him. He's a good guy. I'm sure we'll work well together on *Ghost*. If I wasn't, I'd never have agreed to partner with him. I'm sorry if either of us did anything tonight to upset you."

I shook my head and let out a heavy sigh. "Lately, I've let too many things upset me. I think I must have some seriously unresolved crap complicating my life. My ex-boyfriend is mixed up in there too, but most of my angst centers on Chance and my dad." I paused. "And my store and Stel-Wood."

"That's a lot. It sounds like you need someone to talk things over with."

"Are you offering?" I tensed, realizing how much his answer mattered.

His clear blue eyes seemed to take in every nuance in my expression. "Sure. Isn't that my job as your boyfriend?"

The streetlights around town winked on at precisely that moment, and my heart stumbled a beat. Had I heard that right? "Is that what you are? My boyfriend?"

He moved closer. "Is that okay?"

I leaned into him, touching my forehead to his. "More than okay."

Overwhelmed by the intensity of the moment, I closed my eyes. Something seemed to ease within me. A solid thing—a thing I hadn't even been aware of—felt as though it softened and shifted to make space for Ford. The two of us being together was a good thing. The right thing. The inevitable thing.

I opened my eyes to find him watching me, a slight smile tugging at the corners of his mouth. "You have amazing eyes," he said. "Did you know that? Their cognac color is gorgeous, but it's more than that. When your eyes soften this way..." he shook his head, "...I don't know. It gets me right here." He slid his hand over his heart, and mine thumped hard in my chest.

Damn. This guy was making me fall for him even more.

Too much, too fast.

So, what did I do? I retreated to think, like some frightened airhead who didn't know how to relate. Was I afraid of where our relationship was headed, or did I simply have too much other stuff going on tonight?

"Let's finish up with Zephyr."

He peered at me a moment, and then squeezed my hand. It felt as though he understood I needed to change the subject and was giving me space to breathe, and I really, really liked that about him right now.

I set off for the corner as I interlaced my fingers with his, keeping him close.

My thoughts went back to dinner at Don's. Something about tonight still bothered me. "You know, watching you with your dad reminded me of all the times my own father tried to control my life. Your dad is pretty subtle about it. Mine is more like a Border Collie, always poking and prodding and herding us to make us go where he wants. Grayson and I always did what he wanted, but Chance balked. Dad focused all his heavy-handed manipulation on him. For some reason, my younger sisters got a pass."

"Dad had his own ways of manipulating us," Ford said, his forehead tight with this uncomfortable topic. "I think all parents do."

I arched one eyebrow. "Did he constantly berate and demean whoever wouldn't comply? My dad seemed to love that part. He mostly focused on Chance, but since we're twins, his digs really got to me."

Ford winced as he shook his head. "My dad was more into quiet befuddlement rather than outright disapproval. He was supportive, even when we made decisions he didn't agree with—unless we were doing something genuinely bad for us. When Sean was seventeen and wanted to go skydiving, Dad did every-thing he could to stop him, including refusing to sign a waiver, but as soon as Sean turned eighteen, he went on his first jump. Dad was royally pissed."

"Did he ostracize Sean? Demean him?"

"Ostracize? Nope. That wasn't Dad's style."

"It was *my* dad's style. Especially with Chance. Grayson was Dad's favorite—probably because they had so much in common. They still do, since Grayson does cancer research. Chance was Grayson's polar opposite. Dad shut Chance out entirely. When he died, they hadn't spoken in over a year. I'm still angry about it."

We came to a crosswalk. Zephyr remembered his new training and immediately sat. He looked up at me for approval. I fished a treat from the pouch and gave it to him, and when the light changed, we crossed.

"Chance was never into the sciences," I said. "He was a pure artist. He took after our mom that way. I've never understood how Dad completely accepted Mom's dancing and choreography, but refused to support Chance's art. My sisters got a pass from him too. Maybe it was because they're performers, like Mom."

"In my family, we're mostly the creative type," Ford said. "My big sister Hailey is the exception. She's the accountant of the bunch."

I cracked a smile. "No accountants in my family tree. Only

science nerds and artists—and me, the shopkeeper. I've been thinking about it ever since you made that comment about me being logical. Scientists and artists have two key attributes in common. Creativity and grit."

"Creativity and grit," Ford repeated. "I like that. You're right. You couldn't make a name for yourself in a creative field if you didn't have both."

"Add some inspiration into the mix and you have something pretty special. That was Chance—pretty special. I just wish my dad hadn't been blind to it."

A couple stepped out of a restaurant, and the scent of wood-fired pizza wafted out along with them. The man, one of my regular customers, tossed me a wave as he headed for a nearby car. I waved back.

I squeezed Ford's hand and then let go. "Give me a minute while I work on something with Zephyr."

I walked to the edge of the street. Zephyr changed course and hurried to the curb where he promptly sat down and then looked up at me.

"Good boy." I grinned as I leaned down and scratched between his ears. I gave him another treat and then turned back to Ford. We continued on down the sidewalk.

"Our dream of opening a comic book shop started when we were kids. We planned. We prepared. Yes, I majored in computer science, but I minored in business. Chance studied fine arts as well as marketing. His dreams were to write his own comic book and run the store. My plan was to create awesome video games and handle the store's back end. Chance was supposed to chat with customers about comic books, handle day-to-day sales stuff, and stock the shelves."

"It sounds like your brother had a practical side. Even if he never found an audience for his comics, he could have supported himself with the store."

"That was the idea. Chance wasn't some vague wishful thinker. He had plans. Big ones. Dad could only see him as a dreamer though, and he hated the idea of our store. Even when Chance started having some success, Dad never believed in him. It was heartbreaking. The things he said—they were downright cruel." My throat grew tight, and I had to stop talking.

"Where did all that come from? Why was your dad so against your brother's choices? It doesn't make sense considering your mom is a choreographer."

I shrugged. "I think it has to do with Mom's sister. Aunt Jackie couldn't support herself as a painter and ended up becoming a bank teller. She wasn't happy though. She got evicted a couple of times and ended up staying with us. I liked having her there, but Dad didn't. He'd always use her as an example of how hard it was to make a living off of art."

I focused on a house ahead of us. We'd reached the end of Sewickley's business district, and ahead a tree-lined street with houses beckoned us. I could see a family through the window of the house as they gathered in their dining room. A toddler in a highchair happily stuffed something into her mouth. The other kids and the parents sat down, looking happy to be together.

Mom had always had us sit down to dinner together, too. Sometimes she'd have each of us tell everyone about something we were thankful for that had happened that day. She'd say it was a way to get us to focus on the good things in life rather than always worrying about things that went wrong. Huh. I guess she did that to combat Dad's constant criticisms.

No one was allowed to complain during dinner. She was always there for us, in her own subtle way. When dad broke the rule, she'd always call him out on it, but sometimes the damage had already been done.

I shook my head and turned away as I brushed tears from my cheek. I hated showing weakness. Maybe I shouldn't have started talking about this.

Ford tugged at my elbow, not giving up until I relented and turned to face him. When I met his gaze, I only found sympathy there. He cared. My feelings mattered to him.

I could feel my heart melting into an even bigger puddle.

Ford pulled me into his arms and held me close.

This. Being in his arms. This felt so good. He held me until my breathing steadied once again. I tipped my face up and gazed into his eyes. I liked this. I liked being able to trust him. To have him hold me.

"How about one of my famous back rubs?" he asked, stroking my back.

"I'd love that. I don't think we ever got to it last time." I changed course and pulled him toward the street. I fully intended to jaywalk, but when I reached the curb, Zephyr sat. I took a step past him, and then I stopped and let out a laugh. "Good boy." I glanced at Ford. "He's better at crossing the street now than I am."

"The student has surpassed the teacher."

I looked both ways, then we crossed. "I have to admit, when Chance was killed by that drunk driver, I kind of lost it. He died right as things were finally coming together for him. We were almost ready to open the shop." Where was all this coming from? It was like a dam had broken and all these thoughts and feelings were pouring out. "Chance would run it, and I would stay in Boston and handle the orders."

"You lived in Boston? I don't think I knew that."

"I went to MIT. Destiny was my roommate." The chorus of crickets dimmed momentarily as a car drove past us, then resurged. "When we graduated, we started our own video game company. At first, Dad was nervous about Stel-Wood. He thought we should work for a bigger company to 'learn the ropes' before we started off on our own, but after investors began handing us money, he changed his mind. Then, when Chance and I decided to open a comic book store, he thought the idea was too risky. We ignored him. When Chance died and I sold my half of Stel-Wood back to Destiny, he freaked out and said I was gambling everything on Ghost of a Chance."

"I still think that's a clever name for your store."

I gave a wry smile. "Chance and I had been brainstorming ideas, but we hadn't settled on one. When he died, I realized this one was perfect on multiple levels. It also had the added benefit of irritating my dad."

The corner of Ford's mouth twitched in a smile. "How's that?"

"Because he always told Chance he didn't have a ghost of a chance of making a living with his comic books."

Ford let out a laugh. "I love it even more."

"Switching careers and moving here were big decisions. My dad thought I was overreacting, but I knew I was doing the right thing. I still do. I never could have lived with myself if I'd made any other decision." I shrugged. "Dad still pushes me to go back into the video game industry."

The sun was barely visible now, coloring the clouds with waves of orange, red, and pink. Gorgeous. Peaceful. I let out a heavy sigh. "I have so much more respect for Chance now—with the way he stood up to Dad for so long. The man is relentless."

"You're strong and intelligent. Hardworking, too. I'm impressed with everything you've achieved."

"Thanks." My chest swelled with pride. Ford always made me feel better about myself.

When we turned at the next corner, I could see the awning of my store a couple of blocks ahead. "The decision to leave Stel-Wood was hard. I hated leaving it, but I couldn't abandon Ghost of a Chance either. It's probably why I'm so conflicted about starting another business with Destiny."

"And now? Are you any closer to deciding if you'll accept her offer?"

I slumped next to my front door, wishing things could be more straightforward. Wishing I could somehow divine the future and see how things would turn out. "I really don't know. I feel more confused than ever. How can I give up on my store? It would break my heart."

His gaze swept over my face, taking me in. It was as though he could see something there no one else could. "Success can come in other ways, too. Maybe you need to take another look at the goals you want to achieve with your store and decide if there are other paths to get you there. You might see something new now that a year has passed. I know you'll figure something out. I have faith in you."

I was quiet for a moment. His advice resonated with me as I entered the code on my front door keypad. "That's a really good idea," I said as I pushed open the door. "I'll take a fresh look at everything—tomorrow."

"Tomorrow. Tonight, I want to focus on you and help you relax." He wrapped an arm around my waist, nuzzled my neck, and placed a lingering kiss below my ear that sent tingles of delight coursing through me.

CHRIS PITT?

MARA

When my alarm went off the next morning, I was alone in bed. I could hear Ford moving around in the kitchen. I smiled. He was probably cooking something delicious.

My groggy self only bounced off the wall once as I headed to the bathroom where I took a regrettably brief shower. As I turned off the water, I heard the bathroom door open with a click.

"I already took Zephyr for a walk," Ford said. "I have to run back over to my place to get cleaned up. I'm meeting Chris for brunch in the city."

"Chris?"

"Chris Pitt. He texted me he has the day off from shooting. I need to discuss the screen test with him."

My stomach clenched. Him again. Things were moving fast on the Chris Pitt front. I opened my mouth to repeat my concerns about casting him as Ghost, but instead, I heard myself saying, "Drive carefully."

Wimp.

An instant later, my brain caught up to the first part of what Ford had said. "And thanks for taking Zephyr out."

"No problem." The bathroom door clicked, and he was gone.

I grabbed a t-shirt from the top of the stack in my dresser. One of my favorites. Black with a sketch of Ghost in white ink.

I smoothed my hand over it. I'd brought Chance the black t-shirt and he'd created this for me with a few quick strokes of fabric paint. It was my very favorite t-shirt. Fingers crossed it would bring me luck today.

I tugged on my jeans, shoved my feet into my red Chucks, and then pulled my damp hair into a ponytail.

Running on autopilot, I scurried downstairs, turned off the security system, unlocked the front door, and flipped the sign to read "open." My first customers of the day were already waiting.

My brain was having a hard time processing the idea that my boyfriend was hanging out with Chris Pitt today. Of course, my brain was also currently doing cartwheels about Ford being my boyfriend in the first place, so apparently it was a bit overtaxed.

Ford and I led vastly different lives. He was used to the spotlight. Me... not so much. In fact, I avoided it.

The one brush I'd had with the local news station a few months ago where Doug had arranged to have me ambushed had left me shaken and my business in shambles.

What would it be like to live in a world where reporters were always lurking? Where having brunch with a movie star was an everyday occurrence? Spending time with Ford in our little Sewickley bubble had made me forget he was a celebrity in his own right.

Could I handle living in the ambient glow of Ford's fame? If I wanted this relationship to last beyond a few weeks, I'd need to reconcile myself to the idea that some of that light might spill over onto me.

I grimaced.

At least people didn't obsess about directors as much as they crushed on movie stars. Since directors weren't on screen, they could more easily go incognito.

What about my sister Rachael's growing fame on Broadway? Did it ever get to her?

A few months ago, I had visited her in New York City to attend the show she was in. Rachael had landed the part of Frenchy in Grease and was receiving rave reviews. After the performance, we left through a stage door behind the building and stumbled into a swarm of people gathered there. Rachael glowed under their attention as she walked through the gauntlet of theatergoers and paparazzi, and I was pulled along in her wake as she headed toward our waiting car. At that moment, I was grateful for the lack of attention directed my way.

If I attended an event with Ford, the spotlight would undoubtedly be on him. I could fade into the background and enjoy the evening without being the center of attention. It sounded like the perfect scenario.

A customer came to the register, and from that point on, a steady stream kept me busy.

Just after lunch, three middle-school-aged girls flung open my door and came tumbling into the store.

"Is he here yet?" a girl wearing a pink t-shirt asked. She looked around, searching for someone.

"No one's here but me," I replied, trying to hide my amusement. Did she have a crush on a classmate? Someone should clue her in that stalking was never a good idea. "Who are you looking for?"

"Chris Pitt!" The girl in pink squeaked. Her outburst was immediately followed by squeals of excitement from her friends.

A solid weight settled in my chest. This had Ford's fingerprints all over it. "What makes you think Chris Pitt is supposed to be here?"

"He tweeted it! He said he's visiting Ghost of a Chance in Sewickley and plans to sign autographs for an hour or so. Are we the first ones?"

"It looks that way." I tried to control my irritation as I called Ford. The least he could have done was ask if I was okay with this.

The phone rang twice and then went to voicemail. I stared

down at my phone as my face grew hotter. Seriously? He'd rejected my call?

I hung up without leaving a message, and a moment later my phone vibrated with an incoming text.

Ford: Be there in five minutes with Chris.

My hand twitched and I nearly dropped my phone. For a moment, all I could do was stare at that text. When I finally unfroze, my thumbs flew across the screen.

Me: You're bringing Chris Pitt here? Why didn't you ask me first?

Ford: His idea. He sent out a tweet announcing it without telling me. TTYS.

Talk To You Soon? Seriously?

My hands started shaking. I was freaking out. Flashbacks of Doug's news crew crashed into me. The pushy cameraman. The smarmy reporter from hell, Harry. Harry the hateful.

I'd completely botched that interview. The reporter had twisted everything, editing my responses to make it sound like my store was failing. How could I possibly handle a media event like this with no warning? With a star like Chris Pitt on the premises, Ghost of a Chance would be inundated.

I glanced out the window to see teenagers piling out of two cars.

I let out a frustrated sigh. I'd have to adapt, not that I had a choice. Admittedly, this could give Ghost of a Chance some great publicity if I played it right...

My thumbs flew across my phone screen as I shot off a group text that included my brother Grayson, as well as Conner, Courtney, Lianna, and Scarlet. Rose worked Saturdays at the library, so she wouldn't be able to come help.

> Me: I'm in trouble. I need you ASAP at my store. Chris Pitt just tweeted he's coming here to sign autographs. It will be a stampede. HELP!!!

I stared at my phone, waiting for a reply.

> Grayson: Can't come right now. I'm out of town judging a high school science competition. I'll be gone at least four hours, but I can come when I get back.

My stomach sank. Strike one. I texted back.

> Me: Don't bother, Grayson. He should be gone by then. Thanks anyway.

> Lianna: I'll be right there. Gertrude says she's coming too.

> Me: Thank you!!!

> Conner: On my way.

> Me: You guys are my heroes!

The band of panic constricting my chest eased a bit. I closed my eyes and took a deep, calming breath. With a little help from my friends, I might survive this.

My phone chirped again.

> Courtney: Just finished lunch. Be there in fifteen minutes.

> Scarlet: Chris Pitt? That's awesome! I'm calling Chief Brown to help with crowd control. Be there ASAP. Stop freaking out! This is a GOOD THING!

I shook my head. Of course, Scarlet would be thrilled to have a movie star drop into Sewickley like a bombshell. I tried to remind myself she wasn't wrong. I bet she laid awake at night fantasizing about moments like this.

Over the next few minutes, three more groups of people came into the store asking about Chris. Pretty soon my little shop would be filled to capacity.

Through the front window, I spotted Ford's car pulling into the last empty spot out front. I couldn't make out the features of the man in the passenger seat, but then he unfurled himself—all six-foot-three inches of him. Chris Pitt, in the flesh. A blond-haired, blue-eyed, god among mortals.

As he strode into the store, everyone broke into applause. A huge grin split his face. The man was clearly in his element. "Hello, Sewickley!" he called out, his deep, resonant voice filling the store.

Everyone burst into another round of applause.

I tamped down my anxiety. Right now, my job was to pull off the role of the grateful shopkeeper. My brain scrambled, trying to figure out logistics. Where would I put him? Maybe behind my folding table? I'd need to grab it from the back room.

I pasted on a smile as I approached Chris. "Hi. I'm Mara Stellar. Welcome to my store."

Ford headed into the back room without even glancing at me. What the heck?

"Your brother wrote *Ghost*, right?" Chris gestured toward my t-shirt, and I remembered I was wearing the one with Chance's original drawing. "I read the entire series. It's awesome."

Pride filled me. "Thank you so much." Was I blushing? The heat in my cheeks made me feel like just another silly fan girl. "Chance would be thrilled."

I spotted Ford returning, carrying my folding table. I'd hosted a couple of signings for local comic book authors, and the table had been perfect for them to sit behind while they signed autographs.

Ford caught my eye as he set up the table near the cash register. He grimaced and gave a resigned shrug in what I think was meant to be an apology.

Seriously? He and Chris ambush me and all I get is a shrug? Not good enough. Not by a long shot. Pulling this off could make or break me.

"Let's get organized," Conner called out to the crowd, taking me by surprise. When had he arrived? He'd gotten here fast. I'd assumed he'd be busy handling the lunch crowd down at Not A Yacht Club. "If you all form a line that weaves through the shelves, I think we can fit more people in the store. The ones stuck outside will appreciate the air conditioning."

As people shuffled around to comply, I finally cornered Ford.

"What the frack?" I couldn't help feeling a little freaked out about this. "Why would Chris Pitt tweet he was coming here without checking with me first?" I whisper-shouted. "You know how I feel about getting the wrong kind of publicity. What if this backfires like last time?"

"I know—I'm sorry. I didn't plan this. I think Chris got caught up in wanting to promote your store. He sent the tweet without thinking it through."

I shot Chris a scowl, but his attention was focused on the girl in pink who'd been the first to show up. Chris was using a black Sharpie to autograph her red backpack. The girl stared at him in star-struck wonder.

My anger eased as I vicariously enjoyed her excitement.

"Don't be mad at him," Ford said. "He just wanted to help you out. Give your store the boost it needs."

My eyes widened. "He thinks my store is in trouble?" I asked. "What did you tell him? I told you about my problems in confidence."

He looked contrite. "I told him your store would get a needed boost once people figured out the connection to the movie. I think I said something about turning things around for you. I'm sorry. It was careless of me."

I stared at him, appalled that a casual conversation could

create a media frenzy like this. "We'll talk about this later," I said, then let it go—for now. I had other things to worry about.

Ford was distracting, though. I couldn't help noticing how good he looked. After he'd left my place and gone home, he'd apparently showered and changed into the khakis and collared shirt he now wore, but his jaw was rough with yesterday's stubble. I had to stop myself from reaching out to stroke his cheek. "No time to shave?"

"I was running late. Someone kept me up late last night." Fortunately, he leaned in to kiss me, so I got to feel that soft bristle after all.

When he pulled away, I frowned at him. "I'm still annoyed with you. Especially since you look so much better than I do right now." I tucked a fading, blue-tipped strand of hair behind my ear that had escaped my updo, wishing I'd taken the time to do more than tie it back in a ponytail this morning.

"Mara!"

I whirled around and spotted Courtney at the entrance. A broad-shouldered customer I didn't recognize stood there like a storm trooper on crowd control, blocking her way.

I lifted my arm and shouted, "She isn't a rebel invader! Let her in. She's here to help me."

The big guy shrugged and moved aside.

I glanced at Ford. "Shouldn't someone like Chris Pitt have a bodyguard with him?"

Ford winced. "Yeah, he should. Chris ditched him. Matty is pissed. He'll be here any minute."

As Courtney approached, her self-assured attitude had everyone clearing a path for her. She didn't pause as she passed me and claimed the spot behind the sales counter. "I'll handle the purchases. You deal with everything else."

I let out a sigh of relief. "Thanks, Courtney. You're a lifesaver."

Lianna arrived a moment later with Gertrude in tow. The storm trooper glanced at me. At my nod, he stepped aside to let them pass. They were dressed casually—Lianna in black yoga pants and an athletic top, and Gertrude in jeans and a pale blue t-shirt.

"You had great timing with that text," Lianna said as she reached me. "Gertrude and I had just finished loading my car when it arrived. We moved the last of my personal stuff out of Paul's house today. He and I still need to divide up the furniture, but at least I have all my clothes and personal things." She inched closer to me to let someone shuffle past her. "I'll handle crowd control inside the store."

"Wait, you're dividing up stuff?" I asked.

"We're getting a divorce," she said.

I stared, not sure what to say. Sorry? Congratulations? "Let me know if you need help with anything," I said.

"I can help Courtney at the register," Gertrude added. "I'll bag purchases." She laid claim to the stool next to Courtney.

A flash of sunlight from outside blinded me momentarily. Through the front window, I spotted a large white van pulling to a stop in the middle of the street, and I immediately recognized the logo for W-ZZZ TV.

My stomach somersaulted nauseatingly as my anxiety flared. That was the station Doug worked for—the one that had nearly put me out of business six months ago.

What if his reporter friend was here? What if he tried to sabotage me again? My store couldn't handle another blow like that.

Before I thought better of it, I headed out the front door with Ford right behind me.

Scarlet stood next to the news van, smiling warmly and chatting with the driver. She pointed toward a nearby alley, and the driver nodded. A moment later, he pulled into the alleyway so he didn't block traffic.

A young woman wearing a crisp suit and low pumps exited the van. She smoothed her clothes before holding out her hand to shake Scarlet's.

She had to be the reporter since everyone else piling out of the van wore t-shirts and jeans.

I watched a moment longer, but the man who'd interviewed me six months ago didn't appear. Good, but I hesitated. Should I walk over there, or stand back?

"What's wrong?" Ford asked, his gaze assessing me.

I jutted my chin toward the news van. "That's the station Doug works for. I'm kind of freaking out that they're here."

Ford tensed. "Your ex? Is he here, too?"

I shook my head. "I haven't seen him."

"They're probably just covering the story. With luck, this will bring you some free publicity."

I frowned, still worried. "In my experience, not all publicity is good publicity." Then I let out a sigh as I tried to release some of my anxiety. "But maybe you're right. Maybe this will all work out."

I turned, preparing to follow Ford back into the store, but then I spotted it. A familiar black Camaro tooling down the street.

Doug's car. It pulled into the alley, right behind the news van.

"He's here," I told Ford.

He whirled around.

Doug climbed out of his Camaro, locked eyes with me, and smirked.

Asshat.

Bantha poo-doo.

Disaster waiting to happen.

That man had a lot of nerve showing up here again. I couldn't wait to eviscerate him.

INTO THE FIRE

FORD

Mara looked like she was about to lose it. I hurried to keep up with her as she stalked toward the smirking asshole standing next to a black Camaro.

I evaluated the situation. Considering the news crew setting up just a few feet away, any sort of blowup could become a disaster of epic proportions.

"Mara." I darted around her, inserting myself between her and her infamous ex. "You need to calm down. This is a delicate situation."

"Calm down? Calm down?" She leveled a furious gaze at me. "You do *not* get to tell me to calm down. I'm in this situation because of *you*. You and Chris Pitt!"

I held up my hands in surrender. "Bad choice of words. I just want you to notice the news crew watching us. You need to consider whether you want everything you're about to say broadcast on the evening news."

That seemed to stop her cold.

Mayor Scarlet Smith's bright, airy voice called out, "Doug Aspin. As I live and breathe."

I whirled to see her stroll up to the man, a predatory grin on her face.

"I never expected you to set foot in my fair city again," she said.

"This is a public street." A smarmy grin slid across Doug's face. He glanced at Mara and gave a self-satisfied smirk. "I want my news crew to get the shop owner on camera."

Scarlet's heels gave an authoritative click as she stepped between him and Mara. "Am I right in recalling there's still an outstanding bench warrant for your arrest?"

His eyes widened.

"Ah, I see you remember that. I thought it would be neighborly of me to point out that the police chief is right over there handling crowd management."

Doug's face paled. He took a step back, edging toward his car. "I—I just remembered—"

"That you have somewhere else to be?" Scarlet blinked at him. "How fortuitous."

Doug climbed into his car, backed out of the alley, and slowly, cautiously, drove away.

Mara moved to stand with the mayor. She crossed her arms and bumped shoulders with Scarlet. "Thanks. I think you saved me from making a fool of myself."

"I think he wanted to get under your skin," I commented. "Maybe start something he could get on camera."

"My thoughts exactly," Scarlet said.

Mara scowled and then headed back into the store, ignoring me. Was she still angry? Not that I could blame her.

The last thing I ever wanted was to give Doug a way to hurt her again, but that's exactly what I'd done today. I needed to do something about that guy before he did any more damage.

I glanced at the reporter pinning a microphone to her lapel. She looked harried. At least this was something I could handle. I was pretty good at this part of the entertainment business.

"Hello." I held out my hand.

The reporter's frustration disappeared as she flashed a smile and shook my hand. She cocked her head to one side. "You're Ford Ross, right?"

"I am. I came here with Chris Pitt today. I want to make sure everything goes smoothly. And you're...?"

"Mindy. Mindy Trevor. I'm new with W-ZZZ."

"That might work in your favor. I take it you aren't the reporter who did the piece on this store six months ago?"

She hesitated as she thought. "No. That must have been Harry."

I moved closer as I lowered my voice so that only she could hear me. "Well, Harry got a lot of facts wrong in his story. I'm sure you'll understand why I'm worried about slander."

Mindy's face pinched in a combination of worry and affront. "I assure you I have no intention of slandering you or Chris Pitt."

I kept my gaze fixed on hers, searching for any deceit. "Does that apply to the store owner as well?"

"Of course. I'm not sure what you heard—"

"I heard that a slanderous report caused this business financial harm. I want your promise that nothing like that will happen again before I let you speak to Chris."

"I promise. It's not like that. I'm not doing investigative journalism. Just a bit of celebrity gossip about a star visiting a small town, that's all."

I scrutinized her, but she kept her cool.

I decided to take her at her word. After all, publicity was the entire reason Chris had made that tweet. "If Chris agrees to a quick interview, I'll try to clear it with the shop owner. She has the final say."

The woman's eyes glowed with satisfaction. "Thank you."

After giving her one last look of warning, I headed back toward Mara's shop.

Conner stood outside the entrance, only letting in a few people at a time as others left.

"Thanks for being here," I told him.

Conner shrugged. "Mara said come. I came. I know she'd do the same for me. We always do what we can to support each other. She hosted a Magic the Gathering event upstairs in my restaurant a few months ago, and it was a huge success."

A black Lincoln MKT pulled into a space that opened up. The intimidating man who climbed out wore a dark suit and sunglasses.

"Matty's here," I said. "Chris's bodyguard. He looks furious. Chris ditched him before he made that tweet and set off this chain of events."

Conner smirked. "I can't say as I blame the guy. This is a hell of a scene."

Matty came to a stop directly in front of us, his imposing form blocking out the sun. "This your circus?" he asked in an intimidating, gravelly voice that would stop a heartbeat.

I shrugged. "What can I say? Chris does what he wants."

Matty gave an irritated grunt of agreement. "That's the problem." He pushed past us like a steamroller and entered the store.

"This might be a circus, but Scarlet's doing a great job as ringmaster," Conner commented as the bulldozer did his thing and headed toward Chris.

"Scarlet got rid of Doug pretty easily," I commented.

Conner smirked. "I heard the whole thing. Priceless."

"She looks like she's in her element."

"Dealing with all this stuff?" Conner nodded proudly. "Of course, she is. She's the mayor, after all, and she's damned good at her job. Don't tell her I said that though." He watched her, frowning. "She's a big fish for this little pond."

"Do you think she has bigger political aspirations? State? National?"

"Hard to say." Conner's expression shuttered, and he stopped watching her. "She knows what it takes since she worked on her uncle's campaigns. Talk about a circus. This is nothing compared to that. She'd be under a microscope."

As another group exited the store and headed for a car, I

spotted something seriously wrong. "Why isn't anyone carrying packages?"

"I guess they only came for autographs," Conner said with a frown.

I turned for the door. "That defeats the purpose of having him here. I need to talk to Chris."

Inside, I scanned the room. Lots of people were browsing the shelves. Some were even reading comics while they waited, but Courtney stood slouched behind the register, a sour expression on her face, not ringing up purchases.

When I approached Chris, Matty stood like a boulder in my path, pointedly ignoring me. The man could hold a grudge.

I squeezed past him and spoke to Chris, who gave a curt nod, then stood and addressed the crowd.

"Hey, everyone. Thanks for coming today. I wanted to take a moment to thank the owner of Ghost of a Chance, Mara Stellar, for letting us take over her store today. I doubt her regular customers can even get through the door right now with that long line. Join me in a round of applause for her."

The crowd clapped and cheered. Someone shouted, "Great store!"

"It *is* a great store. I'm glad you said so," Chris said. "I've noticed a lot of you are enjoying her comic books, and even reading them as you stand in line. That's great, as long as you buy them. You'd make me happy if you'd show your appreciation by making a purchase here today. Yinz can do that, right?"

The crowd chuckled at Chris's use of the Pittsburghese word as another round of applause erupted. Within moments, nearly every person in line prominently clutched a comic or some other item.

As Courtney rang up a purchase a few moments later, Mara joined me. She shot Chris a confounded expression. "I can't believe he did that for me. That was really cool of him."

"It's the whole reason he came here today—to give your store a boost. He's a good guy."

Chris posed for yet another photo. The woman next to him looked euphoric as she wrapped her arm around his toned waist.

"You're right." She sounded surprised. "He's nothing like what I'd expected."

"Want help restocking the shelves?"

She looked startled when she noticed how empty they were. "I got it covered. Keep an eye on things out here."

I nodded, and she headed back to her storeroom.

I checked in with Courtney as she rang up another sale.

"Anything I can do to help?" I asked.

"Tell Mara we're running low on bags," Courtney said.

Gertrude smiled at the twenty-something man as she bagged his purchase. "You're Tiffany's son, right? Tell her Gertrude says hi. I hope you stop back again soon." Then she gave the next woman in line a broad smile. "Hi there. I haven't seen you around before. Are you new to the area?"

"No. I live across the river in Moon. My daughter saw Chris's tweet and practically dragged me here."

"We're glad to have you," Gertrude said. "Now that you know we're here, you'll have to come back."

The twelve-year-old flipping through her new comic book glanced up at this. "Can we, Mom? This place is cool."

A few minutes later, Mara carried out an armload of collectible items to replace the ones she'd sold. She set out a Wonder Woman figurine, and a woman in her forties immediately snatched it off the display stand.

"I love this," a woman said, her voice bright with excitement. "Wonder Woman is my favorite." She lifted her sparkly rainbow-colored rhinestone necklace styled as a Wonder Woman emblem.

"Me too." Mara held up her cuff-style bracelet with the "W" design and grinned. "We regularly have unique pieces of jewelry. I have some new items arriving on Thursday. You should come back."

The woman's eyes widened as she handed her credit card to Courtney. "I will."

"You're making a killing," I said to Mara.

"True, and thank you, but I'm still irritated with you." She set a new collectible statue on the shelf to replace the one the woman had just bought.

"I understand completely. Let me apologize to you tonight over dinner and a bottle of wine."

She shot me a sidelong look. "At least you know how to grovel." She hesitated, then relented and said, "Okay, it's a date."

An hour later, Chris glanced at his watch, said something to Matty, and then waved me over.

"I need to wrap this up," Chris said. "Can you tell your guy at the door to make sure no one else lines up?"

"Got it." I headed outside to talk to Conner and was relieved to see there were only a handful of people waiting. I passed on the message.

Conner nodded. "No problem. I'll squeeze this group inside and turn away any newcomers."

Back inside, I flipped the sign to "closed," then noted all the empty spots on the shelves and in the front window. Mara was kneeling as she scraped a piece of gum off the floor.

I dropped down next to her. "Chris is leaving soon."

She sent me a thankful look. "Maybe that's for the best. Not that he hasn't been amazing, but my storeroom is empty. I'm out of nearly everything." She looked exhausted.

Twenty minutes later, the last autograph-seeker left. A few latecomers stood outside, hoping to catch a glimpse of Chris.

Mara approached Chris and held out her hand for him to shake. "Thanks for doing this."

He took it and pulled her into a hug. "You're welcome. Anything for a friend of Ford's. And I'm sorry I didn't run it past you first. I got ahead of myself."

"It all could have ended in mondo-madness," she admitted, "but with my friends pitching in to wrangle the crowd, everything worked out. Give a girl some warning next time."

"Will do." Chris turned to me and flashed that million-dollar smile the camera and fans loved so much. "You're driving me back, right? We still need to talk about that movie you want to make. Let's talk over dinner."

I tensed and glanced at Mara.

The smile left her eyes, but all she said was, "I'll see you tomorrow then."

In a low voice, I murmured, "Are you sure? I promised you dinner."

She shook her head. "I'm worn out, and I'm not exactly in my happy place right now, so maybe this is for the best."

As we headed out the door, Matty stayed close. "I'll follow in the limo." Matty glowered at Chris. "Don't try to lose me, or you'll be looking for a new bodyguard."

A few fans pushed closer, but Matty kept them at a distance. The reporter from W-ZZZ did her brief interview, and then Chris climbed into my passenger seat.

On the drive back, Chris didn't notice that I was distracted, and he kept our conversation going. "It felt great to help a small business," he said. I could tell he was still on a high from all that public adoration.

Once we were in Chris's suite, he turned on the news and flipped channels until he found W-ZZZ.

"I'm going to shower," Chris said, tossing me the remote as he headed into the adjoining bedroom. "Give me a shout when they mention the signing."

Fifteen minutes later, the exterior of Ghost of a Chance appeared on the screen.

"It's on." I turned up the volume.

Chris hurried in, his hair still wet. The scent of lemongrass soap wafted in with him. He plopped onto the sofa next to me.

"Fans of Chris Pitt descended upon a small comic book shop in Sewickley today after the movie star tweeted he'd be there signing autographs," a man's voice intoned.

A customer appeared on screen, and I recognized her as a Wonder Woman fan who'd chatted with Mara. "I'm so excited. I can't believe I met Chris Pitt in person. He's totally hot. And so sweet."

As the camera panned back to show the long line of fans waiting to enter the store, the male voiceover returned. "Our viewers will be heartened to witness this shop's 'rags to riches' story. It was featured in our report on struggling businesses a few months ago." Some silent footage of Mara during the months-old interview came up. She had that deer-in-the-headlights look of someone who wasn't happy with how an interview was going. The man doing the voiceover continued. "Ghost of a Chance seems to be living up to its name as the owner pulls out all the stops in an effort to keep her store from folding. This is Harry Hamilton, with W-ZZZ TV."

"What the hell?" Chris said. "Who's the guy doing the voice-over? I never talked to a male reporter."

"That's because he wasn't there." My heart sank. When a woman appeared on screen for a brief instant, holding out a microphone toward Chris, I said, "She was the only reporter. Mindy Trevor."

The camera zoomed in, cutting Mindy out of frame. Apparently, her interview wouldn't be her big break after all. "Mara's gonna be pissed."

Chris scowled at the screen. "I can't say I blame her. I'll never do another interview with that station. I'll have my PR person rip into them."

I called Mara, and she answered on the second ring. "Ford? Did you see it?"

The panic in her voice hit me like a blow. "I did."

"This is exactly what I was afraid of. Doug is behind this. I know he is. It's totally his style. This is why I didn't want the publicity."

"This should've been great for you. With any other news station, it would've been. I'm so sorry."

"Sorry doesn't stop the rumors." The words sliced into me like a lash, but what cut the deepest was the sound of barely restrained tears in her voice. "Sorry doesn't kill the story Doug and Harry put out—" She cut herself off. "I don't want to argue with you over the phone. We need to talk. In person."

The line went dead.

I stared down at her image on my phone before it disappeared and was replaced by my home screen.

We need to talk.

Mara had been right. There weren't any words more ominous than those.

40

RECUPERATING

MARA

I'd never been more thankful for Sunday to arrive.

I kneeled between my store's shelving units as I slipped the last product label into its plastic sleeve. I'd spent the day reorganizing everything—a chore I'd been postponing for months. Today was the perfect day for the job. I needed busy work to distract me from all this bad publicity.

Since Ghost of a Chance was closed on Sundays, there were no customers—which was just as well, since my shelves were nearly bare.

Those empty, vacant expanses reminded me of the first time I'd walked in here after Chance had died. I'd expected to feel Chance's presence that day, but I'd felt nothing of him, as if the car crash had truly erased him. As I'd walked through the store, hoping to sense him, I'd only felt a deep sense of loss. Everything in the store had been too new, too functional, too unartistic. Chance hadn't poured his soul into this place yet. Not the way I had over the past year.

Maudlin, I know. I was in that sort of mood though. The W-ZZZ news story had been a punch to my self-confidence, making me stagger back a few months to where I'd been just after my breakup with Doug. What if all my suppliers cut off my credit again? I didn't know if I could come back from that sort of setback a second time.

Rationally, I understood that Ford hadn't done anything wrong. The sabotage was all Doug's doing. Even so, I was angry with Ford for opening the door to all that negative media attention. If he hadn't told Chris Pitt my store was having problems, none of this would have happened. Sure, Chris had been the one who'd tweeted, but Ford never should have overshared in the first place.

Someone tapped on the glass, making me yelp in surprise. I looked up to see Lianna peering through the window at me. My nerves must still be raw.

I heaved myself to my feet, unlocked the door, and pulled it open. "I lost track of time," I said as she came inside.

Lianna looked around the store appreciatively. "You've been busy. I like what you've done with the place."

I took in the new layout. "It does look decent. This arrangement gives me better sight lines between the shelves. Plus, my bestselling comics have more space, so I won't have to restock them as often."

"I see you're putting Chance's comics right here up front." Lianna's finger slid over the plastic shelf label for *Ghost*.

"He deserves it. We nearly sold out yesterday. He'd have been thrilled." Of course, once Ford announced that he was making *Ghost* into a movie, I'd probably be selling a lot more of Chance's comics. I needed to prepare for that.

"I'm impressed. You did a great job handling all that chaos."

"Thanks, but it's not like I had much of a choice." Looking at the shop's new layout filled me with a sense of accomplishment. Neatening things up had been a nice change of pace from my normal daily grind.

Grind? Well, yes. This place could be a great big pain in the butt sometimes. Other times, I loved it.

Maybe I should start reaching for more. With the movie, I bet I could leverage the publicity and get Chance's comics out to more people. The publicity would be on my terms, though.

"I'm starving. Are we still going to Not a Yacht Club?" Lianna asked.

"Absolutely," I said, feeling more lighthearted. "It's open mic night. If we get there soon, we should still be able to grab a good table."

"Let's get moving."

A minute later, we were striding down the sidewalk toward the river. The bright June sun beat down on my bare head. It was good to be outside after being cooped up all day.

"Chris Pitt is really nice." Lianna sounded surprised. "Not at all what I expected from a movie star."

"I can't imagine living my life in the public eye like that." I shuddered.

Lianna shot me a look of pity that made me wonder—

"I guess you saw the news last night," I said.

"That reporter was an ass." Lianna wrapped her arm around my shoulders in a quick hug that made us both wobble. "I bet he's friends with Doug. Don't let the trolls get to you."

I could see the Not a Yacht Club parking lot just ahead, and it was only half-full. "I blame Ford," I admitted. "He shouldn't have just shown up with Chris like that." Lianna opened her mouth, but I kept talking over her, not wanting to hear her defend him. "I'm trying to forgive him. I know it was unintentional, but I'm still irritated with him."

"I can see how you could be upset with the whole situation."

What would happen once Ford announced that he was making *Ghost*? Would my store be inundated with Chris Pitt fans? Would everything start to spin out of my control? And what would Doug do to sabotage me once he found out?

I came to a dead stop on the sidewalk. My chest tightened as I suddenly had a vision of what could happen to my life. Ford's movie would mean everyone in the country would know about

Ghost. Heck. Everyone in the world. This movie could shove me into the limelight, whether I wanted it or not.

My back stiffened. "I need to stick to the plan Chance and I made. I can't let anyone sabotage it. Not Doug. Not my dad. Not even Ford." Not that Ford would do it intentionally, but I needed to take control of my end of things. My store. Chance's comics.

It hit me that I needed to talk to his agent, Amy Tate, about all these new developments. Maybe she had some ideas about how I could control everything to keep it from spinning away from me.

"Whoa." Lianna shot me a confused look. "That's a strange list. I get Doug, but your dad? Ford? What have they ever done to sabotage you?"

I blinked rapidly. Lianna didn't know about the movie. Not yet. And Ford hadn't given me the go-ahead to tell anyone. How could I explain how overwhelmed I felt and why I was freaking out?

I cleared my throat as we came to the restaurant parking lot. "Dad thinks I never should have left Stel-Wood. He's constantly undermining me. Poking at me whenever he gets a chance. When I was a kid, he'd go behind my back and interfere in my life. He can't keep his opinions to himself, and I'm getting really tired of his constant criticism. And Ford..." I shook my head, thinking about the movie and the effect it would have on my life. "Our relationship is still new. We're in that stage where we're getting to know each other. Trust is a big deal to me. Ford never should have told Chris about my store's problems." Heck, I was bending over backward right now to keep his secret about the movie. He owed me just as much discretion.

"But your store *is* having problems," Lianna said, still looking confused. "He was trying to help. You're not being fair."

I shook my head. "He went about it in the worst possible way. He got all nebby, telling Chris about stuff that was none of his business."

"Nebby?" Lianna's eyes danced with laughter. "You've only lived here a year and you're already using that word? Our Pittsburgh slang is rubbing off on you." She pushed open the door to Not a Yacht Club.

The garage-sized doors facing the river on the main floor were open and a gentle breeze wafted in. The hostess on duty took us to a table not far from the stage and handed us menus, saying our waitress would be there in a moment.

I spotted Conner doing something with a big electronic console near the stage. He waved at us but kept working while our waitress returned to take our orders.

"I'm still trying to wrap my head around that list of saboteurs you just rattled off," Lianna said once we were alone again. "I get Doug, and now it makes sense that your dad made the list—but Ford? I still don't understand why you'd lump him in with the others. He screwed up telling Chris, sure, but he made a mistake. Your dad and Doug have gone out of their way to be hurtful. Ford believes in you."

I hesitated, wishing I could tell Lianna about the movie deal and the problems I was afraid would come with it, but I didn't want to be a hypocrite and reveal information Ford had asked me not to share. The film was a godsend, of course, but the enormity of the changes I'd be facing terrified me.

Lianna was right, though. I was overreacting. After the way Doug had treated me, I'd become overly sensitive to anything that smacked of meddling. Even Chris Pitt's attempt to help had pissed me off.

I sighed. "I feel like I'm losing control of my own life because of what other people are doing. Chris is the one who sent out that tweet, and yes, I realize it was essentially a really nice favor. What gets to me is that I was afraid the worst might happen—and then it did, thanks to Doug." I sighed. "At least Ford knows how devious Doug can be now. God, I wish that asshat was out of my life."

Our drinks arrived, giving me a moment to think this through. I took a long sip of my mojito. The arguments I offered Lianna were no more than straw men for her to knock down—crappy, empty straw man arguments that had no substance—all because I'd promised Ford not to tell anyone about the movie.

Secrets sucked.

I poked at the ice in my drink, aching to tell her about the movie.

Lianna simply stared at me, making me feel self-conscious.

"What?" I snapped.

"I'm wondering if this is some sort of weird, delayed reaction to you losing your brother and having Doug screw with your life because you aren't making a lot of sense."

The microphone on stage let out a squeal and Conner scrambled to shut it off. Lianna rubbed her ear but continued as if she hadn't been interrupted. "It seems as though you're carrying around a lot of baggage and holding Ford responsible for it."

"Whoa." Her insight hit me hard. Even though I'd just done my best to hide my real concerns, Lianna had cut straight to the root of my problem. I slumped into my chair. How had she figured it out through all the half-truths I'd just fed her?

"I should point out that even though Doug was an ass, you have lots of excellent friends who are nothing but supportive," Lianna said. "Look at how many people showed up yesterday to help you. Not everyone is out to get you. Only Doug. The man's nuts. Please don't hold Ford accountable for someone else's actions."

She was right, of course. I crunched on a piece of ice as I watched Conner step onto the stage. Open mic night was about to commence. "How are you able to see things so clearly?"

"Probably because I'm watching your life rather than living it," she said kindly. "It's hard to be an impartial observer when you're at the center of things."

41

PROGRESS

FORD

I sat in my desk chair in my third-floor home office, on a video call.

"I wanted to give you a quick call to let you know I finished reading through your screenplay," I told my screenwriter, Neil Frank. "It looks good. I marked a few parts I want to discuss with you, but I want to sleep on it first."

"I'm glad you like it so far," Neil said.

The church bell down the road chimed the hour. Was it six already? Where had the day gone? "The author's sister might have some feedback as well. I'll let you know."

Neil looked relieved. "Do you like the approach I'm taking with the inciting event? I thought the story worked better this way."

"It does. You've definitely got the touch." Sure enough, the clock stopped after six chimes. "I have to be somewhere, so I need to get going. I'll call you tomorrow to discuss everything."

"Sounds good." Neil's index finger loomed large on my phone screen as he reached out and ended the call.

I still had a few minutes before Max picked me up for our cooking class. Instead of getting ready though, I stared out my third-floor window. From up here in the former servants' quarters, I had a sweeping view of the neighborhood. An abandoned bird's nest sat on my windowsill. I kept hoping a robin would decide to move in, but so far there'd been no takers.

Working with Neil Frank had been easier than I'd expected, given his fame. But then again, he'd been nominated for best-adapted screenplay last year. The man knew what he was doing. Turning a four-hundred-page novel into a ninety-minute film meant entire subplots and supporting characters needed to be deleted. It took a skilled screenwriter to adapt an existing story and make the appropriate changes while keeping the themes and tone true to the original.

Since Chance had been both an author and an artist, he'd thought visually, and that made all the difference. Even so, the internal dialogue normally conveyed through a comic's thought bubbles would need to be revealed in other ways, and that required changes to the story.

Small changes, yes, but changes, nonetheless.

Would Mara fight them? The way things stood between us, I wasn't sure. I'd broken her trust when I'd told Chris about her problems and he'd made that tweet. It would be hard to come back from that. This was what came from mixing business with pleasure.

The contract Mara signed listed her as a consultant. Any decisions regarding the script were officially mine and mine alone, but unofficially, I knew I'd do anything to make her happy.

I hesitated a moment longer before I called her at her store.

"Ghost of a Chance," she said. "How can I help you?"

"It's good to hear your voice."

She hesitated for a moment, then said, "Hi, Ford."

Not the worst beginning. "Do you have a minute? I just spoke with the screenwriter."

Outside my window, I heard a shout, followed by an excited shriek of laughter. The boys next door darted across their yard, squirt guns in hand. I recalled similar summer evenings like this, playing outside with my brothers while my mom cooked dinner. Usually, we can't recognize how great our lives are in the moment. We can't see the big picture until after it's been erased. I'd never realized how idyllic my life had been until Mom was gone.

"Is he making the changes your dad suggested?" Mara's tone was tense. Professional.

"A couple. His are minor though. You know Ghost's story and themes better than anyone else. I'd like you to read through it and make sure you're happy with what we have in mind."

One of the boys let out another laughing shriek. The sound reminded me of Max as a kid, when Sean would jump out from behind a tree and ambush him, squirting him at close range.

I'd seen my old squirt gun around here someplace when I'd unpacked my office items. I opened one desk drawer after another until—yes. There it was. Red, plastic, and extremely accurate. That was why I'd held onto it all these years.

Mara was quiet for a long time before she spoke. When she did, her voice sounded strange. "It means a lot to me that you value my opinion."

I stilled, my hand tightening around the grip of the squirt gun. It hurt to know she'd doubted me. "Of course, I do. That was our agreement."

"I know, but I always assumed I wouldn't have much input. The contract I signed turned over all creative control to you. That was the logical thing to do, since I don't know anything about making movies."

"You're more than just a script consultant. You're my girlfriend and Chance's sister. Your insight is invaluable. I thought you understood that."

"I did. I do." She sighed. "We should talk."

That phrase again. I swallowed against the tightness in my throat. "I agree. Does tomorrow work? I'll bring you lunch. I have this intense desire to cook for you."

Mara stayed silent for too long. I sprang from my chair and started pacing. My heart thudded louder than my footsteps.

"That sounds nice," she finally said, her tone warmer than it had been before. "Sorry about that. A customer just left, and I'm pretty sure he was eavesdropping. Lunch sounds great. I'm a pushover when it comes to your cooking. What will you make for me?"

Relief broke my tension, and I grinned. "I'll surprise you. But I have one condition." I spun the empty squirt gun around my finger, like an old-time gunslinger from the movies.

"What's that?" Her tone was wary.

"You need to wear one of your Wonder Woman t-shirts." I grinned as I headed downstairs to the kitchen sink.

She hesitated. "I'm wearing one right now," she said, her voice a bit husky.

That caught my attention, and I came to an abrupt stop. "You kill me, Mara. Which one?"

"The dark blue one."

"With the invisible jet?" I asked as I started moving again. "I love that one." It was snug, and the color looked great with her hair.

"Exactly. Will there be anything else?" Her voice had abruptly changed and taken on a cheerful, professional tone.

Someone must have walked up to the register. I made it to the kitchen and quickly filled the gun's little reservoir.

"Nope," I said as I pushed the little plastic plug into place. "You've made me a happy man just knowing you're wearing that t-shirt. See you tomorrow after your lunch rush ends."

"Thank you." She ended the call.

My doorbell rang.

I opened the front door, aimed my water gun, and nailed my brother right between the eyes. He looked stunned. The kids next door would have howled with laughter.

"What the eff, man! How old *are* you?" Max wiped the water from his face.

"I'd judge my mental age to be around ten right now. Your face has sprung a leak, little brother."

"Asshole. I should make you walk to class."

"True, but the Not a Yacht Club isn't far. It wouldn't be much of a hardship."

Max spun on his heel and strode toward his car.

I jogged after him since I wouldn't put it past him to follow through on his threat.

Max glared at me when I climbed in. "Payback's a bitch," he said.

I ignored him. "We're making something chocolate tonight, right? That should cheer you up. It always works with Hailey." Our big sister was an acknowledged chocoholic. Max liked the stuff almost as much as she did.

"Barry's out of town again," Max said, referring to Hailey's husband. "I promised her I'd drop off some of the cake we're making tonight. She's been after me to try my cooking. I owe her for all the times she's fed me."

"I'll go with you. We can give her most of it, but I want to save a piece for Mara. I'm working on getting back into her good graces."

"What? Did you shoot her in the face with a squirt gun too?" Max said dryly.

I gave a laugh. "Nah. She's pissed off about the news story that aired after Chris's visit. It blew up in her face. The whole thing gave her ex an opportunity to dick with her again. The guy works for the station that interviewed Chris."

"Which one was it again?" Max parked his car and turned off the engine.

"W-ZZZ. Her ex works in their sales department."

"I know some people there. I might be able to 'make da guy go away.'" Max gave the last words a bit of a gangster flourish like he was talking about taking a hit out on the guy.

I gave a snort of laughter as I climbed out of the car. "Permanently?" I joked.

"Not mafia-style," Max said as she shut his car door, "but I could probably arrange to have him transferred to another city in their broadcast network."

"That might work," I said as we walked into the Not a Yacht Club. "Let me think about it." After what had happened with Chris, there was no way I'd do anything without checking with Mara first, but she might like Max's idea.

PROMISES, PROMISES

Ford

After cooking class, Max and I stopped by Hailey's house. The kitchen was an empty shell. All the cabinets and appliances were gone. There was a big opening in the rear wall of the house that led to the addition, and the kitchen's new hardwood flooring was about halfway complete.

We found Hailey in the makeshift kitchen she'd set up in the dining room, and Emma sat at the dining room table,

Max set a white box on the buffet.

"I have good news," I said. "Max drafted the press release about *Ghost*. He just sent it out."

"Yes!" Hailey cried as she raised her arms in victory. "That means you'll be living in Sewickley again."

Emma ran over from the table and threw her arms around me. "You're staying! Awesome!"

I hugged her back. "That's one of the best parts. I'll get to see you all the time."

Emma pulled free of my arms, her nose twitching like a bloodhound. She looked pointedly at the white box Max had brought in. "Do I smell chocolate?"

"Good nose." Max grinned as he opened the lid, revealing our Death by Chocolate cake.

Emma's eyes widened. "Is that for us?"

Max slapped me on the back. "Ford and I made it. We think it's great, but we want your unbiased opinion since you're both chocolate cake experts."

Hailey cocked an eyebrow, clearly doubting our skills, but she grabbed two foam plates from a stack on her buffet table, gave a piece to Emma, and took one for herself.

"How long until your kitchen is done?" I asked Hailey.

"Fingers crossed we'll only have to live this way for another couple of weeks," she said. "I hate eating off paper plates, but I won't have a sink or dishwasher for a while yet."

I watched as Hailey took a bite and closed her eyes. A moment later she took another bite and then started nodding. "This is impressive. You two have come a long way with that class. I couldn't have done better myself."

"High praise," I said. "That means a lot, coming from you."

"How are things going with Mara?" Hailey asked. "I hope you're taking her some of this. It'll impress the heck out of her."

I avoided Hailey's gaze by watching Emma devouring her piece of the cake. "That's the plan."

When I glanced back at Hailey, I found her grinning at me as though she'd caught me doing something wrong. I'd forgotten what an annoying big sister she could be.

"You *like* her," she said in a singsong voice. "I can tell."

Emma groaned with happiness as she licked her plate. "This is delicious."

Hailey's playful demeanor disappeared as she shot Emma a warning look. "Use your manners, Em!"

Emma looked up, surprised. "But they're my uncles. We're family."

"Even more reason to behave properly. First of all, licking a plate is gross, and second, you should treat your family best of all. Certainly, better than strangers."

"But my family will love me even if I lick my plate," Emma said, and then licked it again.

"Stop that," Hailey said. "You still shouldn't treat them with disrespect. No one wants to see you licking a dirty plate with your tongue. That's just nasty."

Max and I exchanged glances. "Should I tell her you shot me with a squirt gun tonight?" Max asked in a stage whisper.

"Go ahead," I whispered back, "but then I'll have to tell her about that fake milk you gave me that was made from cornstarch. She won't approve."

Max gave a heavy sigh. "In that case, we should probably keep it to ourselves. We'd only undermine her argument about respecting family."

Hailey held up her hands to silence us. "Nothing more from you two. I know how bad you can get." She swept up the empty foam plates and tossed them in the trash can.

"Guilty as charged," I said, grinning. "But we still managed to make an amazing cake together."

"I guess that bodes well for you two making a movie together. Fingers crossed," Hailey said.

***

The next afternoon, I packed lunch in a picnic basket along with my secret weapon—the Death by Chocolate cake.

As I pushed open the door of Ghost of a Chance, I could only hope my bribe—I mean, peace offering—would smooth things over with Mara.

The scent of newly printed comic books that hit me when I walked in the door seemed stronger than usual today. The store was empty, which worried me. Mara sat on a stool behind the counter as her fingers flew over her laptop's keyboard.

"I like the new layout in here," I said as I set the basket next to her.

She glanced up in surprise. "Thanks. I guess I didn't hear the door chime. I've been so busy today that I've barely had time to work on this coding gig."

The band of tension across my chest let go. "Having lots of customers is a good problem," I said as I unpacked the basket.

"Things have been crazy-busy all day," she told me. "I'm glad I got the shelves reorganized. This works better."

I brought up a website on my phone showing a story about *Ghost* and handed it to Mara so she could read it.

Her eyes went wide. "You made the announcement? It's official?"

"Max sent out the press releases last night."

She heaved a sigh as she handed my phone back to me. "That's a relief. I hated not being able to tell anyone." She glanced down at the Reuben I'd set on her plate. "Oh, my god, I'm so hungry. That smells amazing. You have perfect timing."

When I set the slice of cake next to her sandwich, her eyes lit up.

"That piece is all mine, right?" she teased. "I don't have to share?"

I raised my hands and stepped away from it. "I wouldn't stand between you and Death by Chocolate cake."

"Sounds sinfully delicious."

"It is. Just so you know, the cake is a bribe. I'm trying to get back into your good graces."

"I noticed. Chocolate cake happens to be my kryptonite." She glanced at her watch and raised her eyebrows in surprise. "I can't believe it's already two o'clock. I'm amazed we're alone. I've had nonstop customers all day. Lots of people asked about Chris Pitt. I had to take Zephyr upstairs because he was overexcited from all the attention he was getting." She glanced at the front door. "We probably won't have much time together. I really need to talk to you."

"That's why I'm here." I took a steadying breath.

"All right, then." She licked her lips. "Over the past couple of days, I've been doing a lot of soul-searching, and I've come to realize I have a lot of deep-seated trust issues." She stared down at her Reuben for a moment, but then met my gaze. "I want to trust you, but you never should have told anyone my business was struggling. That was private. I didn't tell anyone about your plans for *Ghost*, and I expected you not to tell people about my problems with my store. I need to be able to confide in you."

I nodded. "I'm sorry. My only defense is that I was trying to help, but the reason doesn't matter. I screwed up. I'd have been upset if the situation were reversed."

She looked directly into my eyes. "I have to be in charge of my own life. I'm the one who has to deal with the consequences, so I have to be the one making the decisions."

"I get it," I said, holding up my hands in surrender. "I wouldn't want anyone making decisions about my life either. The question is, can you forgive me?"

She gave me a mock scowl. "Well, you're here, in my store, groveling. It's hard to stay angry with you."

"I am definitely *not* groveling."

"You made me Death By Chocolate cake," she pointed out.

"That isn't groveling. That's a bribe."

"Po-tay-to, po-tah-to." She grinned, her eyes sparkling.

"Did it work? Am I forgiven?"

Her smile dimmed a little as she considered her reply. "Forgiven? Yes," she said. "I'm still feeling defensive, though. It's something I need to work through. I'm not only reacting to what you did, but to what other people have done in the past. It's all rolled together into one squishy, irrational ball of angst. I realize it isn't fair to you," she shrugged, "but emotions aren't fair. They just are. Give me time. I'll work through this."

"Can we work through it together?"

She put a bite of cake into her mouth and then groaned with pleasure, giving a little wiggle that made me suddenly very aware of how much I wanted her. Missed her. Needed her.

"Will you promise to make more of this cake?" she asked.

"If you wiggle like that, I'll make you a chocolate cake every single day."

"If you make it for me every day, there will be a lot more of me to wiggle." She grinned, popped another bite of cake in her mouth, and gave another wiggle. "Deal. I'm defenseless against this cake."

"Deal."

I pulled the updated version of the script from the basket and handed it to her. "I need you to read through this and give me your feedback regarding changes to one of the characters. If it's okay with you, I'll come over tonight so we can talk."

She tensed. "Changes? I don't like the sound of that."

"I thought you might not. Just read it. There are good reasons for the changes, but you need to read through the entire script first so we can discuss them."

The door chimed as someone walked in.

Mara hesitated. "Eight o'clock," she finally said, and then greeted her customer.

43

CHANGES

MARA

My stomach tightened when I heard my front door open at eight on the dot.

Ford was here. He came into the living room carrying a large canvas grocery bag.

I didn't like this stupid script. His screenwriter had totally messed it up. We needed to talk about it, but I also didn't want things to get confrontational between us right away.

"You're feeding me again?" I asked, hoping he'd brought more of that chocolate cake. That would certainly put us on better footing.

He pulled me into his arms, and I melted into him. Having him hold me felt like coming home after a long time away. Nice way to start things off.

He held me close, letting me know he'd missed this too, but Zephyr's insistent barking finally made me pull away.

"He missed you, too," I said.

"Of course, he did. I bring him treats." Ford leaned over and rummaged around in the canvas bag. "Today I have something new for him."

I gave the long, thin, brown thing a suspicious look. "Dare I ask what that is?"

"A bully stick. The guy at the pet store recommended it. He says dogs love them."

I let out a snort of laughter. "Seriously?"

Ford raised one eyebrow.

"Did he tell you what they are?" At Ford's blank expression, I shot him a devilish grin. "They're bull penises."

Ford's grip on the dog treat failed, and the bully stick fell directly in front of Zephyr, who snatched it and ran off.

Ford looked appalled. "Seriously? A bull penis?"

I let out another chuckle. "At least nothing goes to waste."

"I suppose that's to be commended." He looked doubtful.

"What else do you have in that bag?" I asked.

"I hope my next attempt at bribery doesn't have any unsettling ingredients."

"We shall see."

With a flourish, he reached into the canvas bag and pulled out a small rectangular box. He kept most of it concealed with his hand and then slowly lowered it, like a curtain dropping, to reveal a very familiar dark-brown and white box with a blue logo.

I snatched it from his hand. "You got me Sno-caps?" I said, giving a squeal of joy. "How did you know?"

"You may have mentioned them." He looked inordinately pleased with himself. I couldn't blame him.

I tore open one end of the box. "No unsettling ingredients in here. They're just chocolate chips covered with nonpareils."

"Sounds good," he said, reaching for the box.

I yanked it away. "Ah-ah-ah. I'm not sharing. I just remembered they contain the most disgusting stuff. You'd hate them. Honestly."

He ignored me and grabbed the box, pouring some Sno-caps into his hand.

"Hey!"

He tossed them into his mouth. "Delicious," he said as he munched. "I think you just lied to me."

I snatched the box back from him. "The rest of those are mine. No takebacks."

He held up his hands in surrender. "All yours, Miss Stellar. They're a peace offering."

That brought my irritation with his script roaring back. "I can see why you thought you needed one. I'm not liking your script," I said, folding my arms tightly across my waist.

His lips thinned. "I was afraid you might not."

"Was there any question? This new opening scene never even existed in Chance's story." I grabbed the script from the coffee table. "It doesn't make sense," I said, flipping to the new scene. "In the comic, Jude turns on Christian in the opening scene, and the betrayal hits him hard. It's the main reason Christian becomes Ghost." I thrust the script out to him, jabbing at the page with my finger. "But in your version, they're goofing around while Jude helps him move into a new apartment." I frowned at him in exasperation and confusion. "That never happened."

The muscle in his jaw tensed. "Did you read the entire thing?"

"Of course not." I pressed my lips together in a frown and then dropped the script back onto the table. "Not after that. How could you change something so fundamental?"

Ford dragged his hand through his hair. "I was afraid you'd react this way. That's why I asked you to read all of it." He took my hand and pulled me toward the sofa. "Sit with me. I don't want us to be adversaries."

"Apparently we are." I sat down anyway, but I kept my back stiff and my arms crossed. I didn't want things to be this way between us, but he'd misled me. I'd trusted him, and he'd let me down. Again.

"I'm perfectly aware that Jude's betrayal is a key part of Ghost's backstory. The problem is, if I don't show an existing close bond between him and Jude, then his reaction to Jude's betrayal comes out of nowhere."

I shook my head, keeping my chin down. "Chance made the reader *feel* the pain of the betrayal. I don't understand why you'd want to change that."

Ford ducked his head to look into my eyes. "You have to understand that movies and comics need to tell stories in different ways. Yes, they both use images, but graphic novels are similar to books in that they provide the reader with a character's internal monologue. They can do that by using thought bubbles. Movies can't replicate that. Some directors choose to use voiceovers, but I don't like them. I find them intrusive. I prefer *showing* moviegoers rather than *telling* them. After all, films are a visual medium. Changing the opening scene and establishing the close relationship between those two characters fixes the problem neatly and elegantly."

I heard him, but I still didn't like it. "I don't think Chance would approve." But then I hesitated. Did I really know that? He'd run loads of things past me when he'd been working on the plot, and he'd incorporated quite a few of my suggestions. Did I really know he wouldn't have agreed with Ford?

Then again, I wasn't the only person who loved Ghost exactly the way it was written. "Did I ever mention that Chance won the Russ Manning Promising Newcomer Award for his first Ghost comic?"

Ford raised his eyebrows in surprise. "Really? I'm impressed."

"I don't like the idea of you changing an award-winning story and adding scenes. It smacks of disrespect."

Ford dragged his fingers through his hair. "I don't see it that way. I'm using a storytelling device. I'm trying to convey the closeness of Christian and Jude's relationship in the most natural way possible for the film medium."

He peered into my eyes, and it felt as though he could read all of my fears—of having someone lie to me again—of being manipulated.

He took my hand. "Do me a favor. Read the entire script, and then take some time to consider why I wanted to make a few changes."

I hesitated. How would reading the rest of it make a difference? The opening scene was an affront. If he'd changed much more, I'd only be more furious. When I looked into his eyes and saw how much this meant to him though, I relented.

I gave him a tight, reluctant nod. "I suppose I can do that."

"How about I leave you alone for a while so you can read?" he asked, rising to his feet. "I'll take Zephyr on a long walk."

Zephyr came bounding out from behind the chair at the mention of the words, "Zephyr," and "walk," in the same sentence.

His suggestion made sense. I owed him that much. "Fine. I can do that."

Once the apartment was empty, I turned back to the script. Forty-five minutes later, I was done.

I sat staring at the cover page, not sure what to say to Ford.

What would Chance have thought?

The rest of the changes in the script were minor, but to me, they stood out like a mustache on the Mona Lisa. Well, maybe not quite that egregious. More like red polish on Mona's fingernails.

I sighed, tossed the script onto the coffee table, and grabbed my wine glass. I should read Chance's original comic again to see what Ford was talking about with that "thought-bubble" comment.

A couple of minutes later, Ford came in. Zephyr scampered over to greet me as if he hadn't seen me in days.

"Hi, buddy-boy," I said, smiling indulgently at my dog. "I missed you, too."

Ford approached hesitantly. "Did you finish it?"

I nodded and opened my mouth to tell him about my concerns, but Ford held up a hand to cut me off.

"I'd like you to wait a day or two before we talk. Keep the script. It's your copy. Once you've had a chance to think things through, we'll discuss it."

The knot of tension in my belly eased. The last thing we needed tonight was more conflict between us. With the whole Chris Pitt mess still fresh, we needed to reestablish our connection. "I can do that."

I curled up on the sofa, tucking my feet beneath me.

Ford sat next to me. "Let me say one thing, then we'll set the topic of the script aside for tonight. I strive for perfection when it comes to my movies. There's no way I'd intentionally choose to create an inferior film. I hope you'll keep that in mind when you consider my changes."

"I can do that." I relaxed back on the couch and let out a sigh along with a bundle of tension.

"Chris's screen test is tomorrow." Ford smiled as he lifted his crossed fingers. "Here's hoping it's as great as I think it will be. Want to meet me at my dad's place tomorrow night to watch it with us?"

"Sure. Superstitious much?" I grinned at his crossed fingers.

He shrugged and dropped his hand. "Maybe. I work in an industry where too many things can derail a project that took years to plan. The stars need to align for a film to be a success. I can be a control freak when it comes to my work."

"I'll keep your freakiness in mind." I waggled my eyebrows at him, teasingly.

He waggled his eyebrows right back at me. "Would you like to see more examples of my freakiness?"

My eyes widened as a frisson of excitement shivered up my spine. Sudden images of letting him have power over my body flashed through my mind, like comic book frames. Maybe giving up a tiny bit of control might be interesting… all in good fun.

A slow smile crept over my lips, and I let my eyes drift down his body. "Just so there's no misunderstanding, we're not talking about movies, right?"

His eyes seemed to darken, and the smile he gave me made my breath hitch in anticipation. "I'm talking about us. Now," he murmured.

"In the bedroom?" I managed to ask.

"Precisely." His husky voice sent a wave of desire crashing over me.

He stood, grabbed both my hands, and pulled me from the couch and into his arms. "I'm suddenly in the mood to flex my directorial muscles."

I pressed my hips against his as I peered up at him. I widened my eyes owlishly and then gave my eyelashes a playful flutter. "This is going to be fun."

44

SOLUTIONS AND MORE PROBLEMS

Ford

"One macchiato and one caramel latte," I told the Loco Mocha barista.

As I waved my card over the reader to pay, my phone rang. It was Max, so I took the call. "How's it going?"

"Good," Max said, sounding distracted. "Sorry I couldn't make it to Dad's last night to watch the screen test. I got hung up solving a problem with another one of his films and couldn't get away."

It was hard to hear him over the hissing of the espresso machine, so I stepped closer to the front door where it was fractionally quieter. "Chris was perfect. Even better than I'd expected. Everyone is completely on board now."

"Glad to hear it. I called to let you know my friend at W-ZZZ says they can move Doug to Chicago. Is that still what you want to do?"

I searched my memory, then it hit me. "Doug? Mara's ex?"

"My friend can pull some strings and get him transferred."

"I haven't told Mara yet," I admitted. "Let me check with her first."

"I need an answer by the end of the day," Max replied.

The barista called my name.

"I'll go talk to her now," I said, grabbing the two cups of coffee in a holder. "Thanks again. I owe you."

"Sure thing. Keep me posted."

I stepped outside into a gray sky that had once been sunny. Typical Pittsburgh weather. The city was known for its rain, but it did have a silver lining. The constant showers made everything lush and green. In fact, Pittsburgh was ranked third in the country for the most cloudy days, right after Buffalo and Seattle. But today, there was no time to admire the foliage. I had to get back to Mara.

Two minutes later, I pushed open the door to Ghost of a Chance, the bell above it jingling. The wind followed me inside, giving the chimes an extra zazz. Holding the coffee holder in one hand and my phone in the other, I scanned the room for Mara, ready to snap a photo.

She stared intently at her laptop, frowning at whatever was displayed there, but when she glanced up and spotted me, her expression was transformed as she grinned at me. "Hi."

I took a photo, then stashed my phone in my pocket.

"Hi." I handed her the coffee and kissed her cheek.

"Thanks. You read my mind." She took a sip and pushed her glasses up her nose. No contact lenses today. "I just finished submitting a freelance coding gig. Your timing is perfect."

I looked at her blankly.

"Freelance coding gig?" she asked. "Remember? I occasionally pick up coding jobs. I finished one up and submitted the code on GitHub."

"GitHub," I parroted. "Gotcha." Not really. I peered at her more closely. "Are you doing okay? You looked irritated with your computer when I came in."

She frowned. "Just a little tired. I stayed up late rereading *Ghost* and then had to wake up early to get started on this code so I could submit it on time."

"You look gorgeous, as usual. What made you want to reread *Ghost*?"

She yawned and stretched, then closed her laptop. "I realized you were right about Chris Pitt being perfect for the role, and that made me decide to look at your script changes in a different light. You made a really good point regarding the whole thought-bubble thing. Chance used them a lot in his first comic, but rarely in his later ones. I've been wondering all day if he decided he didn't like them either." She pulled at her lower lip with her thumb and forefinger.

I could tell she was making a difficult decision right now... one that would affect the future of my film. As the moment stretched, I leaned against the counter, focusing only on her.

She finally sighed. "I think your changes are okay. I've decided I'm pretty sure Chance would have thought so too."

I let out a whoop. I wanted to pull her into my arms, but the counter prevented me, so I settled on leaning across it and planting a kiss on those gorgeous lips.

She let out a surprised laugh. "Glad I could make you so happy."

"You have no idea. I hated being at odds with you."

"Me too." She yawned again. Her body relaxed as the tension I'd noticed earlier disappeared. I took that as a sign she was happy with her decision about the script.

"I got a call from Max a few minutes ago," I said. "He has some pull with W-ZZZ. He says he can arrange to have the network offer Doug a transfer to Chicago. It would be the same job but in a bigger market. If it's something you'd like to have happen, I'll tell Max to do his magic."

She raised her eyebrows in questioning surprise. "Doug would move away?"

"Yep."

She stilled. "That would mean he wouldn't be able to show up at my store unannounced. Or pull in favors to twist around news stories about me."

"Exactly."

Her eyes bored into me. "Max could do that? It could actually happen?"

"Max can get them to make the offer, yes. It would be up to Doug to accept it."

She grinned. "Oh, I can guarantee you that he'll take it. He's dying to move to a bigger city."

"Then I can tell Max to go ahead with it?"

"Abso-frigging-lutely!" She beamed, unable to contain her grin.

Me: She's in. Do it.

Max: On it.

"Done," I said, smiling at her.

"This day is turning out to be one of my better ones. Is this the good news you texted me about?" she asked.

I smacked myself on the forehead. "After Max texted me about the transfer, I nearly forgot. It's about Chris Pitt. It's official. He signed to play Ghost."

Mara's eyes widened with delight. "Congratulations. That's great news. He was perfect in that screen test. I wish Chance had been able to see it. He was never much of a Chris Pitt fan, but I think the screen test would have changed his mind."

She came out from behind the counter and wrapped me in a hug. She fit against me perfectly, like a missing part.

She tipped her head back and met my gaze. "We should celebrate."

We were about to kiss when the bells on the door jingled with a rush of wind. Lianna came in. She had to push the door closed behind her against the breeze.

Mara quietly asked, "Is it okay if I tell her about Chris Pitt? I only just told her about the movie."

"Sure," I murmured back. "It's all official now."

"Hi, Ford. Hi, Mara," Lianna said. "I hope I'm not interrupting. You two look adorable together."

Mara darted forward to greet Lianna. "I have the most amazing news," she said, grinning from ear to ear. "Chris Pitt is going to be Ghost in Ford's movie."

Lianna's mouth dropped open. She glanced at me briefly, looking incredulous, and when I nodded, her eyes went wide, and she let out a squeal of excitement. "Oh, my god! That's huge! Is that why he was here last week?"

I grinned, watching the pair of them hold hands and jump up and down like giddy teenagers. When Mara beckoned me over, she pulled us into a group hug.

"This whole movie thing is the best news I've had in months," Lianna said. "I'm so excited for you."

"I've been dying to talk to you about it, but Ford swore me to secrecy until everything was official," Mara said. "He was afraid news would leak and ruin the deal."

My phone chirped with an incoming call. I glanced at my smartwatch and saw it was Dad. "Sorry," I said, stepping away from Mara and Lianna. "I need to take this."

I stepped closer to the door before putting the phone to my ear. "Hi, Dad. What's up?"

"What's up? What the hell do you think is up? You announced that you signed Chris Pitt, that's what's up!" he shouted in my ear. "Do you realize the avalanche of crap you just dumped on me? My phone has been ringing all morning. Why didn't you bother to warn me so I could do some damage control?"

I glanced up to see Mara and Lianna staring at me as they blatantly eavesdropped.

I pulled the phone away from my ear. "This will take a minute," I told them.

Mara waved me toward the door. "No problem. Vamoose. Go unruffle your dad's feathers."

I winked at her, then stepped outside. Not surprisingly, the sun was back, trying to compete with a sky filled with pale gray clouds. "You saw that screen test last night. He was perfect for the role. You knew I was going to sign him."

"I know, I know." Dad didn't sound happy, but more resigned. "He surprised me. The problem is that our biggest backer is threatening to pull out. I need you on a plane to L.A. as soon as possible to do some damage control."

"Shit. Seriously?" I glanced at Mara through the store window. I knew Dad always brought in outside investors, but the situation must be even more dire than he'd let on if he was getting this freaked out.

"With luck, it'll be a short trip for you," Dad said. "All you have to do is reassure him and his partners that everything will go smoothly and Chris's screen test with Kim Curry was sensational."

That stopped me cold. "What are you saying, Dad? How do they know he took a screen test? That was never supposed to get out."

"I might have mentioned something," he mumbled. "You know how things get around in this business."

"Which is exactly why I asked you not to mention it to anyone."

"Well, I did," Dad snapped. "I didn't have a choice, or they would have backed out. Besides, it's not that unusual to want to make sure two actors have chemistry."

I let out a frustrated sigh. This wasn't now how I liked to handle inside information about my films. I'd have to do damage control now. "Book me a flight. I'll run home and pack a bag. I can be at the airport in a little over an hour."

"Good, because your flight leaves in two."

"Text me the flight details." My phone vibrated, announcing an incoming text.

"Already did. Let me know how the meetings go. I already put them on your calendar."

I suppose this was the good part about collaborating with Dad. The man was extremely well-organized.

I waved at Mara through the front window and indicated I had to leave. She nodded and waved.

I'd call her on the way to the airport and let her know what was going on. With any luck, the whole movie deal wouldn't blow up in my face before I had a chance to clear things up with the investor. This movie had to happen. I refused to disappoint Mara.

45

IT'S RIGHT THERE

Mara

After a week apart, I was longing to see Ford again. He'd left so suddenly that we hadn't had a chance to say goodbye. Thank goodness he was finally flying home today. In fact, his plane was in the air right now.

Over the past week, we'd video chatted every night, so he'd kept me up to date on everything he'd been doing. He'd gone to coddle an investor who had cold feet. The guy needed reassurance, but Ford's normal charm wasn't working on him.

Investors could be tricky. I knew that from personal experience since Destiny and I had had them with Stel-Wood. Ford had just won best director at Sundance, though. That should convince them he knew what he was doing.

If Destiny and I partnered on this new game, we'd have to look for backers again, too. Something I dreaded.

I'd been busy this past week, so it was probably for the best that Ford had been out of town. I'd contacted Chance's agent, Amy Tate, and she'd explained various options for distributing the Ghost comics on a larger scale. I wanted to have as many people as possible read Chance's graphic novels. Amy was brilliant. She'd shop the print rights to a few different publishing houses this week. With luck, I'd have multiple deals to choose from and could pick the one that worked best for me, as well as for Chance's legacy.

I had plans to meet Lianna after work tonight, so Ford and I would see each other a little later this evening.

After I closed Ghost of a Chance, I went upstairs to my apartment and changed into a summery leaf-green skirt and a white top, then I headed over to In Vino Veritas to meet Lianna. The new wine bar had become one of my favorite places to rendezvous with friends after work, especially now that summer was in full swing.

I spotted Lianna standing near the entrance, reading something on her phone. Her slim-fitting pink capris, gauzy pink-and-white top, and white flats suited her. She looked more relaxed than I'd seen her in months.

My phone chimed announcing a text.

> Ford: I just landed. Heading to my weekly cooking class. See you soon. Can I bring dinner?

> Me: I'm having dinner with Lianna, but I always love your cooking. Come over when you're finished and bring me something yummy.

> Ford: Will do. Can't wait to see you.

Lianna spotted me and tucked her phone into her pocket. "Hi, sweetie. They're holding a table for us on the back patio."

We headed through the restaurant and back to the garden. It had the feel of an Italian villa, with gorgeous pillars, grape arbors, and a bubbling fountain.

After sending our server off with our orders, I sat back and watched a pair of birds splash and preen in the nearby fountain as I let the stress of my busy week melt away. Lianna's contentment radiated off her.

"I don't think I've seen you look this happy and relaxed in ages," I commented.

Her inner glow seemed to shine even brighter. "I guess it comes from shedding all that excess weight."

I frowned. "Excess weight? What are you talking about?"

"Paul. My almost ex-husband was weighing me down. We filed the divorce papers and now we're in the ninety-day state-mandated cooling-off period. In two months, three weeks, and three days, I'll be single again. Fortunately, Paul was more than happy to buy out my share of the house."

"I know this is what you wanted, but still, a divorce has to be hard. You're handling it well."

"It is. I'll be relieved when this is behind me." She glanced at her watch. "I can't stay long. I'm meeting my realtor soon to look at a place that just came on the market. She thinks it'll sell quickly."

The server dropped off our wine. "Your order should be ready. I'll bring it right out."

"Thanks," Lianna said.

I gave Lianna a slow, disbelieving shake of the head. "I didn't realize you and Paul had already finalized things. Holy awesome, girl. You're amazing."

Lianna waved away my praise. "I only did what I had to do. What's going on with you these days? Any news on the movie? I still haven't forgiven you for keeping *that* a secret for so long, but I'll get over it. Eventually."

I shrugged as I set my sunglasses on the table. "The movie brings a lot of changes with it. My store is finally turning a profit now that I'm getting so many new customers. Plus, I'm working with Chance's literary agent to develop a plan to get his graphic novels into more stores." I sipped my Chardonnay. "Meeting Ford has changed my life. So many opportunities have opened up for me." I set my wineglass on the table directly in a beam of sunlight. It fractured into a rainbow prism on the white tablecloth. I put a fingernail in the pool of colored lights, shifting it from side to side as I watched the colors move across it.

"The two of you are good together."

"I think so too." I glanced up at Lianna. "Ford's amazing. I can't figure out what's wrong with me, though. I'm seeing an amazing guy, my brother's comic is being turned into a movie, my store is finally turning around—it's all so overwhelming."

"You have a lot of changes going on in your life. Of course, you're feeling off-kilter." She lifted her arms and made a sweeping gesture toward herself. "Come on, tell me all your problems. You need to talk through this."

I hesitated. I hated the idea of unloading on someone, but maybe she was right, and talking would help. "Well, since you offered, here it comes, but remember, you asked for it." I gathered my thoughts, but the words that came pouring out surprised me. "Even though these new opportunities have been exciting, everything else is the same. My dad is still a jerk. Running the store has become routine, even though I'm busier now. I can't help wondering if this is what my life will be like from now on." I sighed. "In the beginning, I really loved Ghost of a Chance and conquering all its challenges, but I've lost that feeling. I need to figure out how to get it back."

Lianna settled back in her chair and stared at me for a heartbeat. "What *does* interest you?"

"I'm not sure. Coding, mostly. I love the side gigs I do." I slumped back in my chair and stared at the fountain. One of the birds flitted off, and a little yellow one took its place.

The hostess led a large group to a nearby table, and when I glanced over, I locked eyes with my mother.

"Mom?"

She hurried over to us. "What a nice surprise."

"Hi, Monica. Nice to see you," Lianna said.

"I thought you had a late rehearsal tonight," I said.

"The director had something else going on this evening. Your dad's on call, so I decided to have dinner with friends." Mom said. "You'll come to our show, right?"

"Of course," I said. "Wouldn't miss it."

"Me too," Lianna said. "Congratulations on Chance's movie. You must be excited."

Our server brought our artichoke and cheese spread and our bruschetta and set them on the table.

"Absolutely," Mom said, clasping her hands together. "I still can't quite believe it. I'm absolutely thrilled." Her smile dimmed. "I wish Chance could have been here to see it happen." She blinked rapidly a few times, then glanced over her shoulder to where her friends were sitting. "I don't want to keep you. It was wonderful to see you both." She hurried back to her group.

"Mom's thrilled, but Dad's kind of been a shit about everything," I grumbled. "Big surprise. He keeps talking about bolts of lightning and dumb luck, completely dismissing Chance's years of hard work."

"That's terrible," Lianna said, sounding genuinely affronted.

I suddenly sat bolt upright. "I'm such an idiot. I got an email and I wanted to talk to you about it, but I got sidetracked. I could really use some advice." Butterflies fluttered in my stomach.

"You know me. I'm all about advice," Lianna said with a smirk.

I pulled up an email on my phone and took a deep breath as I handed it to Lianna. "Destiny sent me this a couple of hours ago. Read it."

Lianna scanned the email, then her mouth fell open and she almost dropped the phone. "Is this what I think it is?"

The butterflies in my stomach turned into killer bees. "If you think it's a formal offer to form a new company with Destiny, then yes."

"Tell me you're doing it," she said, handing the phone back to me.

I chewed my lip and didn't answer. Was I? What I wanted and what I felt capable of doing battled within me. I'd walked out on

Destiny once before. How did I know I wouldn't do it again? What if I fell apart under pressure and bailed on her? Besides, Ghost of a Chance was finally starting to do well. Did I really want to abandon it? I'd always said I couldn't take on both jobs and do them well. That had changed.

As the silence between us lengthened, Lianna frowned. "I know you want it. What's holding you back?" She hesitated, then said, "Is it your brother? What you think you owe him?"

I took a big gulp of wine to drown the killer bees. Fortunately, they backed down. "That, yes. Plus, I'm afraid that if I leave, it will fail. Chance was a role model for me. He always stood up to Dad. I've tried to emulate him, but leaving the store to go back to Destiny feels like giving in to Dad's pressure."

"I'm sorry your dad's been such an ass, but don't measure your success using his yardstick." She looked into my eyes. "I met you right when you first moved here. You were grieving. Don't underestimate how much pain you were in, or how much it influenced you." She paused, gathering her words as she chewed a bite of food. "You've taken his legacy farther than your brother ever would have imagined. I doubt he expected *Ghost* would become a movie. That's impressive." She swirled her wineglass. "By any measure, I'd say you've accomplished what you set out to do. No one is going to forget Chance, or Ghost."

I shrugged. "I suppose so, but I can't really take any credit for the movie. That was a fluke."

She set her glass down with a thump. "Fluke! Now you sound like your dad. If you hadn't sold him your brother's comics, Ford never would have read *Ghost*. You've always been your brother's biggest fan. Don't let anyone take that away from you. It wasn't dumb luck. It was hard work and persistence. You showed real grit."

I rocked back in my chair. I remembered Dad telling me the movie deal had all been a fluke. A *fluke*. Exactly the word I'd used. His scorn had weaseled its way into my subconscious.

With a jolt of determination, I ruthlessly purged all of Dad's negativity from my mind. It was easier than I'd expected. Maybe because they weren't really my thoughts.

"How did I let him get into my head that way?" I asked her, irritated with myself.

She lifted one hand. "Habit?"

"I have to admit," I said, rolling the stem of my wineglass back and forth, "it feels good to have other people interested in Ghost. It's social proof of Chance's talent."

"All your doubters will have to admit you succeeded. You're the bomb."

"That reminds me. I have more good news. Doug got transferred to Chicago. Ford's brother Max called in a favor to make it happen."

"What?" Lianna inhaled sharply and choked on her wine. She coughed for a few seconds. "That's amazing. Awesome." Her grin nearly split her face in two. "It'll be hard for him to drop by the store and harass you from three states away."

I chuckled. "Yeah. The man has always been pretty delusional. As if gaslighting me would make me come running back to him."

Lianna arched a single eyebrow. "Who are you to call someone else delusional?"

"Say what?" I blinked at her.

Lianna leaned forward, her gaze skewering me. "You heard me. You've been busy deluding yourself. You know exactly what you need to do to be happy. You keep dancing around the solution when it's obvious to everyone else. I can't understand why you can't see it for yourself. Your brother had the courage to follow his dreams. You need to do the same."

I frowned in confusion. "What are you talking about? Ford? My dad? Destiny? The store?"

Crap. She could be talking about any of those things. Or all of them. I suddenly felt as though I was going through life with blinders on, avoiding any problems I didn't want to confront. Was I really that out of touch with my own wants and needs?

Lianna's phone vibrated, and she glanced down at it. When

she read the screen, her eyes widened in surprise. "I had no idea it was so late." She opened her wallet and set some cash on the table. "I need to get going or I'll miss my appointment with my realtor. I have a feeling this house could be the one."

I could only gape at Lianna as she rose to her feet. Was she really going to leave me hanging like this? I pushed away from the table and stood.

When Lianna registered my confusion, she let out a heavy sigh. "You're a smart cookie."

"I am?" I stared at her in wide-eyed panic, like a kid in the front of the classroom who didn't know how to solve the math problem on the board.

She tapped my cell phone on the table. "The answer's right there. Call me if you need to talk. Don't forget, we have a book club meeting next Tuesday."

A solar flare of comprehension burst into my brain. Of course. The email.

As Lianna walked away, all the puzzle pieces slid into place. It was so obvious. Was I really so blind that I couldn't see what was right in front of me until Lianna literally pointed it out?

Of course not. I was simply an expert at avoiding conflict. And this email from Destiny had conflict written all over it.

It was time to stop avoiding and start doing.

But—could I? Could I make this change?

Ford had once suggested I needed to take a step back to look at my basic assumptions and reframe my problem. That's what I needed to do now.

What did I really want? I'd always told everyone I wanted the store to be a success, but now that I thought about it, I realized that didn't encapsulate what I really wanted. My true goals had more to do with Chance and his graphic novels.

I grabbed a paper napkin and wrote down my biggest goal: Make sure Chance is never forgotten and share his genius with the world.

I held my breath, staring at the words. That was a big goal.

Maybe that was why I'd never framed it that way. It felt too enormous.

With Ford's help though, that's exactly what was happening. The world was about to see my brother's story.

Before I could second-guess myself, I replied yes to Destiny's email and pressed send.

46

REVELATIONS

MARA

When I was back in my apartment twenty minutes later, I got a video call from Destiny.

"Hey, partner," I said, recognizing the living room of her Boston apartment in the background. I'd expected her to have moved someplace fancier by now, what with selling Stel-Wood, but I guess there hadn't been much time. She'd been pretty busy.

"It's official. My neighbors think I'm crazy," Destiny said. "I squealed with excitement when I saw you said 'yes' to my offer. I was downstairs, picking up my mail, and the woman who lives down the hall gave me an 'oh, my.'"

"Don't worry. I already knew you were crazy," I teased. I adjusted my grip on my phone as I sat down on my sofa. Zephyr jumped up next to me. "This is going to be great." I distractedly scratched him behind one ear, and he flipped onto his side for better belly-rub access.

"Aw. Is that Zephyr?" Destiny asked. "I've missed him. You, too. Since we'll be partners again, I'll get to spoil him."

"I'm totally in awe of you. You got investors lined up so fast. Last time, that part took us months, and we weren't even asking for all that much money." Things were moving at lightning speed.

I'd have to find a place to live in Boston. One not too far from Destiny, as long as she didn't end up moving someplace out of my price range. Now that we'd be partners again, I'd have to make a ton of changes to my life. Anxiety tightened my chest, so I exhaled slowly to calm myself.

"Our game is a huge success," Destiny said with a self-satisfied smile. "Investors were lining up for this new one. I was able to negotiate great terms. The whole process was a million times easier since we've already proven we can deliver on our promises."

I winced, feeling uncomfortable. "You're being generous using the word 'we.' Over the past twelve months, I've only done some paid consulting for you. It's nowhere near the amount of work I used to put in."

Destiny rubbed the back of her neck and sighed. "I've been thinking about that too. You need to promise me you're really committed to this for the long haul before we make an announcement."

"Ouch. I deserve that." I sat up straighter. "I've been thinking long and hard about this. I'm proud of Ghost of a Chance, and I'm glad I kept it open and put in the work, but I can't see myself running it long-term. At heart, I'm a coder and a game developer, not a shopkeeper. I did what I had to do after Chance died to keep his dream alive, but it's my turn now. I need to follow my heart. I have to do what I really love."

Destiny peered at me, then offered a tight smile. "You'll stick with me? Promise?"

A sense of confidence filled and strengthened me. This is what I really wanted in life. A weight had lifted from my chest the moment I'd sent Destiny that email saying yes.

"I promise. I'll need to make a lot of changes in my life to make this happen, but I'll figure them out." It would be challenging to start a new business while Ford was filming *Ghost*, but we could do it. Absolutely. Commuting between here and Boston would be a pain, especially since we'd be working long hours.

That meant we wouldn't spend as much time together, but we'd both be following our dreams.

"Let me know if there's anything I can do to help make things easier for you," Destiny said. "We still need to hash out the partnership details. I want us both to be happy."

I nodded distractedly. Maybe Ford and I should discuss making some *other* changes in our lives. What would he say if I suggested we move in together? After all, we were almost living together now, since we alternated between spending the weekend at my apartment and his house, so it wouldn't be that big of a change. Since my new company with Destiny would be based in Boston, I might as well rent out my place over the store. I could spend every weekend with him. Maybe I could even arrange to work from home sometimes—at Ford's house.

Slow down. I haven't even told Ford about the partnership yet!

I'd tell him as soon as he arrived, which should be any minute now.

Zephyr flopped over on his back and wriggled, trying to entice me into scratching him again.

"I'm excited that I'm finally doing this," I told Destiny. "I couldn't be happier. I've missed you and Stel-Wood like crazy." I gave Zephyr's belly a vigorous rub.

"You and me, both. I've missed you, too. We make a great team."

A sharp knock came at my apartment door and it opened an instant later. Ford came in holding a large canvas bag.

Zephyr gave a yap of delight, flopped around like a beached baby whale until he regained his feet, and then darted to the door to greet his new favorite person.

"It sounds like that boyfriend you told me about just arrived," Destiny said. "I'll let you go. We can work out the details later."

Ford pulled another of those special gourmet dog biscuits he always brought for Zephyr from his pocket and gave it to the little beggar. He disappeared behind the sofa with his prize.

"You're spoiling him," I told Ford. I glanced back at my phone screen. "Thanks, Destiny. I'll call you in the morning." I ended the call.

"That was Destiny?" he asked. He set a carryout container and a fork on the coffee table and then sat next to me.

"It was. A lot is happening on the video game front." I wasn't hungry, but the delicious aroma of ginger and soy had me reaching for the fork.

Ford gave a distracted nod.

I took a bite of the Ahi tuna. The stronger flavors of ginger and garlic were softened by notes of lime and something smokey. Was that sesame oil? Whatever it was, it was perfect. "You need to make this again. It's a keeper."

"I'm glad you like it." He rested his head on the back of my sofa and closed his eyes. "It's been a long, frustrating week. It was good to go to the cooking class, but I'm glad to be home. With you. I missed you."

I took in the dark circles under Ford's eyes. The poor guy looked beat, so I paused and reassessed. Yes, I wanted to tell him about my partnership with Destiny, but I could tell he really needed to talk. My news could wait a few more minutes. "I'm glad you're here. I missed you, too. What happened with the investor?"

Zephyr joined us. I could swear he picked up on Ford's mood because he jumped onto his lap and rested his chin on Ford's chest. Ford looked down at him and his grim features eased as he stroked Zephyr's fur.

"He wouldn't budge. He hates my decision to cast Chris Pitt, so he's backing out."

"Oh, no!" I set my fork back in the carryout box and shifted to face him. "That has to be frustrating. I'm so sorry. I was sure you'd win him over."

"It gets worse. He convinced the other investors he brought along with him to back out too. They're saying that having a father and son as producer and director is a bad idea, and pointing to my decision to use Chris as proof."

A cold knot of dread settled in my stomach. What was he telling me? Was the movie deal falling apart? Was my bright, shiny new future about to shatter? "Does—does that mean you might not be able to make *Ghost*?" My voice wavered.

Ford's desolate eyes met mine. "At best, I'll have to delay everything. These guys have lost confidence in Ross Film Productions, and they might be the tip of the iceberg. I'm worried that Dad won't be able to bring in any new money."

My stomach lurched. "How long of a delay are we talking about? Weeks? Months?"

Ford's hand stopped moving on Zephyr's back, and he let out a dejected sigh that sounded like the death rattle of his dreams. "I don't know. Max and I are meeting tomorrow to come up with a plan."

I sat there, stunned, barely able to process what he was telling me. "I never realized your plans for *Ghost* could evaporate like this. You won Sundance. I thought your next movie would have investors lining up."

He stared at his hand resting on Zephyr's back for a long time, and then finally started stroking the little dog again. "When I turned down McCormick's movie, he mentioned rumors that Dad's production company is having problems," he finally said. "The only time I ever had problems with money was when I was just starting out and no one knew who I was."

Tears filled my eyes. When I sniffed, Ford's head whipped to face me, eyes wide. He immediately pulled me into his arms. "I'm sorry. I wasn't thinking. Of course, this would be a blow for you. Try not to worry, though. Max and I have connections too. I'll still make the movie. It just might take a little longer than I expected."

I shook my head. "I know you will, but I had news to share with you, too—I planned to tell you as soon as you got here." I brushed away my tears with the heel of my hand. "Destiny sent me a formal offer to partner with her, and I accepted. We planned to start a new company together."

Ford pulled away to look me in the eyes, and Zephyr jumped

off his lap to stand next to him on the sofa. "That's fantastic news," he said, grinning, but then his smile faltered. "Wait. You said planned. Past tense."

I pushed myself to my feet, needing to put some distance between us. To move. To pace. "I can't possibly do it now. I only decided to accept her offer because Chance's graphic novels would get such a huge boost from the movie. People from all over the world would be introduced to them. But, if there's no movie, then there's no boost. No notoriety. No global attention to Chance's work. I'll have to keep running the store. Keep pushing to get *Ghost* into people's hands."

I pressed my hands to my face as I paced. "Destiny's gonna be so pissed with me. Just ten minutes ago, I promised her I wouldn't abandon her again." I stopped suddenly and faced Ford as I dug my fingers into my hair. "If I back out now, she'll never offer me a partnership again."

I snatched the takeout container from the coffee table and headed into the kitchen. After sticking it in the fridge, I braced my hands against the sink edge and stared out the window into the vacant street below.

Ford joined me, standing behind me and wrapping his arms around my waist. "You should still go through with it. Follow your dreams."

I tightened my grip on the sink, my fingers slipping on the stainless steel. "That won't work. We've been through this before. I have two dreams, and I won't throw one away in order to partner with Destiny. I have to keep working to make Chance a success because no one else will. My other dream will just have to wait." Simply saying the words made my heart break. I'd never get a chance like this again. Not with Destiny. Not if I backed out now.

WHEN IT ALL COMES CRASHING DOWN

FORD

I'd let Mara down. My heart gave a hard, painful thump. I'd given her my word, and then, with a few carelessly chosen words, I'd destroyed her dreams. She'd had everything in her grasp, and I'd yanked it all away.

My phone rang. My sister. I used my smartwatch to reject her call.

"Give me some time," I told Mara as she turned to face me. "Delay things with Destiny instead of turning her down. Buy us some time. I can fix this. I have to."

I wasn't a money guy. I hated dealing with investors. I had always turned that side of things over to other people. If Dad couldn't come through, though, I'd have no choice. I'd have to figure it out.

Mara simply stood there, peering into my eyes. She must have seen my doubt because she started wilting before my eyes. All I could do was pull her into my arms and try to console her.

I kissed the top of her head as I rubbed my hand up and down her spine. "We'll get through this. I promise."

She stiffened, then pulled away, shaking her head. "You're trying to placate me. Just look at my store. I might be starting to break even, but that's only because of the boost I got from Chris Pitt's visit." She shook her head. "Without the movie, I'm not sure what I'll do. Let me process this first. I think I just need to curl up in a dark room and cry for a while."

That pierced my heart. This entire situation threw me back to the night I'd missed my ex-wife's Christmas party. I'd made a commitment to Mara about the movie, and I'd let her down. Not only that, but I'd underestimated how hard she'd take the news. Just like I had with my Chelsea and that work party.

As Mara turned away, the sting of her rejection hit me hard. Was this only about the deal, or was something more happening? I had the sudden premonition that she was turning away from us and everything we'd started to build together.

My phone rang again. As I impatiently lifted my smartwatch to decline the call again, I stilled. I'd missed a bunch of texts from my family, and now Max was calling.

"First Hailey called, now Max," I said, meeting Mara's eyes. "I hope nothing's wrong."

Her eyes filled with worry, and she stepped closer, gesturing for me to take the call.

"Hi, Max—"

"—It's Dad," Max interrupted from my watch's tiny speaker.

My breathing hitched. "What's wrong?"

"He's in the hospital. Something's going on with his heart. They're admitting him."

Mara clutched my arm, her eyes going wide.

My heart began to race. "Which hospital?"

"The one here in Sewickley," Max said.

"Give me five minutes," I said, searching for my keys in my pocket. "I'll be right there." I ended the call.

Mara snatched up her keys from the table near the front door and lifted them to eye level. "I'm driving. You're in no condition."

I gave a nod. We rushed down the stairs and I climbed into Mara's little Mazda.

My brain ricocheted from thought to thought. I didn't seem

able to focus on one particular thing. Had I let Dad down? Missed important clues about his health? What about potential investors? Even current ones? Would the news of Dad's hospitalization get out and destroy his business? And what about Mara? Had I just torpedoed her plans with Destiny? Was our relationship strong enough to withstand all this? I glanced at her. Her eyes were focused on the road, but her knuckles were white as she gripped the steering wheel.

I put my hand on her knee. "I'm sorry about messing things up with you and Destiny. I want us to talk more about it, but I can't think straight until I know what's going on with my dad."

She pressed her lips together and blinked a few times. "Let's deal with that later. Don't worry about me or the movie right now. Focus on your dad."

Mara's soul-deep pain pulsed around her, as it had been since the moment I'd broken the news to her. She was devastated.

When I'd disappointed my ex, she'd filed for divorce within two weeks. The blow I'd dealt Mara had to be a million times worse than anything I'd ever done to Chelsea. Mara had finally found a way to fulfill all her dreams, and I'd ruined it all.

Despite everything, here she was, by my side. Helping me.

Mara parked in the hospital's garage. She led us to a reception desk, and it didn't take her long to learn my dad was in the cardiac unit. When we walked into the waiting room, I spotted Hailey pacing, her fingers clutching her phone.

"Ford, you're here." Hailey flew to me, wrapping me in a fierce hug. I held her close as she trembled, losing her ever-present self-control as fear overwhelmed her.

She held tight until she stopped shaking, then pulled away, wiping tears from her cheeks. "They're running tests," she said. "When they're done, they'll let us see him."

Hailey's phone chimed, and she glanced at it. "It's Max," she said. "He's downstairs. I'll text him where we are." She stepped away as her thumbs tapped at the screen.

Mara moved closer to me and took hold of my arm. "I saw

Mom earlier tonight. She mentioned Dad was on call." She licked her lips. "He's probably with Don right now."

I stared at her for a moment, processing what she was telling me. I hadn't even met her father yet. From what Mara had said, he was a skilled cardiologist, as well as a perfectionist.

After that moment of hesitation, I gave a nod. "I'm sure he'll take good care of Dad."

Max came in and headed straight for Hailey. They hugged, and a moment later a man in blue scrubs came out of the door leading into the cardiology wing. When he spotted Mara, he nodded at her and then headed straight for us.

"You're here for Don Ross?" he confirmed.

We nodded.

"I'm Doctor Stellar. I'm taking care of your father tonight," he said, his eyes flicking briefly towards Mara and then back to me and my siblings. He seemed all business, focused entirely on his patient and our father.

Mara's resemblance to her dad was striking. He had dark brown eyes behind silver-framed glasses, and Mara's eyes were similar but a shade lighter. She had inherited his full lower lip and slim build too.

But I couldn't let myself get distracted. We were here for our father. Seeing Mara's dad in blue scrubs felt surreal, but I needed to focus on the fact that he was a doctor, not just Mara's dad.

"How's Dad doing?" I asked, trying to steady my voice.

"He's resting now, and he is *not* in any immediate danger. No heart attack. He's in atrial fibrillation, which means his heart isn't beating in a proper rhythm. It's making him feel uncomfortable and out of sorts, but we're keeping a close eye on things."

"Can it kill him?" Hailey asked, getting straight to the point.

Dr. Stellar met her gaze. "That's unlikely in the short term. If it continues and goes untreated, it could potentially cause other problems. He was already on blood thinners, so that's helping."

I recalled that when I'd done that Google search on the pills I'd found in Dad's bathroom a few months ago, a blood thinner had been among them.

"We'll monitor your dad overnight," Dr. Stellar said. "He says he's been having symptoms for a while. He really should have gone to see his cardiologist when he first noticed the problem."

I glanced at my siblings, surprised.

"Why wouldn't he see his doctor?" Hailey asked.

Good question. None of us had an answer.

"What's the best-case scenario?" Max asked.

"The best option is that his heart decides to beat properly again on its own," the doctor said. "If that doesn't happen, there are a couple of alternatives. The first is to wait and see if it resolves on its own. The second is to give his heart a bit of an electric jolt to get it beating normally again. Sometimes the electrical signals in the heart get confused. Giving it a shock will reboot things and get it back to normal sinus rhythm."

"Shock it? Is that dangerous?" Hailey asked.

"Not nearly as dangerous as staying in a-fib," Dr. Stellar said. "He could throw off a blood clot. Since he's been having these episodes for a while, once he's stabilized and we send him home, I'll have him wear a heart monitor for a week so we can record heart data. If his a-fib is frequent and persistent, I can refer him to an electrophysiologist, but that's not the first option to consider."

"A blood clot?" I repeated. A clot could be incredibly dangerous. "That could cause a stroke, right?"

"It's nothing to panic about," Dr. Stellar said, his tone soothing my fears. "Yes, strokes are five times more likely when you're in a-fib, but that isn't the same thing as saying one will definitely occur. The fact that your dad is on a blood thinner will reduce his chances of having one. He doesn't smoke and he isn't overweight, so those factors are in his favor too. He needs to be careful going forward though. I've had some patients who have had good results with the breathing techniques they learn in yoga. I'll discuss all this with your dad."

The automatic doors leading into the patient area whooshed open. A woman in scrubs told Dr. Steller, "Mr. Ross is ready now."

"Your dad's back in his room," Dr. Stellar told us. "I'll take you to see him."

We followed him through the automatic doors and down a pale corridor. Someone on the cleaning staff was wiping down the door handles to the patients' rooms with a sharp-scented sanitizing solution.

As soon as we entered Dad's room, Dr. Stellar stepped to one side, giving us an unobstructed view of the bed.

A thin, white blanket covered Dad, and his complexion looked odd—slightly flushed, but sort of mottled. Wires ran from his chest to a monitor next to him. I'd seen enough medical shows to recognize a regular sinus rhythm, and that's definitely *not* what I was seeing on the screen. I could identify his solid, regular heartbeat, but I also saw additional squiggles of activity between each beat.

Dad gave a sheepish half-smile. "I didn't mean to panic all of you," he said. "I was having dinner at the country club when my heart started feeling strange. They insisted on calling an ambulance."

"I'm glad they did," I said. "The doctor says these episodes have been happening for a while. Why didn't you say anything?"

Dad looked down at his hands, embarrassed. "I thought it was stress. All in my mind. It didn't feel anything like my heart attack five years ago, so I didn't bother to call my doctor. Stupid of me."

"We'll get this under control," Dr. Stellar said. He checked Dad's heart monitor and wrote down a few notes.

"How did everything go in California?" Dad asked. "I was planning on calling you tonight."

I hesitated. The last thing I wanted to do was give him something more to worry about. "We can talk about it later. Don't worry about work right now."

Dad waved away my concern. "I'm feeling fine. Just a bit off-kilter from this fluttery sensation in my chest. Besides, Dr. Stellar assures me it isn't stress-related. Tell me what's going on. I could use the distraction."

I glanced at Dr. Stellar, and he lifted his shoulder slightly, giving me permission to talk to my dad, so I went ahead. "The investor pulled out. He's hung up on my casting decision. I guess he really hates Chris Pitt. Worse, he's taking the other investors with him. We'll need to find new ones, which means delaying the film."

With a clatter, Dr. Stellar slid the clipboard with his notes into a slot at the foot of Dad's bed, then hurried from the room.

Dad gave a muttered curse. "I'm sorry about that. That guy's always been a bit of a flake. He's been wanting to put money into one of my films for a while, but I could never find one that suited him, the prickly bastard. I never should have used him as an investor in the first place. This is what I get for doing him a favor."

That took me by surprise. "Why didn't you ever mention that to me?"

Dad shrugged. "I told you he was a prickly investor and had cold feet. I figured you'd charm him." He lifted his hand as if to make a gesture, but when the IV tugged against the blanket, he grimaced and set his hand back down. "I have some other people I can reach out to. It won't take long to replace those guys. I always have people eager to back my movies, and with you as the director, they'll be lining up."

I stilled for a moment, not breathing. His news took me completely by surprise. "I don't get it. When we spoke, you made it sound as though keeping this guy happy was crucial."

Dad's features hardened. "It was. The guy's been after me to put together a superhero film for years now so he could invest in it. I thought this was the perfect opportunity for him." He started to cross his arms across his chest, then stopped again because of all the wires and the IV. He let out an irritated sigh. "What can I say? I was wrong."

My anger and frustration flared. "Do you have any idea what

kind of panic I was in when all those investors backed out? And what about Mara? When I told her I'd have to delay filming, it gutted her. I derailed all the plans she was making for her future."

"Ford, he's in a hospital bed," Hailey scolded. "Let up on the guy."

I stilled. My sister was right. This wasn't the time. "Sorry, Dad."

I glanced at Mara, and only then did I realize she wasn't standing next to me anymore. I'd been so focused on my dad that I hadn't noticed when she'd left.

"You're right," Dad said, "I should have filled you in."

I headed toward the door in search of Mara. She might not have heard Dad saying he could easily find new investors. What if she'd left to call Destiny? What if she was backing out of the partnership at this very moment? I needed to tell her before she did anything drastic.

When I reached the open door, I spotted her, and I nearly sagged with relief to see she wasn't on the phone. Instead, she and her dad were talking.

Well, maybe arguing.

My news wasn't so urgent that I needed to interrupt them. Whatever Mara and Dr. Stellar were talking about, it looked intense. I recognized her strained, overly patient expression. It was the one she made when she was trying hard not to get angry.

Dr. Stellar's back was to me, so he didn't see me. I overheard him say in a scathing voice, "I can't believe you were so naive."

That did it. Mara's face hardened with anger.

48

KNOCK DOWN, DRAG OUT

MARA

I glowered at my dad, so irritated with him that I could barely hold it in. He wanted to pick a fight with me here? Right outside Don Ross's hospital room?

I glanced away, trying to calm down. That's when I spotted Ford standing in the doorway. I could tell he'd heard what my dad had said.

I knew he'd come to my aid at the slightest indication that I wanted him. In fact, he seemed to be restraining himself. I gave him a very subtle head shake to let him know I wanted to handle this on my own.

His posture eased, ever so slightly, letting me know he'd understood.

I turned my attention back to Dad. I could hardly believe he was using this moment to attack me, right when I was the most emotionally vulnerable. With the movie's financing falling through and then the call about Ford's dad, I was reeling from a one-two punch.

My father was a doctor. He should know how worried and upset we all were. That didn't seem to matter though. Dad bulldozed ahead. Apparently, what he wanted right now was all that mattered.

I tried to tap into my inner reserves of calm. It took a gargantuan effort, but I managed to pull myself back from the brink of a freakout. "We're standing outside Don Ross's hospital room. Do we really have to talk about this right now?"

Judging by Dad's panicked, glassy-eyed expression, my words didn't register with him. He wasn't simply angry, he was freaking out. My father was completely losing his vaunted self-control.

"I told you this whole movie thing was a fluke," he said, his voice rising.

The word "fluke" hit me like a slap in the face. Now I could hear how cruel it really was. Cruel and painful—and completely untrue.

"Of course, the investors backed out," he continued. "They knew *Ghost* would flop, just like I predicted. What will you do now?" He stepped into my space to press his point. "Your plan to prop up your brother's ridiculous dreams is going to hold you down for the rest of your life, and you only have yourself to blame. You gave up on Stel-Wood so you could follow through with that childish comic book store idea, and now you're going to double down on your decision, even though Ghost of a Chance is failing. Are you crazy?"

I could hear the fear in Dad's panicked voice. Fear for me— fear for my future. I had to admit, I was afraid too. I might sympathize with him, but that didn't keep my anger from rising. Mom was right, Dad thought he was looking out for me. But his methods? They were hateful.

I put my hands on my hips and lifted my chin. It was past time for me to put an end to this treatment. "Stop it, Dad. I know you're worried about me, but you don't need to keep saying 'I told you so.' You've made your opinions abundantly clear, over and over again. I'll remind you, these are *my* decisions. You need to stop trying to control my life. You need to stop harassing me when you don't agree with me. This has to end."

Dad jerked his head back, stunned. "You expect me to just stand by and stay silent when I know you're making a huge mistake?"

"That's exactly what I expect," I said, staring him down. "If you can't be supportive, then be quiet."

"That's ridiculous," he said. "I'm your father. I won't just watch you make a mess of your life without saying anything."

My dad's abusive and controlling behavior had gone unchecked for way too long.

"It's either that, or I'll be forced to cut off all communication with you. This isn't healthy for me. I can't listen to you constantly berating me and tearing me down."

He stared at me, appalled by my threat. I could barely believe it myself, but it had been the right thing to say. He needed to understand there were limits.

Rather than backing down, I straightened my spine and stared right back at him, willing him to believe me. I continued to glare at him for a few heartbeats, needing him to understand that this was an ultimatum.

Finally, his shoulders dropped an inch or two and he gave a reluctant nod.

I almost wilted with relief, but I knew better. I needed to stay strong or risk undoing all the progress I'd made.

I have to admit, I hadn't expected my threat to work. I'd been fully prepared to follow through on it, but I hadn't been happy about the prospect. Maybe that's why my heart softened towards him at that moment.

"You might be interested in knowing I spoke with Destiny today."

He watched me, his expression grim, clearly expecting bad news.

I inhaled deeply. "We've decided to start a new business together. I've finally managed to put Ghost of a Chance on solid financial footing, so I plan to hire a manager to run it."

Dad gaped. An instant later, he pressed his lips together and glowered at me. "It's about damned time. I've been telling you for the past year that you made a mistake by leaving her."

I leaned forward and glowered right back at him, pushing into his personal space. "There you go again, saying 'I told you so.' *Stop it*. These are *my* choices. *My* decisions. This is *my* life. I've done exactly what I set out to do, Dad. I've made Ghost of a Chance a success. You can call that 'propping up Chance's ridiculous idea' if you want, but I call it grit. Perseverance. Hard work. And I did it all on my own, without any help from you. Don't harass me like that ever again. That was your last warning."

Dad lifted his hands in the air. I wasn't sure if it was a gesture of surrender, or if he was emotionally pushing me away, washing his hands of me. All I know for sure is that he backed down from fighting me in that moment, and it felt good. Really good.

As Dad turned to one side, he spotted Ford standing not far behind him at the door of Don's hospital room. Maybe that's what finally brought my father to his senses. All I know is that he turned back to face me, his expression sober and contemplative. Then, he held out his hand for me to shake.

I stared at it, confused, but still, I took hold of it.

"Congratulations, Mara. On everything. The store. The hard work. The movie. The new deal with Destiny. You've done well."

I closed my eyes, absorbing those long-awaited words of approval. Maybe it had taken too long for him to say them, but hearing them didn't feel as good as I'd hoped.

I sighed as I tried to let go of my anger, and I looked him straight in the eyes. "I'm glad you finally noticed."

He grimaced and then headed down the corridor toward an empty nurses' station.

I moved to join Ford. He opened his arms to me, and I stepped into them. Exactly where I wanted to be.

"Hey there, Wonder Woman," Ford said, holding me close. "You're amazing. Have I told you that lately? I have some great news. Dad says he won't have any trouble finding new investors."

I pulled away to look into his eyes. "Wait, what?" I shook my head, the emotional whiplash of the past hour leaving me confused and doubting my own ears. He couldn't have just said what I thought he'd said, could he?

Ford let out a soft laugh. "I know. I could hardly believe it either. Dad said the guy who backed out was a flake who'd been begging for years to invest in a superhero film. Dad says he has loads of investors who will want in on *Ghost*."

As the news sank in, I felt that knot of dread that had settled in my chest fade away to nothing, and once it was gone, my heart soared.

Shoes tapped as they moved toward us, and I turned to see my dad.

He cleared his throat. "Did I hear you say you're still making the movie?"

Ford frowned at him. "Of course, I'm making the movie. That was never in doubt. I simply thought I might have to delay it, but it turns out I was wrong."

Dad dragged his hand down his face, then stared at the floor, his ears turning red. Finally, he faced me and cleared his throat. "I owe you an apology." He glanced at Ford. "To you, Ford, but mostly Mara."

I looked into his eyes. "Exactly what are you apologizing for?"

He looked confused. "For everything."

I shook my head. "You need to be more specific. A blanket apology won't cut it. I need to know you understand exactly what you did that was wrong."

He pressed his lips together, irritated at being put on the spot, but then gave a tight nod. "I'm sorry I wasn't supportive of you and Chance about the comic book store, and I'm sorry I second-guessed your decisions."

I waited more, but when he didn't continue, I said, "That's a pretty good start. Can you also apologize for constantly criticizing both me and Chance and for saying such cruel things? Like calling me a quitter and naive? For saying Chance was wasting his life?

For calling his success a fluke instead of acknowledging that it was the product of hard work and talent?"

Dad's face turned red as I spoke. I waited, and he blew out a breath. "I'm sorry for all that too. I regret a lot of the things I said to your brother. I didn't want him to turn out like your aunt, but that's no excuse." He glanced down. "You're right. Predicting doom isn't exactly something to be proud of. In fact, I need to tell you right now, I'm impressed with you. Your perseverance and determination made all this happen. You knew what you wanted to make happen, and you did it."

He looked me straight in the eyes. "I'm proud of you, Mara."

49

A NEW WORLD

FORD

A month later, Dad was home and feeling a lot better. No new a-fib episodes, which was a relief.

I checked the small dog door Kincaid had helped me install. The flap swung freely. Last weekend he'd brought over his tools, and we'd made quick work of cutting a hole in the door of the utility room. Now Zephyr would be able to go into the fenced back yard anytime he wanted. Having a friend who owned a construction company had its benefits.

Someone rapped on the front door and then opened it.

"Hi. We're here," Mara announced. As I walked into the foyer, she let Zephyr off his leash. He made a beeline for me, dancing excitedly around my feet. When I crossed my arms, he immediately sat and stared up at me expectantly.

"I think he's looking for one of those treats you always give him," Mara said.

"That's because he's smart," I said as I pulled the biscuit from my pocket and gave it to him. He devoured it with a single crunch.

"I have a surprise for him," I told Mara as I pulled her into my arms. She felt perfect there. Exactly where she was meant to be. I kissed her, tasting toothpaste. God, I was crazy for this woman. The touch of her. The feel of her. Even the minty flavor of her toothpaste.

As we separated, I inhaled, catching the scent of her hair. I loved that too.

"Come on," I said, taking her hand and pulling her toward the back of the house. "Let me show you."

She let out a low laugh. "You're really excited about this."

I took her straight to the utility room, and Zephyr followed. When I pointed at the new dog door, Mara's eyes widened in delighted surprise. "You did that for Zephyr?"

"Of course. He's my favorite dog in the world."

Her eyes softened at that.

I took a high-value treat from my pocket. As soon as he saw it, the little beggar sat without me saying a word.

I grinned up at Mara. "I guess bully sticks incentivize him."

"He loves those things, which is totally gross."

I pushed open the flap on the dog door, and said, "Come get your treat."

As soon as Zephyr's butt left the ground, I let go of the treat so it fell outside the dog door into the backyard.

I had to hand it to him, that dog didn't even hesitate. He headed straight out the door to claim his reward. He even turned around and came back in again with it in his mouth.

"Smart dog," I said.

"He picked up on that fast," she agreed.

"Let's sit outside," I said, pulling open the human-sized door. "I have lunch waiting on the patio."

I'd made a *salad niçoise*, which had taken a lot longer to prepare than I'd expected. Salads should be easy, in my opinion. Boiling the potatoes and eggs, making my own dressing, and cooking the green beans took time, but seeing the delighted expression on Mara's face made it all worthwhile. I loved cooking for her.

"Destiny and I have a business call later today. I need to make a decision about my apartment over the store," Mara said as she sat.

I reached across the table and took her hand in mine. "I'm glad you brought it up. I want to spend as much time with you as possible. I want you to stay here—to move in with me, I mean. I won't get to see you nearly enough once you move to Boston, and I want to make every moment we're together count."

Her eyes lit up and a delighted smile spread across her face. "I was thinking the same thing." She sat forward and leaned across the table to kiss me.

"You can set up a home office, too," I added. "There's plenty of space in the old servants' quarters on the third floor. My office is there. There's a small kitchen and a common area, along with four small bedrooms. One of them could even be set up as a private office or conference room."

"For reals? You'd do that for me?" She sprang from her seat and slid onto my lap as she peppered my face with kisses.

I laughed at her exuberance. She was as excited as a kid who'd just found out she was going to Disney World. "Of course, I would. Don't you know by now I'd do anything for you, Mara Stellar? I love you."

She stilled, then swallowed as tears welled. "I love you too, Ford Ross." She gazed into my eyes with wonder. "I can't believe how lucky I am. You and I are like magic together. I couldn't have found a more perfect man if I'd created him from my imagination, because I never would have dared to imagine that someone like you would fall in love with someone like me."

She melted my heart. "I guess you don't quite get it, then. You're my perfect woman. Kind and intelligent and gorgeous. The whole package. I'm the lucky one here. I've been searching for you all my life."

"And to think, we only met because you came into my store to get out of the rain."

I shook my head. "I actually met you the night before, outside the Not a Yacht Club."

"Nearly ran me down, you mean. That doesn't count."

"As you wish," I told her. "I bow to your wisdom on the matter."

Her eyes softened, and she leaned in and kissed me again. When she pulled away, she said, "My meeting with Destiny is in half an hour. I want to bring up telecommuting."

That caught my attention. "You mean from Pittsburgh? So you could be in town more often?"

"That was my idea. Is that okay with you?" She gave me a playful, sidelong look. "You aren't going to back out of asking me to move in, are you?"

"Never," I tightened my arms around her and pulled her close. "The more time we spend together, the better."

My watch chimed with an incoming call. My dad. My stomach tensed. That last health scare still had me rattled. Mara spotted who was calling and said, "You should take that."

She slid off my lap.

"Hi, Dad," I said.

"Hey, Ford," Dad's voice came through on my watch. "Just a quick call. I wanted to let you know how happy our new investors are. They can't stop singing your praises."

"That's great news. Mara is with me now, and she heard what you just said."

"Hi, Don," Mara said.

"Hi. I won't keep you two," Dad said. "I have a few more phone calls to make."

"How are you feeling?" I asked him before he could end the call.

"I'm fine. Stop worrying," Dad chided.

"That won't be happening for a while," I said. "Not after that scare. Talk to you later, Dad."

Zephyr jumped to his feet, his body quivering with excitement as he focused on something on the other side of the lawn. An instant later, he went tearing across the grass, barking like mad. A squirrel turned tail and scampered up a tree. When Zephyr reached it, he put his front paws up on the trunk and continued to bark for a few more seconds. When he was satisfied the squirrel had been vanquished, he came trotting back to us, head held high.

"That's one happy dog," Mara said. "I think he's gonna love it here."

"That's good since you're both moving in. Think we can get everything packed up over the next couple of weeks?"

She brightened. I wouldn't have thought that was possible given how happy she already was. "That sounds like an excellent idea."

As we ate lunch, we compared our schedules and made some plans. It was easy to decide where we'd put her furniture. I hadn't fully furnished the place yet, so adding her things would be simple enough.

Mara glanced at her watch. "Destiny should be calling soon. Would you like to meet her? It'll be a video call."

"Absolutely."

Mara rinsed our plates as I loaded the dishwasher. We'd just finished cleaning up when her phone rang.

"Well, hello, Destiny Woodward. How are *you* today?" Mara asked in a singsong voice.

"I'm absolutely *fabulous*, Mara Stellar," she replied playfully. "How are you this fine summer afternoon?"

Listening to their banter, I could tell their exchange was typical for them.

"Absolutely amazing," Mara replied. "I just finished an amazing lunch with my even more amazing boyfriend, and he just asked me to move in with him. Life couldn't get much better than this."

"Squee!" Destiny said. "That's so adorable. Good for you."

"Here he is," Mara said, turning and tilting the phone so both of us showed up on the camera. "Destiny, this is Ford Ross, and Ford, meet Destiny Woodward."

We both raised our hands and waved.

"I hear you make movies," Destiny said.

"I do. In fact, I'm working on a new one right now. I'm filming it here in Pittsburgh. That should keep me busy for quite a few months."

"Pittsburgh! That's wild," Destiny said. "I thought everything was filmed in Hollywood."

"Mara said pretty much the same thing when we first met," I told her. "When we finally meet in person, you'll have to tell me some college stories about her. Is it true that all she did was study and hang out in the computer lab?"

Destiny flashed a bright smile. "You better believe it. That girl was a complete nerd. Even if she wasn't, what makes you think I'd spill any dirt about her? As if."

Mara hip-checked me. "Turns out all you wanted was to get some insider information on me."

"You can't blame a guy for trying."

Mara ignored me as she crossed the room and sat at the kitchen table. "We need to finalize some decisions," she said to Destiny.

"We sure do," Destiny said. "First of all, let's talk about where we'll be based. I'd assumed it would be Boston."

"Boston is fine," Mara said. "That's what I assumed too."

"Wait, wait—honestly, it doesn't really matter to me. With that gorgeous man in your life, and girl, how did you not tell me how hot he is? And your family, and that store, you have a lot of good reasons for wanting to stay in Pittsburgh. Since I already planned to move out of this apartment and buy something a bit posher, why don't I leave these Boston winters behind me and head to Pittsburgh? After all, you have all those Carnegie Mellon and University of Pittsburgh grads looking for jobs. It should be easy to hire some uber-talented people there."

"Destiny!" Mara said, bolting upright from her chair. "That would be awesome!" She looked over at me, her eyes glowing with excitement. "But, just to be fair, Pittsburgh has winter too."

"I know, I know," Destiny said. "But you don't get nearly as much snow as we do. I like winter, don't get me wrong. Some parts of it are great. Like wearing leather boots and drinking hot chocolate and snuggling up under a blanket—but these crazy amounts of snow we get in Boston? That I can do without. Thank you very much. I already checked. Pittsburgh gets twenty-eight inches of snow a year. Boston gets nearly fifty inches. Easy decision."

Mara faced me, her eyes filled with excitement. When she saw how relieved I was, she turned back to the phone and said, "Done. I'll even get Ford to give you a grand tour of Pittsburgh when you get here. He's a fantastic tour guide."

EPILOGUE

MARA

The following spring.

Lianna burst into my third-floor office, calling out, "Your front door was unlocked. You didn't answer, so I let myself in. Are you up here?"

I paused my headphones and replied, "Hey, give me a second to finish this video call." I quickly wrapped up my conversation with my lead project manager and ended the call.

As I turned back to Lianna, she was already making herself comfortable. Zephyr sat directly in her path, so she picked him up. The little beggar used the opportunity to lick her ears. "Hi," I said, trying to focus on Lianna.

Lianna grinned. "Look at you, talking about testing and time-lines with a real-life program manager. My little girl is all grown up." She fluttered her hand over her heart, pretending to wipe away tears.

I rolled my eyes but couldn't help feeling a sense of pride. "I feel dirty. This adulting thing is hard."

"Don't try to fool me," Lianna teased. "You love it. I can tell."

With a smile, I replied, "Maybe a little too much."

I stood and stretched my arms high over my head. "I have to admit, I'm in my happy place. Both metaphorically and literally."

Lianna took in my gleaming new workspace. "I can see why. You really pulled out all the stops when you set up your office here. You've completely transformed the place. Does Ford mind being displaced?"

I pointed out Ford's desk. "He sits exactly where he always did, with a view of the backyard. He loves all my high-tech gadgets. There's a high-speed router, three monitors, a top-of-the-line color printer for the artwork the game's graphic design team developed, and, of course, my red couch. It's the perfect place to sit and work through sticky problems."

Lianna gave a sly smile. "I recognize your comfy sofa from your old living room. I'll bet you and Ford put it to good use."

I blushed. "It isn't talking, and neither am I."

"Lucky girl." She gave a saucy grin.

My answering smile flashed into existence before I could think twice. "That, I am."

Lianna glanced at her watch. "Your hair looks gorgeous. You'd better change though. Aren't you supposed to be at Ghost of a Chance in twenty minutes?"

"Max's big media event!" I glanced at the clock. "I lost track of time! Ford's picking me up in ten. Thank god I already showered and did my hair and makeup. Come down to the bedroom so we can talk while I change."

"Dante is catering, right?" Lianna asked. "I'm craving truffle fries. That man better be handing out business cards. He'll get loads of new customers with them."

"They're addictive," I said. I headed down the narrow servants' staircase.

I entered our immaculate master bedroom. The room was perfect. Ford had great taste. The soft gray walls, white coverlet, and silver-painted antique furniture created an oasis of cool serenity that always soothed me. A gray dog bed sat under the bench at the foot of the bed, making a dog den that Zephyr adored.

Lianna sat in one of the matching dove-gray chairs facing a gorgeous, vibrant painting, and I headed into my closet.

I glanced at my watch and winced. Eight minutes until Ford got here.

It only took a moment to strip out of my jeans and t-shirt and slide the delicate dress over my head. I returned to the bedroom and twirled like a model. Pieces of pale silk printed with inked sketches of Chance's artwork fluttered from the skirt, and a pencil drawing of Ghost adorned the bodice.

Lianna's eyes widened. "That dress is so unique. I love it."

Delighted, I grinned. "Ford gave it to me. One of his friends made the fabric and designed the dress. It's my favorite thing ever." I twirled in front of a mirror, admiring the way the bits of silk fluttered as I moved.

"It's perfect." Lianna sighed. "Those gauzy bits of fabric remind me of the pages of a comic book. Lucky girl."

I glanced at my watch again. "No time to waste. I need to touch up my makeup. Come with." I darted into the bathroom.

"Tell me about all the happenings at book group," I said as soon as she joined me. "I miss seeing everyone, but I've been swamped."

"Don't worry about it. We know you're busy. Gertrude and I are coming to your event today, so you'll get to see her. We have another new member you haven't met, Sonya. She's a fifth-grade teacher in town, and she's kinda shy. Scarlet wanted to take a group photo for the local paper, but she refused to be in it. She says she hates social media."

"I feel her pain," I said, making a face as I freshened my lipstick. "It's been tough getting used to all the attention that comes along with living with Ford. I've been dreading this media event to launch filming."

A vibration startled me, and I glanced at the text message on my smartwatch. "Speak of the devil, Ford says he's almost here." I grabbed my phone and shoved it into the pocket of my dress.

"You even have pockets," Lianna said. "I love that dress even more."

"I hate not having pockets. Drives me crazy. Come on. Let's go." I grabbed hold of Lianna's hand, pulling her along in my wake. The layers of black and white silk fluttered as I darted downstairs and out the front door just in time to see Ford pull up. "See you there," I said, giving Lianna a quick hug.

The convertible top on Ford's BMW was up for a change. I glanced up at the sky, noting the darkening clouds. As I climbed in, the breeze picked up, causing the spring leaves to tremble.

Ford leaned over and kissed my cheek. "You look amazing."

"Thanks. It's the dress."

"It's the woman wearing the dress," he said, his hot gaze sparking a thrill in me.

We'd been living together for six months, and the slow simmer of our passion was always ready to turn to a boil in an instant.

He leaned across and kissed me, his lips lingering on mine. I reined in my desire before it could get us in trouble. We had people waiting for us.

He pulled down the street, and a moment later, heavy raindrops splashed against the windshield. The skies opened up, and rain fell hard and fast. I breathed in that delicious, fresh scent of ozone.

The sound of the rain pounding on the roof took me back to the moment Ford had driven us through the tunnel in Pittsburgh. It sounded similar to the whoosh of the tunnel when I'd stood in his car that day. I pulled my phone from my pocket. It took me a moment, but I was able to bring up the song Heroes, by David Bowie. As the first notes filled the car, I grinned at Ford. "Remember this?"

He shot me a pained expression. "How could I forget? You gave me a heart attack when you stood up in the tunnel."

"It's why you keep me around," I teased as he pulled the car into a spot around the corner from Ghost of a Chance. "To keep things exciting."

"Yeah, that's it," he deadpanned. He pulled out a black umbrella and handed it to me. "It has nothing to do with how much I love you." He gave me a wink, then peered up at the sky. "The rain seems to be letting up. Let's make a break for it."

Once the media event ended, Ghost of a Chance would reopen for the autograph seekers. How many people would have started lining up? Not many, I hoped, or they'd be drenched.

I lifted the umbrella over our heads, and we struck out. As we rounded the corner onto the main thoroughfare, I got my first look at the long line of people waiting to enter Ghost of a Chance and I stumbled. Ford grabbed hold of my elbow to steady me.

My stomach flipped. "The crowd is even bigger than last summer when Chris Pitt came here."

"That's because Max got the word out in advance."

Speaking of Max, there he was, holding an umbrella over his head and handing more to people waiting in line.

As we approached, someone called out, "Ford Ross is here." The entire crowd turned in unison to face us.

Creepy. "Yowza. Can you say 'intimidating?'" I muttered. "It's like a zombie apocalypse."

Someone touched Ford's sleeve and held out a pen and a notebook, so Ford signed as his brother joined us.

"Nice weather," Max commented.

"For ducks." I watched Ford autograph the notebook and hand it back to the guy. My man was in his element. He really knew how to handle situations like this.

A moment later, the same guy pressed his notebook into my hands. "Can I have your autograph too?" he asked. "Your brother's comic is amazing. I'm a huge fan."

I froze. I wasn't supposed to be the one on display. That happened to people like Ford Ross and Chris Pitt. Not the likes of me.

Ford grinned as he pulled the umbrella from my clenched hand and handed me a pen. "Aww... your first autograph."

I shot him an irritated glance. "Don't tease." Even so, I couldn't help grinning back at him. He always knew how to make me feel better.

"It is?" Max asked. He pulled out his phone. "We'll immortalize the moment. Baby's first steps."

I arched one eyebrow. "You can be really annoying sometimes."

"Get used to it," Max said. "It's my specialty."

As I signed my autograph, I glanced shyly at my very first fan. He didn't seem too intimidating. Just a comic book nerd, like me.

Maybe this could be kinda cool.

Ford signed a few more autographs, and then we made it inside Ghost of a Chance. It was stuffed with media people, friends, and local celebrities.

I glanced at my Wonder Woman poster on the wall, the one that read "be the hero of your own life." For once, I didn't feel as though she was chiding me. Nope. Today, Wonder Woman was cheering me on.

The display racks had been pushed to the back of the room to make space for all the people here. Sam had draped them with black plastic tablecloths so they wouldn't be accidentally damaged by spilled food or drinks, and then someone had decorated the tablecloths with images from my brother's comic. It looked amazing.

Mom and I spotted each other from across the room at the same time, and she nudged Dad to point me out. He immediately grinned and shot me a double thumbs up.

Dad had been true to his word ever since that night at the hospital. I was starting to believe he'd really changed. He didn't second-guess me anymore. He occasionally criticized one of us kids, but he'd immediately apologize, and that made all the difference.

"I'm driving Chris back to the city for dinner after this is all over," Max said. "Want to join us?"

"Mara and I have plans with Dad and her parents," Ford said as he took my hand. "Maybe some other time."

"You turned me down last time, too," Max said, shaking his head in mock disapproval. A moment later, he stilled. "You're doing something with both Dad *and* Mara's parents? That sounds like a big deal."

I widened my eyes and then shrugged, trying to act casual. "Mom's been wanting to meet Don for ages," I explained, as Ford and I interlaced our fingers. "Today's the first day when everyone was available."

Max skewered me with his gaze that always seemed to see too much. I squirmed, and he shook his head in disappointment. "You'd suck at poker."

Ford squeezed my hand as he stifled a laugh. "That's what I keep telling her. You can read her every emotion."

"Spill it," Max said, wiggling his fingers in a come-on gesture. "You two have news. I can tell."

I pressed my lips together and stayed silent. It was none of his business. At least, not yet.

"Wait," Max said, holding up his hand as if trying to stop me from talking—as if I actually would, "don't tell me. I can guess." He pantomimed holding his hand to his forehead like a mind reader. A moment later, he said, "I have it. You're engaged."

My mouth fell open. "Shh!" I hissed as I stepped closer. "Reporters are everywhere," I whisper-shouted. "Keep your voice down."

Max wore a satisfied grin.

I sighed. "We're getting our parents together tonight to tell them," I murmured. "We'll announce it to everyone else after that."

"Make sure Dad doesn't overdo it tonight," Max told Ford. "I don't want him to get tired." His phone chimed and he glanced down at it with a frown. "Give me a minute. I need to take this. I'll be right back." He stepped toward the back of the store.

"Why is Max so worried about Don?" I asked, watching his departing back. "I thought his heart was back to normal and he was doing great. Should I be worried?"

Ford's eyes tracked Max until he stepped into the storage area. "I think last week's heart ablation procedure still has him on edge."

"Don's doing great, isn't he?" I asked, concerned. "I thought the procedure was a complete success and fixed his a-fib. Is he having problems?" I glanced over to where my dad stood, ready to wave him over for a quick consultation.

"He's fine," Ford reassured me. "Maybe a little pain from the incisions from the catheters, but his heart's doing great. I think Max is beating himself up for not figuring out Dad was having heart problems again."

I couldn't blame the guy. If Mom or Dad kept something important about their health from me, I'd be devastated. I bet I'd also start watching them like a prison guard. "Maybe when he sees how well Don is doing, he'll relax." I glanced up and spotted Don pushing open the front door, with Lianna and Gertrude right behind him. "Speak of the devil, your dad just walked in. He looks great."

Don pushed toward us through the crowd.

As I moved forward to greet him, someone stepped into my path. I found myself face-to-face with a woman in a tailored suit. It took me a moment to place her, and when I did, I gaped in surprise—and horror. This was that reporter, Mindy Trevor. The one who'd interviewed Chris Pitt when he'd made his surprise appearance at my store.

I stood, staring at her in stunned disbelief. What was she doing here? Max had said she was banned for life!

Mindy must have recognized my anger because she winced. Then she lifted her microphone and tapped on the side. I thought she was telling me it was live, but then I realized she was indicating her network logo. That wasn't the W-ZZZ emblem. Apparently, she'd switched jobs to work for one of their rivals.

"I want to apologize for what happened last summer," Mindy said. "I promise you; I had nothing to do with that story."

I searched for something to say, but "that's okay," wasn't going to come out of my mouth.

Max joined me and gave Mindy a welcoming handshake. "Good to see you," he said, then turned to me. "She's good people. She was furious about the way her piece was used to attack you. It made her look bad. When she reached out to apologize, I offered to help her find a position with another network."

Mindy's face glowed with gratitude. "And I love it there."

Doug had left a lot of collateral damage in his wake—no surprise. I finally found my voice. "I'm glad to see you found a new home. Good for you, and—good luck."

It struck me a moment later that I hadn't thought about Doug in ages. Even with today's event looming on the horizon, I'd never once worried he might do something to sabotage me. Having him transferred to Chicago had been a brilliant solution.

Don moved around Mindy and pulled me into a hug. "Good to see you, Mara. This is a great turnout today."

"And exciting, even if it's a bit overwhelming." I took in the crowded room. Dante's waitstaff moved around the room brandishing serving trays of hors d'oeuvres.

Mindy turned to her cameraman and made a rolling motion with her hand. A light on the camera turned green, and then Max nodded at my store manager, Sam.

I narrowed my eyes, wary. Max and Sam had planned something.

The cameraman pointed his bright light directly at me.

Ford slid his arm around my waist. "You look like a deer in the headlights," he murmured into my ear. "Relax."

I moved closer to him. "Or use my poker face?" I murmured.

I tried to look around the room, but the bright light made it so I could barely see. Eventually, I was able to identify friends out there along with my parents. Lianna and Gertrude, of course. Our kickass-mayor Scarlet was plucking a treat from Dante's tray. Courtney was there too, standing next to Rose, the librarian. Seeing them here helped me breathe more evenly.

My new manager straightened his spine. "Hey, Ford." Sam pitched his voice to rise above the chatter of the crowd, "I heard a rumor you're planning to relocate to Pittsburgh permanently. Is that true?" The poor guy's voice sounded so stiff and awkward that it was obvious someone had told him to ask the question. My money was on Max. Then again, Ford didn't seem surprised by the question either, so maybe he'd been the one.

"Lots of movies are filmed in Pittsburgh," Ford said. "Since I have family in the area, I've decided to make this my base of operations. I'm moving back home."

Everyone applauded, and Don clapped Ford on the back, his face shining with pleasure. "That's great news. And about time."

"What about the two of you?" Max asked loudly for the audience, looking Ford squarely in the eye. "Since you're relocating here, does that mean we'll be hearing wedding bells soon?" Max grinned, then leaned closer to Ford. "Gotcha," he murmured. "I told you payback's a bitch."

My eyes nearly bugged out of my head. *That jerk!* I glanced up at Ford to see how he'd react.

Ford looked startled, but a moment later he glanced at me with one eyebrow cocked and a questioning look.

My life was a lot more public now. I'd accepted that when I'd decided this was the path I wanted. I'd have to learn to roll with it. I gave Ford the tiniest of nods.

He laced his fingers with mine. "This isn't the way we'd planned to tell our families, but—I popped the question last night, and she said yes. Mara and I will be tying the knot next year."

This time, the applause was even louder. I searched for my parents and found them clapping along with everyone else.

"Kiss her!" My dad called out, taking me completely by surprise.

Ford heard and pulled me into his arms. As he gazed into my eyes, he asked, "How does the spotlight feel?"

"A bit intense," I said, "but not bad."

"Your dad's right. You two need to kiss," Don said. "Now's the moment."

I cocked my head to one side and raised one eyebrow. "Kiss me, Ford. I don't think this crowd is going to settle for anything less."

Ford, my own real-life superhero, wrapped his arms around me and pulled me closer. The slow, simmering heat that was always present when we were together flared, and I melted into him.

SIMPLE CONGO CHICKEN MOAMBE (AFRICAN PEANUT BUTTER CHICKEN STEW)

Level: Moderate
   Prep and Active Cooking Time: 15 minutes
   Passive Cooking Time: 2 hours
   Total Time: 2 hours and 15 minutes
   Serves: 6

Ingredients

- 3-4 lbs boneless chicken pieces
- 1/2 teaspoon salt
- black pepper to taste
- 1/4 teaspoon cayenne pepper (I leave this out)
- 1 large onion, diced (you can also use frozen onions)
- 1/2 teaspoon nutmeg
- 1 8 oz. Can tomato sauce
- 1 Tablespoon butter
- 1 cup peanut butter, creamy and unsalted (if you use peanut butter with salt, skip adding the salt)
- 2 cups cooked rice

Directions:

1. This is a simple recipe, and kids tend to love it! Be warned though, serve smallish portions since this is very filling.
2. Place your chicken pieces in a large stew pot and add enough water to cover the chicken. Add the salt (if you are using unsalted peanut butter) and pepper. Bring it to a boil, then lower it to a simmer and cook for 1 to 1.5 hours. (If you like, you can do this step the night before and place the chicken and broth in the refrigerator overnight.)
3. Remove the chicken and reserve 1-1/2 cups of the chicken broth.
4. In a large ovenproof skillet, sauté the onion, nutmeg, cayenne pepper, tomato sauce, and butter for 3 minutes.
5. To that same skillet, add the cooked chicken, and the 1-1/2 cups of reserved chicken broth. Simmer covered for 15 minutes.
6. Add the peanut butter to the chicken, then place it in a 350 F oven for 30 minutes, uncovered.
7. Prepare your rice.
8. Remove the Chicken Moambe from the oven, stir it, then serve it over rice.

DANTE'S CHILI

Level: Moderate
   Prep/Active Cooking Time: 30 minutes
   Passive Cooking Time: 2 hours
   Total Time: 2 hours 30 minutes
   Serves: 8 1-cup servings

Ingredients

- 1 tablespoon salt
- 1 tablespoon black pepper
- 2 pounds ground chuck
- 2 tablespoon olive oil
- 1 large sweet onion, diced
- 2 medium green bell peppers, 1" diced (I skip these)
- 1 poblano chili pepper, diced (I skip this as well)
- 8 cloves garlic - diced or pressed using a garlic press
- 1 tablespoon ground cumin (add extra if you want. I prefer lots of it!)
- 1 tablespoon ground coriander

- 1 tablespoon dark brown sugar
- 1 teaspoon marjoram
- 1 teaspoon dried oregano
- 2 cups (16 oz) brewed decaffeinated coffee
- 1 28 oz. Can crushed tomatoes or 10-12 fresh tomatoes, diced
- 1 15 oz. Can red kidney beans drained & rinsed
- 1 15 oz. Can cannellini beans or great northern beans drained & rinsed (a second can of red beans can be substituted)
- 2 squares dark chocolate (70% or more purity)
- Salt and pepper to taste

- *Optional items for serving/toppings:*
- Sour cream or Greek Yogurt
- Shredded cheddar cheese
- Corn chips / tortilla chips
- Cornbread
- Lime
- Cilantro
- Sliced green onion
- Black olives
- Avocado

Directions:

1. Pour yourself a margarita. This should be fun!
2. In a large pot or Dutch oven, heat 2 Tablespoons of oil over medium-high heat. Break up the ground chuck and add about 1/3 of the meat at a time to the oil. Be careful not to splash the oil and burn yourself or

overcrowd the pot. Stir the meat every thirty seconds or so until it is browned all the way through. This will take about 3 minutes or so. Then remove the meat with a slotted spoon and set it aside, leaving the oil behind.

3. Keep the heat at medium and add the onions. You can add a bit more olive oil if necessary. Sprinkle on some salt and pepper and stir it up. Keep an eye on your onions and stir them every twenty seconds or so until they start to turn translucent. This will take about 2 minutes.

4. Sip your margarita. Brew your decaf coffee that you'll be using later.

5. Add your bell pepper and poblano to the translucent onions along with a bit more salt and pepper. Cook all of this down for about five minutes. Make sure you stir it from time to time, so it doesn't burn. Once the peppers begin to soften, it will be time for the next step. You might as well freshen up your drink while you wait.

6. Since you're waiting anyway, measure all your spices into a small bowl so you can dump them in all at once (cumin, coriander, brown sugar, marjoram, oregano, and diced garlic). Take a sip of your margarita while you enjoy the wonderful aromas of your spices!

7. Now that your peppers are soft, add your spice blend and stir. Keep your stirring spoon moving so you don't burn those spices! Heat them for a couple of minutes to bring out their flavor.

8. After two minutes or so have passed, add 1/2 cup (4 oz) of brewed coffee. Quickly, before the liquid evaporates, scrape the bottom of the pan and get those spices and flavors blended with your mixture. Once you're certain you've mixed everything, add the remaining 1-1/2 cup (12 oz) of decaf coffee.

9. Add the can of tomatoes.

10. Lastly, add both cans of beans and the meat you browned earlier. Stir everything together and raise the heat to high. When it begins to boil, cover it and turn the heat to low. Simmer for 2 hours. Stop by every now and then and give it a stir. Check on the liquid level, and if you think it looks too dry, add a bit of water. It would be a shame to let it burn now after most of the work is done.

11. After 2 hours have passed, turn off the heat and remove the lid. Add your dark chocolate chunks and let them melt. They should disappear into the chili in about 2 minutes or so.

12. Taste test time! You can add more salt and pepper now if you choose.

13. Serve! You can provide corn chips, cornbread, sour cream, Greek yogurt, lime, shredded cheddar cheese, cilantro, black olives, sliced green onion, avocado, more chunks of chopped chocolate, shots of tequila... whatever you'd like!

GINGER SOY MARINADE FOR TUNA STEAKS

Level: Easy
  Prep Time: 5 minutes
  Marinading time: 30 minutes (longer if you prefer)
  Cooking Time: 6 minutes
  Total Time: 45 minutes
  Serves: 4
  The marinade can be made in advance.

Ingredients

- 4 medium tuna steaks, 1 inch in thickness
- 2 tablespoons fresh lime juice
- 2 tablespoons soy sauce
- 2 garlic cloves, crushed
- 1 tablespoon fresh ginger, minced
- 2 teaspoons sesame oil
- 1 teaspoon sugar

Directions:

This one will be fun and easy, and it will let you release some of your aggression when you prepare the marinade. Let's get started.

1. First, combine all the ingredients except for the tuna in a 1-gallon resealable plastic bag. This is the fun part. Carefully close the bag, then shake and squish the contents together until everything is well combined. Add the tuna steaks. Seal the bag again and let the tuna marinate at room temperature for at least 30 minutes. If you plan to let it marinate longer, set it in the refrigerator. Your prep work is done! Now you just need to cook them.

2. Preheat your grill to 475 (medium-high if you don't have a thermometer on your grill). Place your tuna steaks on the grill and baste them with half the marinade in the bag (that means drizzle the marinade over the steaks while they're on the grill). Cook the steaks for approximately 3 minutes. Then flip them over, baste them with the remaining marinade, and cook them for an additional 2-3 minutes.

3. Transfer the steaks to a plate and serve.

DEATH BY CHOCOLATE CAKE

Level: Moderate to advanced
   Prep Time: about 40 minutes divided between the 3 steps
   Baking Time: 30 minutes
   Total Time: 1 hour 10 mins
   Serves: 6-8

Note: This cake uses 6" cake pans, which are smaller than the typical 8"
or 9" pans you probably already own. You will need to purchase these
smaller pans if you don't have them.

Ingredients

Chocolate Fudge Cake:

- 3 oz unsweetened chocolate, chopped into smallish pieces to melt faster
- 1/3 cup unsweetened dark cocoa powder
- 1 cup water, boiling
- 3/4 cup unsalted butter, room temperature
- 1 1/4 cups dark brown sugar, packed
- 2 large eggs, room temperature
- 1/3 cup sour cream, room temperature
- 1 teaspoon vanilla extract
- 3/4 cup all-purpose flour
- 1/2 cup cake flour
- 1 teaspoon baking powder
- 1/4 teaspoon fine sea salt
- 1 teaspoon cinnamon

Simple Chocolate Buttercream:

- 1 cup unsalted butter, room temperature
- 3 cups powdered sugar
- 1/2 cup unsweetened cocoa powder
- 1/4 teaspoon fine salt
- 2 Tablespoons milk, or heavy cream

Chocolate Ganache:

- 3 oz dark chocolate (72% cocoa), finely chopped (NOT unsweetened chocolate)

- 3 oz heavy cream

Directions:

You'll make this cake in 3 parts... first the cake, then the buttercream frosting, then the ganache. It takes time, but it's worth it!

Chocolate Fudge Cake:

1. First, preheat your oven to 350 degrees F. Prepare two 6-inch round cake pans by buttering them and lining them with parchment paper.
2. In a small bowl, combine your unsweetened chocolate, cocoa powder, and boiling water. Whisk everything together until it's smooth. Set it aside and allow it to cool. It will be ready to use when it is no longer hot. It can be warm to the touch.
3. Using a larger bowl and your mixer, blend the butter and brown sugar until fluffy and smooth. Add your eggs and blend them in until they are incorporated. Add the sour cream and vanilla and mix until blended. Scrape down the sides and make sure everything is blended together.
4. In a separate bowl, blend together your all-purpose flour, cake flour, baking powder, cinnamon, and salt. Add 1/3 of the flour mixture into your larger bowl containing the butter mixture. Mix it in at low speed until everything is almost combined. Stop your mixer, pour in half of the cooled chocolate mixture, scrape the sides of the bowl, and mix it in. Repeat, adding another 1/3 of the flour, followed by the remaining half of the

chocolate. End with the last 1/3 of the flour. Each time you add something, make sure you scrape down the sides of the bowl, so everything gets mixed together thoroughly.

5. Evenly divide your batter between your two prepared cake pans. Bake for 30 minutes (until the cake is set and a toothpick inserted in the center of the cake comes out clean). Let the cake cool in the pans for 10 minutes, then run a knife or spatula around the edge of the pan to loosen the cake. Gently turn the cake out of the pan and onto a wire rack to cool to room temperature.

Simple Chocolate Buttercream:

1. You can make this while the cake is baking. Using a mixer, cream your room-temperature butter until smooth. Sift together your powdered sugar and cocoa powder and then slowly add them to the bowl while mixing on low speed (starting at a slow speed is important if you don't want to make a mess). Add your salt and milk and blend until smooth. You can slowly increase the speed of your mixer to make sure everything is mixed thoroughly.

2. You can adjust the consistency of your buttercream according to your preference. If it is too thick, add milk — 1 Tablespoon at a time— until you get it to the desired consistency. If the buttercream is too thin, add some sifted powdered sugar a little at a time (up to 3/4 cup). Set it aside until you are ready to use it.

Chocolate Ganache:

Note: You can wait until just before you are ready to assemble your cake to make the ganache.

1. Place your chopped pieces of dark chocolate into a small bowl—around the size of a cereal bowl. Bring your heavy cream to a simmer and then pour the hot cream over the chopped chocolate.
2. Cover the bowl with plastic wrap or a tight-fitting lid and let it sit for 3 minutes.
3. Remove the plastic wrap/lid and stir your ganache until it is smooth. Allow it to sit at room temperature for 8-10 minutes until the ganache has thickened slightly.

Assembly:

1. If you like, you can slice off the rounded tops of your cakes. Since one of those tops will end up inside the cake, I prefer to simply flip over one of the tops so the "top" ends up on the bottom of the cake—face down on the plate.
2. Slice each cake round into two layers for a total of 4 layers of cake. I prefer cutting them in half by inserting my blade only halfway into the cake all the way around.
3. Build your cake by slathering the buttercream between the layers and then frosting the entire cake with the buttercream. Chill your cake in the refrigerator while the ganache thickens. Once your chocolate ganache is ready, pour it over the chilled cake. It won't completely coat the cake but will instead cover the top and drizzle down the sides. Set your cake in the refrigerator for 10 minutes while the chocolate sets. Serve chilled.

BIBLIOGRAPHY

Contemporary Romances

The Way to a Woman's Heart series - the **Coming Home** trilogy

Slow Simmer
Here's the Scoop
From Bitter to Sweet

———

Coming in 2024
The Way to a Woman's Heart series - the **Destination Wedding** trilogy

Too Much On My Plate
Say Cheese!
Turkish Delight

———

Historical romances

Gambling On a Scoundrel

Secrets and Seduction series:

Lady Cecilia Is Cordially Disinvited for Christmas
(A prequel only available through my VIP club)

It Takes a Spy…
Lady Catherine's Secret
Once Upon a Spy
My Lady, My Spy
Along Came a Spy

ABOUT THE AUTHOR

I'm Sheridan Jeane, and I write the **Way to a Woman's Heart**
series of romcoms set in Sewickley, a small town near Pittsburgh.
These books all feature my favorite things: food, books, family,
and friends.
You can also check out my exciting Victorian-era romances from
my **Secrets and Seduction** series. They're filled with spies,
intrigue, and tender, sensual moments.

More about me?
I'm the daughter of an artist/art-therapist/professor mother and
an opera-loving/computer engineer/do-it-yourself father.
Growing up, I assumed parents routinely converted their garages
into well-stocked art studios complete with potter's wheels, kilns,
and every color of paint under the sun. Didn't every second-
grader learn how to weld or nail shingles on the roof of the 2-car
garage their dad built? And what about all those after-opera cast
parties? Weren't they run-of-the-mill too?
No?
Go figure!
That probably explains my quirky outlook on life.

Visit me at www.SheridanJeane.com

CPSIA information can be obtained
at www.ICGtesting.com
Printed in the USA
BVHW031128060423
661868BV00007B/465

9 781633 030206